THE STONE MAG

C000234218

THE GUARDIAN OF MAGIC

ANDREW SHARP

The Guardian of Magic – The Stone Magic Series: Book One by Andrew Sharp
ISBN: 978-1-9169016-0-5

andysharp@penphotopaint.com
andysharp@penphotopaint.co.uk

Cover design and formatting by AuthorPackages.com

Published by

To all those who helped me achieve this, a very big thank you. You know who you are. Including Lucy Rose York for the copy edit, Maria Carter for polishing my manuscript and tidying my words, and Mark Reid for the cover art and graphics.

ONE

Beth sat by the cold stone hearth in the dingy kitchen, listening to her parents argue about her in the other room. A door slammed as her Da left. He would be back later, drunk. There was every chance he would argue again and beat her Ma; and her too if she got in his way. This was her life. She was a failure; inept at everything, a burden to all – and (she often lamented) she was still a virgin, unlike most girls of her age. She wasn't pretty (or so she'd been told), but she longed for someone to save her from her life and whisk her away on an adventure.

Beth replayed her Da's words in her head.

"She's useless. Eighteen years old and still living with her parents. A freak with no magic, no aptitude and no skills. Too fucking ugly to get a husband, too fucking hopeless to get a job, and a drain on our meagre earnings." The floorboards creaked under his heavy feet as he paced.

Beth's Ma did her best to calm the situation. "The Tester said some magic may still show up," she began hopefully.

"Face it, Helna. You've taken her to the Tester every year since she was thirteen and still there's no magic," he snapped. "Not a spark, nothing. She's a bloody freak, that's what!"

In a world where everyone acquired magic at some point in their lives, this was yet another thing that made Beth different. Or, as her father asserted, a freak.

Furniture skidded across the room and crashed into the wall as he said this, and Beth closed her eyes. She hoped he wouldn't storm into the kitchen and start venting his anger at her.

"I'll speak with the seamstress tomorrow," tried Helna. "She said she might give her another try as an apprentice."

Beth's Da scoffed. "She was just being polite," he said. "She won't get another trial. The dumb girl can't even keep a simple cleaner's job. She lasted two days last time. If she was an animal, we'd have had her culled."

"Relax," Helna tried to soothe him, although her voice was anything but relaxed.

"Sod this. I'm going to the tavern. I won't be back till late."

The room shook as the door slammed behind him, and then there was quiet. Moments later, the wood-planked door to the kitchen burst open. Now Helna was mad too.

"Get your shawl!" she barked from the doorway. "I'm not taking another beating for you tonight. You're getting a job – today."

Helna grabbed Beth by the scruff of her sleeve and dragged her through the streets. The unshaken girl had no idea where she was being taken and she didn't really care. Nothing in her life could be any worse as far as she was concerned. But as her mother steered her through the rundown streets of Malad, past the dilapidated shacks that housed some of the poorest citizens of Arities, and towards a small shack set apart from the rest, Beth realised exactly where they were headed.

"This is your last chance, girl. You will take this job and you will keep it – even if it kills you! Your Da's right – you're useless, and I'm not going to keep paying the price for it."

They lived in Malad, one of the poorest districts in the city of Arities. It didn't take Beth long to realise where her mother was taking her, as she steered her passed the ramshackle shacks that people here called homes.

Helna banged hard several times on the door of one small shack, and a lean man in his late forties answered it.

"What the hell's going on? Can't you simply knock?"

"My daughter wants to work in the sewers," said Helna. "She'll do any job and any task, and she wants to start now."

"Hold on! It's not that easy," cautioned the man. "City Hall says she has to sign papers."

"She'll sign them!" snapped Helna, and she pushed through the door, hauling Beth behind her.

The man paused for a moment and eyed them both with suspicion. A single desk and chair furnished the drab interior of the Sewer Office, adorned with stacks of papers held down by rocks to prevent fly-aways.

"Well. Come into the light then, girl. Let me see you."

Beth felt the man's gaze as he looked her up and down. She kept her head bowed so that her dishevelled red hair flopped in front of her face.

"Well, you have a broad back and you look reasonably healthy," he said. "Do you know what this job involves?"

"Yes," replied Helna.

"I was asking your daughter …"

Beth didn't respond so Helna nudged her.

"Well?" he asked again.

"Yes," she muttered, barely audible.

"Good. Well I've got to read this to you anyway, so listen up."

He cleared his throat and withdrew a sheet of paper from one of the stacks on the desk, then continued, "'I – that will be you when you sign this – declare that I understand the risks of being a sewer worker. No matter what injuries I suffer or diseases I am afflicted with, I will make no claim on the city of Arities. I willingly pledge to work in the city sewers. Should I die within them, the city is not obliged to recover my body.' That's it. Do you understand, girl?"

"She understands," replied Helna.

"I need your daughter to answer."

"Yes," Beth muttered again.

"Okay. Well, if you sign this then you'll be contracted," he explained. "If you miss a shift, you'll face a penalty, get sacked – or worse, in some cases."

"She'll be here," her mother said.

"Can you read and write your name, girl?"

"Yes. I taught her myself."

The man scowled at her and stepped towards Beth.

"Well then. Sign this and make sure you arrive back here at first light tomorrow – for your first shift."

Beth nodded and signed the parchment without a

word, then Helna turned and started towards the door, snapping at Beth to follow her.

"Er, M'am? M'am? Can I have a quick word?" called the man as Helna swung the door open. "Let your daughter wait outside."

Helna nodded and turned her back to Beth, closing the door again.

"What is it?"

"I know it's none of my business," he started, "but you do know, don't you, that not a lot of people live long on this job. There's illness, accidents and drownings nearly every day. It's the last place most people would turn to for a living ... It's the last place most mothers would want their daughters ..."

"Is that all you want to say?" Helna sneered.

"Yes—"

"Then she'll be here in the morning."

***

Ten dour men stood waiting outside the office when Beth arrived the next day.

"You must be the new girl. Who'd you piss off to get this job?" asked one of them, his mocking voice full of disdain.

"My Ma and Da," replied Beth meekly.

"Well, looks like you're here now," said another, holding out his hand, but she demured. "I'm Parat, the shift leader. Do what I say and you might just live through your first shift. Now, fall in line with the others. We have a short walk to the hatch, yet."

There was little conversation as the men and Beth

walked through the narrow cobbled streets towards the hatch. Dawn was just beginning to break and some early traders were setting up their stalls, but in general the route was quiet. The hatch he mentioned was just that – a heavy wooden slab in the ground that lifted up to reveal a ladder and a thirty-foot drop. It took two men to prise it open. At the base was a lantern-lit chamber with benches and baskets.

"Climb down and find a spot on a bench near an empty basket," instructed Parat. "That will be your spot every time on this gang, and that will be your basket."

When they reached the bottom, he pointed to a dingy wall lined with crates of clothing and equipment. "Over there are some boots, aprons, hats and gloves. Find what fits you and put them in your basket before you leave. The other gangs have their own chambers so no one should steal your stuff. Not that anyone would want to steal your shit-stained leather," he chuckled.

The leathers stank worse than anything Beth had ever smelled in her life but at least they fitted reasonably well. She gagged as she slipped her feet into the boots but held her vomit down – she was determined not to make a bad first impression.

Parat stopped at the entrance to a small passage, allowing the other men to go through before them into a chamber where several chains dangled from an overhead water tank.

"This is the washroom," he told Beth, pausing for a moment beneath one of the chains. "When the tunnels are flushed, the water tops up that big tank up there," he pointed out. "Pull one of these at the end of your shift and it'll wash the shit right off you."

Beth looked up at the chains and nodded slightly.

"Then stack your shovel over there against the wall with the others," he continued. "You'll go home wet, but most workers don't mind; they appreciate the fresh feeling – although you'll still stink, of course." Another chuckle.

Beth nodded again.

"Now, grab a shovel. Remember you must always use the same shovel too – some of the lads are quite particular about that."

They went through another passage and arrived at the first sewer. Beth had done well to keep her breakfast down so far, but as she entered into the sewage-lined tunnel and was struck by the full intensity of its aroma, she heaved.

"You did well," Parat said, with a subtle wipe of his finger across his nostrils. "Most people spew when they first come down the hatch. I promise you, you'll get used to it."

He turned and stooped his head down to her level. "Now listen up because this is important. This high ledge you're on runs on the left side of every single tunnel. Remember, only on the left side, as that's the side with hatches. There's also a walkway on the right side of the trough, but don't be there when there's a flush."

Beth had to crouch on the narrow ledge because the curve of the tunnel had next to no headroom. The other men had already dropped down onto the walkway below. Between the walkways was a deep trough, around six feet wide and four feet deep.

"A marvel of engineering, these tunnels – or so we're told," Parat laughed. "They're a death trap, really. Literally. Now drop down, then climb back up," he instructed.

11

"You'll appreciate the lesson now rather than when you're rushing to escape the flush."

Getting back onto the ledge was difficult for Beth – it took her six attempts. There was no space for her to haul her body up and over; she had to swing her legs up and roll lengthways onto it, then stand up without hitting her head on the curve of the tunnel and falling back down.

"If you fall, you're as good as dead," explained Parat. "You'll be lucky to drown if the flush catches you. And not so lucky if it drags you along, breaks your bones and spits you out alive somewhere, ravaged, because no one'll come looking for you. Now, get down here. The first rule is we stay together – no wandering off. The second rule is whatever we find, we tell no one – ever. Do you understand?"

"Yes. Tell no one," repeated Beth, now realising how awful her situation was.

"Right, this is how it works, and I'm only telling you this once, so listen up. There will be two lantern bearers walking on the left side of the trough – stay within their light. There are two more on each side of the walkway, and the rest of us are in the trough. Anything that's stuck, or not supposed to be there, or just needs loosening up, we get at it with our shovels. The idea is to make whatever we find small enough for the flush to carry it away. Oh, and just one last word of caution – try not to stand under a sewer-well or pit, as people don't tend to look when they tip out their chamber pots. It might stink down here, but trust me when I say that the fresh stuff tastes disgusting." He grinned widely and looked at her. "Right, got it?"

"Yes," said Beth. His demeanour was breaking through

her resistance, making her not feel so bad about what lay ahead.

"Right. Get in the trough then, young'un, and do what the others do."

***

Two hours passed before the first bell sounded and everyone scrambled for the high ledge. Seconds later, a torrent of water and sewage washed down through the trough and into the walkways.

"That's why I clean and check every bell hung across the trough," said Parat. "We don't get much warning before a flush. The bells are all we have. A broken or missing bell … and we're all gone."

"Parat! Got one," interrupted one of the crewmen.

The shift leader turned towards the man standing in a pool of light over a peculiar pile of rags or sacking as another worker poked tentatively at it with his shovel. The two men lifted up the strange bundle and shook it. Beth screamed as a man fell out and his cold, slimy body slumped onto the sewer floor. But no one paid any attention to her.

Parat leapt towards the dead body with greed in his eyes and started rifling through it. "Been down here a while – weeks, maybe. Looks like the rats have had their turn, too," he said, tracing his hands along the man's soiled lapel and down one leg of his trousers.

"Ahh, we're in luck!" he called. He pulled a pistol and a mouldy purse from the man's pockets. "He wasn't robbed!"

The crew gave a loud cheer.

"Right, have at him, lads. You too, girl, if you want your cut."

One of the other men pushed Beth forward. "You first, girl. We all do this, and no one talks. Get it?"

Beth nodded as she stood over the rotting corpse, unsure of what to do next.

"Chop it up, then" called another, and he gestured towards her shovel. "It needs to be small enough for the flush to carry it away. Like this," and he slammed his shovel down into the man's lifeless body, hacking off a rotting hand.

"Go on. Do it, girl," urged Parat calmly. "The lads need to know you're with them – not against them."

A feeling of revulsion swept through Beth as she realised what she had to do. It wasn't right, she thought – this man's family were probably out there looking for him – but she was scared of what would happen to her if she didn't obey, so she plunged her shovel deep into the body … not once, not twice, but again and again. And soon the others joined in to help.

"Well, you survived your first shift," said Parat as they walked back from the hatch. "Not everyone does, and I've worked in sewers all over the city. We'll all go back to the office now so that the manager can record any deaths. Tomorrow you'll get your cut of the findings. But remember, don't tell a soul – the lads won't forgive you if you do. We make more money from corpses and other things than we do from our wages."

***

Four weeks passed. It hadn't taken long for the sewer gang to accept Beth as one of their own. Back at home too, Beth's father still called her worthless, but he took the coppers she gave him for her keep and the beatings of her mother were less frequent. Her mother, though, tended to ignore Beth most days. On the rare occasions they spoke, it was to ask her when she'd have enough money to leave home, or to find out if any of the men from work were 'interested' in her. Their conversations never lasted long as Beth wasn't able to give her the answers she wanted; none of the gang had shown her the slightest bit of interest so far, and she hadn't earned enough to even contemplate leaving home.

***

"Right, let's get back to the hatch," called Parat after a particularly busy day. "Shift's over."

Everyone sighed with relief and gathered, some of them jumping up onto the high ledge for the long walk back.

"I must admit, Beth, I didn't think you'd last this long," said Parat as they moved along, still down in the trench so they could walk side by side. "The guys are calling you their lucky charm. We've lost no one, had no injuries, and had more lucky finds since you joined the gang!"

Beth's cheeks flushed red. She'd never been complimented before and was glad they were on the edge of the lantern light so no one could see her high colour. She wasn't sure how to respond either, so she said nothing.

"Tomorrow's Stonemorn", he began again. "End of the week and no shift. The lads are all meeting for a few tankards in The Hauling Gausent. You should come. I'm sure the lads would like—" but he was interrupted by a cry from another worker up ahead.

"Flush coming!!"

There had been no bell. No sooner had the man called out then the sound of gushing water filled the tunnel, and a mad scramble ensued as those not already on the high ledge tried to mount it. The torrent raged by for several minutes before subsiding, then only the sound of heavy breathing filled the air. At this point, Parat would usually call out the names of the workers on shift to check everyone was alright – but not this time.

"Parat, you there?", called a crewman called Tem, but there was no response. "Right! Name call! Beth? Sidlemore? Cord? Dreclin? Filpit? Dander? Olber? Gornt? Rusty? *Parat*?" he shouted, pausing between each name.

Everyone acknowledged their name with a "Here!" or a loud grunt and everyone was accounted for – everyone that is except Parat.

"Shit," said Tem. "We must've lost him. Anyone see what happened?"

A slew of mutterings followed, but no one had seen what had happened to their leader.

"Right, we all know the drill. Back to the hatch."

To Beth's astonishment, all of the workers – who, moments earlier, had been laughing and bantering with Parat – dropped down to the walkway and continued on.

"Wait! You can't just leave him!" she cried, loud enough for everyone to hear.

"Sorry, Beth. That's the policy," said Tem, and he kept on walking. "It's too dangerous for us to go searching. He'll be far away by now. The flush probably dragged him for miles."

"But how do you know?" asked Beth. "What if he's close by and injured?".

"It's almost unheard of to survive a flush," replied Tem. "And anyway, we'll get lost if we go outside our sector. We don't know the other tunnels and hatches."

"But it's not impossible, right?" she insisted.

Tem stopped suddenly and turned to face her. "I'm sorry, Beth. I know he's your first loss, but it happens. We've all lost mates before. And even if he's close, the next flush will wash him further away."

"Well I'm not leaving," said Beth, and she folded her arms stubbornly.

Tem sighed. "Beth, this is just what happens in the sewers. You have to accept it."

"No. I'm not going back without him," she cried, and held out her hand. "Now give me that lantern."

The crewmen who'd heard the exchange stopped and glowered at her. Beth wondered if any of them would choose to stay with her and help, but they didn't.

Beth stood firm and Tem realised just how determined she was. "You can take a lantern and some oil, but you're on your own. And I'll have to report you lost, too".

"I'm not leaving him," she said again.

The light of the other lanterns disappeared quickly and Beth was alone, rooted to the spot, fear and doubt creeping into her mind. Why was she being so stupid? So stubborn? Parat meant nothing to her. He'd have left her if it had been the other way around, so why should she risk it all for him? It wasn't like her to be brave. She usually just did what she was told – never challenging or rebelling. That was always the safest and easiest thing to do. For a second she considered going back to the hatch like the others, and forgetting about him, but the moment passed and as she continued down the dark tunnel – away from the hatch and the promise of safety – she knew nothing would change her mind.

She was baffled when she came to an intersection of three tunnels. She'd never been out this far before, and she had no idea which way to go next. A bell rang and she climbed high onto the ledge to avoid the flush. Water charged from one tunnel and diverted into another. Keep going downstream, she told herself. Follow the flush.

She lost track of time but kept going, not seeing anyone else as she passed through the other tunnels. All the other shifts must have finished too. Then, out the corner of her eye, she saw a body. She didn't flinch this time – the sight of corpses didn't bother her much these days. She hoisted the weight up against the wall of the walkway to examine it. It wasn't Parat. She searched through its clothing and pulled a coin pouch from a pocket, which she stuffed into her own before continuing on. A little while later, she came across another body. The imminence of a flush loomed over her so she raced towards it and swiped the faeces from its face as quickly as she could, and there – beneath all the sludge and grime – was Parat's face.

It was difficult, but she finally managed to lift his body onto the ledge. For once she was glad she was so much broader and stronger than other girls her age. She heard a grunt. Was he alive?

A bell rang out, followed by the sound of water crashing through the chambers. And then the wave came. A deluge of thick black slush raced towards her and she knew she had to act fast. She swung the lantern up onto the ledge and had just managed to hurl her upper body onto it when the wave hit. She fought hard against its icy current which gripped at her legs, determined to claim another victim, and with a strength she didn't know she possessed, she hauled her legs up above the furious flood and lay there, holding on tightly as the fast-flowing water overlapped the edge. She shook with the effort as the threat charged below her, but she still held on. Finally it passed and her exhausted muscles relaxed.

She felt the panic rising as she wondered what to do next, then she remembered a passageway that she'd passed several hundred yards back. With a Herculean effort, she managed to reach it, walking backwards all the way while dragging Parat. Sometime later, she was back in a chamber much like their own, where she placed him down as gently as she could onto the floor, then pulled on a shower-chain to wash them both clean. Only then did she check him for signs of life – he hadn't made a sound so far. She pressed her ear to his mouth while watching for the fall and rise of his chest. To her relief he was breathing. Only shallow breaths, but breaths all the same.

"Tough old bastard," she said aloud and started to cry.

Parat coughed suddenly, then vomited a slew of dirty liquid all over the chamber floor. Beth rolled him on his side so that he wouldn't choke and, after a few seconds, the spluttering stopped. When he opened his eyes, his gaze seemed distant – lost – as though his life had left his body but his body was yet to realise that. And then, a spark of recognition. His eyes locked with Beth's.

"Beth?" he croaked.

"I'm here."

***

Together, still dressed in their leathers and carrying the lantern, they pushed open the hatch. Parat looked around them. It was light outside – mid-morning, probably; they must have been down in the sewer all night.

"We're in Cutter District," he whispered.

They climbed out and stood up shakily on the street. They brushed themselves down instinctively, despite knowing it was pointless. Beth handed the pouch to him. "Here, I found this."

Parat took it and chuckled softly. He opened the flap and poured the contents into his palm; two gold coin, some silvers, and some coppers fell out.

"Good god, girl. You really are one serious good luck charm."

The Hauling Gausent was loud and rowdy that evening. The sewer gang sat at their regular long table, making toasts to their lost comrades and wishing them a fond farewell. Tem was the first to see them and Beth's huge smile. He fell silent and turned pale. The others turned round to see what he was staring at and gawped when they saw Beth and Parat striding towards them – her arm interlinked with his, both now looking clean and smartly dressed. It had been Parat's idea to clean up and spend some of the coin they had on clean clothing. "I can't wait to see their faces when we show up both alive and looking dandy," he had chuckled.

"So," said Parat, his cheery voice piercing their stunned silence. "Is no one going to get our girl here an ale?"

Their questions all came at once, and Beth perched herself on one of the benches and readied herself to talk.

Parat told his version of events first; he couldn't recall much other than that he'd drifted in and out of consciousness, trying not to drown. When it was Beth's turn, she told her tale with such calmness and modesty that the others were forced to remind her how much bravery, strength and determination she'd shown – and, of course, stupidity. Beth blushed, and smiled, and laughed. When she'd finished her piece, Parat revealed the purse she'd found, and the whole table roared. Every head in the tavern swivelled round to see what the commotion was, forcing them to dampen their cheers and huddle back down in an attempt to be inconspicuous again.

This was Beth's first time in a tavern, and she thoroughly enjoyed it. She was surprised when Dreclin offered to walk her home at the end of the evening. She wasn't sure if it was because of the ale or because she'd been caught off guard, but she said yes. Dreclin was older than her by at least ten years, but he was far from ugly. He was also the first person ever to show her any gallantry. They walked home slowly, talking nonsense along the way. Beth was bemused, bewildered even, by the fact she had a chaperone, so she prattled on about anything and everything, but Dreclin didn't seem to mind and smiled at her the whole time. When they reached the door of her house and Beth began her thank yous and goodnights, he kissed her on the lips.

"Goodnight, Beth. See you on the next shift."

He left and she didn't move until he was well out of sight. Even then, she was reluctant to give up the moment – standing alone in the night, cherishing the feeling of his lips against hers and wondering what it meant. She had never been kissed like that before. It had been the best day of her life.

Her contentment was shattered when she stepped indoors, where her Ma and Da sat at the kitchen table, with two enforcers opposite them. On the table was a pistol, some assorted silverware and a few other trinkets.

"Here she is, the dirty thief," her Da spat at her when she walked into the room. "She's the one you want. Ask her how she's come by so much coin recently."

"Be quiet, sir. We'll ask the questions." The uniformed female enforcer looked sternly at Beth, then gestured towards the objects on the table. "Have you seen these items before, girl?"

"No. Why? What's going on?"

"We were told a thief lived here, so we searched the building and found these. Are you sure you haven't seen them before?"

"No – I mean, yes," Beth stuttered, "I haven't seen them before."

"Then how do you explain this?" the enforcer asked, and she dropped a leather purse onto the table. This Beth could explain – it was a leather purse she had acquired several weeks ago. She'd kept it hidden in her room and was using it to store her share of the findings from the sewers. It fell open as it clanked onto the table, and several gold and silver coins rolled out. Of course Beth couldn't tell them where she had got the money – she'd been sworn to secrecy. So when they asked her, "Is this yours?" and she nodded, and they said, "So how does a sewer girl like you come across so much coin when you've only been working a few weeks?" she had no response.

"See! We told you. She's the thief!" cried Helna, her voice shrill and full of accusation. "She's the one you want – not us."

Now both enforcers turned to face Beth. "Well, girl? Can you explain?"

Beth froze. She knew she wasn't the thief – not of the pistol, or the silverware, or the trinkets, anyway – but she couldn't bring herself to explain why she had so much coin, or why she'd hidden it away in her room. She just couldn't.

"Last chance … or we'll take you to the cells for further questioning."

And just like that, the best day of Beth's life became the worst, and she was muscled away into the night by the two enforcers.

TWO

The man tied to the chair had his head on his chest. He was sobbing. There was a yellow stain on his pants and a foul smell drifted upwards to reach Valentina's nose. She had tortured him for no more than half an hour, but she was sure she knew everything that he knew. Now he was a worthless man, bloodied and beaten, and scarred by magic. She stood before him, contemplating his demise. Then, placing her hand on his head, she discharged a pulse of magic that fried his brain. The sobbing stopped abruptly and his chest stilled.

Taking a napkin from the table (he had been dining on his evening meal when she arrived) Valentina wiped a few specks of blood from the front of her leather bodice and embroidered britches. The cutlery he'd been eating with now protruded from his dead body. The sliced meat, still uneaten on the plate, looked appetising, so Valentina took a piece and chewed on it as she headed for the front door.

She'd been searching for Orestas Connroy's secrets for a long, long time, and the man she had just questioned had given her what she needed. The end of her quest to find the secrets of the most powerful spellbinder who'd ever lived was finally in sight. She had questioned countless men and women to get to where she was today, but it was all going to be worth it, all that time she'd spent away from her lands and estate, attending to their many problems.

Outside, in the poorly cobbled street, waited her two escorts, Dom and Grigor, big burly hunters whom she had hired back in Ragas. There had been three of them when they set out, but one had fallen prey to a dreken along the way. The bites from the six-foot-long, six-legged, rake-thin lizards are severe and disabling even if treated, but without the antidote the poison is fatal in minutes. Valentina carried one phial of the antidote with her but she wasn't going to waste it on a hired hand. The other two hunters had shown no remorse at the loss of their companion, probably because the generous purse for their services would now be split only two ways.

"We are going back to Ragas tonight," she announced.

Dom opened his mouth to speak. "Ah …"

Valentina shot him a glance and he swallowed whatever he was about to say.

"I hate these backwater villages and towns," she muttered as she strode off.

When the three reached the stable on the edge of the village, Dom rattled the doors.

"Doors locked," he said in a deep gruff voice.

"Stable hand must have gone home for the night," added Grigor.

"Well, break it open," Valentina ordered, growing impatient.

"But—" started Dom and Grigor.

She was in no mood for excuses. "I am Mistress of Castle Worthmere and the stupid rules and regulations of these cities, towns and villages do not apply to me. Break the doors open now."

The interior of the stable stank of gausents and fouled straw. There were only five mounts; the three they had brought and two others.

"We will ride until morning, rest for a while, then ride through the next day and evening until we reach Ragas," Valentina declared as she reached the stall of her mount.

She had purchased her gausent in Ragas and would sell it back to the same stable on her return. Valentina always bought the best mounts available when she travelled outside populated areas. A strong reliable one could make the difference between life and death on the tracks between settlements. The big bull gausent she rode now was six feet tall at its humped shoulders, with a hugely barrelled chest. A gausent's gait, although steady, could be uncomfortable after many miles, so her saddle and pack harness were of the finest quality.

They made good time, keeping up a brisk trot until dawn. Thankfully they encountered no predators on the muddy track they followed. It had started to rain as dawn broke and a rest and quick meal were much needed by the weary travellers.

Valentina let her guides select the best place to stop; they knew the local terrain better than she did. That was why she was paying them. The two hunters set up camp with practised ease. They were in a small clearing, close enough to a watercourse to replenish their flasks, but far enough from the riverbank to avoid being ambushed by coldons. They were known to break cover in groups and charge unwary campers. When they attacked, they struck quickly. Despite being the length of a man, they were almost impossible to see as they scurried along the banks of the waterways because they were so well camouflaged by their slick dark-mottled skin. A third of their length was a powerful snapping jaw that clamped onto their victims and dragged them beneath the water.

The first thing the two men set up was a large thick waxed sheet on two poles. Here Valentina would rest, sheltered from the rain. She watched her two escorts carefully as they tethered the gausents, set a fire and prepared a simple meal. She had no reason yet to distrust them, and observing their competency reassured her that she could risk sleeping after she'd eaten.

The men ignored the rain, their patchwork coats and hats of fur and hide made them impervious to the wet. Dom cast a spell to light the fire. Valentina had seen him do this before, but she had yet to see what Grigor's incant was.

She removed the wide-brimmed capotain from her head and reached into one pocket of her long leather coat. Her familiar was curled up in there, snug and warm, but gave no objection to being roused.

Dom and Grigor eyed the black rat with obvious concern. Valentina smiled mischievously. The familiar was harmless to the two men, but their superstitions gave them cause to fear it. She set it down and placed some scraps of dried food before its nose. It would stay awake while she slept and alert her to any danger.

When they were sated and rested, they set out at a brisk trot once more. Dom and Grigor rode a little ahead, side by side, with Valentina far enough behind to avoid the mud their mounts splashed backwards. She noticed that Dom was asleep in his saddle, slumped forward on top of the pack harness across the gausent's hump. Sleeping in the saddle at a trot was something she'd never mastered.

They rounded a bend and Grigor pulled to a stop. The change in pace woke Dom, who quickly sat upright. In the road, some three hundred yards ahead, was a large vember. Dom drew his bow and nocked an arrow. Grigor readied a lance. Their gausents lowered their horns; generally so timid and calm, they weren't averse to a fight to defend themselves or their riders. With one hand, Valentina drew one of her seedpistols, taking a firm grip of the pack harness with the other. If her gausent was going to join the charge, she didn't want to be dislodged from her saddle.

The vember was sprawled across the road. It was a big male, eight feet from head to flank, idly flipping his six-foot tail backwards and forwards. Watching the riders, he slowly rose to stand on all four heavy sharp-clawed paws. His fanged muzzle and chest were covered in blood. He sniffed the air, taking in the scent of the gausents and their riders. Then he strolled into the trees and disappeared.

They rode at top speed for the next half-mile, putting as much distance between them and the vember as they could. Big males in their prime ran faster than gausents. Then they slowed to a walk and Valentina fell in behind them again. But just because they couldn't see the vember didn't mean it wasn't there – it also had effective camouflage because of its black-spotted grey hide. So they kept their weapons drawn and at the ready. After a short walk, they once again broke into the brisk trot that the gausents were bred for, which they could maintain for many miles at a time.

Ragas came into sight as evening fell. The stables on the outskirts of the town were always open and attended, and this would be Valentina's first point of call. Next, would be a visit to the temple's money-holding cages.

The cobbled streets were smooth here, and lit by lanterns. The Mistress was pleased to be back in a place with some semblance of civilisation. Ragas may not have all the refinements of the cities, but it was an old well-established town where she could restock supplies and rest comfortably before their onward journey.

They were forced to detour from a more direct path to the temple because one of the boroughs of half-timbered houses was being demolished. The old buildings, with thatched roofs and wattle and daub filling their timber frames, were being replaced with modern brick-filled wood-framed homes with tiled roofs. The aim was to reduce the risk of fires, of which there had been several in recent years.

The temple was located at the far end of a large open square, and in the centre of the square was a large statue of the spellbinder Orestas. The stone plinth on which he stood read:

Orestas Connroy

Born Fox10 – Died Fox310

A Glorified Soul of Stellation

Valentina stared at his finely carved features. He was the reason for her travels and the source of what she was seeking. Deceased for over a hundred years, his spellbinding was still legendary.

"Do you think he really lived for three hundred years?" Dom asked Grigor.

"You ask that every time we pass it," replied his companion. "The Temple of Stellation obviously thinks so, as they made him a glorified soul."

The symmetry of the temple set it apart from any of the nearby buildings. Its orderly arrangement of columns, pilasters and lintels, semicircular arches and hemispherical domes, all in pale stone, were in stark contrast to the dark irregularly shaped buildings to either side.

"Wait here," instructed Valentina. She didn't wait to see if they complied. They would obey her. Leaving them in the large open space of the exchange hall, she proceeded into the temple to the vault-access cages.

There were fewer people in the temple at this time of night, but both the vaults and the chapel were open. Priests, temple workers and the Temple Guard were ever-present, watching over the worshipers and attendees of the vault service.

Valentina located the vault-access cages and waited behind a bald portly man who was making a payment on his loan. When it was her turn, she stepped forward to the attendant and withdrew enough gold, silver and copper coin for the next stage of her trip. She secured the coin in five separate leather money pouches that she kept in various inner pockets of her coat.

Away from the cages, she counted out the payment for her two guides. This she put in a front pocket for easy access before setting off back to the exchange hall. She paid the two men and left them to their own affairs.

While Valentina had been away from Ragas, her rooms had been kept at a very cosy boarding establishment. She was glad to go back there and immediately ordered a hot bath and a tray of meats and cheeses, along with a bottle of red wine. She would rest for the remainder of the night and through the next day? before continuing her passage. The secrets as to how Orestas had managed to live so long and stay so healthy were closer than ever to being discovered, and when she had that knowledge she would return to her vast estate and relax again, knowing she had a long life ahead of her.

There was only one more person she needed to question, Rigard Pentwing, another spellbinder and a wealthy man who resided in the city of Fallon. He supposedly held in secret – safely and securely – what she sought. She would travel to Arities and take the airboat from there to Fallon.

THREE

The journey on the coach was not the smoothest of rides. The suspension was hard, and little tax money had been spent on maintaining the roads, so the bumpiness had to be endured.

Valentina had paid for all four seats on one side of the carriage that held eight first-class passengers in total. The second-class seats were in a large open basket attached to the back of the coach. The least privileged travellers sat on the roof along with the luggage, relying on a handrail to stop them falling off; if they did fall off they would be left behind. The first-class passengers, who sat in relative comfort inside the carriage, were promised they would not be abandoned if they fell out of the carriage and would not be abandoned if they were attacked.

The unwieldy vehicle lurched along the rutted roads quite slowly, at an average speed of twelve miles an hour. Coaches were regarded as a safer mode of transport than journeying alone on a gausent or with an escort, because the carriage and the six large gausents that drew it presented too large a target for most predators. There were also three armed guards on board, two on the rear bench and one up front with the driver. Yet it was still the case that not every coach completed its journey.

Valentina sat alone, in relative comfort with her other three seats empty beside her. Occasionally she looked at the four strangers opposite, packed together more tightly than she could tolerate. They were clearly wealthy and polite, attempting to introduce themselves to her soon after they set off. Valentina brushed them aside by telling them her title – Mistress of Castle Worthmere – and made obvious her complete lack of interest in small talk. The atmosphere was frosty for the first couple of hours, but then they began to speak freely amongst themselves. Two of them looked very young and Valentina couldn't help overhearing that they were newly married couple, and making their way to the city to start a new life. They were talking animatedly with an older woman, one Jacobia Jeston, who traded in fashion garments and was off to secure a new contract. The fourth, however, was more elusive. She was a seemingly demure businesswoman called Lissa Tormain. Valentina had her measure straight away. Nothing more than a brothel scout, she thought, out looking for fresh men and women to recruit.

It was going to be a long trip, the next rest stop many hours away. These coaches only stopped every eight hours or so, and stayed put for the same amount of time, and there were three stops between Ragas and Arities.

Six hours into the journey, the coach halted suddenly and the passengers were jolted in their seats.

"There's mist ahead," hollered the driver. "We'll wait

to see if it's moving towards us or drifting away."

The four other passengers became agitated, while Valentina calmly drew each of her three seedpistols in turn and checked that they were fully charged. She relaxed and waited for the update about the mist.

"It's coming towards us, so we're going t-o back up," was the next announcement.

Before the driver could crack his reins there was the clap of a seedpistol, then four more rounds followed in rapid succession. The carriage was struck by something large.

Everyone screamed apart from Valentina. The newly married girl started to sob and held on to her husband tightly. They were going to be no help with whatever predator had attacked the stationary coach, Valentina thought. Then there was the mist to consider, if it was closing in. She climbed out of the coach and assessed the situation.

On the ground beside her lay the coach driver, three passengers from the outside seats, and two guards – each armed with a lance and bow. They were squirming in their death throes. Another guard was recharging his pistol – just one pistol – how stupid, thought Valentina. The other passengers were cowering in fear, except two of them, perched high on the roof of the coach, one a well-dressed man holding a seedpistol in each hand, and beside him a tall blonde woman poised with a bow nocked with two arrows. They were scanning the trees to the right of the road.

Valentina assessed the fallen, and knew they had been attacked by a dreken – one of the giant lizards. Its bites alone were severe and disabling, but without an antidote its poison caused death within minutes.

Now she was out in the open, on the wrong side of the coach, so she would be its next target. The murky grey, swirling mist was billowing towards them. She holstered both her pistols and moved as quickly as she could to the coach driver's seat, grabbing the fallen reins as she did so. The dreken was dangerous, but not as dangerous as the mist and what it may contain. She needed to back the coach up before it came any closer. As she manoeuvred it backwards, the dreken struck again, darting across the road and mounting the coach, snapping and biting at everything in its path. Three more passengers fell.

The man on the roof fired off six shots, and the archer four arrows, two at a time. The guard was still charging and loading his pistol. It appeared that all six slugs and four arrows hit their target, but the dreken didn't slow down. Valentina hoped the arrows were laced with poison. Why didn't the seeder have darts loaded in at least one of his pistols? A big mistake for such a skilled fighter.

Valentina cracked the reins and the coach kept moving. The six gausents hauled the carriage backwards as bidden, and once again she found herself admiring their steadfastness.

But it was too late. The billowing cloud of interlaced shades of grey mist was upon them, from which a mist monster bounded out. With a single hop, it covered the forty feet or so between them and landed inches from the coach, standing upright on its massive hind legs, so that its long-snouted head with huge bell-shaped ears reared over the top of the coach. It swiped at its prey with its two short but deadly clawed front paws, the gaping maw bristling with long sharp canines.

Before it latched onto the leg of the woman archer the dreken was caught off-guard as the mist monster swung around and clamped its jaws into its skull, bringing it to an instant halt. Then, with a single hop and the dreken in its mouth, the monster returned to the mist.

Valentina cracked the reins once more and the gausents pulled the coach yet further from the converging mist.

Several hundred yards down the road the Mistress reined them in. Drawing two of her seedpistols, she joined the other two seeders on the roof to look back at the mist and survey their surroundings, ready for anything else that might emerge. Other monsters and predators could be hiding out there, capable of outrunning the coach. Sometimes fighting was the best option: they would stand fast and fight instead of fleeing.

The mist continued to advance on them relentlessly, but seconds before it engulfed them, it began to dissipate as the swirls of grey wafted to nothing like the smoke from an extinguished candle. Moments later it had gone completely. The fallen people, bitten by the dreken, were no longer lying on the road ahead. The mist had taken them with it.

"Hold on," Valentina ordered, once again taking the reins. The gausents, now pulling them forward, picked up speed.

The seeder guard moved back to the board seating next to Valentina.

"You're not sitting there," the Mistress said. "Get to the back and keep a lookout with the archer."

The guard started to object but the stern sharp look that flashed across Valentina's face with its steely green eyes were enough to make him obey.

"Mind if I have that seat?" came a voice from above her. It was the well-dressed man, the other seeder, who had taken a stance on the roof.

Looking him up and down, and finding him agreeable enough, Valentina nodded.

"By my count we lost nine," he said.

"Why have you no darts in your seedpistol?" she asked him.

"I couldn't afford any if I was to pay my passage on this trip."

"Do you have any slugs left?"

"Yes. Ten. But I don't have any more seedpods to recharge my pistols."

Valentina reached into her pocket and handed him four seedpods. "Recharge your pistols. We may need them again."

The Mistress kept one eye on the road and the other on the seeder. She wanted a better measure of his competency. The man placed two of the seedpods in a charging chamber and with two rapid pump-action strokes of the chamber's casing crushed the seeds, releasing the gas and pressurising the chamber. He inserted the charged chamber's transfer nipple to the injection port at the base of the pistol's grip to move the charge to the weapon and then re-loaded the revolving chambers with four fresh slugs. He repeated the actions with his second pistol.

He seems reasonably capable, Valentina observed. At no time had he left himself without a loaded charged weapon.

They arrived at the coach house early in the evening.

The Mistress pulled the team up outside and retrieved her bag from the roof. She climbed down from the coach, leaving everyone else behind without a second thought or glance.

The eight-hour rest stop would give the gausents much-needed respite and allow them to swap any out of the team that were flagging, provided any replacements were available. Not wanting to mix with the other passengers, Valentina enquired about private rooms for herself. She was in luck. Before her fellow travellers had even disembarked, she was heading up the stairs.

An hour later she had eaten and refreshed herself in her rooms, and could hear raised voices coming from below. Some sort of argument, she discerned, no doubt over the lost driver and guards. Coach houses often had reservists in waiting for such scenarios, but it wasn't guaranteed. She wasn't prepared to delay her journey so, checking the charge in her seedpistols, she left her room to join the fray.

"We have to wait for replacements from Ragas," said one of the survivors, Jacobia Jeston.

A few of the passengers and the seeder guard nodded in mutual agreement. It seemed Valentina would only have the support of the well-dressed seeder passenger and the blonde archer.

"We will be carrying on," she declared, drawing everyone's attention.

The guard was quick to reply as he pointed to the coach-house manager. "The proprietor says the coach cannot leave without a registered coach-line employee, and being the only one left I'm not going on without others to support me."

"These good people ..." Valentina swept her hand towards the newlyweds, Jacobia and Lissa, "know that I am Mistress of Castle Worthmere. If that is not enough to convince you that we will be continuing, then know that I can be very persuasive in many other ways." Her tone brooked no argument.

In the stunned silence that followed, the seeder passenger and the archer took up position beside her.

"I'm certainly not going on," said the new bride, taking a firm hold of her husband.

"I'm not asking who is or isn't going on or staying behind. The coach will leave as soon as the gausents are rested. This is not up for debate."

Valentina headed away from the group, followed by the archer and the seeder, ignoring the proprietor who was quoting the regulations for a second time. "No coach can leave a station without a registered coach-line employee. You can *not* take the coach."

She turned on her heel. "Did you miss the moment I made you aware that I am a Mistress?"

The risk of losing his position at the coach house gave the nervous proprietor enough strength to make a further, albeit weak, stand. "No coach can leave a station without a registered coach-line employee," he repeated stridently.

Valentina paused only briefly at the rebuff. For a second she considered bribing him, but dismissed that idea just as quickly as it had arrived. She didn't need his permission, but would prefer to have the help of his stable hands. A further demonstration of her power was needed. So, taking the familiar from her pocket, she placed it on the proprietor's desk and fed it a few scraps of food.

The proprietor's eyes widened. The blonde archer took in a sharp breath at the sight of it, but the gentlemen seeder seemed unfazed. Then the proprietor's expression transitioned from shock, to fear, and finally to submission; his shoulders drooped and his head hung down.

"I will have the team ready on time, Mistress," he complied weakly. "And I will advise you when they are harnessed."

***

Valentina stood outside in the fresh early morning air. It was time leave. The well-dressed seeder approached her.

"Mornin' Mistress. My name's Enray. Don't suppose I can travel with you?" He adjusted his belt and holster as he spoke. He sounded cocky.

"I'd like to come too," called Lissa, hurrying out from the coach house.

"Decided to join us, then?" Enray was smiling widely.

"Yes. I'm hoping that the next coach house will have reservists and we can continue from there with a full guard and a driver."

"That doesn't make the next leg any safer," said the blonde archer as she sidled up to them. "I'm Abelee, by the way, and I'd like to travel with you too."

"My employer won't be happy if I'm not on this coach," Lisa added. "He's scarier than any beast out there!" The relaxed banter was raising their mood.

"First things first!" interrupted the Mistress. "Apart from myself, who can drive a coach?"

Everyone acknowledged that they could to some extent. Enray raised an eyebrow at Lissa. With her short, stout, full-curved figure she didn't look like someone who could handle a strong team of gausents. She noticed his mockery.

"I have a past that wasn't always about flowery clothes and polite manners," she countered. "I'm also competent with a seedpistol and a blade – but all I have with me is a six-inch dagger and no one inside would give me anything more substantial."

Valentina handed her a finely polished wooden box, which she opened and then gasped in amazement. Inside was a pistol and seed-chamber set.

"Don't lose it," Valentina said curtly. "I want it back."

"They're beautiful." Lissa took out the pistol and turned it over in her hands. "Isn't this that new steel that some smiths are using to replace iron?"

"That's right."

"It must be really expensive."

"Worth your life if you lose it," Valentina replied. "It's also the only spare I'm travelling with, so do not damage it. You will need these, too." She handed over two pouches, one filled with seedpods and the other with slugs. "Whatever you don't use, I want back. There are only four of us so we'll all travel on top of the coach and take turns at driving the team."

Enray couldn't take his eyes off the pistol Lissa was holding, his envy clear for all to see. Then he straightened his back, reaching his full height of five foot nine inches, so that his eyes were at the same level as Valentina's, and took a deep breath to say something. The Mistress cut him off.

"Don't ask," she said. "Here." And she handed him two similar pouches and a rack of six darts. Their tips were sheathed in the body of a leather rack with a fold-over flap to protect the plumes. "The red ones are toxic – one of the strongest poisons you can buy. The single blue one is a tranquiliser that will floor a human almost instantly …" she paused. "Don't look at me like that! None of this means that I like any of you! I merely want to survive this trip and for that I need you suitably ready and equipped. Abelee, you're good with that bow and I can see you have a good supply of arrows, but that shirt and coat won't protect you from anything. You're a bit taller than me, a touch slimmer round the waist, a little heavier in the bust, but this leather bodice should adjust enough to fit you. Its woven lining should prevent slugs and arrows from penetrating."

"Thank you," said Abelee as she accepted the garment.

"Thank you," Lissa and Enray echoed.

They all turned at the sound of the coach drawing out from the stable and turned to watch as the stable hands brought it over to them.

"I didn't think she was this nice," Lissa whispered to Enray, but Valentina heard the comment.

"I'm not nice. I'm just improving my own chances of survival."

They arrived without incident at the next coach house. They had seen some mist not too far away from the road in the early morning light, but it was at a safe distance among the trees and did not overly alarm them.

When Valentina climbed from the carriage she went inside to arrange another private room, delaying long enough before retiring for some rest to speak with the proprietor about their onward journey. Lissa's wish, that there would be some available reservists, was partly realised.

There was a driver and a single guard, both free to continue with them, but they both needed to be persuaded to do so. It was only when Abelee, Enray and Lissa agreed to remain on top of the coach for additional protection that they conceded.

The next stage of their journey began in the early evening, and the rain fell heavily for the entirety of the passage. Valentina was the sole occupant of the inside of the carriage, while everyone else had to endure the downpour. They arrived at the final coach house in the early hours of that evening and left again in the morning, a little before dawn.

During this final leg, the rain ceased and the sun shone strongly and warmly, so Valentina opened the side shutters of the cabin to take in the view. The closer they came to the city of Arities, the more the landscape changed. The woodland and its heavy vegetation thinned out into isolated pockets of scrub, the spaces in between filled by well-constructed hamlets and tended fields, along with plenty of livestock until they dominated the scene. The final indication that they had reach civilisation was when the coach left the dirt road and began to traverse along a smooth stone road. They were just a couple of hours outside the city.

FOUR

Valentina found suitable accommodation in an affluent part of the city, a large luxurious living space with a separate bedroom. She had no reason to restock with supplies. so she went straight to the airboat station and booked a flight to Fallon. The next departure was the day after next. With considerable time on her hands, she wanted some leisurely distraction. She bought herself a ticket to a play that was on in the evening at the city's renowned theatre, together with a green velvet and gold embroidered dress, matching elegant shoes and all the complementary jewellery trimmings.

"Hotel Lanka," she instructed the female barrow-puller, ready at last to rest in her comfortable suite. The show had been every bit as she had hoped for and now all she wanted was a hot bath, a bottle of red wine and a decent sleep.

"Is it alright to take the Tower Road, miss?" asked the barrow-woman once she had started to run, hauling the lightweight wooden barrow behind her.

"Why do you ask?"

"Well, it cuts through Cutter and its much quicker – only Cutter's not the nicest of districts."

Valentina considered this. She was wearing only a single pistol and one sturdy knife because she hadn't wanted to spoil her outfit.

"No. Go the long way."

"Alright miss."

The journey took just over half an hour and the woman's face was dripping with sweat by the end of it and she was breathless from the exertion. Valentina paid her the exact amount for the ride, offering no gratuity. She had no compassion for this type of woman; if this was her chosen profession then she needed to be fitter.

At the reception desk she ordered a bottle of Torborg Red and a hot bath. Not long after, the bath arrived in her room with clouds of steam wafting off the boiling water, just right for her. And the wine was excellent. The bottle and glass sat on a side-table next to the tub.

Crash!

The door to Valentina's room was kicked in and twelve masked armed intruders charged through it. They ran up to the high back of the bath knowing that was where their quarry rested, unaware.

"Don't move or we'll shoot," one of them shouted. "And we have a spellbinder with us! Now get up slowly and you might just live through this."

Clap! Clap! Clap!

Three slugs were fired in rapid succession. The first hit the spellbinder and killed him outright, his hands still glowing with readied magic. The iron ball entered his right temple and exploded from the other side of his head.

The second took the speaker in his right cheek, its lead jacket ripping the skin away from the side of his face as the iron-cored ball ricocheted inside his skull.

The third hit the neck of the largest intruder – a muscular, dangerous-looking beast of a man. He fell to the floor, blood spurting unchecked from the wound.

The other assailants turned to see Valentina standing beside the open door inside the bedroom, dressed only in the loose undergarments she had been wearing before stepping into the bath tub. She wielded a pistol in each hand.

Three of them who held pistols were obviously not seeders, Valentina deduced. They were the next to fall as she fired slugs into vital areas of their bodies. The surviving six charged at her.

After shooting her last two slugs, she dropped her pistols. One slug struck a woman in the chest, but didn't stop her. The other slug missed its target entirely.

Boom!

Valentina released a spell that knocked all the charging assailants backwards, tumbling them to the floor. She casually picked up her third pistol from the top of the dresser on the other side of the open door and took aim at their crumpled bodies. But out of the corner of one eye, she saw a masked seeder concealed in the shadows of the corridor outside the room. She ducked as she dashed from the room and back into her bedroom just as two slugs splintered the door frame.

The six living intruders who had fallen down stumbled to their feet and with angry cries rushed through the doorway after her. She fired all four rounds into the mass of bodies converging on her.

At least one woman dropped. Then, from the palm of her right hand, Valentina released a charge of magic that gripped one of the men. Light danced around him as he convulsed violently before falling to the floor, dead. Then the other four attackers were on top of her. Fight as she might, they managed to subdue her. Two held her down on her knees with her arms locked behind her.

"Don't use any fucking magic, bitch," said one woman as she pushed the very sharp point of a short sword hard into the back of Valentina's neck.

The masked seeder from the corridor entered the bedroom, clapping softly. "Very impressive," he cajoled. "I told Balcoff he needed to send more than twelve, but it seems they were enough. If she tries anything," he directed to her captors, "knock her out cold."

He slowly lowered his mask, revealing a familiar face. It was Enray. "I want them pretty steel pistols of yours," he said, smirking, and picked up the three fallen weapons before rummaging through Valentina's bag where it lay discarded on the bed.

"And I sold you out to Balcoff," he continued. "He's going to hold you hostage until your Castle Worthmere pays him a very handsome sum. I had considered wooing you and stealing them while you slept ... because you are quite pretty ... even though your nose is too thin and I prefer blondes to brunettes," he mocked her. Walking up to her and staring hard into her eyes, he added, "But I think you're too cold to fall for anyone, aren't you. So I gave up on that idea. Plus, you're too old. What are you? Thirty-three? Maybe thirty-six?".

He opened the polished wooden box that held the gun he had so admired. It was empty. "Where's the spare pistol?"

Valentina began to enjoy herself. "The box was empty when Lissa returned it. Looks like she beat you to it."

"You're fucking lying," Enray shouted, and slapped her across the face. "If she had stolen it, you'd have gone straight after her." Another vicious slap.

"Thank you," said Valentina, blood now dripping from her mouth.

"What the fuck for?" he blurted.

"For telling me why you are here and who's behind this. I don't like not knowing who's trying to hurt me – or kill me."

Blood-curdling screams filled the room as an intense ball of flame flashed out from Valentina's hand, burning the flesh from the hands that held her down and that of the woman holding the sword, then their faces frizzled away to bare bones as the flames ate away the flesh. Taking advantage of their shock and momentary distraction, she reached under the mattress of the bed and pulled out the spare pistol.

"Of course I was lying, you idiot," she scorned.

But Enray was fast – even after the shock of seeing the flesh burned from his accomplices. He drew his own pistol. And then, with one resounding crack, both pistols fired simultaneously. Valentina's slug exploded through his left eyeball and splattered the contents of his head across the wall behind him. His slug ripped into her right shoulder.

The one remaining attacker sat on the bedroom chair, quietly, bleeding. He'd been caught in the earlier crossfire and one of the slugs had caught him in the gut. He no longer had the strength to fight. Two of his burned comrades were squirming in agony on the bedroom floor, now gasping and squawking rather than screaming. Valentina wanted to let them die slowly, but she didn't want to risk any surprise recoveries, so she shot them all at close range, the belly-wounded man first, then the burned woman who was still holding her sword, and finally the torched man who still showed more signs of life than Valentina was comfortable with.

Job done, Valentina picked up her seed-chamber and a couple of spilt-out seedpods from the bed and recharged and reloaded the pistol in her hand, followed by a second pistol – something she could do with impressive speed. She calmly stepped over the mess of bodies and left the bedroom to return to the living space. Two of her attackers lay there, wounded and in in no fit condition to fight on. She finished them off with one shot each.

There was another noise at the door. Valentina spun round quickly, crouched down and aimed her weapons as someone appeared in the doorway. A man screamed, but Valentina hadn't fired. It was one of the hotel servants.

"I want a fresh room," she demanded, looking sadly at the broken bottle and glass on the floor beside the bath. "And another bottle of Torborg red."

She paused to make sure he was hearing her. "I also want a fresh bath."

"Y-yes, M-mistress," the man spluttered, and turned to leave.

"Wait!" she called after him. "I have not dismissed you yet." He reluctantly turned back to face her.

"I will pack my belongings and by the time I'm done, my room, wine and bath had better be ready – or there will be more dead bodies in here."

"Yes, Mistress." He was rooted to the spot, shaking visibly.

"Go. You're dismissed now." She let out a small laugh.

Back in the bedroom she waited for her new rooms to be prepared. She opened the bottom drawer of the dresser and looked at her familiar, curled up contentedly, still sleeping. She picked him up and placed him on her bed while she began to pack.

One fresh suite, hot bath and half a bottle of wine later, there was a knock at the door. She opened it, loaded pistol held low by her hip pointing forwards at the ready.

Two hotel servants and three large male enforcers stood outside.

"We've come to collect the tub, miss," said one of the servants, who was physically distancing herself from the enforcers as best she could. Valentina let the servants come past her.

"We'd like to ask you some questions," said one of the uniformed men.

"Come in, do" she said politely. "And I'd like to ask you some too, as it happens."

"Can we sit down?" asked another.

"No. I think not" said Valentina.

"The Commander wants you to come down to the station," said the first.

"Well, that won't be happening."

"But we must insist," was his stern response.

"You've obviously not checked the hotel register, have

you? I am Mistress Valentina Holbrine of Castle Worthmere, and I have no mind for your city rules and regulations. Now my question – tell me, who is Balcoff?"

The enforcers exchanged nervous glances. Was the name Balcoff the cause of all this mayhem? Finally, one of them spoke.

"Apologies, Mistress, we were unaware of your status." Their confidence gone, the three men shuffled their feet.

"So? Who is he?" Valentina folded her arms to emphasis her growing impatience.

The third uniformed man answered. "He proclaims himself the Master of Arities, but he is just a very influential criminal really – because, as you know, there are no Masters or Mistresses of any cities."

"So why have you not apprehended him?"

"As I say, he is influential. The people are scared of him. And his accomplices won't give him up." His tone was apologetic.

"This would not happen on my lands. Criminals are dealt with swiftly, and extremely harshly."

Valentina sat down on an easy chair and fixed them with a stony glare. "Is there a reward for this man?"

"Yes, Mistress." All three responded in unison.

"Well, have it doubled. Dead or alive. When he is dealt with, send word to Castle Worthmere and I will see that the coin is delivered accordingly."

"Yes, Mistress. Of course, Mistress."

There was another knock at the door. "See who that is," Valentina ordered from her chair.

"It's the poultician," announced the one who answered the door.

"Let them in. You can all go now."

The enforcers retreated with their instructions at the fore of their minds as Valentina greeted the poultician with some measure of gratitude. The wound on her shoulder was not serious but there was the risk of infection. The poultician cleaned and packed the wound, and bandaged it up, then applied a cooling ointment to the bruises on Valentina's face. She left some fresh dressings on the table beside Valentina's chair, and a tub of ointment to use over the next few days. She accepted her payment and left.

Alone once more, Valentina retired to bed, placing four loaded pistols beside her pillow, along with a sturdy knife and a dagger and reached for the other half of the bottle of wine. Her familiar lay where she had left it, trusted as always to keep watch while she slept. The hotel had put armed guards outside her room door for the night.

The next morning required a visit to a pistol specialist. It seemed one of her pistols had lost its charge overnight. The hotel leased two guards to Valentina for the day who, they swore, were from a reliable provider. The male was a seeder – tall, thin and dressed in a weave-lined leather waistcoat and britches. The female was a spellbinder – young, pretty and smartly dressed, with a sheathed sword on her hip.

"How can I help you?" asked the pistol specialist in the quiet shop, with her and her two guards the only customers.

"I dropped my pistol last night and it's no longer holding its charge," Valentina told him.

"Hmmh, let me see. Yes, probably one of the seals on the grip has failed. Give me one moment." He stepped into a back room where his workbench piled with sundry tools and clutter was just visible.

While she waited, Valentina admired some of the pistols hanging on the wall behind the counter. All so well designed and ornate. The pistol specialist, it would seem, was quite skilled at his craft. A small slender innocent-looking tube caught her attention. What was it? And why was it hanging alongside the weapons?

After a few minutes the man returned with her pistol. "As I thought. One of the seals has ruptured. It will be fine now."

"What's that tube?" Valentina pointed it out.

The man turned to the wall behind him and gently lifted the device from its rest. "This is my latest creation. It will fit most pistols with the correct clamps."

He handed it to Valentina. She turned it over and over in her hand, attempting to fathom its function.

"Look through the wider end," he instructed.

Valentina put it to her eye and looked out of the window across the street. "Everything is blurry."

"Turn the wheel on the top."

She used her forefinger to locate the tiny notched wheel and moved it a fraction. Everything came into sharp focus.

"Oh! It's a very small eyeglass."

"Not quite … Can you see the crossed lines? And more lines beneath the cross."

"Yes, what of them?"

"Come with me," he replied enthusiastically and signalled with his hand for her to follow him.

Intrigued by his excitement and the mysterious device,

Valentina followed him. He stopped at the workbench and attached the eyeglass to her repaired pistol, then led her through a side door to a shooting range. Ten feet wide, with thick timbers running along both sides, heavy sandbags were stacked at the far end, a few hundred feet away. Three timber-framed targets, each the silhouette of an upright person, were spaced down along the range at various distances.

"Please," he beckoned. "Take a few shots with one of your pistols."

Valentina fired four slugs and then recharged and reloaded.

"I see you are an exceptional seeder, miss. Most seeders are accurate up to around eighty feet, but it takes great skill beyond that. And slugs are not effective over more than a few hundred feet." He reached out and took the pistol from her, and then handed her the repaired pistol with the small eyeglass attached. "Now try this."

Valentina fired a single slug from the pistol without looking through the tube.

"No, not like that!" instructed the man. "Look through the eyeglass and aim where the cross lines meet at the centre."

Valentina did so, reluctantly. "But I can aim and fire more quickly without looking through the eyeglass," she stated, a little disappointed.

"Please give it a go. Fire at the second target, but use the first line beneath the horizontal for your aim."

She indulged him. "Well, that was accurate," she admitted.

"The cross lines are good to eighty feet and each line beneath the cross compensates on average for an additional ten feet. Each pistol is slightly different, of course, but that's the basic principle."

Valentina fired and reloaded twice. It was true – the eyeglass was useful for accuracy over some distance. "It is slower, but the added accuracy is worth it if you have the eyeglass on, say, one pistol for ranged shots."

"Oh," said the vendor, with excitement mounting in his voice once more. "But there's more!" He dimmed the flame of the oil lamp until it was very low and the room darkened and asked Valentina to use the device again.

Valentina looked through the glass and then without it several times down the range. "I can see the targets in the dark!" she exclaimed.

"Well, yes, but not quite. It won't work in complete darkness, but the inside of the eyeglass is coated in a paint that captures any existing light and enhances it. So in low light you can see more accurately through it."

Valentina was impressed. "How much is it?"

"This is the first one I've made and displayed in the shop, so it is unique … and very expensive."

"Can you adapt a holster to carry my pistol with the sighting device attached?"

"I suppose I could try, but a leatherworker would do a better job."

"That is true. I will buy the eyeglass today."

The specialist hesitated and Valentina was puzzled.

"If you did not intend to sell this or future eyeglasses, then why did you put it on display? Tell me your name and I will tell people where I obtained it, and you will become famous."

His seemed interested in this idea. "I am Jorn Ghear."

"Well, Jorn Ghear. I will purchase this one today and commission three others from you."

She paid him for all three in advance and paused at the door on her way out with her two guards. "One last thing – you will have to teach me how to fit the eyeglass to my pistols."

Their next stop was the leather worker. Valentina wore a pistol on each hip, hilts forward so she could draw either weapon with either hand. The third pistol was tucked into her right-side shoulder holster.

"I want a left-side shoulder holster for this pistol," she told the leather worker. "Note that this pistol has an eyeglass fitted and I do not want the holster to dislodge the glass when I draw. Can you do this? Today?"

The skilled craftswoman advised that it would take a few days, but when Valentina offered the right payment, she promptly assured her that the pistol and new shoulder holster would be delivered to her hotel later that day.

"Now show me to the brother called Star Gazer," she ordered her two guards.

Inside the luxuriously furnished waiting area of the brothel they were greeted by a young man.

"I'm looking for Lissa Tormain," Valentina said.

"And may I ask why?" he enquired.

"We are acquaintances and I have need to speak with her. Tell her Mistress Valentina is here."

The man ordered off the scantily dressed women to deliver the message with some urgency. A Mistress in the house would be a valuable client and not one to discourage.

Lissa arrived soon, accompanied by an elderly gentleman.

"It's a pleasure to have a Mistress in my house," said

the old man. "I was unaware that Lissa had such distinguished acquaintances. I am Piero Bloor – at your pleasure, Mistress." He gave a small courteous nod.

Valentina looked straight passed him, at her fellow passenger from the coach. "Lissa, what can you tell me of a criminal named Balcoff?"

Lissa glanced at the proprietor but he ignored her. The Mistress was quietly impressed because he made no effort whatsoever to challenge her authority or position.

"He's callous," replied Lisa. "And ruthless. He has most of the city in his grip. He's rarely seen out in public because he has an army of thugs to do his bidding," she paused. "Was that you that we heard of being attacked in Hotel Lanka, Mistress?"

"Yes, it was. So I'm looking to get the measure of my new enemy, to decide whether I need to deal with him, or if it was just a one-off incident."

"I doubt Balcoff will try again," Piero spoke up. "Attacking a Mistress is foolish and he knows that. I understand he also lost twelve of his people, so even he will struggle to enlist more to attempt another attack. Nor will he hire assassins. Knowing you escaped and that you know he was behind the plot, he will want to avoid all-out war – especially with the Mistress of Castle Worthmere. The loss of face will not trouble him, as not all his entrepreneurial endeavours succeed."

"You know this Balcoff, then?" Valentina finally addressed him directly.

"We had some association in his early days, Mistress. May I ask why you travel without a guard or escort from the castle? I've not heard of other Mistresses or Masters travelling alone."

"I can look after myself. The hotel incident should attest to that."

"Yes, Mistress. Apologies for the enquiry. It's rare that we find a Master or Mistress outside their estate." He paused. "I was wondering if we can be of service to any of your needs?"

"You're not referring to these," Valentina said as she swept her arm, indicating] the men and ladies of pleasure in the room.

The proprietor allowed himself a small smile. "I know the city well, Mistress. And to work with you would be a pleasure and hopefully profitable. Have you been away from home long?"

"Yes. Too long, But I have people who manage my affairs well enough."

"You do not miss your family?"

Valentina's eyes steeled. There was an awkward pause. "No. I have no family. I am alone."

Piero smiled sympathetically, but without giving offence.

"Is there anything else we can offer you, then?" Piero swept his own hand across to the men and women in the room.

"Yes. I think I will partake off your house. A drink and company would be a pleasant break. My preference is for one of each, together – and I like fine red wine."

FIVE

The airboat station was located in the centre of the city. The brand-new symmetrical structure followed the design of the temples, that not only accommodated prayer, but also housed the money cages now rising in every city, their docking towers for the airboats a prominent feature on the skyline. Air travel was still not trusted by most people and it was expensive, but it was by far the quickest way to move between cities – if not the safest.

Valentina wouldn't admit it, but she was a little nervous. This was her first flight. Weight was a serious challenge on airboats, so her cabin, like all the others, contained only a simple berth. The mattress, however, was very luxurious and there was ample space for her luggage.

"You've flown before, miss?"

The man beside her wore the uniform of the boat. Valentina was looking over the edge of the port bulwark at the treetops far below. Deciding that a conversational tone would best suit the situation, Mistress Valentina did not introduce herself or mention her title.

"Actually, no. This is my first flight."

The sun was high and the views in every direction were spectacular. All fourteen passengers on board were up on the deck talking excitedly and pointing at distant objects below them. The deckhands were constantly adjusting ropes and lines as ordered by the first mate on the poop deck.

"I'm one of the spellbinders on the boat," he said. "Our job is to heat and cool the balloons that make the boat go up and down."

Valentina looked up at the rigging masts, which were hitched to three massive sealed balloons. A spellbinder was nesting below each one, applying heat or cooling them with magic from their hands.

"It's a great job," he continued. "But not without its dangers."

The man was flirting with Valentina, she realised. "Oh, and what dangers are there?"

"Falling out of the sky, for one. Spellbinders have the most important job on board. We keep everyone in the air and safe."

"What of the teamsters? Is not their role of steering the unpredictable ections that pull the boat through the air just as important?"

"Driving four huge birds, temperamental as they are, is just like driving a team of gausents. No, the spellbinders are the key to flight."

Their conversation was interrupted by the hollering of a deck office. "Spellbinder Westbourn! Report below."

The man straightened up. "That's me," he confided,

then shouted "Yes, Sir!" and was gone.

"Apologies, Mistress," said one the deck officers as he walked to her side. "Westbourn is new and does not yet know to leave the passengers to themselves."

Valentina nodded in acknowledgement, reluctant to start another conversation, and settled down to watch the world passing by.

"Vered, North East! Vered, North East!" called the lookout, shattering the peace.

That's the last thing we need, Valentina thought.

"Weapons starboard," ordered the captain from his station up in the forecastle, where two teamsters each handled the reins of a pair of ections. The boat's crew gathered to the right of the vessel, armed with bows and pistols, awaiting the next order.

"Vered away," called the lookout.

Valentina could see the massive bird of prey in the distance, and trusted that the lookout knew what he was doing.

"Stand down from weapons," barked the captain. The crew returned to their duties and the passengers began talking again.

Air travel certainly had its dangers. The four tasty ections strapped to the airboat were a serious temptation for the larger vereds. And it was not without its side effects either, thought Valentina, as she heard someone vomiting violently behind her. She looked to the aft side of the port rail to see an elegant woman hurling over the side while her husband held her billowing hair back from her face.

"Is there a poultician onboard?" Valentina asked a passing officer.

"Yes, Mistress. He is bunked by the galley. Are you not well?"

"I'm fine. I need some bandages and dressings to be changed is all."

***

Fallon was a larger city than Arities and the capital of the region. Valentina found the view of the sprawling metropolis, even in the pouring rain, quite breathtaking as the boat approached, flew over, then docked at a tower in the city centre. Arriving at what she hoped to be her final destination after years of searching excited her. Yet she was also apprehensive that her endeavours would ultimately fail.

She struggled to stay patient while carrying out the mundane task of finding suitable accommodation. But when she did, she settled in quickly, bathed, then set out into the city on foot. She had a name and a location, given by a man she had questioned in the last backwater village. After six years of following leads, investigating stories and reading every snippet of information she could find on the life and times of Orestas Connroy, she was close to her goal. Or so she hoped.

Rigard Pentwing was a wealthy, well-respected businessman and Fellow of the City of Fallon. He was Valentina's target. He supposedly held what the Mistress sought. Pentwing was also a well-known spellbinder and a dean for the city's school of testing and magic, the Stara Academy. Valentina needed a plan. The wealth of Fallon and its recent growth as a trade hub for the new lands discovered across the seas to the East and West had begun to create a shift in power. The capital city was currently seeking to create an alliance with other major cities, so that it might rise to challenge the authority of the Masters and Mistresses. Politics in Fallon had therefore become brittle and fractious. Here, in Fallon, her authority as a Mistress might not be enough to avoid penalties for any misdemeanours.

Valentina located Rigard Pentwing at the Stara Academy, but she did not approach him directly. She needed to learn more about him so she could devise the best approach.

Pentwing was elderly, perhaps in his late fifties. He seemed frail of body and possibly in ill-health, yet still sharp of mind. A large muscular young man bearing a sword and pistol seemed to be forever by his side, a guard and servant. Valentina followed the pair of them for the whole day, as they visited the academy and City Hall, dined at an expensive eating house and then returned to a large, walled and gated home in the northern region of the city.

The next day she followed them again. Their routine was exactly the same as the day before.

On the third day, Valentina ceased to follow them when they left the academy and, in the friendliest manner she could muster, started to ask the academy staff discretely about Pentwing. He was both liked and esteemed, it appeared, by those at the academy, and Valentina gained the impression from the locals she questioned that such admiration extended beyond to the city in general.

There didn't seem any gossip or scandal linked to the man – and no opportunity for leverage. The only quirk that arose was that Pentwing had an unusual fascination with the mists that appeared across the land. He had been known to send well-funded scouting parties to investigate the mists, even entering them, according to the rumours. Convincing anyone to do such a thing gave much credit to Pentwing's skills of negotiation.

That night, over a bottle of rich red wine, Valentina pondered over her options. Her initial ideas were either to break into his house or abduct him and force the answers she sought from him directly. It wasn't compassion or fear of repercussions that dissuaded her from this course, rather the frailty of the man. Such an ordeal might kill him before she had her answers. Castle Worthmere had several prosperous trading contracts with Fallon, related to her quarries, mines and crops, but why would she approach Pentwing on such matters? They were dealt with by her own and the city's administrators.

Perhaps she should simply ask him for the truth? No. That approach hadn't worked in the past. Those that had guarded Orestas Connroy's secrets over the last century had an almost cultist pact not to reveal any information. The mist, though – perhaps that had possibilities. She could seek his advice under the pretence that the mist had become more prevalent across her lands. Although there was a risk that this would adversely affect her trade reputation.

A hunt? Yes, that might suffice. Valentina could play the bored Mistress wanting to go hunting in the mist, and in this regard she could strike up a dialogue with Pentwing. Over the course of that exchange she might discover a way to pressurise him or find some other way to acquire from what she sought from him.

The following morning Mistress Valentina Holbrine sent a formal request to meet with Rigard Pentwing, respected Fellow of the City and renowned spellbinder. That same evening came a response inviting Valentina to Pentwing's home the following day.

It was early evening when Valentina arrived. The gates had been opened in readiness and a servant met her at the door.

"May I take your hat and weapons, Mistress?" said the young girl.

"The hat, yes. My weapons, no."

"Apologies, Mistress, but there are no weapons inside the household."

The large muscular young man who always accompanied Pentwing appeared behind the servant, wearing his sword and pistol as always.

"And you are the exception, I suppose?" Valentina addressed him.

"Yes, Mistress," he replied. "I wear mine to protect Dean Pentwing – should the need arise."

"Do you get much that arises?"

He gave no response. Deciding to play the game, Valentina surrendered all four of her pistols, her knife and her dagger. Then she followed her guides through to the library.

"How many spellbooks do you travel with?" Pentwing asked her, raising his head from the book he was studying. His tone was sharp and his eyes bright, hinting at mischief.

The library was lined on all four walls with shelves of books, stretching from the floor to the ceiling fifteen feet above. A solitary table with four chairs stood in the centre of the large room, and this is where Pentwing was seated slightly hunched over.

"Only one," replied Valentina, taking note that Pentwing had not addressed her by her title.

"Please sit," he gestured to an empty chair. "Do you carry it with you at all times?" Despite his frail-looking posture, the clarity and sharpness of his voice defied his age.

"Yes. As do most spellbinders. It is not something I would leave lying around."

"How many spells can you retain at any one time, and for how long?" he asked, and went on without waiting for an answer. "Is your spellbook mainly incants, or do you have a more powerful repertoire?"

His questions were direct and to the point, as had been the others, and Valentina wondered where he was going with this line of enquiry. She did not answer; such things were not generally discussed. The Pentwing before her was not the polite gentleman she had observed outside these walls. There was an edge to him that was making her wary. She checked the location of Pentwing's protector, who stood now at the only door in or out of the library.

"I'm old now", Pentwing said. "I know no one that has lived past sixty-two and I am now sixty. Many of the spellbinders who attended Stara lost their lives long before my age. You do know as you get older that intelligence starts to decline and focus fades?"

"Age can be a cruel thing." Valentina finally took the chair opposite Pentwing, exposing her back to their armed observer. A display of defiance – she was dangerous enough without her weapons.

"However, power always remains," the old man continued "So although age takes away focus and memory, all you need is one or two well-rehearsed spells and all that power can be channelled through them. You just have to remember the necessary symbols and retain enough focus to cast them."

Valentina listened closely, but was acutely aware that she'd not been offered any refreshment or other courtesy normally expected for a Mistress, let alone a Mistress of one of the most powerful castles and estates in the lands. This, along with Pentwing's tone and manner, was a real indicator that he was either warning her, or threatening her. It was time to find out which.

"I suppose with age, though, it is harder to maintain focus, and an assailant, for example, might easily distract an older spellbinder."

"True. Hence the need to be well-rehearsed and practised," Pentwing replied. "Though I do understand that Orestas Connroy never lost his intelligence, focus or power even at the end of his long life … perhaps in the last final days. Maybe a bit. But who would know? I am told he kept diaries, as did his loyal servants and companions." Pentwing didn't flinch as he said this.

"I have heard the same," said Valentina. "And I believe many people have searched for them but with very little success. Many who supposedly concealed and guarded the chronicles have now died – some very painfully, as I understand it."

Pentwing's expression remained neutral, but his eyes retained their sharp focus. "Indeed. Many have searched. To find Orestas' spellbooks would be a valued prize. Worth a fortune."

Valentina fixed her eyes on his. "And perhaps they contain the secrets of how he lived so long."

Pentwing straightened up a little, pushing against the hunch of his back caused by age. "A trophy worth dying for, maybe?"

"Maybe."

"Thank you, Mistress Valentina." His voice was curt. "Your company has been most enlightening. However, I am tired now ... another problem with age. So, if you would be so kind, Becton will show you out."

Pentwing turned his head back down to his book and blatantly ignored the Mistress until she left.

***

Back at the hotel, in the bath with another bottle of wine, Valentina pondered this new challenge. It would seem that Rigard Pentwing either knew or suspected that she was searching for Orestas Connroy's histories. Perhaps others had searched and landed at his door and he just considered her to be one of those. However, Valentina had closed every lead she had found with some finality, not wanting others to follow her steps. The chronicles would be hers and hers alone. Any competition for them would be removed and so far, had been.

The next morning she visited the docks. That area of the city was busy nearly every hour of the day and night, with large ships loading and offloading their cargo into huge warehouses. The wide estuary of the River Ormer connected to the sea only one mile downstream and Fallon's wealth had seen tremendous growth with the discovery of new trade markets to the East and West. The dock fronts and the yards behind it were constantly expanding on both sides of the river. The homes of the poor were demolished and people displaced with very little regard for their welfare. Castle Worthmere had two large storehouse and shipping properties at the docks: one on each bank of the river. Valentina knew the shipping manager, Hichard, who ran both assets well. They had grown up and played together in the castle grounds as children.

"Can you obtain everything on the list?" Valentina asked Hichard as they strode around the warehouse.

"Yes, Mistress, we will have all of these in our own stores."

"I will need six able bodies to help me too. They need to be trustworthy and not talk to anyone now or after. If you have any doubts about any of them, at any time, you must let me know and I will deal with them, as necessary."

"I have six in mind. They grew up on the castle estates and you can trust them. Perhaps I should come along, too?"

Valentina studied Hichard's face. A tall, strong, handsome man. He was four years younger than herself and on several occasions they had done more than play together as adolescents. Those were happier times, before she inherited the title of Mistress, and before she discovered her need to search out Orestas Connroy's secrets. She had at one time considered him as possibly a more long-term partner, but she had finally realised that wouldn't have worked. So when the opportunity arose for him to manage her estate affairs, here in Fallon, she had urged him to leave.

"No, I need you here," she told him firmly. "This new trade line is important."

"Be careful with that!" hollered Hichard at a team of men handling a crated cage clumsily. "Sorry, Mistress.

Geon requested a breeding pair of colian for back home. The larger boars from the west are supposedly very tasty and he thinks there may be a market for their meat. One of those is in the crate those idiots nearly dropped."

"I will let you get on, then." Valentina said. "Have everyone ready for the night after next."

"Yes, Mistress. Without fail. Now I must have stern word with those idiots."

Walking back through the docks, Valentina stopped several times, a little in wonder, or awe or bafflement. Strange animals were arriving from the freshly discovered lands far to the East and West. Strong scents arose from bails and bundles containing newly discovered spices and fauna. A small number of men and women from other lands mingled with the local inhabitants. Their strange clothing, new languages and uncommon skin pigments, ranging from black to pale, made them stand out as they checked their goods on arrival or before departure. These fresh trade routes were as valuable to them as they were to Fallon. The world was changing, and changing fast. With some luck and skill she would be around for a long time to see it all happen.

A familiar face approached her as she stood and observed. "Good to see you, Mistress," said Scribe Harland. "What brings you to Fallon?"

"I'm not here for lessons, that's for sure."

"I doubt I could teach you anything now. You have grown and made such a name for yourself since I was privileged to be one of your tutors at the castle."

Valentina closed the distance between them. "Can we talk privately?" she asked.

"I have an office. Please follow me."

The large room inside the City Hall was bustling with activity. The large cupboard that Harland referred to as his office was cluttered with papers and documents, stacked on his desk, on the chairs, on every piece of floor space and the windowsill.

"My work is to keep records of the new streets, roads, sewers and buildings that are sprouting up everywhere, and also record the demolition of the old ones. There is so much change and growth at the moment that the city is bursting at the seams. Prosperity is a difficult task to manage," he smiled warmly.

"What we are to discuss you cannot speak to anyone about. Is that understood?"

The small, spectacled man was instantly attentive. "Yes, Mistress. You know I am loyal and know the price if I am not."

"I am being careful to ensure I am not being followed," she explained. "But in such a busy city I can never be certain that I'm not. Castle Worthmere has a new enemy – one you would not suspect. Times like these are hard, and difficult choices and actions are required."

"I do not envy you being responsible for so many lives and the commercial interests that support all those that live and depend on your lands."

She got straight to the point. "I need information about Rigard Pentwing's home. Not just the details anyone can find on city records, but the secrets too."

"There's talk that he is dying, Mistress. Only last week he filed a death writ with City Hall. He is leaving his whole estate to his servant, Becton. It is also whispered that they are lovers."

"Becton? That's the muscular man that's always with him, right? Interesting. I've made enquiries myself and did not hear any of this."

"Yes it is. And we may gossip within City Hall, but we keep it inside the walls."

Two nights later the six men and women that Hichard had chosen arrived precisely on time. It was the dead of night and anyone who loitered would have attracted attention from the city's patrolling enforcers. Valentina took this as a good sign.

"Which one of you is Sklyn?" she asked.

"I am, Mistress," said a scrawny young man.

"There will be no names or titles while we do this – for any of us. We will not be together for long and there will be little need for talking, so this should not be a problem."

"Yes, M—"

Valentina interrupted him sharply. "I have a different task for you, Skyln so pass your missiles – bar one for the signal – to the others. Have you all been briefed thoroughly with the information I shared yesterday at the dock?"

Affirmative mutters came from all.

"You're with me," she said, pointing to Sklyn. "The rest of you – you know what to do. Stay alert and do not get caught. At any cost."

Most of the streets were dark, with only small shallow pools of lantern light creating soft shadows. Valentina took Sklyn's hand as they strolled along. It would draw less attention, she told him, even though there were very few people about.

"Once you throw the signal, I want you to keep watch for Pentwing, or his servant Becton. If you see either of them, leave. Follow them. If they split up, go with Becton. I need to know everywhere they go and who they speak with."

Valentina disappeared into the darkness, leaving Sklyn outside the walls of Pentwing's home, quietly counting to himself. Moments later he hurled his burning missile directly onto the roof of the mansion. The glass bottle shattered on impact and the flame ignited the dispersed fluid instantly.

From inside the outer walls of the building, the other five delivered their missiles. Some were thrown through specific windows, deliberately selected for maximum impact; others were thrown indiscriminately. Objective achieved, they escaped over the walls and disappeared into the night.

The fires took hold quickly and spread dramatically. Screams could be heard from the household as servants and a few houseguests realised what was happening and tried to escape. The whole scene was bedlam and panic, with only Sklyn there to witness it from the onset, tucked away in a side street where Valentina told him to wait, watching the house gate.

The blaze was already out of control when he heard the bell from the hauled fire bowser as it approached. Several of the servants, some wearing only their nightdresses, tumbled coughing and spluttering through the opened gate. One young woman's clothing was partially on fire; others forced her to the ground and beat out the flames.

***

The safe room was in darkness. The noise of the

disturbance was very distant, from somewhere else in the city. Muffled sounds of someone approaching the room were heard, faintly at first, before a hatch in the floor creaked open and Becton climbed up, holding a small covered candle that shed very little light. He was partially dressed, wearing long loose night pants and soft slippers, but had clearly managed to pick up both his sword and his pistol before escaping from the blazing house. He placed the candle holder gently on the floor beside the hatch and reached back down the ladder to help Rigard Pentwing climb into the room. They stood up and sighed with relief.

Clap, clap, clap, clap! Four rapid shots.

Becton took the first two slugs in his bare chest. The third slug took him in the face. His weapons would be no use to him now. The fourth shot went through the back of Pentwing's leg, now turning to flee, shattering his left kneecap as the iron ball burst through the other side.

Valentina moved swiftly. She went straight over to injured man and shot out his other knee.

"Focus on that, old man," she said. Then, with a vicious swipe of her pistol, she cracked the back of his skull. Her intention was not to kill him, but she knew that death was always the risk.

She picked up the leather bag he had dropped and clutched it to her chest with one arm.

From the palm of her right hand, a soft white light erupted. The glow spread, in a controlled manner, until it formed a dome over the three of them, Pentwing now writhing quietly on the floor. A rug and some soft furnishings were now visible on the boundaries of the illumination, but the light spread no further.

Valentina opened the bag eagerly. Her plan could have failed. It could have gone catastrophically wrong. She could have lost everything she had searched for over the years. Now she would discover the fruits of her latest gamble.

Inside the bag, she found jewels, and gold, and several books. The first two books were important tomes and valuable to someone – but of no interest to her. The next four, however, showed real promise. She turned the pages of one, and something jumped out at her.

> *Fidlemorn, 3.5.Fox308. Orestas has returned. He is extremely weary and gaunt from his trip. I think he has finally succeeded as he now seems weaker and less himself. I will speak with him more on this tomorrow, when he rises.*

Penned inside the front cover of the second book, she read:

> *Orestas Connroy. From 2.2.Fox308 to …*

The other two tomes also seemed to be journals, with regularly dated entries. Valentina would need to study all four of them closely before she would know for certain whether her endeavours had borne fruit.

She lifted an oil lamp from a nearby dresser and lit the wick with a touch of her fingers. She checked Pentwing's pulse at his neck. Still alive.

Clap!

She put a slug through his brain at close range, and walked away towards the door. She looked back once then tossed the lamp between the two bodies. It bounced. "Tough little bugger," she muttered before shattering it with a slug and the fire began to spread.

The next day the Mistress made plans to return to Castle Worthmere. The six guards provided by Hichard would travel with her. The news of the fire had been grave – seven dead at the mansion, including two young children.

What was suspected to be the body of Rigard Pentwing had also been found in a second burned-out building at the end of the escape tunnel. The jewels and gold scattered across the floor beside the charred corpse, and the size of the body, were the only real indications that it was Pentwing.

The news of the deaths caused some degree of trauma and regret among the six accomplices, so Mistress Valentina decided they would return home with her, and be suitably rewarded, and given time to recover from the events of the night.

The official word on the street was that neither the city enforcers nor the team of fire bowsers had any clue as to why anyone would want to burn down Rigard Pentwing's home.

SIX

Mocrat ran as fast as he could to keep up with Stala and finally dropped to a walk as they reached the end of Tower Road, laughing with the exhilaration of it all. The boy had helped Stala pick the pocket of an obese gentleman, who had given chase, but he'd been no match for the two youngsters. Once they entered the Cutter District their score had given up his pursuit.

"You're slipping, Stala! He nearly caught you with your hand in his pocket." Mocrat put his hands in his pockets and feigned struggling to pull them out again.

"Nah, you bumped him too hard and alerted him." She nudged against Mocrat, knocking him off his stride.

"Don't be daft," he exclaimed, as he pulled his hands out of his pockets to help him keep his balance.

"You bumped into him so hard his fat belly is still wobbling!"

The children ducked down an alley and crept behind some discarded crates to open the purse and check their prize.

"Wow! A whole gold!" squealed Mocrat.

"Told you he was the right score," said Stala, a smug look on her face. "Stick with me and I'll make you rich." She placed a hand caringly on his shoulder.

"What you going to do with it?"

"Da says to break gold coin into smaller silver and copper as quickly as possible if we want to use the money. So I think I will treat us to some honey bread."

"A store baker won't take a gold from us though," the boy said despondently.

"No, but the street vendors will," smiled Stala. "I'll just say I'm on an errand for someone."

***

Mocrat stared back at the woman as she looked the two children up and down. They looked like street urchins to her, the type always up to no good ... but the girls was holding out a gold coin, and they were buying an entire loaf of sweet honey bread. The vendor couldn't resist. She took the money and handed over the loaf, and then the change – plenty of it, mostly silver.

Later that day, the two kids went down to the docks. They had stolen a few small trinkets but nothing of any real value. They had only taken them because they could, and for Mocrat to please Stala.

"Look. That warehouse has a broken board. We can squeeze through that gap." Stala grabbed his small hand and tugged him.

"But remember what happened last time – and it's getting late and dark." Mocrat's challenge was weak.

"We won't get caught this time and you won't take a beating."

She was off, letting go of his hand, and Mocrat followed as he always did where Stala was concerned.

Inside the warehouse it was dark and quiet.

"No guards. No sentry animals. And they've closed up for the night. What a score!" Stala exclaimed.

"There's nothing here for us," Mocrat replied. "It's all big bundles and too heavy for us to take." He wanted to leave. It was too risky.

"But what's in the bundles?" she said excitedly. "Let's open some!" as she took a small candle and a firestick from her pocket and lit it.

Mocrat followed Stala closely, and used his knife to slice open each bundle she indicated.

"It's all leaves from some strange plant," he said. "Nothing for us, like I said. Let's get out of here."

"Just one more, then we'll go," said Stala as she scanned the high stacks of bags around her.

"Hey! Who's down there?" A gruff voice shouted from somewhere above them.

"Hide!" Stala whispered loudly.

A lantern was lit, and a man came down a ladder, grumbling and complaining to himself as he did so.

"If I get my hands on you, I'll fry you alive. That's my incant, so you'd better be scared."

Mocrat started to creep towards the broken boards in the wall and hoped Stala was doing the same thing.

"I know you're still here," called the man, weaving between the bundles with his lantern held high, cajoling them. "I'll be easy on you if you show yourself ... but if I have to hunt for you, that won't be the case."

Mocrat reached the gap in the boards and stuck his

head outside. Stala was not there.

He heard a scream, and instantly turned back to the dark interior.

He heard the man shout "Gotcha!" gruffly, and headed for the voice.

"Only a young thing. Pretty, though," the man said. "You've got titties too, so you must be old enough for some fun, eh? What do you say, girlie? I'll let you go without a beating for some playtime."

Mocrat could hear Stala struggling, and the man laughing at her efforts.

Finally reaching the scene, Mocrat saw Stala was being restrained and the grotesque man was leaning in, kissing her hard on the lips. He had placed the lantern on a nearby bundle and was starting to undo his belt. Stala kicked and screamed at him, but he was too strong, and determined. His britches fell to his ankles and he pushed her against another bundle, groping her chest aggressively, then he jammed his arm across her throat and started fumbling with her britches. All the while Stala tried to fight him off, but she was not getting away.

She looked up at his face in despair, losing hope, then the man stopped abruptly and the light went out of his eyes.

"Get off her!" yelled Mocrat, his arm thrusting as he stabbed the man in the back, again and again. The body fell to the floor and the boy went with it, still stabbing frantically.

"He's dead," said Stala. She coughed and massaged her throat. "Let's get out of here."

She led Mocrat away from the docks to a quiet spot by the river.

"You need to wash that blood off before we get back to the city. Are you alright?" she asked.

"I should be asking you that. Yes, I'm fine. It's not the first sleazebag I've killed. You know that."

"Da says every killing takes its toll. You sure you're alright?"

"Yes!" Mocrat stood up defiantly, having cleaned himself down. He wasn't going to show any weakness in front of the girl he adored. "Are you sure you're good?"

"Yeah. Must admit, I was scared. So thank you. I don't want to lose it that way. I was hoping for a nice boy in a nice bed, safe and secret," she replied with a seductive smile.

Mocrat looked longingly at her, and realised that his jaw had dropped and he was staring. He coughed and stepped away, turning sideways to hide his blush.

"We should get back to the city, then. You know what your Da's like if you're out too late and he doesn't know where."

***

His bolthole was well hidden, and as far as Mocrat knew no one else was aware of its existence. Recent work in the area had separated and blocked off this section of the old sewer to make way for a new tunnel that would run beneath the city. This was his home, but it didn't come without risks. The standing section was partially collapsed inside and getting in and out was a challenge at times.

Here he slept relatively peacefully, away from the other gangs of children. He lit a lantern without fear of the light being seen by anyone else and scanned the area for intruders and rats. He didn't mind rats but they chewed everything so he had laid traps and poison to keep them at bay. Happy that he was alone, he dropped into the channel and climbed out on the other side. Here he lit a small fire, more for light and comfort than for warmth. Then he checked his stash of food and water; no rats had got to his edibles.

He sat down on his bed of straw and blankets. Now that he was alone, he went over what had happened earlier. The killing of the man scared him. He had lied to Stala, not for the first time. He often made up stories out of bravado, to impress her, but this was the first time he had actually taken someone's life. He started to chastise himself. He had panicked, had been frantic – out of control. What must Stala have thought of him? Yet he had saved her, and she had been grateful. But what if she told someone what he'd done? What if there was a bounty on his head now? What if the man had friends or family that would hunt him down? The killing he could justify, to himself at least, and he'd always known that he would need to do it at some stage of his life. Because that was how the world around him functioned. But he had plans to escape this life.

Again he checked that he was alone, even though he knew there was nowhere for anyone to hide. Rising from the bed, he moved to the far wall and carefully removed the bricks that hid his hoard. What it offered was a way out from this sorry existence. He specialised in stealing spell books – not an easy thing to do; it was the only thing he had never told Stala about. If any spellbinders who lost their books ever discovered that it was him, he would be hunted and no doubt cruelly punished. He counted the first six books and then counted the rest, up to three. He couldn't add the numbers together and decided to ask Stala to teach him how to count to ten again. They must be worth a small fortune, he thought. When he found a buyer that he could trust, they would give him enough money to get out of the city and start afresh. As long as Stala would come with him. Also in the cubbyhole with the books was his reserve of coins – a tidy sum, he guessed, but he didn't know the exact amount. He added his share from the day's efforts to the pile.

***

Stala was late the following morning but he waited patiently in the alley that few people ventured down. He would wait all day if necessary. When she did arrive, she was carrying a large beer tankard.

"What's with that?" asked Mocrat.

"Da made me practise – just watch."

She placed the mug on the cobble-stoned ground and stood back. She focused hard, a frown set on her face. The tankard lifted two feet into the air and stayed there for several seconds before falling with a dull thud.

"See! Yesterday I could only lift a small coin! I'm getting better." She picked up the tankard and turned to him. "You'll need to get tested soon."

Stala had turned thirteen a couple of months back and been sent to her own testing. She had learned the lifting spell as her incant.

Mocrat didn't know his own age. He told people he was twelve, but suspected he was only a little over eleven when he compared his physical size to other boys his age; too young for any magic to have manifested yet.

"Na, I'm not ready yet. I just know it." He stood up

and smiled at Stala. "So what are we doing today?"

"I overheard Da talking about a man with black skin who is opening a new store today. He's selling new clothes but not like anything we've seen before. I want to see them."

"Clothes? Really? You want to look at clothes?"

Stala pouted and faked a sad face.

"Alright, you win. Clothes it is."

Stala beamed a smile and Mocrat's heart fluttered.

"I brought you these," she said, dropping a bundle at his feet.

He opened the wrapping. "Clothes. What is it with clothes today?"

"We'll need to go inside the store. And you are dressed in … well … rags. That just won't do. Put these on."

Mocrat noticed that Stala was wearing a pretty dress rather than her usual britches and laced-up top and jacket. She was more beautiful than usual, he thought, but then she was beautiful every day.

"You want me to get changed here? In the alley?"

"Yes, Mocrat."

"You going to turn around?"

"No." She set her feet firmly and gazed expectantly at him.

"But I'm naked under this tunic and britches."

"So? You don't want me to watch? You're not shy with me, are you?"

Mocrat dropped his britches, allowing the tunic to hide his dignity.

"Ah, no," said Stala. "Tunic off too – before you put the new ones on."

He hesitated just a moment before complying. He could feel his penis start to harden so he dressed into the fresh clothes as quickly as he could.

"That was nice. You show real promise," Stala teased as he pulled on his new boots. Then she kissed the top of his head.

Keeping his face turned to the ground and his eyes on his new boots, Mocrat blushed scarlet. He could still feel the burn on his cheeks when he finally stood straight.

"Very handsome," Stala declared. "Come on, let's go."

The store was boring and Stala wouldn't let him steal anything, but he feigned interest to keep her happy. Everything was long and flowing and brightly coloured.

"These will be all the fashion soon, you'll see," said Stala – more than once.

Frankly Mocrat couldn't see the attraction. He was starting to feel hungry and wanted to be somewhere more fun or more exciting.

Finally Stala bought something. When she was handed the parcel, the two of them left the store.

"Can we come back tomorrow?" she asked.

"Ah …" he muttered.

"It's alright. I'm just teasing. Thank you for coming with me." Then she smiled that certain smile that melted Mocrat's heart.

They were soon back in Cutter. Stala wanted to take her purchase home and get changed before they went anywhere else. As they turned a corner into one of their usual shortcuts, a much bigger boy walked straight into Mocrat – accompanied by six of his cronies.

"Watch were you're going, brat," said the boy, as his buddies laughed.

"Leave him alone, Frig!" demanded Stala.

"Girl got to protect you, brat? You running scared?"

"I'm not scared of you, Frig," Mocrat said, squaring up to him. "You need all this back-up to confront me?"

The boy grunted. "Stala won't always be watching your back. You'll see." With that he turned and left, the gang of boys trailing behind.

Stala watched them leave, her concern evident. "He really doesn't like you," she said. "Do you know why?"

"No. No idea. I think he's just a bully." He turned away from her so she would not see the lie on his face.

"Da likes him, though. Say's he has promise."

***

Day after day for the next three weeks Stala and Mocrat got up to mischief. Stala was always the instigator and if there was a price to be paid Mocrat took the pain or the beating. That was how it was between them. Then one day Stala did not show up at their meeting place. He waited every day, but she didn't show up until a week later.

"Where've you been? You alright?" He asked with genuine concern showing in his every gesture.

"Yeah, sorry." She smiled warmly. "Da stuck me back to schooling. He says I need to be educated. But I've snuck out today to see you."

Mocrat instantly forgave her. "I was worried." And he too smiled, happy to have her back.

They weren't alone for long.

"Thought you'd be here." It was Frig, striding brash

86

and bold into the alley. "Your Da sent me to fetch you, Stala – and no arguments, he said."

Mocrat instantly squared up to him and his smile turning to a scowl.

"Well, I'm not going back yet, so you can just say you didn't find me," she huffed.

"Can't do that. Can't leave you with this brat." He sneered and indicated Mocrat with his thumb.

"And why's that?" Her defiance was apparent in her stance.

"Oh, he's never told you then, has he? He's going to marry you one day, he says. Your Da won't like that," he scoffed.

Stala cast a questioning but amused look at Mocrat.

"Frig and I got drunk one day and I blurted it out," Mocrat explained, trying to conceal his embarrassment. "Seems Frig wants to marry you, too. That's why he doesn't like me."

"Shut up!" Frig yelled. "You can't tell her that!"

"Just did."

Frig stepped forward and hurled a heavy punch at Mocrat's face. He may have been smaller, but he was quicker, and no stranger to fighting. He ducked and moved into Frig's sturdy body and punched him hard in the groin. Frig doubled over but he did not fall.

"Stop it you two!" Stala shouted.

Frig stood up. "You shouldn't have done that."

He pulled a knife.

Mocrat's knife came out too.

The boys circled each other as Stala implored them both to stop.

Throwing his weight into the move, Frig advanced and tried to overpower Mocrat. They held each other's knife hand by the wrist and began to wrestle. Stala joined in and tried to push them apart. The trio fell to the floor and Mocrat bounced up first, but neither Frig nor Stala rose to face him.

"Get up, Stala!" Mocrat yelled, the adrenalin still pumping high.

Slowly, Frig stood up, his face ghostly white. He was no longer holding his knife. Both boys stared down at Stala. At Frig's knife, sticking out of her chest, out of her heart. Blood coursed over her shirt and her eyes stared blankly into the sky.

"You killed her! You fucking killed her!" screamed Mocrat. He charged at Frig, determined to kill him for what he had done.

Together they tumbled into the street. Raw rage gave him enough strength to roll on top of the murdering animal beneath him. His knife held high, it started its downward arc. Morcat was beyond caring if anyone saw him deliver the final strike.

Thwack!

A cudgel cracked the back of his skull. Mocrat fell on top of Frig, stars blurring his vision and sounds suddenly distant. His knife struck the ground well clear of its target.

"You alright, Frig?" Mocrat heard someone ask.

Three uniforms stood over the two boys and one reached down to lift the smaller boy off the other.

"Yes. I'm fine. He just lost it. He killed Stala and then went for me. Look …" He pointed to the entrance to the alley where Stala lay.

The enforcers saw her. They could tell she was dead from where they stood.

Mocrat watched, his head still reeling, and shock taking a hold of him, only managing to stay upright with the forced aid of the enforcer holding him up by the scruff of his new clothes?. The blow had almost knocked him out, but he fought to hold on to consciousness, his only thought to kill Frig. But his body wouldn't respond the way he wanted it to.

"Shit. Her Da's going to be pissed," said one uniform.

"Get him locked up," ordered the senior enforcer. "Frig. You better go tell her Da. And you," he said, signalling to the other uniform, "guard this alley until someone comes for the body. Bale and I will take this murderous horror to the cells."

SEVEN

The holding cells beneath the enforcers' building were not a welcoming place. Buried underground, they had no windows, the barred walls gave no privacy, and the lighting was sparse. Each cell had one bucket for use as a toilet and one cot, but at busy times they would be shared by three or four people. There were six cells inside each of the four thick-walled barred sections. This is where they took Beth.

She was crying out loud, though she tried to hold the sobs back, not wanting to draw any attention to herself. Beth hadn't looked up once since she'd been escorted into the enforcers' offices. Even now, standing in her cell, apparently alone, she hid her face behind her red hair.

"You need to pull yourself together quickly," said a strident female voice. "The other prisoners and the guards, they prey on the weak."

Beth tried hard to stop sobbing and finally managed to, focusing instead on listening. Then she lifted her head and looked at her new companion in the same neighbouring cell.

"That's better. You're in luck – well, other than being in here. There's only three of us in this block. They took a load away yesterday for trial or sentencing. My name's Abelee. What's yours?"

"Beth."

"Well, Beth. Come over here so I can get a proper look at you."

Beth stood and shuffled to the bars dividing the two cells.

"Okay, first thing: don't do everything you're told. And stay beyond arm's reach from anyone in an adjacent cell."

Beth looked up at Abelee in the dim light. A tall, athletic woman with blonde hair who was smiling kindly.

"It's never safe here," she continued. "Don't trust anyone."

"You too? Are you not to be trusted?"

"Look, I'll do what I can for you in here, but that won't be much given the bars – and the place." She cast her gaze around the dismal space around them. "Just act a little tougher. Weakness draws the bullies. With some luck, you'll be out of here soon. Why are you here, anyway? You don't look like a criminal."

"They say I am a thief, but I'm not." Beth started to cry again.

"Look – the tears will only get you in trouble."

Beth swallowed her sobs and once again raised her face to look straight up at Abelee.

"Can you prove you didn't do it?" the woman asked.

"No. It was my own parents that said so. They just let the enforcers take me—"

"Oh, shit," uttered Abelee as the keys rattled in the cell-block door. "Sit as far back in the darkness as you can, and don't make a sound."

Two burly guards entered the cells carrying a lantern.

"There's fresh meat in the corner one," said the shorter of the two.

"Alright. Let's take a look," said the taller one.

They pressed themselves up against the bars at the front of her cell.

"A girl … Hey, girl. Stand up. Show us your face."

Beth did as she was told, too frightened not to, even though Abelee had told her not to do everything she was asked.

"Mmm, not my type," said the taller one.

"Nor mine. Anyway, let's get to it."

The guard held the light up to the blonde woman's cell. Abelee stood strong and stared back hard at them both. Hatred raged in her eyes.

The two men moved on without a word.

Beth watched as the guard raised the lantern to another cell. A small body lay on its cot, unmoving. The guards readied their cudgels, unlocked the door and entered. They prodded and poked the prone form but got no reaction. The smaller guard struck the body on the bed hard and elicited a weak groan.

"I'm first," said the taller man.

The two men stripped the prisoner – just a young boy. He offered no resistance as he was bent over the cot naked, his bare bottom prominent. Beth wanted to scream *Stop!* or *Help!* or *Don't do that!*, but she was terrified. What if she was next? The big guard was first to sodomise the small the frail-looking boy, beating their victim across the head repeatedly as he did so. The next guard was no less gentle as he took his pleasure. When they were finished they simply left the boy where he was, lying across the cot, still naked, and locked the cell when they left.

The taller man walked towards Beth's cell and she started to sob and moved as far back into her confined space as she could. "Please, no," she managed.

"I like that. Begging. Maybe you do show some promise."

"Leave her for now," said the other guard. "We don't know who she is yet and we don't have permission."

The guard blew Beth a kiss and winked. "Maybe soon, then."

"They're gone," said Abelee after a while. "Those two do that to him every day. They're obviously targeting him for a reason. I've been here for a week now. For six days they have raped him without mercy. The first two days he fought back, but they just beat him to the floor – and enjoyed that too. He's not said one word since and now he doesn't even try to fight back."

Looking over to the cell in the gloom, Beth could see that the boy had dressed himself and climbed back onto his cot.

"Why?"

"I don't know, but they're picking on him for a reason." Abelee sat down on her cot.

"Am I next?" asked Beth. She approached the bars, closer to the woman.

"You have to be stronger. Show them you're willing to fight them."

"But they'll just beat me."

"Fight with everything you have. Don't just punch and kick. Gouge their eyes. Bite them. Go wild! Make them regret anything they do." Her tone was steely and determined. She spoke as one who'd learned what it took.

"Didn't the boy do that to begin with?" She looked over to his cell.

"Yes, but I think someone has ordered the guards to torture him daily. Or someone is paying them to."

"Who would do such a thing?"

***

Twice more Beth endured the ordeal of the boy and both times the taller guard came over to her cell afterwards and teased her. He blew kisses and licked his lips and gyrated his groin but he never entered her cell. Beth had taken to imitating Abelee, standing tall and looking as menacing as she could.

Then the cell block door opened at an unusual time. Abelee was on her feet instantly. Having no other role model, Beth copied.

"Mistress Valentina? What are you doing here?" she said.

"I might ask you the same, Abelee"

A Mistress. Beth had never seen or met anyone so important. Why was she here? She certainly looked intimidating, dressed all in leather with a long coat, a tall wide-brimmed hat and armed with pistols that managed to glint even in the low light.

"They let you keep your weapons, I see," Abelee remarked, eyeing up the pistols.

"It wasn't their choice."

Then the woman turned to Beth's cell. "Are you Beth Reach?"

Beth was too startled to speak.

"Answer me, girl."

There was no response. Valentina watched her face expectantly.

"Yes, Mistress."

"You're coming with me. I have had your sentence commuted to an indenture."

Beth looked from the Mistress to Abelee, confused, hope flickering through her mind.

"Mistress Valentina has bought your sentence," Abelee explained. "You belong to her now, until you have served your indenture period."

Then Abelee turned to face the Mistress. "Apologies, Mistress. She's green – very green."

"Not a worry. It's a shame you're in here, Abelee. I could do with some reliable people at present. Why *are* you here?"

"Murder, Mistress. I killed a man in broad daylight." The disclosure was matter of fact and conveyed no regret.

"Silly thing to do. Did he deserve it?"

"Yes" There was a finality to the response.

"Shame. They will not indenture for murder."

Valentina looked around and her eyes fell on the small form in the other cell.

"A young boy, Mistress. He hasn't said a word all the time we've been here. Two of the guards rape him and beat him daily. He's obviously upset someone," Abelee told her.

Valentina ignored the boy's situation. "Can you pick a lock, Abelee?"

"Sorry, Mistress. Not something I am particularly good at."

"Another shame, especially because I happen to have such tools on me at this time." She patted a pocket.

"I can." It was the boy – his voice surprisingly strong and determined.

Valentina approached his cell, where he was now standing at the bars.

"How old are you?"

"Twelve."

"Why are you here?"

"Murder." It was a cold statement.

Beth felt a shift in the atmosphere. The boy was defiant, still. If they were trying to break him, they were having the opposite effect.

"What would you do with these tools?"

"Whatever you tell me to do." He held his hand out.

"Why would I trust a young murderer who is locked in a cell, no doubt soon to see the gallows?" Valentina started to turn away from him.

"They won't let me see a rope for a long time yet," he said. "And I can pay you."

She returned her attention to the boy. "I don't see a purse in your cell. And you don't look as though you're from a wealthy family."

"I have spellbooks. This many." He held up six fingers and then three.

"So you're a spellbinder too?"

"No. A thief – and a good one." The cold flat tone had returned.

"But apparently not so good at getting away with murder."

Valentina looked back over to Abelee, and then back to the boy.

"Take these, then, and hide them." She passed him a small wrapped bundle, then went back to Abelee's cell.

"Did you notice where they take the shit-buckets?" she asked.

"Yes, Mistress."

"In two nights' time I will have someone meet you outside. They won't wait for long, and this is the only chance I am offering. Do you want it?"

"Forgive me, Mistress, but what is the price?"

"Do you want to hang?"

Abelee didn't reply and Valentina did not wait for an answer. Instead, she took the keys from her pocket and opened Beth's cell.

"If you run, I can promise you there are worse things than me shooting you in the back."

Beth sat on the cot, still confused as to what was happening.

"Well, move, girl! I've not got time to waste here."

The next morning Abelee watched as two more prisoners were locked up. An old man in the cell across from the boy, and a hard-looking man with a scarred face next to her cell. All three later witnessed the rape of the boy, but none of them reacted with the concern or fear that Beth had shown. The young lad remained as stoic as always. Other than the few words he had used to address the Mistress, he stayed silent.

"Let me feel your tits, woman," the scarred man leered.

"I reckon I can get my dick inside you through these bars, too, if you bend over for me. Just like the boy did before."

Abelee rose from her cot and pushed her clothed breasts up against the bars. The man, practically salivating, grabbed at them. She reached through the bars and started to caress his head and he moved closer, rummaging through her clothing for bare flesh. She took a firm grip of the man's skull and yanked hard. The first impact against the bars burst the man's nose and claimed a couple of teeth. The next was so forceful that it may have fractured his eye socket. The third, fourth and fifth blows were Abelee demonstrating her control. Then he was allowed to drop to the floor.

"Not one for making friends then," stated the old man from across the space dividing their cells.

Abelee ignored him. It was time to leave.

"Boy," she called out. "It's time."

The child rose from his cot without a word and quickly unlocked his cell door with the tools Valentina had left with him. Then did the same with Abelee's.

"What about us?" asked the man with the busted face between rasping breaths.

"I'm leaving you alive, aren't I? Or would you rather a different solution? Oh ... and if you raise an alarm, you will regret it."

***

The boy unlocked the cell-block door with ease. Beyond was a corridor lined on both sides with many similar doors. They turned right and headed for the stone stairs that led up to the surface, and the sewer well. Again, the boy made simple work of the next door that led to the yard. From this point it would be a little more precarious. The well was around fifty feet away in the open ground of a well-lit, high-walled compound.

"Now what?" muttered Abelee.

The boy pointed sharply. A head had popped out of the well, only briefly, but someone was most definitely inside it.

"I don't see any—" Abelee began, but the boy didn't hear because as he took off at speed directly for the low-walled sewer well.

Throwing caution to the wind, she followed.

A rope had been secured to the inside of the well. As quickly as they could, the two escapees descended into the darkness below. Abelee almost vomited when the pungent odour assaulted her senses, but she held back, noting that the boy seemed as completely indifferent to these surroundings as he had to his cell.

"Listen carefully," said a muffled voice in the darkness. "Hold hands and follow me. Once we have moved on a little, I will light a lantern, but be quick – a flush is due."

The masked speaker emerged from the shadows. "Climb on to this ledge and hold on tight," he said. "This ledge is the only safe place when the flush comes."

A bell rang and they watched and waited as the torrent of rushing water flowed past them. Then they moved on silently. The guide led them left and right through a maze of tunnels and ensured they always had sufficient time to mount the ledge before flushes. Finally they emerged from a passageway into a chamber with hanging chains scattered throughout it.

"Shower here," he said.

Outside, above the hatch, waited Beth.

"Thank you," she said, hugging the masked man.

"You stay safe, Beth. We know you didn't do it. Just serve your indenture and one day we might see you again."

Then, without a glance back, the man departed. Beth hoped one day that she would see Parat again.

"Here, put these on." Beth handed over thick, hooded cloaks to Abelee and the boy. "Now, follow me and stay close."

***

The receptionist at Hotel Lanka let Beth and her hooded companions pass without questions. Upstairs, two warm baths awaited them.

"This will dye your hair; one is black and one red," Beth instructed them. She gave the red bottle of dye to the boy and the black to Abelee.

In the large living area, two cots had been set up. Beth gestured to them and said, "Here is some expensive clothing to put on. We are Mistress Valentina's staff now and she tells me that no one will look at you twice while you are in her service, but you shouldn't test that by making any show of yourselves. I suggest we all get to sleep soon as the Mistress says we are travelling tomorrow."

With that, she turned and went into the bedroom, closing the door firmly behind her.

It was barely light when a servant knocked at their door. "The Mistress says you have twenty minutes to be ready and outside the door of her rooms."

***

Beth knocked on the thick wood-panelled door and

Mistress Valentina opened it, signalling them to step inside. She looked them up and down, at their dark britches and light-blue cotton shirts covered by a short-cut jacket.

"Not the standard I would normally accept, but you look presentable enough. Keep your hats on at all times, unless I tell you to remove them." she instructed. "And keep your heads bowed so that the brims hide your faces – I don't expect you to be so stupid that you walk into anyone or anything."

She waited for a response, but no one spoke.

"This may be more difficult for you than it should be, but the correct response is 'Yes Mistress'". Her tone was one of despair.

Beth looked to Abelee for a cue.

Abelee took the lead. "Yes, Mistress," and the other two followed in turn.

"Well, it's a start," Valentina said dismissively, then with more vigour: "Beth, fetch my two bags. You will carry them. You need to improve your fitness and this is your chance. There will be two barrows waiting out the front for us. Our first stop is the spellbooks."

She looked directly at the boy. "What are we to call you, then?"

"Mocrat, Mistress." He stared back at Valentina, but Beth was certain he meant no disrespect.

"So, where are we going for these books?"

"To City Hall."

"Now I wasn't expecting that reply."

The barrows pulled up at the steps of the large civic building. Valentina and Mocrat alighted and engaged in quiet conversation.

"Mistress Valentina," called the senior official, loud enough to be heard but not enough to seem impolite. "What brings you to Arities City Hall? I assume it is business," the official continued as he approached. He was referring to the Mistress's attire of britches, bodice and long coat, topped by her distinctive capotain.

"Fellow Echeck, how nice to see you again." She seemed genuine. "Sadly, it is neither business nor pleasure that brings me here. My stupid servant here dropped something by the City Hall yesterday and we are here to see if it can be found."

"Oh, if that's the case should I summon assistance and I can organise a search party?"

"No, that won't be necessary. The boy will do it alone – it will teach him an important lesson. Now go boy, and don't take long," Valentina demanded, giving Mocrat a little shove.

Mocrat normally only approached his hideaway at night because it was located beneath City Hall. Scruffy street urchins were chased away in these parts and often beaten by the hall security staff and servants, but today he was dressed in a uniform and was starting to feel the authority and anonymity if afforded him.

He raced to the rear of the building. Deep inside a highly sculptured row of thick green bushes he located the disused sewer well. The well had been filled in, but not very thoroughly and a crack in the low wall allowed him access. He crawled over the broken rubble, barely managing to squeeze through, until he reached his bolthole.

***

"Oh dear," said Echeck when Mocrat returned to the group. "It seems the boy has found the package, but at what cost to his attire?"

Mocrat was covered in dry dust and dirt. But he was holding a small sack.

"What indeed," said Valentina. "It would appear that learning one lesson now requires teaching on a new one. Get on the barrow, boy. We will discuss this shortly. Please forgive me, Fellow Echeck, but I must now be going."

"Of course, Mistress. If you need anything, though, please do return – and ask for me. I would be more than happy to assist you in any matters or to aid you in your business affairs."

***

"Nice to have you on board, Mistress Valentina. Four months, I believe, since we last had the privilege."

Valentina vaguely recognised the airboat officer from her last trip to Fallon. "That is correct, officer. The airboat saves so much time moving between the cities."

Her servants were below decks, in the hold, with the cargo and luggage that was not for the cabins.

This time it was much colder at altitude, the rain more frequent in the icy chill. However, she needed to return to Fallon for more research. The boat was not as busy on this trip, probably because of a recent incident in which a vered attacked one of the ections as it hauled the craft through the air. No crew or passengers had died, but the teamster found it necessary to cut the captured bird loose and allow the bird of prey to take it. This had forced the boat to land mid-journey so the other distressed birds could be settled, and necessary adjustments made to the boat's rigging and a reduced haulage team. Not surprisingly this had led to further distrust in air travel, even though the airboat service still boasted they'd never lost a passengers during a flight.

"Vered, North West. Vered, North West," called the lookout from the crow's nest above the balloons.

"Weapons port," ordered the captain from the forecastle as he approached the rail and looked down onto the deck below to ensure his orders were being obeyed. He was a large-framed man, made more of muscle than fat, recalled Valentina, who had spoken with him on her last voyage. She had learned that he was confident and experienced, and felt certain that they were in reliable hands.

The boat crew and some passengers gathered on the left of the vessel, joining Valentina, armed with bows, javelins and pistols.

"Vered heading towards us, Captain," came a shout from above.

Now Abelee and Mocrat appeared at Valentina's side. The tall woman had acquired a bow and a dozen arrows from somewhere, and the boy wielded a strong-looking catapult loaded with a spiked ball.

"Beth?" asked Valentina.

"She's still below, Mistress," replied Abelee. "Apparently she doesn't know how to use any weapon."

"Good. Make sure she stays below. She's valuable to me," Valentina said, turning back to look over the side of the airboat.

"Vered flying parallel, Captain," came the update.

"Everyone stay ready," ordered the captain.

"Passengers with weapons – be sure you do not hit the balloons above."

"You need to get on deck," an old woman, a servant to another passenger, said to Beth who was sitting on a pile of luggage, looking nervous. "Here, take my pistol. I cannot see a damn to use it anyway."

The old woman did not look well. She had been sick more than once on the journey. Couldn't get her air legs, she said.

Beth hesitated. She had already told Abelee that she didn't know how to use a weapon.

The woman pushed the pistol into her hand, forcing her to take it.

"They need every able person on deck. If that vered takes an ection, we will need to land, or worse, crash. That puts us on the ground with all the other predators. Thank the gods the bird hasn't yet discovered the balloons or it might take them out and then we'll just fall."

"Vered above, Captain," came an increasingly alarmed voice from above.

Beth heard the call and the woman's words were now unnerving her.

"Shit. We can't see it or fire at it because of the balloons," said one of the deckhands, obviously panicked.

"Diving, diving!" screamed the lookout.

Beth arrived on deck to hear the clap of pistols and witnessed the sudden flight of arrows and javelins alongside the bursts of magic issuing fire and energy released by the spellbinders nested below each of the three balloons.

The giant bird of prey was by the forecastle. Everyone who'd been able to had taken their shots. Beth's panic grew

— it seemed they'd all missed the target. It had been hurtling at speed and only visible for the briefest moment, before disappearing. The airboat lurched violently. One passenger, too close to the port rail, nearly fell overboard, but a crew member caught him just in time.

"Can't see it, Captain. It must be in the cloud," the lookout hollered.

"Stay ready. It will return," the captain responded.

"Starboard side! Starboard side!" shrieked the lookout.

The bird was huge, each talon large enough to scoop a person off the deck and carry them away. It tried to cut across the deck but at the last minute got tangled in the rigging. The impact dragged the boat hard over to one side and everyone scrambled to keep their footing. The vered screeched and raked its talons and beak at the ropes that entrapped it. One of the balloons was being pulled towards it, within the range of its claws.

Clap! Clap! Clap! Clap!

"Stop firing," ordered the captain. "You'll hit the balloons."

Everyone looked at the source of the shots. It was Beth. She was aiming the pistol at the bird, no more than thirty feet above her. Somehow she had not only missed hitting the bird but also the balloon close to it.

Valentina saw an opportunity. The bird was flapping frantically and with one final pull freed its talon from the grasping rigging ropes. She had a clear shot. Steadying her aim through the eyeglass of the pistol, she let two slugs fly. The vered let out an angry screech of alarm as both slugs found their target. The two projectiles alone weren't usually enough to kill the creatures, but Valentina had aimed them at its wickedly curved beak. Its weak spot. The vered would never survive with a damaged beak and its instincts came to play – all it wanted to do was escape.

"It's gone, Captain," announced a flat voice from above.

The captain sighed, his demeanour still cool. "Thank you, Mistress Valentina," he said graciously. "You may well have just saved all our lives."

The crew and passengers voiced their appreciation with cheers and clapping, and followed them with a swarm of congratulations and thanks.

"However, Mistress Valentina," the captain leaned in close, "please could I ask that your servant remains below for the remainder of the trip. How she managed to miss the bird – and more importantly the balloon – at that range is astonishing, but very lucky for all of us".

***

"Were you aiming to miss?" Abelee teased Beth, when things quietened down. She gave her a friendly nudge.

"No," bleated Beth, not sure where to look, as most of those around her were still giving her disapproving looks.

Mocrat smiled and squeezed Beth's hand. She stared at him, totally surprised by his comforting gesture. The boy had not spoken more than three words to her since they had met.

EIGHT

Mistress Valentina sent Abelee and Mocrat to Hotel Farsight as soon as they disembarked from the airboat. They were to secure rooms for their stay in the city. As they had arrived mid-morning she didn't want to waste the day, so she and Beth took a barrow to the Stara Academy.

The school of testing and magic was an old tall building with a ribbed central chamber supported above by pointed arches. Yet it was very bright inside, with high stained-glass windows that rendered an astonishingly sun-mottled interior. From the main chamber, a maze of corridors and doors led off to a network of smaller surrounding buildings. Stara Academy was now the home of magic. Here, spellbinders came to enhance their learning and skills. Others came to be tested and achieve their incant. Over the last ten years, Stara had linked itself to all the other places of testing and schooling, establishing itself as the principal hub for all their knowledge and records. Its library was now considered to be the largest of its kind; the librarians had acquired by many and varied means all the books and records they could pertaining to magic, mystery, adventure and discovery.

"Mistress Valentina! How may I accommodate you?" declared the major librarian, a small elderly man, balding patchily and sporting a wispy grey beard. He wore a dark grey suit with a pair of white gloves hanging from the pocket of his jacket. Around his neck on a ribbon was a large magnifying glass.

"I am researching a matter," Valentina responded. "I understand some books and other documents were recovered from Rigard Pentwing's home after the fire." Valentina's posture and tone conveyed that she expected complete compliance.

"Yes, that is true. Such a sad event. The city lost a well-respected and honourable man." He looked around him anxiously.

"May I see these works?"

"They are presently under lock and key while our own scribes and scholars study them."

"That is not what I asked," she retorted.

"Apologies, Mistress, but they are not yet available to the public."

Valentina stepped up close to the man. "Are you referring to me as 'public', Major Librarian?"

The old man shuffled nervously. Valentina appreciated that he was used to dealing with powerful spellbinders and prominent people, but doubted he was rarely challenged or questioned on his role or duties by a Mistress.

"We have not yet catalogued them or decided where they should be housed on the shelves."

"Again, that is not what I asked."

The man had started to cower under Valentina's intensity. "I'm sorry, Mistress, but you would need special permission to view those documents."

"Whose permission?" she demanded.

"M-mine," he stuttered.

"Well, isn't that so very convenient. Here you are before me, able to grant such a thing." She stepped back, displaying herself, challenging any form of contradiction.

The librarian studied the floor and finally sighed heavily.

"I will have an assistant escort you to the room where they are currently being studied."

Five studious-looking men and women sat around a long table loaded with books. At first, they expressed alarm when Valentina and Beth were ushered into the room, but the assistant assured them that they had the correct permission to be there.

"Well, you all might just save me some time," Valentina said to the disgruntled scholars. "I am looking for any and all references to mist and Orestas Connroy, especially where they are linked together."

There was a sudden buzz of conversation and enthusiasm as each scholar voiced their findings with obvious excitement.

Beth had no idea why she was there. She sat uncomfortably for the next eight hours on a hard chair in a corner of the room. Occasionally she paced around the table to stretch her legs or take a drink from the refreshments table. Once she asked where the toilet was, but was shushed back into silence. Later when one of the scholars also needed such a break she took the opportunity to be shown where to go.

Mistress Valentina scribbled notes and copied images from the books into her own records, using magic. At first this fascinated Beth, but after seeing the Mistress lay her hand on one page and then lay it in her own notebook more than a dozen times the novelty wore off.

The next two days were a repeat of the day. Mistress Valentina went over all the findings again, ensuring that she had all the details correct. It was apparent to everyone in the room how much appreciated the work of the scholars – all eight of them, as three more had joined them – who willingly explained their discoveries and theories. Beth herself had heard so much that she felt that she now knew everything there was to know about mist and Orestas Connroy, but she had no real interest in any of the revelations. The mist still frightened her and she had not heard of Orestas before visiting the room of scholars.

After a third day in the library, and another two in Valentina's rooms, watching her Mistress study her notes and ponder over maps.

"Mistress, why am I always accompanying you?"

It had taken her days to muster enough courage to say this. She was restless. Abelee and Mocrat had been allowed to explore the city during the days, and each evening, when all three were back in the suite they shared, she listened to them discussing with delight the intricacies of Fallon: the docks, the poor districts, the rich districts, the taverns and eating houses, the civil buildings, the foreigners, and the strange and wondrous imports that were pouring into the city.

Valentina didn't raise her head from her work. "You're important to me, Beth, and I want you safe and in my sight as much as possible," she replied.

"But why, Mistress?" The question came out before Beth was aware she had spoken.

Valentina stopped marking locations on the map before her and looked up.

"I will need to go on a trip soon and you will need to come with me."

"Into the mist?"

Valentina paused, and Beth wondered if she had said something wrong.

"So you've managed to work that out while you've been sitting with me. That's good, but you cannot tell anyone else about it yet."

"The mist is dangerous. There are monsters in the mist that will hunt and eat us." Beth started to perspire as she spoke and her voice trembled. She was truly scared now. "I can't go into the mist, I will die. I don't want to be eaten."

"You must have heard when we were at the library that Rigard Pentwing sent expeditions into the mist, and they returned," the Mistress said.

"Not all of them, Mistress. In fact, very few returned. Even that Orestas fellow said the mists were very dangerous, and he was supposed to be an all-powerful spellbinder." Her voice quivered.

"I will need you to be brave and trust me," Valentina responded calmly.

"But I'm useless. If I even so much as look at a mist, I nearly piss myself. I can't fight, I'm not brave, and I'm too heavy to run quickly. I will be the first one to be eaten by a monster." Her head was down and her face hidden by the brim of her hat.

"They are not monsters. They are simply animals and beasts, such as we have in our own lands. They are from somewhere else, is all. When have you seen a mist? I thought you had never left Arities?"

"When I was a child, Mistress. The other kids tried to push me into one." The memory still frightened her and she wrung her hands together.

"I doubt it was a real mist. Cities and towns tend to be built away from areas where they are known to form."

"It was still very scary to me. Why do we – I – have to go into any mist?" She looked up now, pleading with her eyes.

"That I will tell you later, but for now I think I need to change our focus for a few days. Tomorrow we will head to the dockyard so I can send some of these notes and documents, and the spellbooks from Mocrat, to my home. Then we will spend some time with Mocrat and Abelee. I must congratulate the boy, too, as his spellbooks contained a few useful snippets – mainly incants, but still new and useful."

***

Beth stared at the caged animal. She was unsure if it was a bird or something else entirely.

"They say that you can ride a fully-grown one in the sky," explained Mocrat. The last few days he had begun to come out of his shell and was engaging more and more in conversation. Beth had attributed this to Abelee, who seemed to have taken the boy under her care and protection.

"That's not fully grown?" asked Beth.

"No, no. A sailor told us that a full-grown one is bigger than a gausent." He stretched out his arms to demonstrate.

"Have you seen an adult one here?" Beth looked about, wondering if there was one nearby.

"No. Something about they can't or won't travel on a ship, the sailor said."

"Beth. Do not wander off," called Abelee, who was standing with Valentina and Hichard, the shipping manager. Beth had stepped away, looking for other cages that might hold an adult creature.

"I finally get out of Malad and I can't see anything," groaned Beth.

"Want to sneak away? We can, you know," Mocrat whispered close to her ear.

"No, I can't. Mistress Valentina would not be happy." She looked over to Valentina, who always seemed to be watching her.

"Look, if you are so valuable to her, what is she going to do to you?"

"I don't know. Lock me up, maybe? Put me on a leash or chain?"

"Come on, Beth. We can explore. I've had a look round before, so I know where to go."

"Not so fast, you two." Abelee had crept up on them. "I can hear your mischievous minds from way over there."

***

The shooting range in the back of the pistol store was available for Valentina to use whenever she requested it. Abelee proved to be adequate with a pistol but professed that she preferred a bow, as she was quicker and more accurate with that weapon. Neither the boy nor Beth had ever fired a pistol before, other than in the episode on the airboat. Mocrat learned quickly; being so young and small he had some difficulty handling the weapon, but he showed real promise. Beth, on the other hand, was useless. After firing twenty slugs, she was yet to hit even the nearest target.

"And you cannot use a knife, sword, bow, spear or anything else?" questioned Valentina.

"No, Mistress. I've never needed to." Beth was looking at the floor and shuffling her feet with embarrassment.

Mocrat offered his catapult and the Mistress took it and handed it to Beth. She took several attempts before she was able to fire her first stone, as she either dropped the projectile or let the band slip as she drew it back. When she finally released a stone it simply fell out of the front of the catapult. The next stone flew backwards – to everyone's amazement.

Abelee offered her bow. Beth's attempts to use it were worse than with the catapult.

"Have you never been in a fight?" asked the Mistress.

"Yes, but I was always beaten up. I don't think I've ever hit anyone."

"Mistress," said Mocrat. "Mistress."

Valentina looked at the boy, who was pointing at her left shoulder holster.

"She can't be any worse with this, I suppose," the Mistress said as she handed the sighted pistol to Beth. She held it, looking lost.

The Mistress explained what the sight was for and how to use it and then faced Beth down the range with the weapon. After what seemed an age of fiddling with the sight, Beth finally fired her first slug. Splinters erupted from the nearest target. Then the next target further down, and then the next, and then finally the furthest one.

She turned to hand the weapon back to Valentina. Her three companions stood motionless, watching her in silence.

"Do that again," said Valentina eventually.

She showed Beth how to load the pistol and charge it. Once again she fired down the range and every slug hit its target.

"Again," said Valentina handing Beth more ammunition and seed pods. "Again. I need to be certain," repeated Valentina.

"Thank the gods for that. We've found a weapon you can use," she said with relief. Then she removed her holster and handed it to Beth. "I have a second holster, sight and pistol in my rooms. This one is yours now. At least you can now defend yourself in some way. But now try to do the same with the darts."

***

Beth accepted the seeds and a seed-chamber from the Mistress, along with some ammunition she'd purchased. She also bought a pistol and holster for the boy. Their reactions were in stark contrast. Mocrat beamed, and didn't stop fondling the forward-facing grip of the weapon on his left hip. While Beth physically recoiled from the weapon in her shoulder holster and constantly fidgeted, as though they irritated her.

It was a fresh clear day so Valentina decided to walk for a while. She took the lead down the narrow street, with

Abelee at her side, and Mocrat and Beth following close behind them.

"Mistress, what is all this about?" asked Abelee.

Valentina studied her companion for a moment. "We will be going on a trip that will be dangerous. I need to find something that's been hidden for a long time."

"What kind of dangerous?"

"We need to enter the mist."

They walked along in silence for a while.

"Mistress!" Abelee raised her bow, an arrow already nocked. A blue dart was lodged in the back of Valentina's hand. She looked at it with glazed eyes for the briefest moment before collapsing to the floor. Eight masked assailants rushed at them, four from either side of the street. Abelee put an arrow in one of them, but then they were too close for her to release a second.

Nearby onlookers fled and one woman screamed as her male companion dragged her away without a look back. There was a blinding flash of light that stunned everyone for a moment, except for Abelee. Her incant disorientated the assailants, giving her time to unsheathe her serrated knife. Two more attackers died within seconds. The aggressors recovered quickly though; two had taken hold of Mocrat and a third punched Beth in the face, knocking her to the floor. The boy fought back and cut the man and woman he was wrestling with. His pistol lay on the floor. The remaining two men turned to face Abelee, both had holstered pistols, but approached with knives drawn.

Clap!

The head of the man nearest to Abelee exploded. Beth, still on her knees, had fired her pistol. The woman who had punched her turned on Beth and kicked her viciously in the head, knocking her into a sprawl on the ground. A blow with a cudgel knocked Mocrat facedown.

Now Abelee faced off against the four of them on her own. They circled her quickly, avoiding the thrusts and slices of her knife.

The roar of a charge caught everyone's attention. Two fresh bodies joined the fight. Most of the people on the street had already fled, and a few watched from afar but two of them, a seeder and a spellbinder, had decided to come to Abelee's aid. Slugs were fired from each of the pistols in the seeder's hands, killing two of the attackers with headshots. The female assailant closest to Abelee convulsed as light crackled around her and she fell dead to the floor. Abelee struck the last one hard across the temple with the hilt of her knife, and the woman joined her companions on the hard stone cobbles.

"You see to the Mistress," the spellbinder instructed Abelee as he looked at Beth. The seeder rushed over to the boy.

Beth and Mocrat were conscious and on their feet again by the time half a dozen enforcers arrived on the scene. They initially wanted everyone to accompany them to the station, but Abelee refused on the grounds that Mistress Valentina would not be very appreciative of such a move. The seeder and the spellbinder also declined; their posturing made it quite clear that there was a chance of more violence if the enforcers insisted on doing that. Finally, it was agreed that the enforcers would call on Mistress Valentina later, once she had recovered. The seeder and the spellbinder would also receive a visit at their accommodation later in the day. So, leaving the bodies to the enforcers, the seeder and the spellbinder, who had given their names as Loate and Nyser, helped carry Valentina to a barrow.

Two hours later the Mistress awoke in her bed, still fully clothed. She was not happy. Beth watched through blurry eyes as Abelee recounted the incident. Beth was sobbing constantly in a corner of the room. Valentina demanded that she cease, but to no avail. On discovering that one of the attackers was still alive, Valentina decided to confront the woman herself, and ordered Abelee to accompany her to the station. Beth and Mocrat were to stay locked in the room and were not to leave or answer the door to anyone. Beth was more than happy with this arrangement – she never wanted to go outside again.

"Mocrat, if anyone enters these rooms other than me, shoot them without question," Valentina instructed as she left.

Not saying a word, the boy took Beth's hand and sat beside her. It was several minutes before Beth spoke. "I killed that man. I killed him," she sputtered between sobs.

"It was needed. They attacked us." His tone was soft and sympathetic, a trait Beth had not yet seen in him.

"I … I … I didn't want to do it. It just happened." Her sobs started to subside.

"It's not nice, killing. We hear so much about it. People die every day and it's not until you take a life you that realise how fragile we all are."

Beth noticed his gaze wander off and wondered whether he was actually referring to another incident.

"Have you?" she asked. "Killed someone?"

"Yes."

"But you're so young." Now she felt sympathy for Mocrat.

"Life on the streets of Arities is not easy. I've needed to kill more than once. I'm not saying it's a good thing, but we need to survive."

Beth held Mocrat in a huge embrace while she cried openly. "I'm so sorry," she said feeling for him, but also comforting herself.

***

"I demand to see the prisoner! Now!" Valentina repeated.

"She's not talking. We have tried," reiterated the commander.

"I need to know who came for me and why, and I am not leaving until I see her. Do you want to see what I can do to this city if you get in my way?"

"No, Mistress. I am most certain that you can harm us through trade and a great many other ways." He let out a long sigh. "So be it. I will have you escorted to her cell. Will your companion go with you?"

"Yes … Leara will come with me. She's my personal escort." There was the slightest hesitation in her voice at the change of Abelee's name.

The female assailant was alone in her cell, but two others shared her cell block. Removing her weapons and handing them to Abelee, Mistress Valentina entered the cell. The guard closed and locked the door after her. The prisoner was bruised and her clothing was torn. Valentina could see no evidence of any sexual abuse, but the woman had obviously been rigorously questioned.

"Do you know who I am?"

There was no response. Sat on the cot with her legs scrunched up to her chest, still and silent.

"You're tough, obviously – the guards do seem to have tried to persuade you to talk. I could do more of the same, but I have another idea. I am assuming you know who I am. Why would you come after me otherwise? I have a great number of enemies. Some openly, but others plot and scheme in silence and darkness. Being Mistress to possibly the most powerful, richest castle and lands and resources in the whole of Parablion is not without its risks and dangers. But I walk freely and alone often without concern, as most that conspire against me are cowards and I have a great many ways to hurt them."

The woman watched as Valentina paced leisurely up and down beside the cot. Her eyes were alert, ready for the next blow or act of violence.

"I also assume you have a family, friends, loved ones. Maybe even children. You see, what I am proposing is that I leave your loved ones alone if you talk to me. Perhaps you don't have anyone close to you, but I suspect you do have someone … and I will find them and they will suffer."

The woman hid her face against her knees.

"I have almost limitless resources," Valentina went on. "I can send people to every corner of the land to search out any links to you. I can use your dead associates to gain leads on you, because someone will know them and they will speak out. It's only a matter of time."

She stopped pacing and stood in front of the woman. "All I want to know is who sent you? For that information, I will leave you here with the guards, but more importantly,

I will not hunt down everyone you care for."

"Balcoff," the prisoner said softly.

The Mistress sat on the cot and looked into the woman's eyes. She was satisfied that the woman spoke the truth.

Valentina did not share her discovery with the commander of the enforcers, but she left content with this new knowledge.

**

"Thank you, Mistress," said Abelee as they rode the barrow together. "I take it you saw the wanted posters for me and the boy. The commander was looking at me very suspiciously."

"I should have changed your names earlier. From now on you are Leara and the boy is Remy."

Hotel Nonook was a low-grade accommodation, with an attached tavern occupying one corner of the building.

"Room six, Mistress," advised the receptionist when Valentina asked about Loate and Nyser.

It was Nyser, the seeder, who answered the door with a lowered pistol in his hand. He welcomed Valentina and Leara, as she was now known, into the small room. Apart from the bed and a small dresser, the only other furnishing was a round table with four hard chairs. Valentina accepted the offered seat and all four sat at the table.

"I came to thank you and reward you for your intervention today. I am not often caught off guard, but I have been a little preoccupied of late."

"We were glad to be of assistance, Mistress," said Nyser.

"So who are you, and what can I offer by way of a reward?"

The men explained that they worked together as

independents. They took on any role that paid for their talents with pistols and magic. In the main, they were reputable and legal, but they admitted that they often encountered very grey areas in the course of their service and contracts.

They were in their late twenties, Valentina decided, and both of them appeared fit and healthy, and able. After talking for a while about a couple of their recent professional activities, Mistress Valentina brought the conversation back to the subject of a reward. Neither man expressed a desire for any compensation.

"Perhaps I can offer you employment, then?" said Valentina.

"We're listening," they replied, and leaned forward, suddenly more interested by the direction the conversation had taken.

"I have a dangerous trip planned and I will need reliable men and women with me. There is a good chance that not all who accompany me will survive, but the pay and treatment you will receive will more than compensate for the risks," outlined Valentina.

"What kind of trip?" asked Nyser, cautiously.

"That, for now, is not up for discussion. Are you interested or not?"

"Surely a Mistress such as yourself does not need to hire independents. Do you not have your own army and guards to accompany you?"

"They are all employed – to protect my interests, and my home and other matters. I choose to leave these tasks with the men and women I trust and have grown up with. This trip will be my own private excursion."

The two men looked to each other and then Nyser spoke. "We would be very interested. What do you need of us now and where are we to go?"

"Leave this room tonight and I will have a room waiting for you at Hotel Farsight. Tomorrow we can discuss the matter further."

"Your incant – that takes no small amount of power," said Valentina to Leara as they rode back to the hotel, sitting close beside each other on the barrow.

"Not really, Mistress. It is just that I have a knack for that particular incant," Leara replied. "The tester said my power is weak and very slow to regenerate."

"It is a rather uncommon incant. Have you tried other spells?" Valentina turned to look her in the eyes.

"Like most people I can only learn a simple incant because my focus is not well attuned to magic." Leara held her Mistress's gaze. "I have tried other spells and I definitely do not have the power. It often takes a day or more for me to recover enough to use the incant again. I did have a little success in the early days with igniting a flame, but I couldn't hold the spell in my focus every time."

"Hmm, perhaps we can work on that if we have some time." Valentina smiled softly.

Mistress Valentina walked into her rooms to be greeted by two pistols pointing at her. Mocrat sighed with visible relief and lowered his own and Beth's weapon. Beth was sleeping on one of the cushioned chairs.

"You show more promise every day," Valentina told him. "Leara, please take Beth and Remy to your own rooms. I want a hot bath and wine. I will call for you all in the morning."

"Who's Remy? Who's Leara?" asked Mocrat.

"I will explain shortly," said Leara as she lifted the sleeping girl from the chair, not without some effort, as Beth had a solid frame for someone of her sex and age.

"Mistress," said Leara as she was leaving. "Loate knew you as 'Mistress' when he first came to our aid – before any introductions. It only occurred to me while we were at the Hotel Nonook."

"Thank you. Don't worry about that for now. We have more pressing matters."

NINE

The next morning Mistress Valentina revealed to her small team that they were heading to Anding Town, a prosperous settlement where the manufacture of clothing and leather goods was the staple trade. Having never walked outside city walls, this excited both Remy and Beth. However, there was currently no coach service so the journey would need to be made overland by their own means. Beth's excitement shifted to apprehension and it was Remy who held her hand and reassured her that everything would be fine.

Valentina intended to purchase some gausents and equip everyone appropriately. Hichard should have taken care of the arrangements; she had sent him a message the day before, following her recruitment of Loate and Nyser. They would leave Fallon early in the afternoon, giving them the whole morning to close any business in the city and pick up any personal supplies that they might need. In light of the events of the day before, none of them were to be alone at any time. The Mistress paired Remy with Leara, Loate with Nyser, and herself with Beth.

Once Nyser and Loate left, Valentina gave additional instructions to Remy and Leara. They were to follow the seeder and the spellbinder and remain undetected, to see if they could learn anything that revealed more of whom the newcomers were, and whether they worked for or with others. The challenge excited Remy. He had tailed people before in the streets of Arities, and suggested a plan whereby he could get close to the seeder and spellbinder unnoticed. Valentina approved and instructed Leara and Remy to act accordingly.

***

Leara was some distance back watching Loate and Nyser, who in turn were now watching Valentina as she left the messaging station. Fallon had three such offices and it was obvious to Remy that it had been a pure coincidence that they'd all arrived at the same one at the same time. Remy was much closer to the seeder and the spellbinder, close enough to hear them speaking. His disguise as a dirty street urchin allowed him to go unnoticed, provided he didn't offend or accost anyone and stayed out of any respectable establishments.

"Well, that would have been awkward," said Loate, indicating Valentina and Beth climbing into a waiting barrow.

"Let's get our business done quickly," replied Nyser. "She might come back."

Remy watched the two men cross the busy street and enter the messaging station. He knew all too well that he would not be able to enter in his current attire, so he waited.

Leara did not disappoint him. She approached him and took time to sort some coin in the palm of her hand before handing the few coppers to him, as if giving alms.

"They are in the messaging station," Remy advised her quietly. "You should find out what they're doing in there."

"You make sure you get a warm meal," Leara told the street urchin, as she left him.

"Thank you, miss," he replied, then in a softer tone, "I will follow them when they leave."

The tavern adjoining the Hotel Nonook was busy; the poor-quality ale was cheap which suited the miscreant clientele that frequented it. Remy had followed the two men back to their hotel, relieved that they hadn't taken a barrow – probably couldn't afford one, he decided, as he mingled into the hustle and bustle of the crowd.

The single ground-floor serving room was dimly lit, even in daylight, the tables and chairs creaking and groaning with age, and the constant hum and buzz of conversation made it difficult to hear any specific thing that was going on. Loate and Nyser had found a small table to themselves, close to the centre of the room. Remy heard them say that it wasn't really to their liking, but it beat standing in a dark corner. However, their location meant that they were constantly being bumped and jostled by the passing patrons and serving staff.

They were on their second ale when a dubious-looking character joined them.

"So, you're in with the Mistress now?" he said from under a wide-brimmed hat that shadowed his face.

Remy tried to find a better position to see the new arrival's face but was forced in another direction by the natural flow of the people through the room. He knew he should follow their movement in the space so that he wouldn't stand out. So far, he had managed not to get himself noticed by anyone while remaining within earshot of his two marks.

"It wasn't intentional, Evritt," Nyser said to the hat-wearing stranger.

"So what's the plan now?" the man asked.

Remy managed to find a new spot just as the man removed his hat. He was older than both Nyser and Loate by a good number of years, his skin extremely wrinkled and especially craggy around the eyes, but Remy knew his sort. He might be older but he would still be a dangerous man to get into a fight with. Remy didn't recognise him, but the two miscreants did.

"We will stay with the Mistress until an opportunity arises, Evritt" said Nyser.

"Master Brigges might not like that," Evritt replied.

"We sent him a cryptic message earlier. You can maybe explain to him that we can't back out now. We have to work with what we've got. If we hadn't teamed up with her, it would have made her suspicious the next time she saw us."

Several people pushed past their table, knocking it sideways. "Oy! Back off," complained Evritt, then turned his attention back to the men. "Where are you heading?"

"Anding Town," said Loate.

"Hmm. I'm not sure I want to follow you there alone, overland. That road's dangerous and known to have mist." Evritt scratched at his thick grey stubble.

"Then head back to Arities. Chances are we'll end up

there at some point, too. Right now, though, we need to be going," Nyser got to his feet.

***

Valentina, Beth and Leara waited for Remy at Hotel Farsight. The only nervous one among them was Beth. There was no knock at the door as it opened and a dirty street boy quickly sneaked inside.

"They're back," said Remy.

"So spill," said Valentina.

The boy reported what he had seen and heard. After leaving the messaging station, Loate and Nyser had gone to the tavern and there he overheard the names Master Brigges and Evritt. Evritt seemed to be their accomplice for something they were planning. But he was now going to Arities.

"Is there more?" Remy asked Leara. "What happened in the messaging station?" He was keen to piece more of the puzzle together.

"Not much, I've already told Valentina and Beth. They sent a message. That's all. I tried to bribe the clerk, but he got offended and called the proprietor, so I left quickly. However a man approached me outside and for a silver he told me he'd overheard them saying the name Master Brigges."

"That must be who they're working for," said Remy.

"Let's not jump to conclusions," Valentina cautioned him. "Something is amiss, agreed, but let it run its course and we will watch them – but without rousing their suspicions."

Remy nodded in agreement.

***

The North Stables held the gausents and supplies sent by Hichard, and with them was one of the shipping manager's hands to ensure nothing happened to the provisions. Mistress Valentina handed the man a message for Hichard and then the six of them rode out of the city. For the first mile, Leara spent her time instructing Remy and Beth how to ride. Remy was a natural in the saddle. But Beth was … her usual self. Even after the first mile she still looked like she might fall off at any time.

Valentina set a comfortable pace, allowing Beth to gain some confidence as they rode. The road was a well-used by trade caravans and in most places it was even and maintained.

"Relax a little, Beth. Stop clamping so tightly with your knees and legs," said Loate, who'd moved alongside the girl. "The more relaxed you are, the more the gausent will be, too."

Beth looked at the spellbinder. On his shoulder sat a small brown bird.

"Ah, this is my familiar. Rather unusual, I know. Most are rodents or small burrowing animals, or anything that can be easily kept out of sight in a pocket or pouch. I get a bird."

"Why is that unusual?" Beth asked.

"Well, I've yet to meet another spellbinder with a bird."

"Does that mean yours is special?"

"A familiar provides the same, no matter what it looks like. My problem is that I need to let her out to fly and that exposes her to risks that I'd rather not have to consider."

As dusk approached they came alongside a caravan of four wagons setting up camp beside the road, heading towards Fallon. Valentina spoke with the wagon master and it was agreed that they could prepare their own camp for the night opposite the caravan, on the other side of the road. Loate told Beth it was a common practice – safety in numbers against predators. Beth wondered why the spellbinder had taken a liking to her, and if it was part of his plan?

Several hours into the following day's ride they hit a problem. Lazing in the roadway were six hacros, so intimidating because they were more than twice the size of a gausent and had sturdy horns protruding from the crowns of their heads. They were in the main harmless but, being short-sighted and extremely stubborn, they could be easily panicked or roused into aggression. This meant that they would charge anything with little or no provocation. Their hides were thick and tough and slugs wouldn't penetrate them in most places. Across from the six riders were two caravans, both at a standstill, one tailing the other; until the hacros moved on, they would all have to wait.

"Keep an eye on the trees," said Loate, once again riding beside Beth. "Hacros may be herbivores, but they are prey to a good variety of carnivores that would as soon eat us as well."

Beth watched Valentina and Leara for guidance. Leara had her bow ready. Recognising the flight and arrowhead style, Beth knew that the tip was laced with a lethal toxin. Her own pistol was loaded with two slugs and two darts. Valentina had explained that most predators were difficult, if not impossible, to bring down with slugs but the poison was effective, at least for a short period of time – that was provided you hit a spot where the toxin could enter the bloodstream.

Everyone waited, with varying levels of patience. The minutes went by slowly and the group of beasts showed no indication it would soon be moving on.

"We're going around them," instructed the Mistress. "Not too deep into the treeline but enough not to spook the hacros."

"Kerns," called out Leara. Loud enough to get everyone's attention, but not so loud as to startle the hacros.

"Which side?" asked Valentina, a pistol now in her hand.

"Right. I only glimpsed one, but where there's one there's always a pack."

Nyser and Loate readied the lances slung from the sides of their gausents. Beth looked at the two lances secured to her own mount but decided she couldn't ride *and* fight, so she drew her pistol, for comfort, and held on tightly to the harness. Fear started to rise inside her and her palms began to sweat; she worried her hold would slip, but she dared not let go to wipe her hands.

The hacros were now all on their feet, alert. The pack of kerns erupted from the trees on both sides. Over a dozen of them, howling and yapping as they raced towards the hacros. The heavy beasts bolted, herding tightly together, towards the stationary caravans. The pack nipped at their hoofs and flanks, dodging kicks and horns, harassing the larger animals. One hacro stopped and turned and the kerns were on her. The big animal shook off the predators that bit at her legs, ears and snout, then charged back down the road, trying to toss aside any kerns in her path.

Before Beth realised it, the hacro and kerns were bearing down on her. She was aware of arrows being loosed, the clap of pistols and the energy of magic being cast, but she froze. Her gausent, however, rose to the occasion. Head lowered, it charged, meeting both pack and prey in the roadway ahead. A larger kern leaped on the back of her mount, snarling and snapping with savage teeth, and the grey-coated predator's head would have reached Beth's waist if she had been standing. It was almost as heavy as her. It brushed past her, almost unseating her, with its muzzle just inches from her face so that she felt its breath. The leather of the harness and reins cut into her hands as she held on for her life. The gausent barged onwards, past the racing hacro, crushing Beth's leg against the beast.

One of the kerns had a firm grip of the prey's snout and the animal tumbled to the ground. The rest of the pack closed in for the kill, including the animal that had just mounted her gausent. Beth sped on, risking a backward glance, and leaving the scene behind her. Ahead, two wagons were overturned, battered by the rest of the herd as they fled. One gausent lay dead and three people were injured, or dead. She couldn't be sure. Once past the wagons, Beth's mount slowed and stopped. In the distance, the herd raced on, no longer hunted by the kerns.

"You alright?" asked Remy, coming up alongside Beth who was shaking and sobbing. "Wasn't that exciting!"

Beth couldn't bring herself to speak, and suddenly threw up the contents of her stomach onto the road beside her. Her mount snorted and moved away from the splattering.

"I shot two kerns," said Remy. "I know I hit them but they didn't even slow down. I think the herd killed one of the wagoneers but the rest seem to be alive."

"I thought I was going to die," cried Beth.

"But you didn't."

"I can't stop shaking."

"That's good – it means you're still alive."

"My hands hurt and my leg's sore."

"You look fine to me. I saw that big kern jump up behind you and nearly shot it, but it was too close to you. Leara was so fast with her bow and I've never seen so much magic at once!"

Beth's breaths began to slow down. She took a moment to look back down the road. The fallen hacro was gone, dragged off by the kerns. The caravan teams were busy sorting out their stock and transport. Valentina remained on her mount, talking to people in the midst of the chaos.

"Leara said they won't be very long. They're offering assistance and she's recovering arrows, but she said the wagoneers won't want any help."

When everyone was together again they moved on. Leara had a dead kern slung over the back of her gausent and tied. "Tonight's meal," she announced, assuring everyone there was no toxin in the animal.

Loate caught up to ride alongside Beth, enquiring about her welfare. She was glad of the opportunity to talk and vent her fear and frustration at being so inadequate.

***

"You're doing really well," said Leara, sitting next to Beth at the evening camp.

"I feel useless," said Beth, on the verge of tears once more.

"You need to take a moment and look at what you've done so far."

"You mean *survived*." Beth's shoulders sagged.

"Well, yes, that too. It all makes you grow, if you think about it. Could you have dreamed before of escaping prison, or even being in prison? Then to be travelling with a Mistress?"

"No. I thought I would die in the sewer." She paused momentarily. "Leara, I don't know if I should ask this, but why did you murder someone?"

"It's a long story, Beth. For now, let's just say he deserved it and he was the only reason I was in Arities."

"Do you know what Remy did? Why he was in prison?" Beth looked over to the boy who was adding logs of wood to the fire.

"No. He hasn't spoken about it and I don't think it's something we should push. He's a hard young lad and he seems to have shut out the prison and whatever came before, and we should let him."

A couple of days later, one day's ride from Anding Town, Valentina halted the ride. "We are not going into the town. Instead, we are going some way into the forest and open areas off the road. We should make camp by nightfall, provided we don't encounter any trouble."

Beth started to feel physically sick at the thought of entering where predators prevailed. She looked to both Leara and Remy, who had simply accepted the change in course, while Loate and Nyser questioned the Mistress's logic.

"You two can turn back," Valentina said. "I will see that you are paid for your services so far."

The spellbinder and the seeder exchanged glances, before falling inline, quiet once more.

"Stay low in your saddle. Hug your gausent's back. Do not create a silhouette of yourself above the animal," Leara advised Beth and Remy. "If anything does happen, hold tight to your mount and trust the gausent. They are very capable intelligent animals."

The Mistress led the way off the road into the thickening vegetation and trees. Almost immediately everything changed, in more ways than just appearance. The fear and tension were palpable. They were not being quiet as they moved through the flora, the large mounts trod on leaves and snapping branches as they pushed through the thick brush and web of trees. They weren't much of a hindrance to the strong beasts, and they easily forged a path forward. However, with cover capable of concealing predators on both sides, and low branches above them, everyone was nervous. Beth knew that you never left the road unless you were a skilled hunter.

They pushed on for an hour. Valentina, it seemed to the others, knew exactly where she was going. Without any indication from her, they broke out onto a manufactured track. The low tree branches had been cut back and there were two to three feet without any undergrowth on either side of the gausents. The earth had been packed tight by more than passing hooves, and the tunnel through the brush was obviously well maintained. They continued on this way, crossing clearings here and there, and picking up the track again. The five of them had relaxed a little when they came across the clear passage, but Beth was soaked in perspiration nonetheless. Her hands were both blistered, and the sores burst with her unyielding grip on her reins and harness. As nightfall approached, her anxiety increased to levels she couldn't believe existed. She wanted to scream, to run, but where could she go?

"It can't be long now," said Leara softly to Beth, as she brought up the rear behind her. In front were Nyser, Remy and Loate, and at the head, Valentina. The track had been cut in long straight lines wherever possible, so at most times they'd had each other in their sights.

It was at that moment that Nyser screamed. Those that were quick enough caught sight of a large black corllet disappearing into the darkness, its long thick tail the last thing to vanish. A predator from the same family as the vember, but not quite as big, it had tried to claw the seeder from his gausent. Valentina didn't hesitate. She urged her mount into a gallop, and the other gausents followed instinctively.

A short burst of speed and they raced into a clearing, only to meet further mayhem head on. The Mistress hauled her reins back strongly, bringing her ride to such a hard stop that its haunches dragged on the ground. The riders behind her veered in every direction to avoid a collision.

The roar was deafening. Ahead of them was a huge dark-furred basila. It reared up on its hind legs, shocked by the sudden and violent intrusion. Valentina barely stopped before crashing into the beast. The basila dropped back on to all fours and with a powerful swipe of its long sharp curved claws it ripped into the head and neck of the gausent. Although marginally lighter than the gausent, the basila had delivered a fatal blow. Valentina barely managed to leap to safety as her gausent collapsed to the ground.

The poorly sighted basila charged the next threat – Beth. In the scattered and confused entrance into the clearing, Beth had overtaken everyone. Now the surprisingly agile basila was only feet away from her. Her gausent faced the charge and braced to meet the basila's slavering maw and brutal claws. Beth hung on tightly as the two heavy creatures slammed into each other. She had no idea what to do, so she simply held on for her life. A claw raked her left leg and she screamed. Hot breath and spittle from the basila decorated her cheeks and hair as she tried to bury herself in the back and shoulder of her mount. She was vaguely aware of magic erupting and the clap of pistols, but the onslaught of the attack, of which she was the centre, did not ease.

A wild, loud hollering penetrated Beth's mind and the savage fight eased; then ceased. Her gausent grunted, snorted and beat his hooves on the ground. Steam rose from its back and with it the smell of blood and sweat.

"Beth. Are you alright?" Remy reached out to her from his own ride, nudging her in the back for a response. "Beth, speak to me."

She peeked up then lifted her head. In the dark clearing, a multitude of torches burned bright. Other riders had joined them. She saw the brown-furred rear of the basila crashing back into the woodland.

She sat up, slowly. More than a dozen riders in uniform were urgently seeing to the needs of everyone in the clearing. Beth touched her left leg and brought her hand to her face. A dark liquid coated her palm. It took her a moment to register that it was blood, an instant before the pain hit her. She thought she screamed out then, but Remy later told her that she simply collapsed.

Beth awoke in a strange shelter, part canvas tent and part log cabin. On the cot next to her lay Nyser, sleeping peacefully.

"You're awake," said Remy, from his seat at the foot of her bed.

"Where are we?"

"Mistress Valentina's secret campsite. There must be eighty soldiers here. We should be safe, they've put up spiked barricades to keep predators out."

"Is everyone else alright?"

"Yeah. Only you and Nyser were injured. He's got some nasty claw marks across his back. You were both lucky. Apart from some heavy-duty scarring, you will both be fine."

Beth tried to sit up but struggled. Remy rushed to aid her. Her leg was heavily bandaged.

"The poultician says your bandages can come off tomorrow and he will put lighter dressings on. For now, the thick stuff is to stop you pulling out the few stitches he had to put in." Remy gripped Beth's hand, helping here sit up on the cot.

"How long have I been here?"

"It's mid-afternoon now. We got here last night. From what I've heard, this camp has been watching the mist near here. Their presence has caused predators to hang about nearby, but they've not lost a soldier yet. They've been sending out a night patrol to the road each night, just in case the Mistress arrived. That's what saved you."

"Is this where we are going into the mist?" asked Beth.

"So you know about that? I heard some soldiers talking about it, but I wasn't sure they were telling the truth." He let go of her hand now that she was sitting steadily.

"Yes. We are going into the mist. Valentina is looking for something in there."

"What?"

"I don't know." Then after a brief pause, "but it's to do with a spellbinder called Orestas."

"Oh, I've heard stories about him. Didn't he live like forever or something?" said Remy.

"I don't know much. Only that he lived a long time ago and was supposedly the most powerful spellbinder that there has ever been. He died a long time ago, though."

"Ah, glad to see you're awake," remarked the poultician as he entered their room. "I suggest you move about and get the blood circulating. It's not good for you to be lying about with a wound like that. Here, chew some of this when it's painful." He gave her a few lumps of compressed sio leaves.

Beth asked Remy to help her to her gausent. She wanted to thank the animal for her life. Remy acted as her crutch as they moved to the corral at the centre of the camp, surrounded by over a dozen wooden huts behind the barricades, all in various stages of completion. Beth's gausent came up to her almost as soon as they reached the pole-bar fence. She buried her face in the it's shaggy neck and cried. The gausent did not move until Beth was finished pouring out her gratitude. Then it nuzzled her and wandered back into the penned area.

A soldier hurried towards them. "Mistress Valentina is

looking for you two," he said. "She's in the only finished log cabin on the far side of the corral."

"These are the Mistress's own soldiers from her castle," commented Remy as they worked their way around the fencing. "They've been here for over a month already."

"Good to see you on your feet," said Leara as the soldiers on guard allowed them to enter the cabin. She was sitting with Valentina at a round table before a small hearth in the comfortable, if not a little cramped, building.

"Sit down," instructed the Mistress. "I need to assure you both of a few things if you are to be of use to me. I've already discussed this with Leara, but I feel you need to know it too."

Beth guessed from the glance between the two women that this sharing had been Leara's proposal.

"You both no doubt know by now that I intend taking us into the mist. Beth spent time with me back in the library at Stara Academy so she knows much of this already, but you, Remy, probably know nothing." Valentina rose from her seat and began to pace the small room.

"The mists are not mystical, nor are they full of monsters," she began.

Beth thought for a moment that Valentina might be nervous about something, pacing up and down like that, but she realised it was because she wasn't used to explaining herself to others.

"They are a path to other lands," said Valentina. "Others have researched them too and all the information I have gathered confirmed it. The library had some good sources of information, as did the collection from Pentwing … but they are missing an awful lot of details."

Valentina stopped pacing and directly addressed them as they sat at the table. "I've been researching this for many years now and I have obtained much that neither they nor seemingly anyone else knows." She took a deep breath. "Yes, it's dangerous, but I am telling you this so that no silly superstitions scare you and panic you, because I will need you to be focused in there, on the other side. I've spent a long time getting here, to this specific place and this specific mist, and I need you both to be strong."

"You mean I'm going too?" asked Remy.

"Yes, the four of us. And Loate and Nyser. With half a dozen of my guard."

"When?" he said, a slight squeakiness in his voice.

Beth turned pale and looked close to fainting.

"Alright, Beth?" asked Leara.

"Y-yes," she stammered. "It's just the pain in my leg." She started to chew a small lump of sio leaves.

"What're we looking for, Mistress?" asked Remy.

"For now that's not your concern, but what I can tell you is that there are people on the other side of the mist that we need to meet, and befriend. There are also dangerous beasts, but nothing more than we have on our side. They are not monsters." Her tone changed to a more serious note. "You cannot talk about this with anyone. Either of you. Do you understand?"

Beth and Remy nodded.

"The day after tomorrow we should be going."

"Why wait?" asked Remy.

"The mist needs to arrive here – and it has to be the right mist, too."

"There's more than one?"

"Yes, there's more than one, but I'm not going to go through that now. My soldiers have been monitoring the mist nearby and the right one should be here the day after tomorrow."

"The day after—," Beth did not finish her sentence. Instead, she fell from her chair with a thud.

TEN

They stood on foot, surrounded by mounted soldiers. The mist had started to appear mid-morning and very quickly they had moved out and travelled the quarter-mile distance to a small clearing where the mist was known to be at its densest. The six of them wore leather backpacks and utility belts along with their weapons. The accompanying guards bore heavier packs and two each pulled a small travois loaded with additional supplies and equipment. All twelve of them wore light clothing barely suitable for such a cold morning, but Valentina had told them all that they would thank her once they crossed through the mist.

No beasts or large predators came with the grey swirling mist – a good sign that this was the one they were waiting for. It thickened quickly and lingered for over fifteen minutes. As it started to dissipate, the Mistress ordered them forward.

Beth glanced around at her companions. She seemed to be the only one who thought this was stupid and dangerous.

Even Remy looked entirely comfortable. Once again the sweat that came with fear and apprehension lathered her. Why was she doing this, not even trying to run away?

Then they reached the other side, and found themselves in another clearing – but one so very different. They had left behind a relatively quiet woodland with birds softly calling and very little else to be heard; here there was a cacophony of noise – bird song, insects buzzing, and the bellows, cries and hollers from myriads of mostly unseen creatures. The air was very hot and damp and if she hadn't already been drenched from fear the heat and humidity would have done the trick.

Not too far in every direction was dense foliage, the likes of which she had never seen. Beyond the clearing were enormous trees, more than two hundred feet high, and those nearer by had trunks greater than sixteen feet in circumference. They bore broad leaves and in their dizzy heights there were animals leaping through the canopy's maze of branches. Below the trees was another dark layer of plants reaching twelve to twenty feet upwards, blocking out any daylight to the ground below. Here there was a large concentration of insects, and almost no plants grew on the carpet of decaying fauna. Beth had no doubt that they were no longer in Parablion.

"Remember, the smaller creatures here are the deadliest" said Valentina. "They slither, crawl and hop on every surface and they have toxins in their bites and on their skin. So do not touch anything. And if anyone shows themselves to us, we do nothing aggressive. I need these people to see us as friends."

As if on cue, a solitary figure appeared at the treeline,

and was quickly pointed out by several in the group.

"Stop pointing and stay calm," instructed the Mistress.

The man was small, dressed only in a loincloth, and his skin was black. He carried a small bow and a soft quiver hung from his hip. He stood in plain sight, expressionless, simply studying the new arrivals. Minutes passed, and no one moved. Then the small man disappeared into the darkness of the forest.

"Now we wait," said Valentina. "But be ready to move off at any moment. Don't get too comfortable."

Comfortable, thought Beth. She was so scared she was physically shaking.

Remy took her hand. "Relax, Beth. You've been through worse than this and you're still here. The Mistress knows what she's doing."

Beth nodded, more to reassure herself than anything. She also kept hold of the boy's hand, again for her own comfort. She glanced at him, so confident and fearless for one so young. Then she recalled what he had endured in the prison cell and her admiration grew further. She wished she had even a little of his strength.

A tense hour passed, during which they glimpsed many wild animals of all sizes moving through the darkness below the trees. Everyone remained alert to potential dangers. A lumbering creature, maybe three feet tall with a long pointed snout, crossed the clearing. Its whole body seemed to be encased in armour. It ignored them and continued on its way. Several long-armed, long-tailed furry animals with hands where they should have feet huddled together and studied them for a while. Having satisfied their curiosity they also soon moved on.

The small dark-skinned man returned and with him were others of his kind. Beth counted ten but she was sure there were others lurking in the darkness. They did not speak together or move from the treeline for some time. Eventually one of them stepped forward and confidently approached Valentina. The Mistress towered over him; he had a small frame and stood a little under five foot.

"Greetings," he said slowly. The language was obviously not his own.

"Greetings," replied the Mistress, remaining still, obviously wanting to avoid any movement that might be misinterpreted.

"From Par-ab-lion?" He pointed back to where the mist had been.

"Yes, Parablion."

"We have not seen you kind for long time." He swept his arm in an arc, indicating those before him.

"You are the leader here?" asked Valentina.

"Yes, I am Speaker." The man showed no fear, Beth noticed.

"We come to trade and talk." Valentina ushered forward the two travoises and the guards laid them flat before the Speaker. "These are for you and your people."

"And in return?" he asked.

"We simply want to spend time with you and your people."

"How much time?"

She shrugged her shoulders slowly and evenly. "As long as you will have us."

The Speaker gave a simple signal and his companions, both men and women, moved forwards towards the travois.

Carefully they went through the supplies and distributed them among themselves, placing them into empty sacks they carried. Beth watched intently as they quickly, silently and efficiently divided up the trade goods – iron pans, simple tools, small bales of mixed fabrics, mirrors, beads and other trinkets. Those laden with goods walked back into the forest, only to be replaced by others of their race on the treeline.

"Name?" asked the Speaker.

"Valentina."

"Val-ent-ina. My name Copo. You follow me now."

The men and women that were to escort them quickly disappeared into the forest ahead. Occasional glimpses revealed that they were never truly far away, just difficult to see most of the time. Copo walked at the lead, without a backward glance or uttering a word, seemingly indifferent as to whether his guests kept up or not. However, he set a comfortable pace, for which Beth was thankful, as she found it unsettling walking on the soft bed of rotting leaves and mosses.

Even more disturbing were the creatures she now saw. Long worm-like creatures, brightly coloured, slithered along branches and – she guessed – the ground below. She knew they were not giant worms because they had eyes and mouths, and tongues that constantly licked the air. She would later learn these were called snakes, collectively, or at least that was the closest Parablion word for them - their individual names could not easily be translated. They were a creature not known in Parablion. Insects buzzed around their heads persistently, but not Copo's, and despite slapping and brushing themselves constantly they were repeatedly bitten. Beth yelped when she saw a spider, not because she feared them, but because she had never seen one so large. It spanned over twelve inches in diameter and rose up defensively on its front legs as they passed by. She had chased away and squashed many big spiders at home, back in Malad, but none bigger than an inch. She was sure this one would fight back. The constant noise of animals all around them soon became ordinary, but when the raucous suddenly ceased she was scared. What was so terrifying that everything in the forest went silent? Then, as quickly as it had stopped, the noise returned.

The village had no fences or barriers to keep predators out. The huts made of leaves, dirt and branches were stitched into the forest, connecting the ground to branches and brush. A labyrinth of well-trodden paths linked the huts together. It was impossible to see how many lodgings there were. As they progressed into the community, dozens upon dozens of the small dark-skinned people watched them silently – even the children remained quiet – giving their procession a scary and daunting air.

When they stopped, Beth could not see what lay ahead of them, but gradually the people spread out unevenly into a collective gathering before one man.

"This Chief," introduced Copo.

Beth could not estimate the age of the man before them. He neither looked young nor old. He was draped in colourful cloth with obvious Parablion origins, and his neck, wrists and forehead were adorned with beads and other small trinkets.

Copo spoke in a strange tongue to the Chief. The only recognisable word was 'Valentina'. Beth had never heard another language being spoken. In truth, she had not even considered they existed before the new lands of Nadreaca to the East and Abeerian to the West had been discovered. For a moment she forgot all her fears and discomfort and felt awe. Here she was in a strange unknown world, listening to an alien language, surrounded by probably thousands of possibly deadly creatures, and she did not feel out of place. Perhaps she did have some of Remy's strength; she had gotten this far, after all. The wound made its presence known again when it itched. And not without trial and injury, she reminded herself.

The Chief said something unintelligible, loud enough that it was obviously some kind of announcement.

"Chief Mimambae welcome you, Val-ent-ina," translated Copo. "He thanks the land of Par-ab-lion for sending you here. It has been many, many seasons since we see you people. We will make you home and you stay with us."

Offering no physical greeting, Chief Mimambae turned and walked a short distance before entering a partially obscured hut.

"We see Chief again soon. Now we make you home."

For the next two days, the villagers literally made their guests their own homes, huts like their own. Valentina encouraged the Parablion people to work alongside the Delines, and this was enthusiastically welcomed by the locals. Men, women and children all got involved in the creation of the new structures. Beth was paired with Remy to work on their own lodging. Nyser and Loate were also paired together, as were Valentina and Leara. The guards were grouped and homed together in threes. Everyone's huts were in separate areas of the village, apart from each other.

Only a very small number of the locals spoke any Parablion at all and one of them always stayed with each grouping to help explain what was going on at any time. Copo visited constantly, but over the first two days neither Beth nor Remy saw much of their companions. Food and water were always provided. The food was very different from anything they had tasted before but it was obviously still meat, vegetables and fruit. A woman started to slather Remy and Beth with a slimy lard substance that was rather pungent at first. Remy fought against it until their translator, Tiid, told them it was to keep the insects away and reduce the swelling of the numerous itchy bites they had already endured. It didn't take long for Beth to completely forgot about the snakes, spiders and other dangers around them; the people were so friendly and Tiid was so free with information that she started to feel at home with them.

"You seem happy," said Remy.

They were lying in their finished home. Their beds consisted of a woven lattice of leaves and branches twisted into a mattress that was surprisingly comfortable. On one side of the lodge they had several pots that held water and fruits, and on the other were baskets containing their belongings. Other than that the space was sparse. Before leaving for the night, Tiid addressed some safety concerns, about how snakes and spiders might crawl into their hut and how to prevent it. Tiid had been amused by their boots – they always went barefoot – but he had pointed out that they should empty them out before putting them on as they were prone to attracting unwanted visitors when left unattended.

"I think I am happy," Beth replied. The sentiment was clear from her smile and her voice.

"I'm glad." His tone held genuine concern. "You seem to have found it hard so far." He was staring up into the leafy ceiling in the evening light.

"And you've not?" Beth shifted so that she was looking at Remy.

"Me? No. This is an adventure and exciting, and if I wasn't here I would more than likely be dead now. Hung for a murder I didn't commit." His gaze remained upwards.

"Do you want to talk about it?"

"No, not yet. I like to forget about it most of the time. It still hurts. But I will return and get them all for what they did."

Beth felt sorry for him, but where she might have once sobbed a little she now refrained easily. She had noted the subtle anger in his voice, so she changed the subject.

"What do you think we will do tomorrow now our huts are finished?"

"I'd like to go deeper into the forest. See some of the wild animals. Maybe go hunting." Now he rolled over onto one side, to face her.

"I'd like to learn their language. I think I've picked up a few words already," said Beth.

"Do you know why the Mistress has brought us here?"

"All I know is that it's to do with that spellbinder Orestas Connroy." Beth sat up, crossing her legs to face him. He mirrored her position. "She's been studying him for years. That's why we're here – he must have been here, too. Whatever he brought here, or left here, I think Valentina wants it."

"Do you know what 'it' is?"

"No, but I think it's a spellbinder thing."

"Maybe a spellbook?" suggested Remy.

"I don't know. I just hope that if we find it, we don't need to hurt anyone to get it."

The next morning Beth and Remy went to find their kinsmen, only to discover that Nyser was ill. His wounds from the corllet's claws had developed an infection due to the hot, damp climate. Loate was at his side constantly while the villagers treated his wounds with ointments and maggots. One of the guards was also in a delirious fever caused by insect bites, and again the locals were treating her with local remedies.

"Have you checked your seedpods?" asked Valentina when she saw Beth and Remy approaching.

Both of them shook their heads.

"You need to keep them dry. Do not expose them to this damp climate too often. This humidity rots them quickly, making them inert and useless." She glared at them as she spoke.

"We will bring some small tins with us next time to store them – they're better than pouches," added Leara, more softly. "But for now, keep them wrapped up and dry."

"Mistress, do you know that Nyser and one of the guards are ill?" asked Beth.

"Yes, Copo advised us as soon as their symptoms appeared." She did not seem to be concerned, Beth observed. "He wanted permission for their healers to treat them and I agreed."

"What do you want us to do today, Mistress?" Remy enquired.

"Leara and I have asked for an audience with the Chief." Valentina indicated back towards the largest hut. "Copo says the Chief will want his council with him and so when that is in place I want us four to attend together."

"Exciting," said Remy. "Do we know when it will be? We'd like to explore today if we can."

"I don't want Beth exposed to the forest dangers, so no exploring." The hard edge returned to Valentina's voice.

"I'll be fine," said Beth. "Remy is safe company, and we have our pistols and will go only with people from the village."

If Beth's challenge was a surprise to Valentina, she gave no indication, but neither Leara nor Remy could hide their astonishment.

"I do not want to risk you," Valentina said.

"Perhaps it would be a good way to increase our good standing with the villagers?" suggested Leara. "I could ask Copo to make sure they were safe at all times. They might also learn something valuable or useful when they're outside the village?"

Valentina paused for a moment, considering the suggestion. "Alright. I will leave it with you to sort out, but when the council meets, we all need to attend."

***

"Did you hear what I heard?" Remy said as they walked away towards the denser foliage accompanied by a small group of guards.

"Hear what?" Beth asked.

"One of the guards saying that the Mistress and Leara

155

are lovers. I'm guessing that's true now, having seen how they are together. And you too, back there – wow, you stood up for yourself!"

"I like it here. It feels like home for some reason. Even though there are no similarities whatsoever to Malad District."

***

"Whatever danger, stay still," one of the guides instructed them. "We will deal with it and keep you safe."

The meeting with the chief and his council was scheduled for the next morning. The council needed to check signs and prepare before sitting with Valentina. Beth had no idea what 'signs' were or what preparations were needed, but she was glad because they had been allowed out into the jungle for the rest of the day. Their escort consisted of six villagers, including Tiid to translate for them.

"Copo say we take you to Stones," explained Tiid. "This spiritual place for us, so do no-thing more than we say to you. Understand?"

The two acknowledged their diminutive guide. He seemed younger than the other five escorts, but he obviously had some authority, as it was he that instructed the others where to go and what to do.

If Beth hadn't known better, she would have thought the three of them were alone in the jungle. She rarely caught any sight or sound of the other escorts as they progressed. Tiid stopped time after time to show Beth and Remy certain plants, leaves, small insects and animals and explain a little about them and he named them in his language. Beth was like a sponge to all of it. It fascinated her. Remy started off feeling the same way but soon wanted to see something bigger – or more dangerous.

"Hold," suggested Tiid as he passed a three-foot-long snake to Remy's open palms.

"Oh! It's warm and dry. Not slimy at all." The brightly colour banded snake wrapped itself around his arms. Its tongue flicked out near his skin.

"More danger," said Tiid. "If she bite you, you dead in very short time."

Remy's expression changed. Fear replaced interest and he stopped moving, became a statue.

"Will it bite?" asked Beth quietly.

"No, if you not harm, not threat to her. You too big to eat, so safe." He smiled at her.

Beth took the snake carefully from Remy and it coiled around her own arms. "She has a lump in her belly."

"Last kill. She swallow whole and eat while inside."

Beth gently returned the snake to the branch where they had found her.

"You should have seen your face!" she teased Remy.

"He could have told me first. I wasn't scared, just surprised." He turned his face to hide his expression.

"Remember the Mistress said the small things here are the deadliest," Beth teased.

"I still want to see a monster! A big predator." His enthusiasm had returned.

"You want see big animal?" said Tiid.

"Yes, can we?" Beth and Remy called together.

Tiid led them to grey swirling bank of mist. The mist no longer held the superstitious fears that it had only a few days earlier for Beth and Remy. They now knew it was simply a curtain hiding another place. However, that didn't make it any less dangerous. They still had no idea what other lands or people or monsters lay on the far side of the mist curtains. The mist often brought large predators to its boundary, after all, looking for prey in Parablion.

Remy watched in amazement as a loxorn, a local predator Tiid told them, galloped through the brush ahead of them. It was so low to the ground that its entire thirty-foot length was rarely even partially visible. It raised itself up on four well-spaced stubby legs and then powered forward. A thick long muscular tail, a third of its length, helped to propel it forward. They couldn't help noticing the massive long mouth with sharp teeth protruding at all angles, easily capable of taking the young child in one bite.

"Will be more. Stay close," advised Tiid. "Water animal dangerous on land. Ambush prey."

The loxorn darted into a patch of mist only to return moments later with a three-horned deer, the likes of which neither Beth nor Remy had seen before.

"Much sand other side of mist," explained their guide. "Water hole too bring loxorn."

As they crept forward Remy put his foot on a fallen log. It moved. Huge jaws opened as the hidden loxorn turned on the boy. Tiid stepped between Remy and the certain death that the savage rows of sharp teeth were about to deliver. At the last moment, the maw snapped closed, empty.

"Stay close. You not protected," said Tiid.

They watched now as more than six loxorn darted through the grey curtain, each returning with more prey.

"This good feed. Not always find prey. This good for them for while."

"How many mists are there?" asked Beth.

"Many. I not know your count, but many."

As the patch of mist started to dissipate so did the loxorn.

"Now we go to Stones." Tiid pointed off into the jungle. "Stay close. Mist unsettles all for while but jungle soon calm."

"What did you mean by we're not protected?" asked Remy.

"You Parablion people have incant." The small man weaved through the growth around, hardly brushing anything aside, with each step to reveal a clear path. "Delines have place in jungle where magic protect us. No incant but magic."

"You mean no predators hunt you?" asked Beth.

"We safe if we treat jungle well."

"Have you been through all the mists?" asked Remy.

"We not leave jungle, but we do see to other side and get visitors through mist."

"More like us?" asked Beth.

"Like — but not like. Many different people but not often. We here now," he waved his arm ahead of them. "Only do what I tell."

Neither Beth nor Remy could see any stones. All that was around them was more of the same jungle. Their hidden escorts appeared and formed a half-circle around them. Tiid led Beth and Remy out of the half-circle to the side where only vines and undergrowth blocked their way. After only a short push through some dense growth they entered a cave. There they waited.

"Eyes see soon."

Gradually Remy and Beth began to see the rock face around them. They could not be certain if the light was coming from the walls or if it was their own vision adjusting; or perhaps a bit of both.

"Walk behind," Tiid said and set off down a narrow pathway. They circled inwards for some distance before entering a large chamber, in the centre of which a great number of huge green pillars rose from the ground. The columns ranged from ten to thirty feet in height and five to twelve feet in circumference. Above them was only darkness.

"Stones," announced Tiid with some reverence.

"What are they?" asked Beth.

"Stones."

"But what do they do?"

"Sacred place. Place magic."

Remy moved forward to get a closer look.

"No. Stay behind. Dangerous for you."

"Dangerous? How?" asked the boy, taking a step back.

"You wait here. Not move. You — come." Tiid indicated that Beth should follow him.

Beth left Remy and walked with Tiid towards the standing stones and then followed their perimeter.

"Stones dangerous. Stay still," called out Tiid, his voice echoing across the chamber.

Beth looked at him with curiosity.

"Remy creep toward Stones. I hear him. He still now," he explained.

They were moving closer and closer to the green columns as they circled the chamber. Beth was nervous but felt none of the anxiety that previous situations had caused her. She trusted her guide and her curiosity outranked her fears. Eventually they came within arm's reach of the outer stones and Tiid stopped.

"You touch Stone."

"I didn't," replied Beth, thinking it was an accusation.

"No — you touch," he repeated, motioning for her to touch the stone.

"But aren't they dangerous?"

Tiid said nothing, but gesticulated again.

Beth reached out but hesitated inches away from the nearest green pillar. Her escort simply waited. Tentatively she edged closer until finally her fingertips brushed the stone surface. It was warm. Feeling no other sensation but that warmth she pushed her hand firmly onto the surface. It was hard, yet receptive. Her other hand reached out and soon she was brushing, almost caressing, the green surface.

"Now we go. Tell no one you touch."

They finished their circle around the cavern and returned to Remy.

"Are you alright? What happened?" he asked.

"We just walked around them. There are so many," Beth replied.

"Why couldn't I go?"

"I don't know."

Remy asked Tiid the same question.

"We go back to village now," was the only reply he received.

That night Beth struggled to keep silent about the fact that she had touched one of the green pillars of rock. Thankfully Remy was too excited by what they had experienced together and was keen to do it all again the next day. However, they needed to attend the meeting with the Chief first, and his council. Remy began to speculate on what might happen at the meeting and as they pondered over the possibilities they both drifted to sleep.

The inside of the meeting hut was larger than any they had seen so far. The Chief and his six councillors sat on one side of a brazier hung over a low burning fire. Sweet scents rose from the pot over the flames and lingered in the air. Valentina and her own three companions sat on a log bench facing the villagers.

Beth was glad to see that Tiid was part of the council. Around the fire sat three other villagers. One tended the fire and sprinkled something into the brazier from time to time. The scents changed each time she added new components. The other two were facing them and it soon became apparent that they were translators, as the Chief addressed them in only his own language, as did any other member of the council when they spoke. On this occasion, none of them wore elaborate costumes, only loincloths; the women's breasts were wrapped in similar material.

Greetings, compliments, thanks and recognitions were all passed between the two groups, followed by silence that lasted for several minutes. Valentina had instructed her own escorts not to speak unless she addressed them herself, so the pensive silence held until the Chief broke it.

"We not seen people from Parablion for many seasons," one of the translators began, his words faltering as if he hadn't spoken the language for some time. "Our beasts not stalk mist to your lands, so this surprise us."

"We have other mists in Parablion that do have predators. It took some time to find your mist," replied Valentina.

There was a short untranslated interaction between the Chief and his council.

"You cross into these other mists?"

"We haven't, but I have reports from those that have. They go to other lands and not your own. The other lands and their predators are extremely dangerous, according to these reports. Some are barren lands where nothing survives. Others are so cold that a man can freeze to death in moments, or they are so hot they ignite."

Another short untranslated interaction between the chief and his council followed. Beth could sense that this annoyed Valentina, but outwardly she showed no sign that it did.

"Why you come to us now?" The Chief looked at Valentina as the translator enquired.

"We seek to know you better." The Mistress met their gaze.

The scent from the brazier turned bitter.

"Why you come to us now?" repeated the Chief, maintaining what was close to a stare.

"I seek knowledge of a man named Orestas Connroy," answered Valentina, unwaveringly.

The air returned to a gentle sweet odour.

"This man we know." The Chief broke eye contact. "He was last of your people to visit us. What do you seek?"

"He brought secrets that I seek to understand."

The air once again turned bitter.

"He brought spellbinder knowledge that I seek," she added quickly, and the air sweetened. "Perhaps in the form of books?"

Remy nudged Beth subtly in a gesture of *told you so.*

There was a further short untranslated conversation between the Chief and his council.

"We know nothing of books he may have brought." The chief was staring intently at her. "Orestas visit us many times. Long enough to learn much of our language and ways. Perhaps these books are not here."

"It may not have been books." Valentina looked at each of the council in turn. "His writings use the words 'knowledge' and 'magic' and it was my assumption that he had transcribed this knowledge to spellbooks or journals."

"Only Stones here have knowledge of magic. Orestas visit Stones, but it is sacred dangerous place."

"Could I – could we – visit these Stones?"

The Chief and his council went into a longer untranslated debate than before. At times, the members studied the faces of those on the other side of the fire. Even without knowing their language, they were obviously in debate, although the discussion seemed to be without malice.

Another question from the Chief. "If you not return, who will come look for you?"

Valentina looked to the woman tending the fire and brazier. The woman continued her task, seemingly oblivious to the intense discussions around her.

"I am a person of power in my lands. I have an army and other powerful people that would seek to find me or discover why I had not returned." Her tone was calm, indicating there was no threat.

"That not wise for your people."

"If what I seek is not here, Chief, then I will not return once I leave." Beth sensed that Valentina was being careful to keep her attitude neutral.

164

"If it is here?"

"Then I would want that knowledge for myself."

"And if you not obtain what is hidden?"

"I can only try. I mean you and your people no harm."

The scent in the air became flat and dry; neither sweet nor bitter.

"Gathering now closed," the translator conveyed the Chief's final words. "We respond to your request soon."

The two translators stood up and indicated that Valentina, Leara, Beth and Remy should leave the hut with them.

"We saw those stones yesterday," said Remy as soon as they were outside.

"Could you find them again?" asked Valentina.

"I don't think so. Tiid took us through the jungle. They could be anywhere out there. It all looks the same."

"They were in a cave and there was no obvious path to them," added Beth. She wanted to be part of the conversation before Valentina quizzed her. She didn't want to reveal that she had touched one of the green stone pillars.

"Right. Then, for now, we will wait to see what the Chief decides."

Two days passed. The villagers remained as friendly as always. Beth and Remy ventured out each day into the jungle with Tiid and an escort of villagers who disappeared from view when they entered the dense vegetation.

Valentina hid her frustrations well, but those close to her knew that her patience was wearing thin. But what could she do if the villagers decided not to help her? The jungle was not a place where her army would do well, she thought. Even if the villagers didn't fight any invasion, the local jungle was an inhospitable enough foe, and the villagers might just disappear.

Copo came alone to Valentina's hut late on the second evening. He brought news that Valentina could visit the Stones but stressed that it was a sacred place and neither she nor any of her people were to enter the area within the Stones – nor were they to touch them.

Very early the next morning the Mistress met Copo, Tiid and another escort, with Beth and Loate at her side. Nyser was well enough to travel now, but Valentina only wanted Beth and Loate to accompany her.

The walk through the jungle was silent. Tiid did not point out any plants or wildlife this time, or try to explain where they were in the jungle. Copo walked as close to the Mistress as the path allowed and when they finally reached the cave the hidden escort of villagers appeared two or three at a time and created a semicircle in front of the entrance.

"You may enter," instructed Copo, indicating that the three should go forward alone.

Beth saw Valentina looking at the wall of vegetation before her, seemingly unsure of what to do next. Beth stepped forward and pushed her way through and into the cave. Valentina and Loate followed.

"Stand still for a moment," she told them. "Let your eyes adjust to the darkness and then we can move on."

She showed them to the cavern, where Valentina and the spellbinder were fascinated by the multitude of green pillars.

"Why are these dangerous?" asked Loate.

"I don't think they are. I think it's just a local superstition," replied Valentina.

"There are so many of them."

"You can walk around them all – they form a circle," said Beth.

The Mistress led the way as the three of them took the journey around the Stones and back to the cavern's entrance.

"Women cannot go past the perimeter," said Valentina once they had completed the circuit. "But the men of the village can."

Beth held her tongue. She was not sure of the truth of the Mistress's statement, but hadn't been privy to all of her conversations regarding the Stones. Certainly Tiid had not let Remy close to them.

"There is probably something in the centre of them," said Valentina. "I think you should take a look, Loate. I would go, but we might not be alone and I don't want to upset the beliefs or customs of the villagers."

The spellbinder hesitated. "Are you sure it's safe?"

"Remy and Beth came here a few days ago and they're fine. It's just local superstition. I need to know what's at the centre, though. If you would." She waved her open palm towards a gap in the stones.

The spellbinder moved forwards. He paused briefly at the threshold then stepped into the confines of the green pillars. He managed three quick paces before stopping suddenly, as though caught in an invisible web. He turned slowly, his face a frozen visage of anguish and pain, a muted scream fixed on his face. A second later he exploded into a cloud of green dust that dissipated quickly. The spellbinder was gone.

Beth clapped her hands to her mouth, holding back a

scream. She did not want to draw the others into the cavern after them. What had they done? She feared now for all their safety. Had they broken some divine rule? Would the villagers now cast them out?

"So that's what he meant," said Valentina. "Your turn now, Beth."

"No."

The Mistress drew her pistol and raised a hand charged with magic. "I can make you, or you can go willingly. Orestas' writings said that only someone without magic can retrieve his secrets. Why do you think I searched for you and indentured you? This is why you are important to me. This is why you are here. Loate was just a test."

Beth's hand moved fractionally towards her own pistol.

Valentina's eye followed the movement. "Now we both know that won't do you any good, don't we?"

Get shot or scorched by magic, or perhaps the Mistress's magic could make her walk into the Stones. Beth considered her options. No matter what, there was little chance of her leaving the cavern alive. At least if the Stones didn't kill her she might have a chance. She had already touched them and survived, so perhaps she might be alright.

She turned and marched directly to the spot where Loate had disintegrated. There she stopped. The pain was excruciating, her head throbbing as if her skull would explode. Her nose ran and her mouth was suddenly parched. Beth wiped her nose, only to find her hand smeared with blood. She turned and tried to leave the green pillars but her steps were heavy, painful and slow. The

Mistress was calling to her and had her pistol aimed directly at her, but Beth could hear nothing over the pounding in her ears. Finally, she broke free of the Stones' perimeter and collapsed to the ground.

"You're alive, then," said Valentina as Beth slowly regained consciousness.

They were still in the cavern, Beth still lay on the ground where she had fallen. Mistress Valentina had not approached her or, more likely, she had not approached the Stones. This was the first time Beth had known the Mistress to be frightened of anything. She had done something that the mighty Valentina could not do. Even if the experience had nearly killed her.

Valentina looked lost in thought. "Perhaps you just need to get stronger before you can reach the centre, but it still doesn't tell me how Orestas got there. The villagers must know more than they are saying, that's for sure. Now get up!" she snapped at Beth. We can return tomorrow."

Beth didn't have the strength to stand so she crawled a few feet forward, then Valentina finally walked up to her and lifted her. They left the cave together, where Tiid was waiting for them. He immediately took hold of Beth to support her, holding her upright with ease while offering her some water with his other hand. His strength astounded her.

"Find knowledge?" asked Copo.

"Only more questions," Valentina replied.

Beth's strength returned quickly once they began the walk back to the village. Tiid walked silently beside her but closer than ever before. Copo and the Mistress followed, their escorts once again hidden within the jungle. No one asked after Loate.

Remy raced up to Beth the moment that he saw her – full of his own questions: What had they seen? What had happened? Did they see monsters? Was there magic? And, finally he asked, "Where is Loate?"

"Gone," replied Beth.

Valentina walked away to speak with her guards and Leara, leaving Beth and Remy alone. They went back to their hut, where she told him everything that had occurred. He was fascinated how the spellbinder had died. Beth emphasised how the Mistress had wanted her to do the same.

"No." said Remy thoughtfully, touching Beth reassuringly on the arm. "She knew you would survive. Isn't that why she brought you?"

"She didn't care, Remy!" Beth stood up with a burst of temper. "She just wanted answers."

"No … the Mistress has looked after us. She cares." Remy took her hand as if it would help her to believe him.

"We mean nothing to her. All she wants is what's inside those Stones."

"She looks after you. Looks after me. I know she can be heartless, but she has a castle and lands to rule. She has to be tough." The boy pulled Beth back down to sit next him.

"She wants me to do it again tomorrow."

"Maybe she's right. Maybe you just have to get used to it."

"The pain was horrible. The worst I've ever known."

"Maybe tomorrow there won't be any pain."

"Remy – she didn't care if I died or not. She was going to shoot me!"

The next morning Leara woke them up to go to the Stones. This time she was going to accompany them, along with two of Valentina's guards, and they were to leave immediately. Copo left the village with them, but he disappeared into the jungle with the other villagers. Tiid was their sole escort.

"They are impressive," said Leara when she first saw the green columns.

"Tiid told us they were dangerous," added Remy. "But he didn't say why."

"Gordhien, you go to the right with Leara and Remy. Yorgone, you come to the left with me and Beth," Valentina instructed the two guards. "Leara, you know what to do."

Gordhien was a female spellbinder who served the Mistress all her life, having grown up in Valentina's homelands. Yorgone was an enlisted soldier serving under the Mistress's banner. They had been told that today they were here to protect everyone from an as yet unknown danger. Both were totally loyal to her and, for this reason, Gordhien never questioned her order to enter the green pillars as her Mistress and Beth observed. Less than two steps into the Stones, Gordhien disintegrated, along with all her possessions, just as Loate had done. Shortly after, back at the cavern entrance, Leara reported that the same fate had befallen Yorgone.

"He had the smallest incant I've ever known," replied Valentina. "So it would appear no magic at all can enter. Remy, your magic has yet to surface, hasn't it?"

"No!" screamed Beth. "You can't send Remy in there!"

"I've had the signs," replied the boy. "But I've not been

tested, so I don't know."

"I'll do it," insisted Beth. "I just need to get stronger."

And without any further direction, she walked straight past the perimeter of the green pillars.

The pain returned – no less than before – but now she had a reason to push on. Remy didn't deserve such a death. She needed to keep him alive. A further step and there was a new pressure in her chest; her heart felt as though it would explode, like her head. She took one more step and began to feel faint and disorientated. Too far, she thought, so she turned back.

She couldn't remember exiting the Stones, but she woke up barely outside the ring to hear Remy calling her name. The others were only a few feet away, but like before they did not approached her. Perhaps they thought she still carried whatever it was that disintegrated magic. She slowly got to her feet.

That night in their hut Beth tried to convince Remy that Mistress Valentina had been about to send him to his death. The young boy at first disagreed, but by the end of their discussion he had was less sure. At that point, he agreed to Beth's plan.

***

Nyser had been placed under armed guard when he had learned of Loate's disappearance. Valentina ordered for him to be confined to prevent him searching for his friend. His weapons had been removed, and he sat shackled to a large log by a metal chain around his wrist.

"Mistress Valentina said we could visit him," insisted Beth for the third time to the sentry at the hut's entrance.

"If you don't believe me, go and ask."

The man, one of the Mistress's own Guard, was on duty by himself. Beth knew he would be reluctant to leave his post and she could see the doubt on his face.

"Right, I'll go get her myself and she can tell you …" she said.

"No. If you leave your weapons outside you can see him."

"We didn't bring any."

The guard quickly gave them a cursory search and then allowed them inside the hut.

"What's happening?" the bedraggled prisoner asked. "Why am I shackled and guarded? Why can't I search for Loate?". His fever had gone and he now looked far healthier.

Beth sat next to him and took his hand in hers. Then, as calmly as she could, she explained what had happened to Loate and the other two soldiers, and what had nearly happened to Remy. She didn't tell him that she had entered the Stones.

Nyser cried a few gentle sobs, then composed himself. "Why are you here?".

"I need you to teach Remy an incant," Beth said.

"But I'm no spellbinder."

"But you're the only person we can trust at the moment," she pleaded.

"Why does he need an incant now?" The seeder looked the boy up and down.

"If he can demonstrate magic, Valentina won't send him into the Stones."

"I've felt the signs real strongly recently," Remy added.

"I think I'm ready."

"I don't have much power myself. My incant can produce a small light for a few seconds, but I could maybe go through the steps that I was tested under." Nyser looked thoughtful. "That might be enough, if you're ready."

"Then let's begin," said Beth.

A few hours later, the guard standing outside was relieved. The three of them knew they had very little time before they were discovered.

"What's all this about?" demanded Leara, rushing into the hut.

"It was my idea," blurted Beth before anyone else answered. "Remy needs magic or the Mistress will kill him."

Leara didn't seem surprised by the accusation, nor did she challenge it. "And why does that bring you here?"

"Show her, Remy."

The young boy snapped his fingers. Nothing happened.

"Focus, Remy," encouraged Nyser.

The boy snapped his fingers once again and the snap was accompanied by a small spark.

"See! His magic has manifested," said Beth. "So the Mistress doesn't need to send him into the Stones."

Leara seemed relieved for a moment, but then became stern again. "Well, you can go back to your own hut now. don't let me find you in here again."

Beth slept restlessly that night. When she awoke Remy was gone, and it was already close to midday. Copo sat beside her, his hand gently covering her hand.

"Bad dreams?" he asked.

"Where's Remy?"

"He fine. He play with other boys in village."

Copo's hand was cool and calming but Beth pulled away – slowly – so as not to offend him.

"You dream of Stones?"

The memory of her dreams was fading quickly, but she could recall them briefly, as though they were a person calling to her.

"I think so?" She looked at Copo questioningly.

"Mistress ask if we enter Stones. I tell her no as we perish if we do," he continued.

"She doesn't believe you, does she?" Beth's head dropped at the thought of more forced deaths.

"She want to see herself," he said.

"What are you going to do?" Beth met his eyes again.

"We show her."

"But someone will die," she gasped.

"Stones sacred to us. Where we go to die. We all enter Stones one day."

"But someone will die!" Beth took both his hands in hers.

"She want to see when we go. I tell you it not a problem. Person who enter Stones is ready. You not interfere."

"When are we going then?" asked Beth, now resigned to the inevitable.

"Soon. They come for you now," said Copo as he left the hut.

Tiid escorted Mistress Valentina, Leara, Beth and Remy as usual, but this time, when Copo and the others disappeared into the jungle, an older villager remained with them. Beth tried to talk to him but he didn't speak their language; all she could ascertain was that his name was Quee. When they entered the cavern, this time accompanied by Copo, he remained calm and relaxed. Beth was torn between preserving his life and the inevitability of his actions. She knew that without this sacrifice Valentina would find another way to test the villagers – one that wasn't so peaceful.

Copo spoke in his native tongue to the old man with a tone and pace that could only be part of some ritual blessing. Then, without any further preamble, the old man walked towards the green stone pillars. He didn't hesitate or look back, simply walked purposefully over their perimeter. Six paces later, he disintegrated into a cloud of green.

Valentina seemed satisfied with the result and turned to Beth. "Your turn again."

Beth knew well enough now that if she disobeyed her, someone else would be forced to enter – until Valentina had exhausted all possibilities.

The pain was just as intense as it had been before. The pressure in her chest took her breath away, and she felt as if she was drowning in the open air. Feeling faint again, she turned back, but this time she had gone too far towards the centre and collapsed inside the Stones. She knew no one could help her and as she blacked out she accepted her end.

"You need to get up."

The voice was familiar to Beth, clear and calm, but she didn't recognise who had spoken.

"You must leave now and return again later."

Beth opened her eyes then. Lying face down on the cold floor of the cavern, the intense pain and pressure still assaulted her. She raised her head enough to look forward and saw Valentina and Leara watching her stoically. Remy was calling out to her but the pounding of her own heart deafened his cries. Copo was standing calmly as he looked on, his gaze relaxed but intense. She knew he was willing her on; could feel the power of his encouragement to move forward. To leave the Stones.

One hand pressed into the ground beneath her, then the other, and she slowly began to crawl. Every pull and push motion took immense effort, as though she carried ten bodies on her back. Finally, she cleared the perimeter and there she collapsed again. Still no one came to her aid. She was too close to the pillars. When her breathing returned to normal she stood up carefully. She was soaked in perspiration and the dirt from the cavern floor clung heavily to her skin and clothes. But she was alive, although she wasn't sure whether that was a blessing. Valentina wouldn't stop sending her beyond the green pillars until she either died or succeeded in reaching the centre.

ELEVEN

They stood on the other side of the mist, back in Parablion. A group of soldiers in the camp were looking at them curiously, but in the main ignored them.

"I don't think they know who we are," said Beth.

"Some might," replied Nyser. "So we'll keep our heads low and avoid any challenges."

That morning, very early, Tiid had distracted the guard who stood outside the captive seeder's hut while Beth used the key he handed her to release Nyser's shackles. No sooner had she expressed her desire to make her escape than the trustworthy villager explained how she might do so, with so smooth a plan that he must already have thought it through. Beth doubted that Copo knew nothing about Tiid's actions.

Her decision to leave Remy had been very difficult, but she knew his loyalties were still strongly with Valentina and she couldn't risk him exposing her intentions to escape.

"There are so many more soldiers here now," she remarked as they strolled through the encampment.

"She must be planning to invade the jungle," said Nyser.

"Then we should go back and warn them."

"I suspect the villagers know already. Right now, we must get away from here before they realise we've gone."

An hour later they were riding newly acquired gausents on the road away from the camp. They had no doubt they would be pursued so they pushed their mounts harder than they should have, with no time to consider the risks lurking and prowling amid the woodland and brush alongside the road.

Their main hope was that anyone chasing them would assume they'd head for Anding Town, rather than Fallon. They had several days' of riding ahead of them, and the seeder told Beth they wouldn't be getting out of the saddle to make camp at any time until they reached the city. She would have to learn to sleep in her saddle. Their only stops would be to relieve themselves and water the gausents. He assured her that their hardy mounts could easily manage such a journey.

Beth was so glad to reach the city without incident. They were both exhausted, and every part of her body ached in a way she'd never before experienced. They had traded for food and provisions with some of the trade caravans they encountered along the way and so avoided having to forage or hunt. Before they had left the mist, Tiid had secured Nyser's weapons and pack, and handed over a small pouch of coins. Without his assistance, they could not have succeeded.

She wondered many times as they fled what would become of Tiid and the village. She had little doubt that

Valentina intended to invade the jungle now – why else would she amass so many soldiers?

When they neared the stables, they released their gausents to wander freely, knowing someone would see them and capture them. Then the seeder led them through the streets to a boarding house he knew, and took Beth to a room, where she wearily dropped her bags and took off her boots before collapsing on the bed.

She had no idea how long she had slept for, but when she finally woke she was alone. The bed across the room from her was crumpled. Nyser had obviously returned and slept there at some point. When she tried to raise herself so she could sit her body revolted. Every muscle screamed and seized up tightly to prevent her from moving. She persisted though, with considerable effort, and finally got her boots back on and stood up. She desperately wanted to return to bed but knew that would be a mistake, so she focused on pacing the floor of the small room, stretching her sore muscles. By the time the seeder returned, she had recovered reasonably well.

"I've secured us passage on the next airboat to Arities, Beth. It leaves soon so we need to move now. No doubt Valentina will have people watching out for us, but we have to risk it. They probably won't try to snatch us openly if there are others nearby watching." He was busy picking up a few loose items and tucking them into their bags.

"I don't think that would put the Mistress off," Beth countered.

"Well. I'm hoping she's still in the jungle and her agents will not be as rash as the Mistress herself." Nyser was ready to leave.

"Do we have a choice?" asked Beth, as she pulled her coat on, aware of the cold air on this side of the mist.

"No. We don't. But if we can get to Arities, I have friends there that can hide us."

"How did you pay for the airboat?"

"Ha. Mistress Valentina may be powerful and have lots of influence, but so does my employer – Master Brigges."

"Oh yes. Brigges. We knew about him before we left Fallon," she told him.

"I guessed that might be the case when I was suddenly shackled. But it's good to know the truth of it. It might help us. Masters and Mistresses rarely engage in open conflict, so her knowing about Brigges might gain us some protection."

They shared a small cabin on the airboat. Nyser slept on the floor, giving Beth the single cot. Once they were airborne, they both relaxed a little. Beth watched the city fall away behind them in the crisp clear morning air. She was going home, but she was still not a free person. She wondered whether she had forfeited her indenture, and whether the local authorities would be looking for her, perhaps waiting for her when they landed. Had she served her purpose to Mistress Valentina? What would happen to the villagers and Remy back in Deline? She also wondered who this Master Brigges was, and why Nyser was taking her to him.

Later that day, up on the deck, a well-dressed man, very slim and with a narrow pinched face, approached Beth.

"Mistress Valentina would like you to return. She has sent word ahead and people can meet you and take you back."

She was taken aback, but remained outwardly calm. "And if I don't go back?" Beth replied.

He paused for a moment. "We have the Mistress's permission to enforce her will – as long as you are not left dead." He touched the sword and pistol at his hips.

"There's nothing you can do while we are in the air, so I have some time to think. Don't I?"

"I suppose so," he replied, but looked nervously around to see if someone was watching them.

"How did you recognise me, sir? We've never met."

"There is a description of you – and the seeder." He glanced across the deck at Nyser, who was gazing at the view over the boat's side. "Seeing the two of you together gave me a hunch it was you."

"So you weren't sure until I replied to you just then?"

"I was fairly certain, but as you say I may have been wrong."

A familiar cry came from the lookout. "Vered, North East. Vered, North East."

And a familiar response from the captain on the forecastle. "Weapons port. Sharpshooters to posts." He ordered.

"Not again," muttered Beth, but she drew her pistol and crossed over to the balustrade. Now, with the sight attached to her pistol, she was confident that if she had to shoot she could do so without risking the entire airboat and everyone aboard.

"That's new," said Nyser as he joined Beth to prepare for the onslaught.

She looked in the direction he nodded to, and saw many seeders, positioned strategically, with sights fitted to their pistols similar to her own.

"Business must be good for Jorn Ghear," she quipped.

"Who?"

"He makes these," she replied, tapping the sight on her pistol.

"Vered veering away. Vered veering away," shouted the lookout.

Beth had to tell him what she'd just found out. "That guy knows who we are," Beth said, pointing at the slim stranger.

Nyser followed the line of her finger and picked him out from the crowd.

"He says there are people waiting for us who will take me at all cost – provided they don't kill me."

"Well, Beth. We knew they would catch up with us eventually. Gausents can't outrun messenger birds."

"Vered out of sight. Vered out of sight," the lookout announced. "Stand down everyone. Crew, back to your posts," the captain replied.

Crisis averted, the passengers began to relax again, but the two escapees had some serious issues to discuss.

"I have people waiting too," Nyser said. "This isn't over yet. We need to talk …"

***

The airboat station at the centre of Arities city was a prominent building, the docking tower a significant feature of the skyline. Anyone waiting for new arrivals would be in the large hall at ground level. Beth felt nervous as they descended, but was unwavering in her determination not to return to Valentina. She had to rely on Nyser for now, but if anything went wrong below, she would flee alone and solve any issues as they arose.

The passenger stairwell to the hall was wide, giving the passengers enough room to meander down casually. The hall was split by a barrier to allow the new arrivals unrestricted egress until they finally joined the people who were waiting to receive them. As they descended the final flight of steps, Beth could see no more than twenty people waiting in the open-floor space immediately in front of the exit to the streets and city beyond. Already there, talking to a group of other individuals, was the pinched-face man she had met earlier.

"I can see Evritt. He has two others with him. Remember what we discussed," said Nyser.

Beth nodded, realising that she felt almost calm. Her adventures to date had hardened both her character and resolve. This self-recognition further bolstered her determination to escape Mistress Valentina and whatever the pinched-faced man below was preparing.

"Evritt will keep his distance, but be assured he will cover our escape."

Nyser and Beth waited until all the other passengers had exited the hall, until they were the only ones left on their side of the barrier. On the other side were seven men and women now accompanying the pinched-faced man, obviously working for Valentina.

"Are you coming through?" urged the barrier attendant.

"Are you ready?" said Nyser, looking to Beth.

Beth nodded and they crossed to the other side. Almost immediately the waiting party started to close in on them.

"Stay back," ordered Nyser as he grabbed Beth and

held his pistol to her head.

"If you don't know already, I work for Master Brigges and my orders are to deliver the girl dead or alive. So be assured I will shoot, as will the men waiting outside."

The approaching group with the pinched-faced man hesitated, looking to a burly man who stood among them for guidance.

"There are more of us than you, and I don't think you will shoot," said the big man.

Nyser kept on his way towards the exit, then he turned to face the barrier, with his back to the streets and the hesitant party.

Beth saw the eyes of the burly man and the others dart to the doorway. Something had caught their attention. The burly man went for his pistol, but at that split second Nyser shot him. The others grappled for their weapons and Beth was aware of more pistol fire from behind her as they turn towards the exist of the hall.

Nyser grabbed her hand and ran, pulling her behind him. As they sped through the doorway into the street, they passed three men and a woman who were rapidly firing back into the hall. A slug tugged at Beth's shoulder as shots were returned.

"The barrow!" shouted Nyser. They rushed over to a waiting carriage and no sooner did they climb in than the two men pulling it set off at speed. The pistol fire quickly faded behind them, but the alarm bell of the docking tower was now ringing out loudly.

They were taken down several side streets, changing course at almost every turn, until the barrow came to a halt outside a fine-looking tavern.

"Inside," said one of the runners, indicating a green-painted door.

They ran through and slammed the door shut. A short curvaceous woman sat in a luxuriously furnished waiting area, and several other scantily and provocatively dressed men and women were dotted around the room. They were inside a brothel.

"Evritt said to expect you," said the woman. "Come this way."

They were led through to the back of the building, passing through its very elegant interior in which a number of guests were enjoying the fine food, drink and company on offer. At the far end of the building they entered another smaller, opulently furnished room, where they were then alone with the woman in what was obviously a quiet office space with an ornate desk and chair dominating one wall and a large sofa in another. An array of bottles and glasses adorned a tall dresser unit, which functioned as a bar.

"My name is Lissa Tormain," she said in a soft voice. "Master Brigges is a rare patron of this establishment here but very generous when he is here. I have been instructed by Piero to aid you as requested by Evritt."

Her eyes widened when she looked at Beth closely for the first time. "Oh, you're bleeding," she said.

Beth looked down to her right shoulder. Blood had soaked the upper part of her arm and she remembered the sting of the slug. Adrenaline had masked the pain until now, but seeing the patch of red she suddenly became aware of a burning sensation.

When she looked up again, Lissa was holding a small

sharp dagger which she used to rip away the fabric over the wound.

"It's only a flesh wound," she stated, prodding at the injury. "There's no slug in there. But we will need to clean and dress it before you move on. There are some fresh clothes and further instructions for you in the bag over there." She gestured to Nyser to pick it up. Then she went to the bar and produced a bowl and pitcher of water and some bandages. "Sit down and I will clean the wound".

The seeder read a note that had been tucked inside a pocket of the bag before disrobing and donning a fine shirt, jacket and breeches, along with a wide-brimmed hat that effectively shadowed his face. He discarded his other clothes and transferred his weapons into his new attire.

There was a knock at the door.

"Enter," said Lissa as she wrapped a dressing around Beth's shoulder.

Two men bumped their way in carrying a large wooden travel chest.

"Barrow's outside and waiting," said one of them.

"I'm done here," said Lissa, finishing off. "Now you need to get inside this chest."

The men opened the hinged lid wide and stood back, clearly waiting for Beth to climb inside. She looked questioningly at Nyser.

"They are looking for a young woman, Beth. Not a dandy like me with a heavy set of luggage," he said by way of explanation.

Nervously, but seeing no other option, Beth climbed in. She had to pull her knees up to her chest and slink her back against the base, but she wasn't in too much discomfort. Then the lid closed down on her and the darkness and confinement raised a panic inside her. Wanting to call out, she opened her mouth but then stopped herself. She felt the chest being lifted up and braced herself against the sides.

For several hours she endured the journey. The barrow journey had been the easiest part. Then someone hauled her off and she found herself suspended vertically, her head facing downward and her knees driving into the narrow space either side of her head, before being roughly shoved onto another surface, thankfully on her back again. She heard the muffled voices of strangers around her but it was impossible to make out what they were saying. She drifted off to sleep for a short while, despite getting several spasms of cramp, and only awoke when she heard a series of knocks on the lid.

"You can come out now." Nyser said as he opened the lid. She saw clear sky above his silhouetted face.

She uncurled slowly, gradually extending her sore limbs and rubbing them to relieve the numbness. The returning circulation caused sharp pains, pins and needles, but still she tried to stand up. She fell immediately and the seeder caught her, helped her to climb out of the case on to the roof of the carriage. She looked behind them to see six mounted soldiers accompanying them. To the front, a team of four gausents led the way.

"One of Master Brigges' coaches," explained the seeder. "The escort's his, too. We're heading to his castle. Three days and we will be there."

The remainder of the journey was almost pleasant. The interior of the carriage was comfortable and Beth was the only occupant so she allowed herself to stretch out. Nyser sat outside, on top of the carriage. They stopped several times to rest, and were always given food, drink and heightened protection for her; she felt relatively safe. However, when she was alone inside the carriage she became more and more pensive. Having escaped Mistress Valentina, was she now a prisoner to Master Brigges? She wasn't sure why he was helping her or, for that matter what Valentina was going to do about it all. Her thoughts turned also to what might be happening back in the jungle, with Remy, with the Stones?

TWELVE

On their approach to the castle later that afternoon, Beth had been awestruck by its immense size, and the number buildings and houses surrounding it that formed a township. They were all in good repair and the place looked prosperous. The people they passed along the way looked friendly and healthy – well cared for, she thought.

The suite of rooms assigned to her in Master Brigges' castle was luxurious. She had been provided with a hot bath on arrival, and a change of clothing – the finest boots, britches and an intricately embroidered blouse.

It was now evening and other than a couple of servants she had seen no one. She sat on the bed and reflected on the last couple of days, the platter of meats and cheeses and the pitcher of wine laid out on a side table as yet untouched. She was too nervous to eat until she knew more about why she was there. She had twisted the handle on the door to her chambers but found it locked, giving her even more reason to be anxious. Sometime later, the door opened and a young servant girl walked in.

"Master Brigges will see you now," she said.

Beth rose immediately and followed her through the long twisting carpeted corridors lined with glazed windows, some were clear and others depicted elaborate scenes in stained glass. Between the windows, many artworks hung from the walls. They stopped after a few minutes and the servant knocked on a door.

"Come in," came a voice from within.

It was Nyser. He was alone.

"I thought I was meeting Master Brigges," Beth said.

"You are – shortly." His head dropped for a moment. "I'm here to say goodbye to you and thank you for getting me out of the jungle."

"You're leaving?" Beth was surprised.

"My contract was to secure you, and I've done that. Master Brigges thought it would be best if I said farewell rather than simply disappearing."

"Yes, I understand, but where are you going?"

"I've been asked to go back to Arities for a little while."

"For Master Brigges?"

"Yes." He didn't elaborate further.

Then a side door opened and a tall bald man entered, his stature was chunky, verging on fat, some loose flesh discernible beneath his clothes. He reminded Beth of how she had looked what seemed like a lifetime ago. In the days since being arrested she had shed all her fat and become more toned; her face had thinned down, losing its plump cheeks and jowls. When she had looked in the mirror in her chambers earlier to tie back her red locks of hair, she barely recognised herself. She wondered if her parents or any of the sewer gang would recognise the woman she was now.

"If you would take your leave now, Nyser …" the man said.

The seeder crossed over to Beth and kissed her on the cheek. "You take care, Beth. And if we meet again, I hope we can be friends."

When Nyser left, the man stood by the door, without introducing himself or attempting to make conversation.

"You're not Master Brigges, are you?"

The man made no response.

Then a second side door opened on the other side of the room. This time a mature woman entered, finely dressed but still obviously a servant, pushing a wheelchair, in which a frail man sat with a blanket covering his legs, barely a skeleton with loose skin hanging from his frame.

"Thank you, Saftreena. You may leave us now."

Despite his frailty, his voice was strong, deep and confident, in direct contradiction to his appearance.

As soon as the woman left the introductions began.

"It's good to meet you finally, Beth Reach. I am Master Brigges and my aid over there is Bardowlion. I suppose you're wondering why you are here?"

Beth nodded; she didn't yet know if she was among friends or enemies. Her weapons had been taken from her and even though she was not overly confident with them she would have liked their reassuring presence.

"I am a researcher; some call my kind Searchers. Have you heard the term before?"

Beth shook her head.

"Well, I'm one of the growing number of people starting to question what we regard as 'normal'. And what magic is and why there is magic. Why some trees shed leaves while others do not. And, more in line with my own works, why some people fall ill while others do not. You will have noticed that I am frail and my condition is deteriorating – which brings me to you."

Brigges gestured to Bardowlion, who stepped forward and wheeled his chair behind the desk.

"Please, sit." Brigges pointed at the chair opposite him, across the desk. The aid returned to his position at the main door of the office, behind Beth.

Brigges rested his lower arms on the top of the desk and continued speaking in a gentle voice. "I have been monitoring Mistress Valentina for some time and I am aware that she has spies in my lands. We share a common interest in the mist. I'm not really sure why she studies this phenomenon, but as for myself I am looking for new cultures, new plants, new animals and much more. I have failed to find a cure for my condition anywhere in Parablion, but the lands beyond the mist may have something else to offer. Then suddenly she took a great interest in you."

His eyebrows raised. "Did you know that she sent a letter to every magic-testing station looking for someone who was devoid of magic?" he asked, eyeing her closely.

Beth started to say no, but her throat was dry and her voice failed her. She coughed and tried again. "No."

"I knew it was in relation to the mist, but I had no idea why," he went on. "After all, there is no such thing as a person devoid of magic … or so I believed. Then you came onto the scene and at that point I commissioned my own agents to locate you."

"You mean, to locate me then take me," challenged Beth.

"I suppose that's a fair assumption," he conceded. "But the politics of the situation is complicated. Mistress Valentina holds possibly twice the power, wealth, lands and influence that I do, and so I needed to be careful in my approach."

Obviously not too careful, mused Beth.

"You are here now, though, and that is good for me, but there may still be consequences." He looked Beth up and down and she wondered if he was considering whether she was worth the risks he was taking. "What I still do not fully understand, however, is what Valentina is searching for, and what these Stones are that Nyser told me about."

"And you want me to tell you." Beth considered how valuable the information might be to him, and how safe she would be if she offered what she knew.

"That's correct."

"And if I don't?" Beth replied, folding her arms and trying to keep calm.

"Well … your stay here can be pleasant or not so pleasant, so what do you have to lose?"

"Once I've told you, what will happen to me?" She looked back at the guard at the door.

"Then, Beth, you will be free to go."

It wasn't the answer she'd been expecting. "But I have nowhere to go," she said.

"Then you can stay here and I will find a use for you," he offered.

Beth considered her new options. So far as she was aware, she knew nothing about Valentina that was secret.

The Mistress had been searching for the works of Orestas Connroy and that was why she studied the mist. She believed that the ancient spellbinder had left his works at the centre of the Stones, where only a person with no magic could retrieve them. What was the harm in telling Brigges all this? Her decision made, she explained what she knew, and answered a few of his questions. Then she waited to see what would happen next.

"Thank you, Beth," the Master said when their conversation had run its course. "Bardowlion will now take you back to your rooms and we will talk some more tomorrow."

Back in her chambers, the heavy door was secured with a resounding clunk of its lock. Beth stared at the solid barrier for several minutes, tears starting to well in her eyes. Slowly she walked to her bedroom and sank into the mattress, curling up tightly, letting the tears flow. She was still a prisoner and had nowhere and no one to turn to. She was all alone.

Her dreams were disjointed. The Stones were a prominent feature and mumbling voices interrupted her constantly. At one moment she was running towards the green pillars, and the next away from them. At times she endured again the intense pain they'd inflicted as she walked amongst them. Copo, Tiid, Remy, Valentina, Brigges and Nyser all made appearances, but none of the dreams made sense when taken as a whole.

"You need to return," stated Copo clearly at the end of the last dream.

Beth awoke with a start. She was still clothed from the night before. The morning light came through the high windows. She rose and looked out across a bright morning from her high position in the castle, other walls climbing even higher outside her chambers. Below she could see parts of the castle grounds and other buildings dotted about. From another window she had a view of the main gate, and the town beyond. Further in the distance, she saw cultivated fields, one of which she recognised as a seed crop, and on a hill in the far distance was the lift wheel of a mine.

Breakfast had been laid out for her on the table in the main living area. This time she enjoyed her meal, finally satisfying her hunger. While she ate she reflected on parts of the dreams that remained with her. Why did she have to go back, as Copo had said? There was only more pain waiting for her, possibly death, if she returned to the jungle or the Stones. Yet her dreams had sown the seeds of possibilities and other options. What if there was something significant at the centre of the pillars? Perhaps it would be enough to buy back her freedom. And why was she the only person who had been able to enter? If Valentina found someone else who could go into that space, what would happen to her?

Sometime in the middle of the morning a servant arrived and escorted Beth to another section of the castle. They climbed two storeys higher and finally entered a bright wide room set out with benches and equipment and an array of plants, small caged animals and many stacks of boxes and crates. A dozen or so men and women in white gowns moved between the benches, while others were submerged deeply in thought, studying whatever lay on the bench in front of them.

"Morning, Beth," said Brigges cheerily as Saftreena

wheeled him towards her. "This is one of my laboratories. Here we study what we find from beyond the mists, and now also what we gain from Nadreaca to the East and Abeerian to the West – collectively now referred to as Illyana, after the captain who discovered Abeerian, the first of the new lands over the seas. As you see, we have an awful lot to research."

Brigges pointed to one end of the room and Saftreena turned his chair and pushed him in that direction. Beth watched them move away. Not having been instructed otherwise she decided to follow them. As she passed each bench she saw plants and animals partially dissected and equipment she could not identify being used to further examine the dissected parts. Volumes of notes lay on each bench; some pages completed while others were still being created.

At the end of the room Bardowlion was waiting, flanked by four soldiers. These soldiers were dressed in different uniforms to those that had escorted the coach and those of the guards on duty inside the castle. Their attire was entirely red, even their leather belts and holsters and the scabbards housing their blades and pistols. Each of them held a five-foot-long narrow lance. She couldn't help noticing another distinct and disturbing feature of their armament – the shackles hanging from their belts. Beth felt her anxiety rise when she saw these.

She followed the Master into the next room, another laboratory very similar to the first, and again they walked its full length, followed by all five armed men. Beth saw more men and woman working at the benches, though there were fewer than in the previous room. They, too, wore white gowns, but many of these were partially spattered with red. Beth paused to look more closely at a dissected specimen on one of the benches. It was a person, a young girl in fact. Beth let out a short scream involuntarily. Two of the guards ran at her instantly and grabbed her while a third swiftly shackled her ankles together.

"There's no need to be afraid, Beth," Brigges said as Saftreena turned his chair back to face her. "The restraints are for your own safety. Here we study the people from beyond the mists and those of interest from Illyana, too. How am I to find a cure if I don't explore every possibility?"

Beth was dumbstruck, but when Saftreena and Brigges resumed their progress through the room, she shuffled along after them, all too aware of the two guards who had a firm grip of her arms and shoulders. She suddenly realised how much she had changed – she was not afraid, and she wouldn't dream of giving up; instead she was considering how she might escape.

Brigges began speaking again. "Of course, very few people are aware of my work here – I wouldn't want to frighten anyone off now, would I?"

Beth thought she heard him chuckle softly.

The next room they reached was a much smaller laboratory, housing just one bench and one large chair. The chair was reclined and fitted with thick leather belts. The soldiers eased Beth into the seat and strapped her in very securely. Escape at that moment was impossible, she thought, but her time would come. She still felt no fear, just more determination to escape. Ideas of revenge popped into her head too.

"You are quite unique, you know," said Brigges. The servant who'd been pushing him left the room, and he rolled the wheelchair himself to stop in front of her. "If it is indeed true that you have no magic, then that is a significant find." He looked her up and down again with a malicious glint in his eyes. She realised she was merely some kind of specimen to him, not a person anymore.

"Also, these Stones intrigue me now," he said as he turned his chair and began to move away from her. "The mists are linked to magic, of that I'm sure."

He scratched his chin, while using his other hand to swivel back to face her. "There are doorways to different lands scattered far across Illyana. I suspect magic is linked at play there too."

He paused in thought as he waved at Bardowlion, who seemed to know what he wanted.

"Every mist seems to be well guarded by predators in a manner that does not seem natural. That is, other than the one currently guarded by Valentina. I intend to study you, Beth. Perhaps you will lead me to a cure, or simply allow me to discover new secrets, but a unique specimen such as yourself needs to be studied."

Bardowlion had drawn a low trolley to the side of the chair on which a range of ominous equipment was mounted. While Brigges was talking, he started to cut away the fabric of her sleeves to expose her arms. He took two long needles from the trolley, attached by tubes to glass jars, and deftly stabbed one into a vein in each of her arms." She winced, but didn't make a sound, although her anger was evident in her eyes. She watched as her blood quickly started to drip into the glass receivers.

"Unfortunately, you must know by now that I cannot let you leave my castle," continued Brigges. His tone was calm and civil, as it had remained throughout his discourse.

Other than her first impulsive scream – when she'd seen the grotesque specimen laid out on the bench – Beth swallowed all further cries. She clenched her teeth as she watched her life flow from her. Her mind was racing, intent on nothing more than escape and revenge. She *would* escape – and make Brigges pay. She was no longer the fat ugly girl from the Malad District of Arities; she was Beth Reach, the only person who could enter the Stones on the other side of the mist. There was no one else like her. She had faced vicious predators, explored a hostile jungle, learned how to fire a pistol and how to kill, and had been shot and gored. She would not curl up or cry or die. This time she would fight back.

"That's enough blood for now, Bardowlion."

The aide removed the needles and placed a dressing over the two small wounds.

Beth felt faint but was still conscious, and through the haze she glared at Brigges. He, in turn, surveyed her with indifference.

"I see we are no longer friends, Beth. No mind. As I said, you can stay here as long as you wish and I will find a use for you." He turned away from her. "Bardowlion, bring the vessels over to the bench and let's start work. Guards, take her below – with the other one."

The guards dragged Beth, too weak to stand, from the room and down several flights of stairs, through a heavy door and into a holding cell area. Unlike the cells she had stayed in in Arities, these were well lit by lamps in recesses and extremely clean, with polished stone walls and floors. A comfortable-looking cot ran along one wall and there was a seated bucket for a toilet. The bars of the cages were gleaming as if they'd been recently polished. The guards shackled her to a thick iron ring on the back wall of the cell and dropped her on to the cot.

"At least you'll have someone to talk to," scoffed one of the guards, jerking a thumb into the space behind him. His companion laughed and they left promptly and fastened several locks on the door behind them.

Beth fought against the sleep that wanted to claim her. They had taken a lot of blood, so much that she thought they were going to drain her dry at one point. She rolled off the cot and crawled on all fours, dragging her chains behind her, to the gate of her new cage. Her vision was still blurred but she could see enough to establish there were four cells in total, in pairs, facing each other. A dark figure stood in the cell opposite hers. A man, judging by his imposing outline, big and strong.

"Who are you?" Beth croaked.

There was no response.

"How long have you been here?"

"Jallon," came a reply in a thick voice with an unusual accent.

"Is that your name?"

"Jallon," the word was accompanied this time by others, but in a language Beth could not comprehend.

"Jallon it is, then. I'm Beth." She managed to pull herself up to her feet using the bars of the gate.

The dark figure opposite her was not in shadow as she'd thought, but had dark skin. He wasn't as dark as the people of the jungle, but he was most definitely not from Parablion.

"You don't know what I'm saying, do you?"

The man was still silent. With concentrated effort, Beth managed to focus on him and saw that he was dressed only in soft britches. His naked torso and arms were well-muscled. She gazed at his face. His dark hair was cropped short and he was young, perhaps a little older than she was. Handsome, too, she thought, before finally slipping to the floor unconscious.

She had no idea how long she had slept on the hard stone. There were no windows to see the passage of the sun, only the constant flickering light of the recessed lanterns.

"Beth?" called the man in the cell opposite in his heavy accent.

"Yes. I'm Beth."

The man said something unintelligible.

Beth looked across at him. He was pointing at something in her own cell. A few feet from where she lay was a tray of food and water. The man gestured with his hands that she should eat. She agreed – she needed to get her strength back quickly. The mug that held the water was metal, as was the plate, but there was no cutlery. Yet the food was good and the water clean. She quickly finished off the meal, then looked at the toilet bucket in the corner. That would have to wait, she decided and took a seat on her cot.

The main door to the cells opened and six red guards entered. They ignored Beth completely and, using their lances, forced the man backwards, away from the door of his cell before entering. They took hold of him and shackled both his wrists and his ankles before releasing him from the iron ring on the back wall. They must consider him dangerous, thought Beth. Keeping him tightly restrained and constantly on the point of a lance, they took him away.

When Jallon returned later his head was facing down and his shoulders sagged, but even though he was visibly weakened the guards remained as alert as they had when they collected him. He was completely naked now and Beth could see shallow wounds on his body. She almost looked away but maintained her intense gaze. He was indeed handsome, in every way. A servant had entered his empty cell early and placed clean breaches on his cot, which the guards allowed him to put on before once again shackling his leg to the ring on the wall.

Then they locked his cell and turned and walked away, but instead of leaving they approached the gate of her cell and unlocked it. They shackled her wrists and ankles at lance-point before releasing her from the ring. They were still efficient in their duties, but obviously didn't consider her to be as dangerous as her fellow prisoner. Slowly, Beth climbed the staircase in her shackles, and they led her back to the room where her blood had been extracted. Brigges, Saftreena and Bardowlion were there, waiting for her, which she had anticipated. What she hadn't expected were the six white-robed laboratory staff.

The whitecoats immediately took charge of the situation. They stripped Beth naked and placed her on the chair. Once again they secured her using the belts, but added another broad strap to secure her head. She was totally immobilised. Then they began their task, prodding and poking at every part of her anatomy, taking measurements and recording their findings in a book on the bench. They put stinging drops in her eyes, some foul-smelling fluid up her nose and pricked her with needles in delicate areas. They spared her no dignity; one of them explored inside her vagina and rectum, finally declaring that she was a virgin.

Beth lay helpless and silent throughout it all. Finally, when they finished their work, she was once again shackled and led back to her cell, naked, as Jallon had been. A clean white gown lay on her cot. The guards shackled her back to the wall ring and left.

Jallon stood watching stoically, never taking his gaze off Beth, but after the indignity she had just suffered that was now irrelevant to her. She slipped the gown on and sat down on the bed with her knees bent up tightly to her chest and her face hidden. She didn't cry, but silently raged against what had just happened and swore again that Brigges and his accomplices would pay for what they had done and were doing – not just to her and Jallon but to countless other victims.

Three meals passed before anyone returned to the cell other than the servants who carried their food trays back and forth. During that time, Beth and Jallon attempted to strike up a dialogue. Beth tried a few of the words that she recalled from the jungle villagers, but nothing registered with him. Two Parablion words did seem to register with him though – 'wound' and 'heal'. They had arisen because Beth could no longer see any evidence of the lance wounds on his body, nor the shallow cuts he'd had on his return to the cell. Yet no matter how persistent they were in trying to find a common language, neither could clearly communicate with the other.

They knew they were due a more sinister visit at some point, but Beth couldn't help flinching slightly when Bardowlion came through the door. It seems he had come to gloat. Beth was aware how evil he was as he wallowed in telling her the details of what would happen next to her and Jallon. He delivered the details slowly, pausing frequently for dramatic effect.

She would be taken in the next days to be systematically raped by guards and male whitecoats. Bardowlion might also take his turn. She would be raped until she fell pregnant.

"Purely in the interests of research, you understand" he clarified.

Brigges wanted to know whether her lack of magic would be passed on to any child she bore. The mass rape ensured that no one could form an attachment as a possible father. Bardowlion admitted it was a long-term project – the Master might not live long enough to see whether the child wielded magic or not, but his hope kept him planning ahead. Then, when the child was born, she would undergo more 'penetration' work. Some of that might be for pleasure, sneered Bardowlion, but in the main it would be to examine as much of her as possible, and she would be cut and dissected while alive – until she wasn't alive anymore. It would be a painstaking process and would have to be done over a long period of time. Bardowlion salivated at the prospect.

There was more in store for Jallon, too, and his suffering would be greater than anything he'd been through thus far. Bardowlion justified this by telling Beth that the foreigner was also unique. His magic manifested itself as rapid healing. No matter how often they cut him, he healed quickly and perfectly, with no scarring. So the next cuts would be deeper into his body and would include his critical organs; they were interested to see how well he would recover from wounds to them. If he survived, the Master wanted to breed from him too, to see whether his particular type of magic was passed on.

Bardowlion took great pleasure in sharing this with her, and walked off with a broad smile on his face, calling over his shoulder: "Tell him what's coming, if you can." Then he laughed as he exited the main door.

Beth felt her anger rise to a new level, and only hoped she could be so impassioned when she meted out justice on them.

Around an hour later Saftreena appeared. She seemed frightened and skittish.

"We need to do this very quickly," she said to Beth. "I work for Mistress Valentina. I've been here since I was a child and have had no contact with her for years – until now. All my family are cared for by the Mistress, and to ensure they remain well it has been my task to gain Brigges' trust and get close to him. I've done that, and have many regrets, but now I get to go free. I have to help you escape no matter the cost. Do you understand?"

Beth nodded. "Him, too," she said, pointing at Jallon. She would have to trust the woman for now. What alternative did she have?

"I thought you'd say that. We don't have long. They're coming for both of you tomorrow morning, so we only have a few hours to get ahead of them."

She fumbled to unlock Beth's cell and took some time to find the right key to release her from her chains and the ring. Then she handed her a small bundle wrapped in linen cloth.

"I was able to get your pistol and utility belt, but you had nothing else worth bringing. Can you tell him," she meant Jallon, "that I'm a friend … before I open his cell? He's killed more than ten guards since he's been here."

"Give me the keys. I'll release him." Beth held out her hand and Saftreena passed the keys and another bundle.

"Here, these are for him."

Jallon didn't react at all when Beth opened his cage and released him from the ring. But when he opened the bundle his face lit up. Inside were two sheathed blades in a harness which he quickly fastened to his back. He drew them both, and Beth noticed they had two opposing blades. Eight-inch long, the daggers protruding from the base of the hilt had one razor sharp side and one serrated. Forward of the hilt, the blades were narrow and thick, fanning out into a sword shape that Beth had never seen before. The ends of the blades turned in a wide crescent-moon shape, honed sharp. Jallon rolled his shoulders, feeling the weight and reassurance of his weapons. He smiled for the first time.

"Now what?" Beth asked their unexpected rescuer.

"There are no guards outside the cells or on the stairway, but there are some in the corridors, and the people in the laboratories. Once we get to Brigges' own laboratory we may be seen," she explained. "But there are passages – hidden passages – and I know many of them, probably better than anyone else. The Master has me use them often because he can't – there are too many steps. But he knows them, too, so will send guards into them when he realises I'm involved."

***

They made it without incident to the small room where the empty belted chair and bench stood menacingly. Their next move was to run down the patrolled corridor, a twenty-foot dash where they couldn't afford to be seen. Saftreena put her head against the laboratory door and listened until she heard the guard approach, then she stepped out cautiously. If the guard saw her, he made no comment. As soon as he had passed, she opened the door and ushered the escapees out. They raced quietly along the corridor and Saftreena halted them beside a large wall lantern. She pushed into a stone and a small hidden door opened inwards. She pulled down hard on the lantern's hook and took the lantern with them as she led the way through and down the spiral stone stairs.

She turned to Beth and whispered slowly and clearly. "We still need to be as quiet as possible. Sounds carry to the rooms and corridors outside. We go three levels down then have to cross another corridor. There are four corridors to cross on the route I've planned, so we can switch to different networks of passages. Then we will be at ground level. Beyond that, I don't know what we will do."

"We are out and at least have a chance now," Beth said. "Thank you for that. I doubt Jallon will be taken without a fight, and neither will I." She held her pistol ready and checked that her knife was within easy reach.

They crossed the first two corridors successfully, Saftreena listening carefully before opening the doors. Then the castle's alarm bells sounded.

"They know we're gone," Saftreena said, her eyes widening.

"Stay calm," Beth said, and placed a reassuring hand on her shoulder. "Stick with your plan and we'll deal with anything we encounter."

Getting across the next corridor proved to be more difficult. Guards and soldiers were racing along it in both directions.

"We can't stay here," Saftreena hissed. "We need to keep moving,"

She waited for a lull in the movement outside and finally stepped out.

"There she is!"

Beth recognised Bardowlion's voice. She wasn't going to leave Saftreena, though – not only because she was the only one who knew the way out, but also because she didn't deserve what they would do to her. Beth stepped out into the unknown without a second's hesitation, pistol and knife at the ready. Jallon stepped out behind her.

Less than ten feet to either side of them were a dozen or more guards, ready to pounce, with Bardowlion in front of them, pushing Master Brigges towards them in his chair. Beth raised and sighted her pistol and fired. The slug hit Bardowlion between his eyes and felt a surge of satisfaction as he fell. She didn't pause to gloat over her excellent shot, just fire three more times quickly in succession. Her aim was not as good this time. None of the slugs hit her target – the Master – but two guards who stepped into the line of fire were wounded.

Beth leaped at the nearest one and hacked wildly with her blade. Saftreena immediately advanced on a second guard with her own dagger.

Beth tasted blood and hit the floor hard, her vision

blurring for a moment. A heavy foot pinned her to the ground. She could hear the escalating fighting all around her, and realised that they wanted her alive. With renewed strength, she struck her knife deep into the leg that held her down. The leg pulled away and she jumped to her feet.

The fighting had stopped. Beth surveyed the scene. Jallon had dispatched all the guards with his strange weapons. He was covered from head to toe in blood. The fresh corpses lay there, wounded heavily, with heads, legs and arms severed. Jallon was indeed dangerous.

The Master was alone. He attempted to turn his chair to flee, calling for help as he did so. But the dark warrior closed in on him and delivered a single blow. The sword sank deep into his chest and broke through the back of the chair. There was a brief moment in which Brigges looked down at his wound, eyes wide, then the top part of his body slumped forward and he toppled onto the floor.

"This way," called Saftreena, out of breath and raspy, as she opened the next hidden door.

Beth and Saftreena went through, but Jallon didn't follow. Beth was about to return to the corridor when he walked through, dragging three bodies, one foot of each tucked under his strong arm. Saftreena closed the door and slumped to the cold stone floor.

"What are you doing?" Beth asked.

The warrior started to strip one guard and indicated Beth should do the same with one of the other bodies.

"Disguise! You're smart as well as handsome! Isn't he, Saftreena?"

But Saftreena was not moving. She was bleeding heavily from her stomach. They dressed her wound as best they could with their discarded prison gowns and breaches, and started to dress her in a guard's uniform. As they struggled to pull the clothes over her, she pushed a book into Beth's hands.

"You'll need this," she mumbled.

Beth took the small notebook and hid it beneath her new leather armour. Jallon picked Saftreena up and slung her over his shoulder then they moved on. The next corridor was quiet, so they reached the final flight of steps safely. When they reached the bottom, Jallon gently placed Saftreena down on the floor. Beth held her head on her lap and looked at the blood seeping through the edges of Saftreena's armour. The castle bells began tolling again, but with a different rhythm.

"They're … telling everyone … the Master of the castle is dead," Saftreena struggled to speak through the blood spilling from the sides of her mouth. "Go … through this door … then you re outside. I had no plan … beyond here."

"Which way do we go to the gate?" Beth asked.

But Saftreena didn't reply. Beth moved the lantern closer to her face. She was dead.

Having seen how the other doors had operated she quickly found a stone with some give. She pushed it while heaving on the wall bracket. Then they stepped out into fresh air. It was dark outside, though the sky revealed that dawn was imminent. They were facing an open road that seemed to run around the castle and another tall wall rose up beyond that. They were obviously still inside the castle grounds. Turning left, quite randomly, they started walking with a guard-like gait.

A massive crowd of people appeared ahead of them, in

turmoil. Chaos had descended. These people were sundry folk from the town outside, not soldiers or guards, and there were cries of "What happened?!", "Is it true?", "We want to see the body". The crowd was growing by the second, and increasingly turbulent – almost riotous. Beth took hold of Jallon's hand and they pushed against the flow, and kept following the road and the wall. Before long, the main gate was in sight. And it was open. The guards were unable to stem the flow of people barging through into the grounds. So they were unchallenged when they walked out into a town in a state of confusion and mounting panic. Twenty minutes later, they were racing away from the Master's land on two strong stolen gausents.

THIRTEEN

T wo days later there was still no sign of any pursuit and they began to relax, while remaining vigilant at all times. Beth was increasingly impressed by Jallon. It seemed he was accomplished at everything. He hunted with ease, avoided confrontation with large predators, and regularly found clean fresh water. He also built them a shelter and nurtured a fresh fire every evening. He was so efficient that it made Beth feel a little useless. But suddenly that all changed.

It was on the third night. Jallon was hunting, searching for meat and edible roots for a meal. Beth was tasked with lighting the fire. She struggled with the flint and cursed when she cut her finger.

"If only I had the incant," she muttered. And then the fire lit. The initial flame was small, but it quickly took hold. Beth stared at the growing fire in bewilderment. She knew the right symbols to do the incant from her many failed testing sessions, but she'd almost forgotten them now. Pushed a few small twigs into a pile, she focused on remembering the symbols and the right configuration. The bundle of kindling ignited. She put the flame out before it could take hold. She had magic!

It was astonishing, but now what? Presumably she was no longer of any use to Valentina. She wouldn't be able to enter the Stones now. She wondered how powerful she was – did she have just one incant, like most people, or could she be a spellbinder?

Jallon returned shortly with two skinned rodents and a large tuber, already washed in clean water.

"Magic!" she said with excitement, then repeated the word in Jallon's own language. The notebook that Saftreena had handed her was a phrasebook of his native tongue. The words were written phonetically, so she could read them out, a much-needed boost to their communication, which was improving daily.

The man watched here as she ignited the small kindling bundle again.

"Magic?" questioned Jallon.

Beth flicked through the pages of the book. "First time," she finally announced in his language.

He gave a small nod of acknowledgement, then carried on with the task in hand, dropping a rodent into a metal pot over the fire, along with the chopped-up root. Then he skewered the second kill and placed it over the flames. They had stolen the small supply of equipment and clothing from the town along with the two gausents, which they had released the day before, quite sure that the animals would return to the town. Stealing a mount was a major crime in most places and they didn't want to be caught red-handed. Their plan was to hide out for a little while and avoid all contact with people – Jallon's skin colour and inability to speak the local language would make them stand out. Beth assumed they were now being hunted for the murder of Master Brigges, and she still found it surprising that there was no evidence of pursuit.

"Day, new camp. You ... work," said Jallon.

"I *do* work!" replied Beth indignantly. Then she realised he more than likely did not mean 'work' but something else. She would need to wait, she supposed, for the next day to really understand what he was saying.

***

Valentina had summoned Leara and Remy. The village was barely recognisable. Large areas had been cut back, as it was gradually being transformed into a camp more familiar to the scores of Parablion soldiers that gathered there to serve the Mistress. The villagers had fled, disappearing into the jungle as soon as the large armed force crossed through the mist. Valentina arranged daily patrols to capture any of the locals, but there were never any prisoners, either dead or alive. A contingent of soldiers now guarded the entrance to the Stones, with orders that no one but their Mistress could enter.

The invasion had not gone totally in Valentina's favour. Many soldiers had died from poisonous bites received as they charged through the undergrowth in the jungle. And still the number of casualties grew. When the patrols came back each day, they nearly always suffered losses and injuries as the strange predators caught them off guard. Others became ill from insect bites and yet more had fevers from unknown sources. Valentina, however, showed no signs of pulling out or reducing the number of patrols or the headcount of soldiers in the jungle.

She no longer used the simple woven-branch structure that the villagers had provided for her to live in. A more substantial building was required, made from hefty logs that her army sought out for her.

"Sit down," Valentina instructed when Leara and Remy entered her safer space. They took chairs at the table.

"You are both going back to Arities today," she informed them.

Remy turned to Leara, a look of concern on his face.

"Yes, yes. I know you are both wanted for murder there," she went on, "but that was some time ago and interest in you will have subsided by now. Even so, I've taken additional precautions. Balcoff has dropped the reward for you, Remy, and the commander of enforcers was happy to take payment to remove and destroy the posters of you both, and to forget the charges."

The surprise was evident on both their faces, and Remy's expression brightened.

"Balcoff and I have come to an understanding," the Mistress continued. "He will meet you both in Arities at the Star Gazer brothel."

"No!" cried Remy. "He will kill me!"

"He will not, Remy. After you told me why you were wanted for murder, how it wasn't you who killed his daughter, I reached out to him. I had something else to offer him – a significant offering. He will not kill you now."

Remy shook his head, obviously not convinced, but he stayed silent.

"*Why* are we going to Arities?" asked Leara.

"You must find Beth."

"Don't you have a small army of agents doing that already?"

"Here's what you don't know yet," she explained. "Beth was apparently shot while fleeing the airboat station. There are rumours that she died from that wound. There are other rumours that she was taken, in secret, to Master Brigges' castle. The next surprising turn is that Brigges is dead. Again, it's only rumour, but it is said that he and a dozen guards and his personal aide were slaughtered by a young woman, who may well have been Beth, as she escaped the castle."

"That's impossible!" Leara exclaimed.

"Nevertheless, the rumours may be true," replied Valentina. "Now Beth is on the run, and she is alone, with no one to turn to. She will know she is being hunted for murdering Brigges, and for absconding from her indenture. Or … she is, in fact, dead, either from her wounds or from something that happened out in the wilds. If she's alive, the only two people she is likely to trust are you two. That is why you need to go and find her." She stopped talking to let Leara and Remy take in all the possible scenarios.

"I've heard of Balcoff – and I agree with Remy. He cannot be trusted," Leara finally replied, sitting upright to emphasise her point. It was apparent that they were both concerned about Beth, but there were other factors to be considered too.

"He will behave," stated Valentina firmly. "And another thing. With Brigges' death there is an opening for a new Master at the castle. You see, he had no blood heir. This means that the remaining eleven Masters and

Mistresses in Parablion need to select a new Master or Mistress. I have offered to support Balcoff as the next Master. There is no guarantee of success, but the rules are that the successor must not be allied with another Master or Mistress. They must contribute to and continue our ways and principles and not threaten our way of life, and they must also keep our secrets. This offering to Balcoff is enough to buy his obedience for now."

Valentina glowered at them. She would not tolerate any more opposition. "None of the other Masters or Mistresses travel much outside their lands and I sincerely doubt they will offer a more suitable candidate," concluded Valentina.

"And if he does not become the next Master?" enquired Leara cautiously.

"The vote is already taking place. I will have the result before you reach Arities and convey the outcome to you on your arrival there."

"Any idea where to start looking for Beth?" asked Remy.

"None. But I have little doubt that she will return at some point to Arities because it was her home. But when – assuming she is still alive – no one can predict. I will ensure you have enough funds for whatever you need." She left a long pause.

"And another thing. There are in fact no charges against Beth for the murder of Brigges, nor for fleeing her indenture. She is a free woman. We, the Masters and Mistresses, have collectively agreed to this. Now go and see the quartermaster. He has everything you need. I need to go now. I am taking a few people to visit the Stones."

***

Beth found out what Jallon meant by 'work' early the next morning. Training. Physical exercise with a blade. His daggers were too cumbersome for her so she used a wooden replica of a Parablion-style sword. The warrior wasn't easy on her. When she complained, he pushed her harder. "You work to survive," was the phrase he adopted as the days passed by. Not only did he teach her swordsmanship, but he began to take her hunting with him. If she didn't kill or scavenge, they didn't eat.

During the next week Beth was so tired in the evenings that she slept soundly, trusting Jallon to guard the camp. Then, slowly, she adjusted until they were both able to sit by the fire late into the night and continue teaching each other their languages.

To Beth's amazement, she discovered she could perform other incants. The symbols and patterns she had learned now came into sharp focus, and where she had failed at her many testings with the local Tester, back home she now succeeded with ease. She worried about how this would be received by Valentina, as she had no doubt that the Mistress was still looking for her.

***

Beth stood at the centre of the green pillars. They were significantly taller than she recalled, rising up so high that they disappeared into the darkness. There was no agonising pain now when she was amongst the Stones, only a strangle tingling throughout her body.

"You're not here, Beth. It's only a dream."

She turned in every direction, looking for the source of the voice.

"I am not here either. I am just your own mind talking to you."

"How is that possible?"

"It's the simplest way for you to understand what is happening without sending you mad."

"But I don't understand what's happening."

"Then you need to return to the Stones."

"But I have magic now. I will just become another cloud of dust."

"Is that what you really think will happen?"

Beth woke up. Jallon was sleeping deeply across from her. The fire had almost died, so she tended to it in order that they might eat a light meal before the day's training. The man opened his eyes, and seeing that the noises were just Beth moving about he closed them again. They had both become so accustomed to the sounds of the trees, brush and animals around them that they could sleep with ease, trusting their instinct to wake them if there was any danger. They could never totally relaxed, though, as they often found the tracks of large, probably dangerous, predators when they were in the jungle.

"Now we look mist," said the warrior. "We must find good mist."

Beth had given up questioning his seemingly random statements, knowing that his true intent would be revealed soon enough. So she nodded and finished her breakfast.

The next day Jallon located a mist with surprising ease. They found a safe spot under cover and watched the amorphous grey cloud develop and expand. Beth was surprised when a large number of predators gathered and crossed through the curtain, returning not long after with prey, prey that looked like the creatures back in the jungle.

"Bad mist," stated Jallon and they moved on.

Over the next few days, they continued to travel, searching for fresh pockets of mist. The few they found were deemed to be 'bad' by Jallon. Then, after more than a week of searching, they came across a 'good' one. Beth couldn't agree with Jallon's assessment that this particular mist was 'good' after seeing a succession of bulky but surprisingly quick lizard-type creatures emerge from the other side. They were close to the size of a gausent and their long tongues shot out, over thirteen feet Beth estimated, to target rodents and burrowing animals, sometimes larger ones. Anything their sticky, clamping tongues captured was rapidly drawn back and swallowed hole after a few munches with their wide jaws.

This mist began to recede, as did the lizards, then – without warning – Jallon took Beth's hand and started running directly into the grey cloud. Beth kept up with him, and when he let go of her hand she followed, trusting his actions. He drew his blades so Beth drew her pistol and wooden training sword. The visibility was extremely poor within the mist, so she stayed close behind Jallon, watching his silhouette at all times, hoping she didn't trip up and lose sight of him. Then they burst through the other side.

The air was damp and carried a heavy aroma of wet dirt. There were no trees in sight, just large plants rising twenty feet or so above them, with gigantic broad-leafed leaves unlike anything Beth had ever seen before. The damp ground was soft and covered in thick moss. The tails of three lizards caught Beth's eye as they walked on through the vegetation. Jallon stopped still suddenly, seeming to gather his bearings, then he turned and moved off towards the setting sun, which could occasionally be glimpsed through the leafy canopy.

The terrain didn't change for the next couple of hours, and the softness of the ground slowed their progress. At one point, Jallon halted and took a wide circular route around a stretch of ground that they could easily have crossed. Beth followed his diversion without question and realised why he had done it when she spotted an antlered animal protruding from the ground they'd avoided. It was a bog, but the surface looked no different to the other ground around them. Jallon seemed to have some instinct for it. Even as they passed she saw its shoulders sink down further, until only the head remained visible.

Before darkness fell, Jallon found a suitable spot to rest. To Beth it looked no different to anywhere else they had been, but because he had taken his time to choose it, Beth knew it must be the safest place.

"Night very dangerous," he said as he hacked down two of the enormous leaves. "Inside. Not come out if hear," he pulled a fearful expression and Beth understood. Then he lay on the ground and rolled himself up inside one of the leaves, which was larger than his body. He unravelled himself and stood up, signalling for Beth to do the same. Once she was wrapped up, he lifted her up and checked her over to be sure that she was fully covered by the leaf before tucking over the top and bottom until she was completely cocooned. Not long after, she felt the weight of his body alongside her, she guessed that Jallon was now wrapped in his own foliage.

The nights were far noisier than the days, filled with

strange cries. At one point, Beth was sure some creature was nosing at her green envelope, but it neither stepped on her nor exposed her. She barely slept, snatching the odd bit of rest, with short dreams haunted by the Stones. It was a common theme of her dreamscape now.

She was aware that it was getting light and the warm weight beside her moved away. She hoped Jallon was rising, that it wasn't anything more sinister. Then she was being unwrapped.

"Day we climb," Jallon announced, gesturing to an enormous mound ahead of them. It could have been a mountain for all Beth knew; she couldn't see the top. The climb was almost vertical in places, flat in others, and Beth noticed there were no stones or rocks or other hard surfaces anywhere. The same moss of the lowlands covered its entire surface, which made it easy to grab handholds and footholds, but it was still hard going, and the moisture soaked through to her skin.

They sat on a ledge to rest. Beth was tired, hungry and thirsty. Her soft britches, thin shirt and flimsy jacket were soaking wet, as were Jallon's. They still wore the robust boots they'd taken from the guards in the castle, having found nothing better during their quick forage in the town. As well as a utility belt, she carried a small satchel, while the warrior had a large pack slung over his back to hold their limited equipment.

Beth began to unstrap her satchel to get out some food and water, but Jallon stopped her instantly.

"No," was all he said, his tone final.

"Why?"

"Poison."

Once again she had no idea what he meant. Was he referring to what they carried in their bags? Or something else, nearby? They needed to work harder on their communication, she admitted, even though they'd achieved a lot so far. Jallon was able to grasp her language far more easily than she did his. Maybe they should talk more often in his language, if they were to communicate better.

The rest stop was only brief. They set off again, but Beth was finding the pace very difficult now.

"Quick!" Jallon urged. "Must go before night. No leaves ... no protect."

Beth found a much-needed reserve of energy and ploughed on. If the darkness scared Jallon, then she knew she should be afraid too. They started zigzagging across the great mound as dusk approached. The warrior looked more worried with every passing minute and his apprehension terrified Beth.

"There!" he shouted.

Beth looked in the direction of his pointed finger. Fifty feet away, almost invisible in the descending darkness, was a small pocket of receding mist. They raced towards it as fast as the soft earth permitted. Still Beth was struggling, so Jallon swept her up into his arms. Even though he sank deeper with every step, they made faster progress. The warrior dived through the curtain just as it began to disappear.

They found themselves lying on hot sand that stuck to every part of their soaking clothing and instantly gathered in every orifice. Untangling themselves from each other they stood up and took in their surroundings; a long sandy beach, with the sea behind them stretching to the horizon. The sun was high above them, so it was close to midday. A vista of low hills and rolling grassland overlooked the beach. Beth stared out at the blue water and the rolling waves. She had never seen the sea before and found it beautiful.

Finally, she looked around at her companion. "No predators?"

"Place we left guards of here."

Recalling the real worry she had seen on his face, Beth didn't doubt him.

"Here safe. Town there." He pointed out over the rolling hills.

Then he stripped naked and carrying all of his clothing and equipment he walked into the sea. "Wash all and toilet!" he called over his shoulder. Without embarrassment, she too stripped and followed his lead.

***

When they were refreshed, rested and their clothes were dry again, they walked towards the town. Their journey was pleasant. The grass was low, the ground firm and the hills gently undulating. They crossed a few small streams. Small wildlife on the ground and in the air was in abundance. They came across a grazing herd of thick white-coated animal, only knee-high, with twin curved horns that looked dangerous, but Jallon assured Beth there was nothing to fear.

"Few predators here," he assured her, gesturing to the land around them.

"Where are we going?" she asked, switching to his language.

"Town," was the reply as he too switched tongues.

"No, I mean where are we going after that?" Beth struggled a little with the pronunciation but was certain she had spoken correctly.

"Then we go home. To my land." He smiled broadly at that.

"Your home?" asked Beth, to be sure she had understood correctly.

"Yes. I have been away far too long now. I need to show them that I'm still alive."

"And me?"

"You are with me. You will be welcomed by my people."

"No. I mean ... when do I go home?" Beth felt the foreign words roll smoothly off her tongue. She smiled at herself proudly.

"You can go home from my home," replied Jallon. "But maybe you will stay a while with me and my people?" He faced Beth and looked deep into her eyes. It was a genuine request. She was content that this time she would not be anyone's prisoner.

"Through the mist?" she asked.

"No. The mist to your home is back where we have been. You use the Stones, I think."

"You have Stones? Green pillars of rock?" She couldn't hide her astonishment.

"Yes, we have green rocks." He answered, seemingly unaware of the surprise in her voice.

Beth went silent for a while as they walked on. More stones. What did that mean? No matter which train of thought she followed, it still made no sense.

"The town," announced Jallon pointing ahead.

She looked ahead. In the distance were large, stubby wide stone-built stacks pushing up out of the ground. Hundreds of them, spread out as far as her eyes could see. As they got closer she determined that they were about twenty feet in diameter and twelve feet high and were almost identical. Soon they were walking amongst them. There was a gap of one or two hundred feet between each one and they all had wide stone steps running up their outer wall. Beth noticed writing painted at the base of each one, illegible to her, presumably signposting something.

Jallon led them up a flight of steps, and over the wall of one of the stacks, where another flight descended for almost thirty feet and finished in a broad street where people bustled by on foot, their skin pale, similar to Parablionions, but with narrower eyes, broader faces and well-defined cheekbones. They were dressed in colourful light robes, men, women and children alike. Beth saw no pistols or weapons of any kind. And they paid no heed to the two strangers in their midst.

Reflective surfaces were set at regular intervals along the street, capturing the light of the sun and bouncing it off other similar devices to provide lighting. This street, like all the others she had seen, ran in a straight line, connecting with other stacks in every direction.

"This way," Jallon said. "Do not touch anyone, Beth," he continued in his own language. "Touching briefly is safe but prolonged contact can be fatal. This is a peaceful place. No weapons are used here. All mist walkers are supposed to come here in peace, but that is occasionally challenging, as not all explorers are peaceful. The authorities here will become aggressive with any outsiders that break the rules."

The route they took was lined with market stalls. Brightly painted wooden doors led off the street to a mix of shops, homes and taverns. Jallon knew where he was going and was obviously not a stranger here.

"Where is this place?" she asked, trying to look everywhere and take everything in at once.

"The land is Rishan. This town is Cember."

"Where are we going?" she asked, wanting to slow down but had to run to keep up with his long strides.

"To a money trader."

Beth continued to follow him, looking around in constant amazement. She could never have dreamed such a place existed. It was not so long ago that she regarded mist as dangerous and full of monsters. Now she was in this marvellous new land, with a handsome stranger, and enjoying herself.

Jallon opened a door and they entered a shop. The walls and ceiling were painted white to reflect as much light as possible. Thick wooden beams stabilised the structure, with narrow timbers adding support. A flight of stairs to the right led down to another level. Although they were underground now, Beth wouldn't have known it from the room's interior. Rows of low shelving and a counter ran along the far side, sporting an array of items for sale – clothes, tools, packs and bags, and weapons, and much more.

Jallon greeted the shopkeeper in what Beth guessed was a local dialect that she couldn't grasp. There was a brief exchange, then the shopkeeper went into another room behind the counter. He quickly returned and handed Jallon a small purse of coins.

"Find clothes and anything else you need," Jallon said to Beth. "There are 'softer' supplies below. Once you have what you need, bring it to the counter."

"Did he just give you money?" Beth asked.

"My people leave what we do not need here in the form of currency." He showed her the purse. "This way if we arrive with nothing we can always resupply, but we only take what we need and leave the rest here."

"This is a bank too, then?"

"What is a *bank*?" asked Jallon, substituting the word into his own language as Beth had done.

"It doesn't matter. Can we get a bath here and a good night's sleep?"

"Not here. But yes, on another street."

Beth hadn't meant in the money trader's establishment, but she let the matter go and went to browse the shelves. Thinking practically, not wanting to take anything excessive, she shopped smartly, or so she thought. Two changes of clothing, more durable items than the ones she was wearing; a real sword, similar to the wooden one she carried, along with a belt and scabbard. She placed them on the counter and then returned to the shelves. A small roll of waterproof canvas would be useful, as well as a thick blanket and a fresh pair of black knee-length boots. There was an outside sheath and clip on the right boot, so she searched for a dagger to fit, then went down the stairs to see what else she could find.

Now she realised what Jallon had meant by 'softer' supplies. Here she found jewellery and trinkets for both men and women, not of any great value but attractive nonetheless. There were also soaps, ribbons and combs and various devices she didn't recognise but assumed had a cosmetic purpose. She almost cried with joy when she found soft absorbent towels for her menstrual cycle; there was even a dry bag to hold them. For so long now she had made do with whatever she could find. Then one particular brooch caught her eye, a circular piece, only small, but the green stripes at its centre reminded her of the Stones. She added it to her selection on a whim.

Back at the counter, Jallon waited. Her pile had been reduced. There was only one change of clothing now. The blue outfit was gone but all the black remained. The blanket and waterproof canvas were also missing. She deposited her remaining goods on the counter and waited to see what would survive. The soap was moved to one side. The towels and comb accepted. Jallon studied the brooch. To Beth's surprise, it went in the good pile. Then he handed her a fresh backpack and indicated that she should put her goods into it.

The shopkeeper and Jallon discussed the trade and a deal was reached. The warrior handed back the purse, keeping some coin.

"Bath now?" she asked.

Several streets away, they entered an establishment totally dedicated to bathing. Two levels, each equipped with eight large circular tubs in individual rooms. Jallon parted with some more coin and they were led to a room. The female attendant pulled a chain and hot water poured into the chest-high tub. Before leaving, she added oils to the flowing water and left a fragrant bar of soap on the bath's ledge.

Jallon stripped naked and climbed into the bath as it

was still filling. Beth joined him, a little relieved at first that the oils had created a foamy layer across the surface, then deciding that clear water may also have had its benefits. There was a platform for sitting on inside the tub. The water was hot, initially almost too hot, but once it stopped flowing it became comfortable, so comfortable that Beth soon fell asleep.

Jallon woke her softly and handed her the soap. "Wash now." He then climbed out of the bath and towelled dry. Once he was dressed, in a front-laced green shirt and matching britches, he pulled on his new brown mid-length boots and secured his swords. Picking up his pack, he left behind his old clothing and exited. "I will wait outside. There is no hurry."

Washed and dressed, Beth heard a rumble in her stomach. She hadn't eaten in quite a while and now she realised she was famished.

"Feed me!" was all she could say when she caught up with Jallon in the lobby.

He laughed and led her outside.

Lamplight now enhanced the fading sunlight and the streets took on an eerie but rather relaxing glow. They walked only a short distance before entering a tavern. The room was larger than Beth expected, with thirty or so round tables, each suitable for four, scattered randomly throughout. There was no bar providing drink as there would have been back home, but the serving people moved across the floor taking orders and delivering food and drink as ordered by the patrons. She quickly counted fifteen people either dining or drinking and they all seemed to be locals.

Jallon found a table where they could sit with their backs to the wall and ordered for them both in the local dialect. The drinks came first, large tankards of a pleasant-tasting ale. As the waiter left their table, Beth noticed a fellow Parablionian enter. He surveyed the room, then noticed Beth, and made a direct line to their table.

"You're new," he said.

Beth looked the man up and down and checked to see if her companion was giving any indication of what she was supposed to do next. Jallon sipped at his ale and ignored the situation.

"Where in Parablion are you from, and which Master or Mistress do you serve?" the man asked. He was grubby from several days' travel, but not excessively so. He wore light travel clothing and dried blood across one of his shirt sleeves suggested he'd encountered trouble of some kind recently. He was in his mid-thirties with short brown hair and a heavily stubbled chin. Beth noted his single pistol and small dagger, probably for throwing, and another larger knife. He had no bags or utility belt.

"You first." Beth said. She thought that having Jallon at her side she had little to fear and could afford a slightly balshy response. After all, this was neutral ground – in the main.

"I'm Radent. I work for Master Brigges. Been out here for three months now. Started with six of us but lost two coming across the mosslands. Told them we shouldn't have gone that way. Then lost another in Tember and the final two trying to poke our heads into Fernish, his land." The man pointed rudely at Jallon and then seated himself at their table.

"So how did you get so friendly with a savage like him? Does your Master know?"

"Mistress, actually. Mistress Valentina."

"Oh, one of the high and mighty. Does she know about him?" He pointed at Jallon again. Beth decided that she definitely did not like him.

"Master Brigges is dead, by the way," Beth said. "Slaughtered in his own castle, I believe."

"Never!" Radent was wide eyed.

"True."

"Damn! Who's going to pay me now?"

"You didn't take money upfront?" asked Beth, feeling glad if he hadn't.

"Brigges doesn't … didn't work that way."

"Why were you sent here?"

"He wanted a specimen from Tember. A young girl, if possible. Didn't care what her magic was – 'just alive' was all he said."

"I don't see a girl."

"We failed, so we thought we'd hedge our bets by getting one of his kind." Another pointing finger at Jallon.

A server approached and the man ordered an ale. Beth wanted to send him away but her curiosity overruled her emotions. This was a chance to learn more of what was actually going on behind the mist.

"How long have you been doing this?" Beth casually enquired, hiding her eagerness to find out more.

"You mean mist-walking or kidnapping?" He laughed. "I've been a mist walker for three years now. Not long after the Masters and Mistresses realised there were lands beyond. This is my tenth journey. You?"

"Third time." She answered confidently.

"So where did you get *him* and why is he so well behaved? Those savages only know how to kill." He continued to point at Jallon as he spoke. "We normally stay away from them unless we have numbers on our side. People rarely get into their lands, but occasionally we manage to pull one out for Brigges. He pays well for them."

"Do you see many other mist walkers?" Beth asked, swerving his question.

"From Parablion? We meet a few every now and again. Those from other lands more often. They've been crossing the mists far longer than we have, although I think they only discovered our little pocket of Illyana about the same time the Masters and Mistresses started sending us through. There are one or two mercenary bands occasionally. Ran into a group sent by Rigard Pentwing once – some rich guy out of Fallon. The Masters and Mistresses won't be able to keep this secret much longer, I'd say. So go on, where did you get him, and is he for trade?"

"Ask him yourself," she replied curtly.

"Can't. Don't know the garble-wobble they speak and they're not bright enough to understand us. Know how to use them swords and other weapons, though. Proper killers, they are."

"Oh, he understands every word you're saying."

"Get lost!" Then, suddenly turning pale, he asked, "You're having me on, aren't you?"

"No, she is not." Jallon sat casually, his expression neutral, as he continued to gulp his ale.

"It wasn't me!" he exclaimed. "I've never tried to take any of your kind!" He stood up quickly and left the

234

premises, abandoning his half-drunken ale on the table.

"Well, you certainly made an impression," Beth said to Jallon.

"I wanted to kill him, but you don't deserve the local authorities coming after you."

Their meals arrived. The meat, vegetables and mash were divine, as was the thick crusty bread that came with it. When Jallon told her the names of what she was eating she was none the wiser, but admitted it was delicious. After two more tankards of ale, Beth yawned. She was suddenly so tired. The food had assuaged her hunger, and the ale was stronger than she had expected.

"Don't we need beds for the night?" she asked.

"I have already made arrangements and paid for somewhere to sleep, along with the meal."

Beth studied the room. There were no stairs going up or down to another area.

"Here?"

"No. The rooms are separate doors along the street. Our room is named Tarjin."

"Our room?"

"Are you ready, then?"

Beth nodded. Although Jallon had already paid he left a coin on the table.

Four doors down on the right, Jallon swung open a door. He had no key and it wasn't locked from the outside. Once inside he slid the bolt. There was one large comfortable-looking bed. Beth explored the second door at the rear where she found a large seated toilet bucket. Behind that was another door, and behind that a tunnel running the length behind the rooms.

"Bolt the back door if you don't want the bucket collector to disturb you," said Jallon over her shoulder.

Beth returned to the bedroom, also bolting the bucket-room door behind her.

Jallon stripped naked and climbed into the bed. Beth sat on the edge slowly undressing. She had no idea what to expect next. Were they just sleeping? Did he get only one bed just to save money? Or were they going to have sex, or make love, or ignore each other? She knew which option she preferred.

Beth climbed cautiously in beside him. He carefully reached over her and kissed her on the lips. Beth didn't argue and embraced the situation. The next morning, she would no longer be a virgin.

After the first time she thought it was enough for her, but the second and third were no less pleasing.

***

The following morning Jallon informed Beth that they would be leaving Cember and his homelands were several hours' ride away. They would be there that evening. It came as no surprise to her; she'd known all along that was their destination. But what did surprise her were the mounts they were going to ride.

In the early hours, they were back on the outskirts of the town, on the surface again, at a stable managed by one of Jallon's kinsmen. The man in charge, who was named Koana, greeted Jallon enthusiastically. He was older by a good few years but still very able-looking and the two swords he wore similar to Jallon's. Beth was sure they were in capable hands.

"I knew you weren't dead, Jallon," said Koana. "You're too stubborn for that! And far too young yet."

"I need two mounts." Jallon was very matter of fact.

"Two? You are taking a woman home?"

"Yes," Beth chipped in. "I'm travelling with Jallon."

Koana smiled broadly. "And she speaks our language, too. My, you have been busy."

The stable housed six maleks across twelve stalls, slender-bodied animals with long legs and necks, short tails, small heads and large, pointed ears. The first thing Beth noticed was their friendly gaze.

"Don't let that soft stare fool you," warned Koana. "They spit and bite when they are annoyed."

Jallon told her more about them, with pride. "They are native to our homelands in the north, an area of craggy cliffs, ravines and canyons set amongst hot sand dunes. They are the most surefooted of any animal. They may look small next to one of your gausents, but they are strong and full of stamina and they can carry you across treacherous sheer rock faces with ease."

The saddle was small and set high up on the shoulder, close to the base of the neck. Koana showed Beth how to set the saddle on her woolly white, orange-patched malek and gave her some basic riding instructions. The main difference between riding a malek and a gausent seemed to be that you could let the animal go where it wanted to. Reins had little effect because their long necks afforded them enough self-control to ignore most instructions transferred through reins. They could simply roll their strong neck against the pull of rein. Gentle pulls were all that was required, to point the mount in roughly the right direction and suggest a direction of travel, then it could be trusted to go that way, picking its own path. This was key, especially on sheer rock faces, if you didn't want to fall. The high stirrups pulled the rider's knees close to the nape of the neck, allowing you to control speed and direction a little more effectively than with the reins; but again it was only a suggestive action as the malek would pick its own path and gait on the rock faces. The foot grips were purely for the rider's safety.

"So I simply hold on, point where I want to go and hope she takes me there?" Beth concluded.

"That's right. You've got it!" said Koana, laughing.

Jallon and Beth covered a few miles during the lesson. The animals' gait, even at speed, was gentle and the ride smooth, with barely any rise on the animal's back. Jallon demonstrated how to sit when crossing rocky terrain, instructing Beth to place herself in the malek's front centre of balance. "Just let her do all the work and enjoy the ride."

They made good time over the grasslands of consistently firm ground and hills that always sloped gently. Eventually, Beth could see the sea ahead of them, a bright blue line meeting the intensely blue sky on the horizon. They were returning to the coast.

"The mist here is quite regular and consistent. My homelands have very few mist banks. They really are very sparse compared to anywhere else. This one will take us to my homeland in the north. When we emerge on the other side, we will step out onto potentially sheer rock, so trust your mount. You may want to close your eyes, too, if we are particularly high up. Nearby there will be more of my people patrolling the mist. We do not permit anyone to enter our lands. If we get separated, show no signs of threat and tell them that you are travelling with me."

The sun was setting as they reached the sand where gentle waves lapped at the shore a thin mist was drifting at the water's edge. Jallon led the way as they walked their maleks through the curtain into bright hot sunshine, and onto a perilous rock ledge.

Beth immediately closed her eyes and scrunched up in the saddle as she had been told. She wouldn't have been able to stand on the thin outcrop of rock that barely protruded from the steep face, but the malek had no problem. The drop below them was significant, onto an even more rugged rock face. The malek walked, leaped and slid and each move brought Beth's heart to her mouth; she expected to tumble to her death at any second. Finally they halted and Jallon told her to open her eyes.

They were now on a rough pathway high above the distant ground below. Ahead of them sat two other riders, bows loosely in their grips, arrows nocked.

"Who's that with you, Jallon?" one of them called out.

"A friend. I am taking her to Aving."

The rider who had spoken stared at Beth for a moment. "You know the rules."

"I do, and I believe she is entitled to be here," Jallon replied.

"Then she's your responsibility."

"I'm aware. I will watch her at all times."

"Good to know you're still alive, anyway," the rider said, directing his mount sideways to let them pass.

The route down the mountain was a mix of loose rock, craggy outcrops and precipitous drops. They passed and leaped over ravines of varied sizes and shapes until they entered a high-walled canyon set amongst hot sand banked up against the walls.

"We live in caves here. Lower down across the desert the people have tents, but inside the canyon there are occasional rockfalls so caves are safer."

The caves were not what Beth expected. Both sides of the canyon had buildings, wide stairways and other architectural and design features carved into them, and elaborate artwork and statues. As they started up the first stairway people were already staring at the newcomer.

They handed their mounts over to a keeper at a stable, then began the walk up the various tiers. The cave homes were all bright, with large open shutters allowing in the dry hot air and sunshine. Jallon told her that malek fur was used extensively, for clothing, bedding, curtains and dressings, woven in a variety of forms and colours. She saw many of these items on the market stalls they passed, which were carved directly into the rock and covered with timber canopies. People continued to stop and stare as Beth came there way.

"I'm guessing you don't get many strangers here?"

"Very few. And those they normally see are prisoners who never leave."

"I'm not a prisoner, am I, Jallon?" The thought that she might be a captive or trophy hadn't crossed her mind recently and it frightened her. She had no idea how to return home other than back the way she had come, and she doubted she could make that journey alone.

"No. You are not," Jallon said.

The path levelled out and widened, leading to a single

three-story building carved into the rock, its facia heavily decorated with painted carved images of distinguished-looking people.

"This is Aving's place. He is our leader and I suppose you would call this his castle."

The door was open and unguarded. Inside was a large, bright reception hall carved deep into the canyon wall, its walls decorated by finely detailed paintings and carvings. Several staircases led both up and down.

"So you're not dead!" said a man who was walking down a wide stairway towards them. He wore a thinly woven knee-length gown and a short sword sheath on his leather belt. He walked barefoot, with an athletic gait and casual manner, and no obvious trappings of power or authority.

"Seems everyone thought I was," replied Jallon with a polite nod.

"Well, you have been gone for some time."

"I was held prisoner."

"They caught you?"

"A lucky shot with a poisoned dart from one of their pistols."

"I suppose that's possible. And who is this with you?"

"This is Beth. I am bringing her to you and Orldrey. Beth this is Aving."

The introduction surprised her.

"Orldrey, you say? Do you think she's the Guardian?" asked Aving, smiling warmly at Beth.

"I have no proof as yet, but yes, I do," answered Jallon, standing a little taller as he spoke.

"Does she know who you think she is?" Aving was looking at Beth as he asked.

"No," replied Jallon, as he turned his attention back to Beth.

"What's a Guardian?" asked Beth, but her question went unanswered.

"She speaks our language! How long have you two travelled together?" queried Aving.

"Quite some time now," Jallon's smiled reassuringly to Beth. "I have also been training her, but she needs more preparation for the journey."

"A wise thing … if indeed she is who you think she is."

"What's a Guardian, Jallon?" Beth repeated.

"I will let Orldrey discuss that with you," replied Aving, smiling at her warmly. "We should seek him straight away. There are questions that need to be answered quickly here."

The three of them left the building together, and walked back down the wide pathway before turning upward up the side of the high-walled canyon. Other people started to follow them, keeping their distance, their low murmurs increasing in volume as the thong grew in size. When they breached the top they were on a very large plateau. The view was clear to the south and its distant sandy horizon; to the north and south, cloud-covered mountain peaks. To the east, another long line of tabletop plateaus like the one they now crossed.

They walked on to the centre of the plateau where, as Beth quickly estimated, there were over forty green stones pillars. They were nowhere near the size of those in the jungle of Deline– the tallest was only waist height to Beth. Off to one side of the field of green, at the farthest edge of the plateau, was a long single-storey stone building, outside which sat a grey-haired elderly man at a table covered with books. With him was a young woman.

The crowd that had kept following them stayed at the plateau's rim while Aving, Jallon and Beth approached the old man. Beth noted how they skirted the Stones at a safe distance. Here, too, she suspected that entering them was fatal.

"There's only one reason that you would bring a stranger here," stated the old man, Orldrey. He closed the book he was reading and stood up. He was only wearing a pair of light britches, exposing his muscular chest and arms.

"Please, approach the Stones," he said to Beth.

They were now as far from the green stones as possible. Beth looked across the distance and back to the old man, who repeated with gestures that she should approach the Stones.

Beth hesitated. She now had magic, and anyone with magic, as she knew, perished when they entered the Stones. Everyone waited for her to make her decision and the crowd of onlookers watched in silence. She considered her options as she took her first tentative step, gradually picking up pace until she was within reach of the first pillar.

Slowly, painstakingly slowly, she reached out towards the green surface of a stone that was no taller than her knees. She paused a hair's breadth away, mindful that this could be the final thing she ever did. She wasn't ready to die, now that she loved Jallon – something she hadn't realised until that very moment. If she didn't proceed, she might lose him. If she did proceed, she might lose him. There was only one thing she could do. The surface was warm to her touch. She felt no pain, only the hard stone that seemed to soften and become receptive to her.

A low murmur rippled through the crowd.

Beth stepped past the first perimeter of stones and laid her hand on top of the next green surface. The pain came then, but not as debilitating as the pain she'd experienced in the jungle. The sensation grew, climbed up her legs, into her torso and down her arms. She stumbled then, and the crowd gasped. She forced herself to get up, prompting a buzz of encouragement from those around her. Two more steps, and she fell again. Climbing back onto her feet seemed impossible, so she turned on her hands and knees and began the torturous crawl back to the perimeter. She collapsed as she neared the boundary, still within their grip, and was acutely aware of the pensive silence that fell across the plateau – and knew that no one would come to help her. Pulling herself forward again, she reached the perimeter, and crossed over it, finally leaving the Stones and the pain behind her. Jallon ran over to meet her, coming perilously close himself to the stumpy columns. He lifted her into his arms and carried her back to the building. The crowd cheered as one, and began chanting and singing. Beth remained conscious just long enough to hear it before reaching the others and drifting off into a sound slumber.

***

"It must have taken a good number of our people to create this," said Orldrey, flicking through the language book Saftreena had given to Beth.

"I suppose so," replied Beth.

She had soundly slept for a few hours and woke to find herself inside the stone building, with only the old man for company. He had fed her a bowl of broth and draped a woollen blanket over her shoulders, explaining how cold it got after dark. He had asked who she was and how she had come to meet Jallon, and she told him everything, how her mother forced her to work in the sewers and let her be imprisoned for a crime she didn't commit, how Mistress Valentina indentured her and took her to the jungle of Deline, how she met Copo and Tiid and saw the Stones, how she ran away with Nyser, how she met Jallon and their ordeals at the hands of Master Brigges, how they escaped from the castle and how Jallon trained her in the wilds. She even told him that they had slept together. The old man listened intently, moving only to light a fire in the hearth as the night closed in.

When she finished her tale they both sat in silence for a while. Beth looked around the huge interior of the building, which stretched back into darkness. It was cluttered with hundreds of books and artefacts obviously from places outside Jallon's land, which she now knew was called Fernish.

"Who are you?" Beth asked, finally breaking the peaceful silence.

"I am the Keeper of the Stones. I record my people's history and offer wisdom when asked. And you, Beth, I think you are a Guardian of the Stones."

Beth wasn't surprised by his last comment. "Exactly what is a Guardian? What am I?"

Orldrey lifted a poker and made some adjustments to the fire so that the flames grew taller. "My great grandfather was a Guardian, too" he replied. "The first and only one my people have produced."

"Did he live for hundreds of years?" asked Beth.

"No. Why do you ask?" He focused on the young woman, curiosity evident in his features.

"I think Orestas Connroy was a Guardian," she said. "He apparently lived for hundreds of years. He's the reason Mistress Valentina is interested in the Stones. She wants his secrets, his spells and incants. I don't really know why – perhaps for power? Or maybe she just wants to live a long time, too."

"Orestas ... That name is familiar." Orldrey wandered off into the darkness of the room and returned with a leather-bound book.

"Yes, he was a Guardian," stated the old man, pointing to a page that must have held confirmation. "He even visited here once, although he never left the circle of Stones when he spoke with one of my forefathers. He shared some interesting facts, too." He read on a bit. "He preceded my great grandfather, it would seem."

"Are there other Guardians?" asked Beth.

"There is only ever one at any time," he said, placing the book on a table and taking his seat near the hearth and Beth.

"So please tell me, what exactly is a Guardian?"

"The Stones are the source of all magic in every land. They store it and take it back when people pass away. They create the mists. They need to grow and be nurtured. They need to be in balance, otherwise sickness and rot will become prevalent."

"How do you know all this?" Beth was intrigued.

"We have always held the Stones as a place of power and so we have protected them. At first, we didn't know why, but generation after generation passed on the legacy.

Perhaps long ago they knew what we know now, but it was forgotten until our own Guardian taught us of their function and importance."

"Why do the Stones need a Guardian?"

"It is the Guardian that is the focus of that balance."

"How so?"

He smiled softly. "Only a Guardian knows that."

"But I don't know."

"One day you will, Beth. The little I do know is that you are expected to visit as many of the Stones as possible."

"How many are there?"

"The records here indicate at least five groupings, but exactly how many there are I do not know."

"Why do they cause so much pain?"

"A Guardian is born without magic, then the Stones infuse him, or her, with magic. That is the pain you need to endure."

"Will they always cause me pain?"

"I am uncertain about that, but I suspect not. Once you are in balance I think there will no longer be any pain. But in truth, I do not really know."

"Can you tell me what I'm supposed to do as a Guardian?"

"I think it is as simple as visiting more and more of the stone groupings."

"Where are these ones you know about?"

"Spread across the lands. This is one of the purposes of our mist walkers. Unlike others, our people only want knowledge of the other locations, but to do this we also need to trade and protect ourselves. Our mist walkers will now gladly serve you."

"Serve me?"

"Yes. We understand the importance of the Stones and their Guardian. Even if we do not know the precise role of the Guardian. Finding a current Guardian is a great sign of hope, and of peace and continuity for our people, and our way of life."

FOURTEEN

emy and Leara arrived in Arities by airboat. Accompanying them were two of Valentina's guards, for both protection and credibility. Leara's blonde hair had been cropped close to her scalp, giving her an entirely different look than with her long flowing locks. She was dressed in a soldier's tunic in Mistress Valentina's colours, a light blue with darker blue edging and trim to the seams and pockets, but she was without any rank insignia. She wore a pistol and sword at her hips, not her preferred weapons, but they fitted the overall effect of the uniform. She still carried her bow and quiver. Remy wore a similar tunic, with pistol and sword. He had grown over a head taller since he had left Arities and filled out considerably. Their appearances did not bear any resemblance to the bounty posters they had seen on the public walls and landmarks of Fallon.

Their first port of call was the messaging station; they intended to retrieve any news from Mistress Valentina. Two notes awaited them. The first confirmed Balcoff's selection as the new Master of Brigges' lands and Castle Sults. The second indicated that Beth was probably still alive as she had been confirmed as the one to escape from Brigges' clutches. Their next task was to secure rooms at Hotel Lanka before visiting Star Gazer brothel.

Inside the brothel, later that day, Lissa Tormain greeted Leara with a huge hug, commenting on how different and how well she looked since their last meeting. She also welcomed Remy warmly, teasing him that it was alright to look at the 'merchandise' but not to touch. Then they moved to the office to discuss their mutual business, leaving the two guards outside in the hallway. Already waiting for them in the office was Piero Bloor.

"Such a turn of events," he said, once the introductions had been made. "Balcoff and I were once partners in a few small ventures and now he is to become a Master at Castle Sults!"

Leara studied the elegantly dressed elderly man. He didn't look like a street criminal, and she decided he could be trusted, for now at least.

"You already know about Balcoff, then," she said.

"News travels fast!" Piero poured himself a small glass of liqueur as he spoke and pushed another glass towards Leara. Leara declined politely – she wanted to keep a clear head.

"He now openly walks the streets of Arities," continued Piero. "The authorities are not willing to arrest him and upset any existing trade deals with Castle Sults." He finished his drink quickly and placed the empty glass beside the bottle. "Plus, there was never enough evidence to prove he did anything illegal, although everyone knew he was a criminal with a reputation for brutality. The castle has already sent him a guard of six men, and now awaits his arrival, but I believe he has to conclude some business with you on behalf of Mistress Valentina before he departs for his new residence."

"Yes. Hence that's why we are here. Mistress Valentina and Balcoff agreed this was a neutral meeting place and I would ask, on her behalf, whether you would facilitate the meeting."

"I would be glad to. May I ask what business is to be discussed?"

"We are looking for a young woman," explained Leara, glancing at Remy. "She came this way with a seeder not so long ago."

"She was wounded at the airboat station," interjected Remy. "You may have heard of this?"

"Well I never!" exclaimed Lissa. "The woman you are looking for came here! I myself dressed her wound. She was with a gentleman – yes, he was a seeder – and a man named Evritt who paid well to have her leave the city in secret. I knew Evritt was on Brigges' payroll. What a coincidence all this is, what with Balcoff now the Master of Castle Sults … He may now know where your woman is."

"We have had a report that the woman, her name is Beth Reach, escaped Brigges and fled from his castle," said Leara. She watched both Piero and Lissa closely for any sign that they already knew this, but they gave no such indication. "We are here to find her and enlist the help of anyone that might aid us in the endeavour."

"And if the woman is no longer at Castle Sults, why do you need to enlist Balcoff?" asked Piero.

"His people can offer more insight into how and when Beth escaped the castle," Leara replied.

Remy had more to say. "And he has agents here in Arities. They might know a few things too."

"And now he will have even more serving him under the title of Master," added Lissa.

"The more people looking," said Remy, "then the greater the chance of finding Beth Reach."

Leara could hear the hope in the young man's tone. "We believe she will return here at some point because Malad District was her home."

"I will put the word out, then," said Piero, indicating to Lissa that she should take care of that for him. "Any assistance I can offer Mistress Valentina would be my pleasure."

"Thank you, Piero. When the meeting with Balcoff has been arranged, will you send word?" asked Leara. "We are staying at Hotel Lanka."

***

Leara and Remy shared a suite of rooms. She took the bedroom while he slept on the sofa in the living space. The two guards had the rooms next door. Remy was still nervous about Balcoff. He knew the man's reputation, had even seen him on a couple of occasions, but he doubted the man's word that he would be safe, despite Mistress Valentina assuring him that she'd told Balcoff of his innocent. This was the reason why Leara kept him close to her at all times.

Another message arrived later that evening with news of the meeting. It was set for tomorrow in the office of the brothel. Leara and Remy were to arrive mid-morning and

Balcoff would show up once they were there. Remy hardly slept that night. He woke sobbing on several occasions to find Leara comforting him. The ordeal he had suffered in the holding cells all that time ago was replaying in his dreams more and more. Once he woke up with a start, calling out Stala's name. He had been so fond of his childhood friend and he still hated Frig for taking her from him. And hated the prison guards for what they had done to him. His desire for revenge was almost as powerful as his fear of Balcoff, and of what Balcoff would do to him if he did not believe his story.

When morning came, Remy was up early to check his pistol repeatedly. He was stronger now, of course, and had a much steadier aim than when he had first fired a weapon. He had also been training with his sword alongside the soldiers in the jungle, but he preferred the pistol or the slender dagger that was tucked inside his tunic.

"You won't need that, Remy," Leara said when she joined him. "And don't do anything stupid, will you. Stay calm. If anything goes wrong, I will stand with you ... but nothing is going to go wrong."

Remy's palms were damp and although he was sweating as he and Leara waited in the office of the Star Gazer, he felt cold and numb. Valentina's guards were outside the door, as were several of Piero's own security staff. Balcoff would soon be standing in front of him; close enough to strike. The door finally opened and a short, burly bald man strode in. He was perhaps fifty years of age. He closed the door behind him, not once taking his piercing gaze from Mocrat. In his hand he carried something wrapped in cloth.

253

"Master Balcoff," said Leara. "Please be seated."

He pulled himself up straight and adjusted his fine black gold-trimmed jacket. "I will remain standing, thank you. Let's just get right to the matters at hand, shall we?". His attention rested on Remy. "Tell me what happened, boy."

Remy couldn't find his voice. His eyes flitted from the pistol holster on the new Master's right hip to the large knife on his left. He had considered himself brave and adventurous since leaving Arities and journeying with Valentina. Now he felt like a small boy again. He began to cry.

"Give him a moment," said Leara as she moved closer to Remy and put a steadying hand on his shoulder.

His sobs subsided, and he began to speak. "Me and Stala used to run together ... but you know that." He paused, sniffled, and met Balcoff's gaze. "We used to meet in an alley in Cutter." The tears had stopped now and he wiped his face and drew in a deep breath. "She hadn't shown up for a while and I was worried about her. Then she turned up and said you had got her back to schooling and she had sneaked out."

Balcoff remained stoic, never taking his eyes from Remy. Leara remained silent at his side.

"She'd only been there a minute when Frig showed up – said he was taking Stala back, on your orders."

Balcoff gave a small nod. "Stala told him she wouldn't go back with him, so Frig got angry and called me out, telling Stala that I wanted to marry her one day.".

Remy lowered his gaze for a moment, considering his words, and trying to recall the details. When he was ready he locked eyes with Balcoff again. "We – Frig and me, not

254

Stala – had got drunk together one day and I told him then, but he had said it too, that he wanted to marry her, so I threw that back at him. Then Frig pulled his knife and went for me. We fought, and I had my knife out too. Stala tried to separate us and we all ended up on the floor in a bundle. I was first to get up, before Frig and Stala. Frig was lying on top of Stala and still holding his knife, which was buried deep in Stala's heart. I lost it so I charged Frig. I wanted to kill him. I had him, and we must have ended up in the main street. Next thing, I was struck on the back of the head before I could stick him. Then I was taken to the holding cells."

Remy had started his story with tears in his eyes, but when he finished he was dry-eyed and glaring back at Balcoff with pent-up anger and hatred, not directed at the man in front of him, but no less intense. No one spoke for a bit. The silence was disturbing. After what seemed an age, Balcoff backed up to the door and opened it.

"Bring him in," he called into the corridor.

Two exceptionally large, mean-looking men dragged Frig into the office by his arms. Balcoff closed the door behind them. He was tall and strong, more man than boy now, and yet he seemed smaller than Remy remembered. He was not restrained in any way other than by the two men holding him, but Remy noted his empty pistol holster and dagger sheath.

"Frig here told me that you fought. His version is that Stala separated you both but you stabbed her in cold anger and charged at him, looking to murder him too," Balcoff said.

"That's a lie!" said Remy, motioning towards Frig, his

fists already clenched. Leara's firm grip on his shoulder halted his progress. Frig glared at him smugly.

"He says that when he arrived in the alley, you and Stala were arguing," Balcoff went on. "She had told you she never wanted to see you again and you were shouting at her."

Leara gripped both of Remy's shoulders now as he tried to lunge at the liar in front of him.

"I had the guards in the cells torment you because I wanted you to suffer before I killed you myself. But first I wanted to cremate my only daughter," said Balcoff. He paused for a moment, swallowed hard. "You escaped before I could question you. Then, a little later, after I had burned Stala and failed to get hold of you, I started asking more questions. The enforcers who stopped you that day were very informative. One of them even kept the knife that had been pushed into Stala's heart. This knife."

Balcoff unwrapped the cloth that he had been holding. "It's quite a big knife, isn't it? Perhaps too big for the small boy I recall who fled the city. Then, I thought, if you had left your knife stuck in my daughter, where did you get the second knife? And where was Frig's blade?"

"He took it from me!" Frig exclaimed, his voice high pitched, his smugness gone.

"A fact you've never mentioned until now," Balcoff asked him. "So is this your knife I'm holding – or his?"

"It's his," insisted Frig.

"Then this smaller blade must be yours," replied Balcoff, continuing to unwrap the cloth to reveal a second knife. "This is the one the enforcers took from him." He pointed the blade at Remy.

"Yes, that's mine. He took it off me when we fought," insisted Frig.

"I've known you a good while now, Frig, and I've never, in all that time, seen you with anything but a big, wicked-looking blade. So are you certain this is yours?"

"Yes, yes! He took it from me and—"

Before he could finish, Balcoff moved with lightning speed and drove the heavy knife that had killed his daughter deep into Frig's chest.

"I've waited a long time to do that," he said calmly, with a tone of sinister satisfaction.

"I was surprised when I heard that you killed Stala," he said, turning to Remy. "She spoke of you often. And we argued about you often. I didn't want her out with you – it was too dangerous – but she always insisted on it, even snuck out to meet you sometimes. I got the impression that she was extremely fond of you, and you of her. Then, when you left the city, I only had one version of what happened that day. Today I think I heard the truth."

Remy had wanted to kill Frig himself, and he wanted to kill Balcoff for having him raped in the cells; he also wanted to kill the guards who had abused him. Yet he simply stared at the slumped bloody body before him and felt nothing but coldness. There was no satisfaction in Frig's death because he hadn't delivered the final blow himself.

Balcoff waved the guards away and they left the room dragging the now lifeless body.

Leara sat Remy on the sofa and took a firm grip of his hand, but no words passed between them.

Balcroff was the first to speak. "Now. I understand we have other business to discuss."

"We do," Leara replied.

"We do, *Master*," Balcoff reminded her.

Leara explained that Mistress Valentina was searching for Beth, and that they needed to know more about what had taken place at Castle Sults. She told him that they needed his resources both inside and outside the city to help find the young escapee, and Balcoff agreed to do what he could to aid the Mistress. He didn't bother to ask why Beth was so important to her.

Back in their suite at the hotel, Remy finally came out of his subdued mood. He shouted, swore and kicked and smashed random pieces of furniture and ornaments. He raged wildly for nearly twenty minutes. Leara simply left him to it, turning the guards away from the door when they came to enquire about the racket.

In the early hours of the morning, she heard Remy rise from the sofa, get dressed and sneak out of the room. She followed him discreetly, but he was very good at blending into the pre-dawn shadows and he kept turning round to check that no one was following him. On more than one occasion Leara thought he'd seen her, but Remy continued on his way. It wasn't long before Leara figure out where he was going -the enforcers' station.

The boy stopped in a hidden corner and watched the main gates. Shortly after his arrival, a group of men and women finishing their work shift came out. Remy followed them as dawn was breaking. His targets laughed and joked as they moved into the city and gradually dispersed. He stayed with his mark, a solitary man, until he was alone. When he stopped at a door that was most likely his home, and turned the key to enter, Remy's pistol was aimed and steady, but before he could take the shot Leara pushed the barrel of the gun towards the ground. Remy struggled to raise it again as he struggled with her, while the man went inside, out of sight.

"What are you doing!" The heat of Remy's anger was obvious, and there was venom in his eyes.

"This is not the way," Leara said calmly.

"It is! Balcoff took Frig. There's nothing I can do about that now, but I can get the men that raped me," he raged.

"Light's coming now, Remy. There's little you or I can do now on that matter, but come back with me and we can talk."

"I don't want to talk." He looked at his pistol, still in his hand.

"If we can talk, I may be able to help you. You are a free man now, after all. Valentina and Balcoff will ensure everyone knows that Frig murdered Stala, and that will clear your name. You can be Mocrat again. So don't commit another murder when you have just become a free man."

Leara noticed that passers-by were staring at them. "We're getting attention," she said. "We need to move."

When they got back to the hotel, the mess and damage to the suite had been rectified. The guards were waiting outside the door, questioning expressions upon their faces, but Leara ignored them. Once inside, she sat Remy down and pulled over a chair for herself so that she was facing him.

"Revenge is not the answer, Remy."

"It's all I have."

"But it won't make the pain go away. It won't heal anything. And you have all your life ahead of you."

"I was so angry when Balcoff killed Frig. *I* wanted to do it. He took Stala from me! Stala was the only good thing in my life – ever. She was beautiful. My best friend. And he took that."

"It hurts, I know, but if you take revenge it will change you. And the next time something bad affects you, taking revenge will become easier, until it becomes your only solution to any problem. It will darken you in places that will be hard to light again. And killing those guards will not bring back Stala."

"They don't deserve to live," he said, shaking his head. "I remember their faces so well, laughing and joking when they were on top of me. Their smell, too … they stank of stale ale and sweat. They can't be allowed to do that to anyone else ever, and I know they will. Killing them will give me the satisfaction I need. I know it will."

"Look, Remy. Let's get out of the city for a while. Everyone is looking for Beth and we could take a trip to Castle Sults on the chance we run into her."

"I'm not going. You can't make me. I'm free now, so I don't need you or Mistress Valentina – or Beth. I can do what I want, and no one can stop me."

Leara stood and paced the floor. She stopped at the table to pour herself a glass of water from a pitcher, then turned to face the boy again.

"Tell me, what will you do once you've murdered these men? Where will you go? How will you make a living?"

"I lived on the streets before. I can do it again."

"So becoming a lifelong criminal is your ambition?"

"I could get a trade. I've not been tested yet. I might be a spellbinder. Or I can become a seeder for hire."

"Can you read and write?"

"You know I can't. But I have learned a little with you and Beth, so I could learn more."

"Still, your best place is with the Mistress."

"She doesn't really care for me, Leara. I know that. I'm not stupid. She only keeps me around because Beth likes me."

"When Beth comes back she will want to see you, and regardless of what Valentina thinks of you, you will have a place in her ranks."

"She was going to make me go into the Stones. I know that now. Beth saved me. The Mistress is ruthless – all she wants are Orestas' secrets and she'll sacrifice anyone to get them."

"She does have a softer side, you know. And once she has what she wants, everything will change."

"Just because she likes you, doesn't mean there's a place for me," he murmured.

"And remember, where else will you learn – freely – the skills you need to survive? Be given a pistol, a sword, clothing, or training, even education?"

Remy sat quietly for a moment. "Doesn't matter. I've made up my mind. I will get those guards and then … and then … I don't know. But I will be alright. I was before!"

Leara sighed. "I can't believe I'm saying this … I will help you kill the guards, but we do it my way. So we don't get caught."

"You will?", his mood changed immediately. "Why? How? You got caught last time!"

"I did. But only because I felt like you do now and didn't act rationally."

"Why? Tell me about it."

"I killed a man in broad daylight, surrounded by witnesses. He deserved to die. He was the only reason I came to Arities. I had tracked him for many weeks with only one purpose. And when I finally saw him, the rage was too much. I drew my bow and shot him through the head. Then I simply dropped my bow and waited for the enforcers to come and get me. I didn't care what happened to me from that moment on. But then I met you, and Beth and Valentina, and I had a new purpose. And I decided I didn't want to hang on the gallows and I didn't want you up there next to me, so we escaped."

"What did he do, this man?"

Leara paused before she spoke. "I had a daughter, a little older than you. This man … raped, beat her and left her for dead. She was all I had – my whole world – and I failed to protect her. I already knew his face and warned him to stay away from us. And I thought he'd taken my warning seriously but then, a week later, maybe just at an opportune moment, he took Carra …"

Leara took a few sips of water before continuing. "He took her to some isolated place, then abused her, tortured her, and left her for dead. When I found her, she was barely alive. I nursed her for one day. She told me what had happened … and then she died. I think she had lost the will to live. So, like you, I wanted revenge – at any cost. I had no other purpose left, so I didn't care how it happened, just that it had to happen. Now, having you and Beth, with so much life left to live, I can't let either of you waste it. My daughter has gone, but I can protect you."

Leara was crying now. Her face fell forwards, over her

lap, tears splashing on her britches. Remy reached out and his arms encircled her. After allowing herself the briefest of moments of grief, she pulled herself together and stopped crying.

"So, if I help you, Remy, will you come back with me to Valentina and make something of your life? Agree?"

"Agree," he replied.

Over the next couple of days, leaving Valentina's colours out from their attire and their guards out of their actions, they tracked the two enforcer guards. They followed them to their homes and watched who they interacted with, where they ate, drank and socialised. Remy wanted a bloody death for them, and he wanted them to know why they had to die. His plan had moved on from a simple shot in the back, to cold protracted murder. Leara tried to convince him that dead was dead, but he didn't fully accept that. At least neither man seemed to have a family, which Leara was thankful for.

They drank heavily and staggered home early in the afternoon to sleep before taking their shift at the enforcers' station. Leara was inside one of their houses, hidden behind the open bedroom door, Remy beside her. They had broken into the house a little earlier and checked all the rooms before finally deciding their ambush would be upstairs. Remy felt nervous and a little scared. Doubts plagued him while they waited in silence. Then they heard the front door open and the man staggering in, colliding, by the sounds of it, with pieces of furniture as he made for the stairs and his bed. The boy's resolve hardened – he was doing this.

The bedroom was dark, with thick curtains drawn to keep out the heat of the afternoon sunlight. The bed smelled as if the sheets hadn't been washed in months or years. Then the fresh stink of ale preceded the man who stumbled into the room and crashed into the bed, holding onto the footboard to steady himself.

Leara's hand on Remy's shoulder held him back. He had his pistol and small dagger at the ready. The darts loaded in his weapon were extremely toxic and would make significantly less sound than the clap of a slug. The man continued to fumble in the darkness, moving around noisily, then their noses were assaulted by the smell and sound of him crapping in the bucket on the far side of the bed. The faeces splattered into the bucket, releasing a foul odour that made Remy gag. Leara released her hold on him and he stepped out from behind the door.

The man still sat on the bucket, head down, on the verge of dropping of.

Remy walked close up beside him. "Remember me?" he said.

The man didn't move, and gave no indication that he had heard the boy.

"Hey! Remember me?" repeated Remy, louder this time.

The guard looked up, trying to focus through his drunken vision. Then he panicked. He stood too quickly, tripping over the pants around his ankles and tipping the bucket in the process. The piss and shit spilt to the floor and he slipped in it, and stumbled towards Remy. He grabbed for the footboard of the bed again, steadying himself with one hand, and the other stretched out to grasp Remy by the front of his shirt. He pulled Remy within kissing distance so quickly that it caught Remy off guard.

Then the hand gripping the bed released its hold and swung to knock the pistol from Remy's hand, causing a dart to fire. In the darkness, Remy had no idea where the projectile, or his pistol, had landed. A split second later, the guard's hands were wrapped around his throat. Lifting him from the floor, the guard began to choke him with adrenaline-fuelled strength. Remy's eyes closed as he struggled for breath.

He felt warm liquid splash across his face. Leara had stabbed the monster of a man in his neck, and now blood erupted from the wound. The kill was not to be his, again, thought Remy fleetingly, and the realisation fuelled his anger and determination. He stabbed out frantically with his dagger, again and again into the man's chest and abdomen. His quarry fell to the floor, taking Remy with him, and the grip on his throat fell away.

Light flooded into the room when Leara opened the curtains. Remy stood up slowly. His upper half was covered in blood, his lower half in urine and faeces. His pistol lay in a pool of human waste.

"Are you hurt?" Leara asked.

"No," he croaked, massaging his throat.

"You were simply to shoot him – not warn him!"

Remy looked at the mess on the floor, and the mess he was covered in, and gulped back a wave of vomit. He couldn't stop staring at the lifeless body at his feet.

"We can't go after the other one now," said Leara. "Look at the state of you!"

"I thought you said it would be best to do both today. So he wasn't warned," Remy replied, wiping ineffectually at the stains on his britches.

"You can't go into the street like that."

Remy looked around the room. "I can clean up here and take one of his shirts ... if he has any."

"You need to clean up anyway. Then we'll decide."

***

They set off in the general direction of their next victim, sticking to the back streets. Remy's britches were wet where he had washed away the fouling, and they were heavily stained as a result, and the oversized shirt smelt pungent and stale. Leara had rough-hewn the over-long sleeves to length with her knife. He looked more like a street urchin now, but there were no signs of blood on him or his clothing. In the end they had decided to stick with the original plan.

They had chosen to target this guard second because the rear door of his house was hidden from view and the lock was broken, so they would not have to pick it. However, when they arrived it was barred from the inside.

"The window," suggested Remy.

It would be a tight squeeze for him but he could flip the shutter's latch and climb through the opening to the kitchen, then remove the barricade from the door. Soon Remy was standing inside the dark room. He froze when heavy footsteps approached.

"I'll get us a drink," called the man to someone in the other room as he stomped into the kitchen. He was stark naked, and not a well-kept man. Every part of him was fat and flabby, but he was easily more than twice the size of Remy.

"Thief!" the man yelled when he spotted Remy. "I'll frigging kill you."

Remy didn't have chance to draw his pistol or his dagger before the man was on him, but he managed to duck beneath the clumsy grab. The naked man spun quickly and charged once again. Remy had nowhere to go in such a small space and found himself crushed between a high sideboard and a grossly fleshy belly. The pair of them slid to the floor, with the naked man on top, straddling him and pinning him to the floor. A flaccid penis and bouncing testicles abutted Remy's chin as the man punched him hard on the side of the head. Remy bit down hard. The man let out a high-pitched screech but Remy held on, shaking his head side to side like a wild animal ripping flesh. Then something gave. The man on top of him became a dead weight.

"Get out of there, Now!" called Leara.

He squirmed from under the body which was pinned to the sideboard by an arrow through its left temple. Remy spat chunks of flesh from his mouth and something spherical bounced across the floor. He gagged in disgust.

"Everything alright?" a female voice called from upstairs.

"Now! Move!" Leara hissed.

Scrabbling as quickly as he could, Remy tumbled out of through window into the back yard. Leara stopped Remy from running so that they didn't draw unwanted attention. Entering the street at a fast pace, they took the first turning they found, but no sooner were they out of sight that they heard a woman's screams. The mutilated guard had been discovered. "Murder!" came the hysterical cries. "Get the enforcers! Murder!"

They slowed down to a casual walk and Leara wiped a

smear of blood from Remy's face.

"Slowly, now, Remy. We've done nothing. If we are followed or caught, we did nothing. We are agents for Mistress Valentina."

Leara glanced behind her, towards the source of the screams. No one was pursuing them, but not wanting to leave it to chance, she steered Remy as they made several more turns, breaking up a straight-line escape as they distanced themselves from the scene of the crime.

At Hotel Lanka, Leara ordered two hot baths. While she held the receptionist's attention, Remy raced upstairs and disappeared from view.

"Are we done now?" called Leara, reclining in the hot tub in the bedroom, feeling quite exhausted. "Is it out of your system?"

Remy was soaking in his own bath in the living space.

"It wasn't like what I thought it would be like," he called back.

"It never is. There's always going to be something unexpected. But at least is it finished now."

"Yes. It's done," he said, mostly to himself. Then, after a pause, "You're right, though. It does change you." Another pregnant pause. "I don't feel anything now. It's like it never happened. Now I don't care if they're dead or not. But then it's too late, isn't it?"

"Drink your wine, Remy. It might surprise you how well it takes the edge off everything. We'll see how you feel tomorrow."

FIFTEEN

Beth sat outside her own stone building on the top of the plateau. It wasn't as large as Orldrey's, but it belonged to her. Inside there was a bed, a table and some chairs and a cosy hearth. She'd been living among Jallon's people for many weeks and they had made her feel very welcome.

Her days had fallen into some semblance of a routine, starting with training sessions with the local mist walkers who were between visits to other lands. There were twelve of them, both men and women. It was a great honour to reach the position of mist walker, one that only the most able people could achieve that goal. And it was widely regarded as an extremely dangerous pursuit.

Beth spent the lunchtime hours and her evenings in the main building with Orldrey and his young apprentice, Rettia, a pleasant young woman who was only a little older than Beth, and who was totally absorbed by every conversation between Beth and Orldrey. During the afternoons she would be near the Stones and, under

Orldrey's, gaze occasionally enter them. Jallon was not always around, but when he was they slept together; it was common knowledge that they were a couple.

Beth's sleeping patterns were extremely erratic. She suspected, and Orldrey agreed, that being in such close proximity to the cluster of Stones was having a direct effect on her psyche. Her dreams often made no sense, and often involved her talking nonsense to herself in the third person. Yet, in the days following a dream, certain realisations would come to her. It might be some revelation about a magical symbol that she'd not known previously, or some new understanding about how the magic and the Stones and the mists were connected. But acting on such discoveries was an extremely slow process.

Her pain when entering the Stones was fractionally less, so minute a difference that it may just have been that she was getting used to it. Her magic, power, focus and learning, however, had definitely improved. She could create heat and cold, like the spellbinders did on the airboats, and lighting a fire was a trifle now, as was creating a globe of light around her to guide her in the darkness.

More recently she had learned how to levitate books, and this ability got better with every attempt, so she was now moving increasingly heavy stacks. She recalled spells that she had seen spellbinders use in combat, such as the mind blast – a gripping energy charge that held a person in dancing light, causing them the convulse; and the knockback that boomed and pushed things back with force; and the fire that ignited a person. She also understood the concept of other spellbinder-type spells that she'd never witnessed at first hand, but she hadn't mastered any one of them; her attempts always resulted in some sort of effect but nothing on the scale of a trained spellbinder.

On this morning, she woke with a start, sitting bolt upright. Jallon wasn't beside her, nor was he anywhere in sight in the room. As she struggled to wake up properly, he came through the door carrying a stack of dried malek manure for the fire.

"Thought you'd appreciate the fire. You normally do when you've dreamed so physically."

Beth knew what he was referring to. Some of her dreams caused her to thrash about the bed violently. There was nothing Jallon could do for her on those occasions – he could never wake her up.

"Same dream?" he asked.

"Yes. And it's becoming more and more vivid. I think I wake just before I die. I go so far inside the Stones that I can't return and I think I perish there."

Jallon raised the flames of the fire and went over to the bed.

"Maybe you should stay out of the Stones for a little while?"

"I don't think I can. There's still so much that I don't know." Beth's gaze went distant as she pondered her choices. She knew she couldn't stay away from the Stones. "Orldrey and I talk of it often and Rettia writes down every word. We're certain that the Stones generate the mists, but are they supposed to be doorways? Or maybe they serve to balance the wildlife and prey? Do the predators guard the mist curtains?" she looked into Jallon's eyes, wanting him to understand her cause while knowing at the same time that he did.

"Every mist we know of has a guard of sorts. Whether that is people like yours or the Delines, or dangerous places like the mosslands or vicious predators. Some people have travelled through them for generations, whereas, where I come from, they are a place of monsters to be avoided at all costs. Yet, the Masters and Mistresses have used them for some years now. Why is that?"

Jallon sighed. He didn't have the answer.

"Then there's the magic – it's so different everywhere," she continued. "Parablion spellbinders have casting magic that seems primarily for conflict. But our people have 'traits', as you call them. Then there are the Rishan, whose skin is toxic. It's all so confusing."

"It's not a race to understand everything," said Jallon.

"But it might be … I still don't think Valentina will have given up looking for me. You don't know her like I do. She is relentless and merciless in her search for Orestas' secrets."

"But I don't understand why."

"I don't know either. I really don't. Power, maybe?"

"Hmm. Try to sleep again, Beth. There are eight of us in the village at the moment, so tomorrow's training will be hard going for you."

"We'll see," said Beth and she caressed his chest and buried her head against his warmth.

As sunlight started to move across the canyon floor the mist walkers and Beth were already training. Strength, form, flexibility, speed and stamina were the core areas they focused on, with drills and exercises designed to enhance and increase each element. After over an hour they partnered up for sparring. They called it light work, but for

Beth it was so close to real fighting that she had struggled in the early days. Then, as she realised her own abilities were no match for the control each mist walker possessed, she fought with greater vigour, understanding that each opponent was taking it easy on her to allow her to progress. She doubted they were ever in any real danger when she assaulted them despite her intention to hurt them.

In recent sessions she was always partnered with Jallon – when he was home, that is. She asked him why and had liked the response she got. She had improved so much, apparently, that the others thought one day she would break through their defences and wound them. Jallon was the only one with the regeneration trait, which gave him the ability to heal quickly. Today was no exception. Fighting against her regularly, against the same opponent, had made Jallon a little lazy, especially because his opponent was his own beloved.

Beth realised that sometimes he was showing off to her. Some of his moves were too flamboyant, moves that he never used when fighting with the others. One particular move followed when he parried her sword and knife attacks together; he would twirl both of his own heavy blades simultaneously in a showy display of triumph. If he was showing off, he wasn't helping her train for any real-life situation; it was time he took her seriously. So she formulated a counter-attack that he wouldn't expect.

Lunging with all her might, her sword held high and her knife held low, she struck hard at his head and stomach. He reacted as she predicted, deflecting both blades and beginning the fancy swirling of his swords. This time, Beth held back on her balance, which he would have noticed if he was really trying. She had a low stable stance, whereas normally she was off balance for long enough for Jallon to begin his triumphant flurry. So, executing a simple flick of her wrist and forearm, her knife flew, impaling his right foot to the ground. He was so shocked that he froze – only for the briefest fraction of a second – but that was enough. Beth stabbed him with her sword over his heart and drew blood, deliberately controlling the thrust so it didn't inflict serious damage. Then she stepped back, pleased with her work.

Jallon pulled the knife from his foot and charged at her, his weapons delivering an unending barrage of attacks from every direction. The other mist walkers and anyone who happened to be nearby stopped what they were doing and watched. Beth fought harder than ever before. Her partner was angry, and not sparing her any consideration; he was trying to harm her, maybe even kill her.

Steel rang on steel. Beth ducked and parried and countered. She thought the rage might leave him, so she defended, but he kept coming at her. He attacked again, and again. If he wasn't going to calm down, she needed to beat him. Both took many cuts as they engaged in battle. Beth applied everything she had learned, simply to stay alive and take her opponent down. She didn't want to kill him, but she knew she might have to seriously wound him if she was to conquer his rage.

They clashed up close, body tight against body. Not only were their blades in play, but they used their feet and legs to try to sweep each other to the floor. They elbowed and headbutted. Beth was no match for his size and strength, but she managed to roll herself around him and exited their deadly dance by skipping to his rear, where a single sweep of her sword opened a wound across his back. Had she applied more pressure it would have been a serious injury, but either her touch was light, or he had created enough distance between them for the sword to fail to bite deeply. She would never know. Jallon spun around, one sword high and one sword low in a pincer move. Beth ducked the high blade but the slap of steel on her legs took them away from her. She was off-balance and the blow was sufficient to make her crash to the floor in a heap. Her recovery was good, but not before Jallon's blade hit her throat.

He pulled back just as the sword connected, but the faint line of blood declared the blow to be a fatal success. He stepped back from her with a wide grin on his face, the widest she'd ever seen. The mist walkers applauded … and as she stood up she realised it was her that they were cheering. And she realised that if Jallon hadn't just slapped her with his blade – but cut – she would have lost both her legs as well as her head. She had lost the battle, but she was acutely aware that Jallon had needed to fight her as viciously as he had done to win. He hadn't held back in the main; just enough to not kill her on the spot. And it had given her the opportunity to prove herself in front of her peers.

"You bastard," she said with affection when they embraced.

"My foot's going to sting for a while, you know."

"You deserve it. I really thought you'd lost control."

"Not with the woman I love. That will never happen."

Beth heard his admission of love but the moment passed quickly because the mist walkers converged on them, lavishing them with praise and acclamations. He had never professed his feelings before. She loved him, but had been too frightened to ask whether he felt the same, for fear of rejection. Later on, she asked him to affirm the sentiment, and he did.

Her wounds were not serious, but they needed attention and dressing. The village healers didn't treat mist walkers' wounds unless it was absolutely necessary. Instead, they watched over them as they treated their own or those of fellow walkers. Beth dressed Jallon's wounds. His foot had already started to heal, but to keep it clean she washed it then bandaged it. She had little doubt that the dressing would not be needed by nightfall. The other cuts she had inflicted on him had already closed over, but she washed them anyway. Her own cuts needed not only washing but ointments to prevent infection and minimise scarring. Jallon covered them, much to the satisfaction of the attending healer.

"I need to practise," Beth told Jallon, who nodded and went outside.

At the base of the canyon, Beth had mounted several targets, person-shaped silhouettes. Here, against the back wall, she practised with her pistol. The local mist walkers declined to use such a weapon, preferring their bows, spears and throwing blades, but Jallon understood Beth's need to be familiar with the weapons she was used to in Parablion.

She needed to ration her slugs and darts and the seedpods necessary to charge the weapon because there was no way to replace them while she was on the plateau. So she practised her speed at drawing the pistol from her holster, first while stationary and then while moving and rolling.

She took aim and imagined her shots. She removed the sight from the top of the barrel because she no longer needed it to focus her aim, but she spent some time learning how to attach it and detach it quickly – the enhanced sighting and partial dark-vision would still come in handy.

Loading and charging the pistol was something else she practised, again while stationary and moving; not that she'd ever be a match for a true seeder, though with no one to compare herself to on the plateau, she allowed herself the possibility that she might. It was rare for her to actually fire a slug or dart when she trained, but her aim was confident. Today she allowed herself four slugs at the end of her session. Each one landed exactly where intended.

***

"Jallon told me you had the dream again last night," said Orldrey who was waiting on her porch.

"Yes. It's becoming ominously repetitive now."

"You think you die and that is when you wake up?"

"That makes sense to me."

"What if you don't die, though? What if you're supposed to stay inside the Stones until you wake?"

She considered this. "But what if I don't wake up?"

"What if you do?" Orldrey said and walked away. He had sown a seed for thought.

"I'm leaving again tomorrow," said Jallon as they ate supper by the open fire that night. "I need to return to Parablion. We – me and Orldrey – still think there must be an outcrop of Stones in your lands. He's made a couple of suggestions about where they might be and I'm going to check them out with Kynew. We'll only be gone a week or so."

Beth knew the risks involved. Her heart saddened every time he left, but stopping him was impossible. This was his life, and the mist walkers had become even more dedicated to the task of seeking out new Stones. Kynew was a strong woman and an experienced mist walker; together her and Jallon could face anything.

"I'll be here when you return."

Lying by Jallon's side in bed, Beth made a decision before drifting off. She slept peacefully and deeply. Jallon had to wake her up for her training.

The training intensified. Beth knew how important it was, as though their mock battles were real. Today she wasn't partnered with Jallon but took a turn with everyone. It felt so different, so much better; more challenging and at the same time exhilarating.

"I'm not training any more today," Beth remarked as they sat together, tending to their wounds.

"Why's that?" asked Jallon.

"I need you all to come with me to the Stones. I've decided to enter them and not leave when the pain threatens my ability to escape."

"You're going to collapse inside? Won't you die?"

"Maybe I won't?"

The mist walkers exchanged nervous glances. Then they all nodded and left, taking the healers with them. Leaving Beth and Jallon alone.

"I love you, both as my Beth and as my Guardian," Jallon said. "I don't want to lose you but I don't understand what you have to do or why. My place is to accept it and to serve. I won't leave the Stones until you do. So I'll wait as long as it takes for you to exit. And if you perish," he gulped, "then when my day comes I'll ask the others to cast me into them so that we might be together again one day."

They embraced for some time before approaching the Stones. The whole village was waiting. There was nothing to be said, no speeches, no farewells. Everyone watched in sombre silence as Beth walked directly towards the perimeter of the Stones.

The pain came, as expected, and Beth dropped to her knees, but rather than turn back she pushed onwards, towards the centre. Crawling along the ground, her face in the dirt, she pulled herself on until the darkness overtook her.

"Hello. It's you talking to me again. Us, I suppose," said a voice from somewhere.

She was nowhere. There was nothing to see about her. Her eyes were closed but she knew it wasn't dark, and it wasn't light either.

"Am I dead?" she asked.

"I don't know." A pause. "I only know what you know."

"The pain has gone."

"Maybe. I don't really know."

"I wonder if my body's still lying in the Stones?"

"The only way to know that is to wake up."

Beth forced her eyes to open. It was light. She looked up to the sun. It had hardly moved across the sky. She could only have been out for a few minutes. She took to her feet and looked across the plateau. All twelve mist walkers stood silently watching her. In the distance, Orldrey and Rettia stood on their porch looking in her direction. The crowd of villagers had dispersed.

She stretched her body. Her muscles ached, but the intense pain was gone, and she felt her whole body vibrating subtly, almost humming. She waved to Jallon, but he didn't respond. Couldn't he see her? She walked out from the Stones towards him and embraced him, noting that he was crying softly, without a sound, while tears ran freely down his cheeks.

"I thought you were dead. You've been lying there motionless for five days."

SIXTEEN

Balcoff arrived at Hotel Lanka with pretentious grandeur, escorted by ten guards in new black and gold uniforms that matched his own attire – the obvious colours of choice for his new estate. A man who previously couldn't walk the streets of Arities for fear of reprisals or arrest, he now paraded himself openly, flaunting his new title. He'd sent a message in advance to Leara to inform her of his arrival and telling her he had the news she sought on behalf of Mistress Valentina.

"Master Balcoff, it's good to see you again," Leara said as he entered her suite accompanied by another man, grimy from several days' travel; he'd obviously not had a seat inside the coach. His light travel clothing had seen better days and there was a dried bloodstain on one sleeve of his shirt. In his mid-thirties, Leara guessed, with short brown hair and his chin heavily stubbled. He deferred completely to Master Balcoff.

"I have refreshments ready for you," she said.

"Not necessary," Balcoff replied. "I have other more

urgent business to deal with. This man is Radent. He was the last person to see this Beth Reach you are looking for. He was working for Brigges and came to the castle looking for payment after the old git was killed. He didn't get the name of the girl he met, but she fits the description from the castle, as does the man she escaped with. I understand you already know the secret of the mists, as does he, so I won't waste more time – the girl is no longer in Parablion."

"Do we know where she is then?"

"My best guess is Fernish. Radent's been there before, so I'm handing him over to you now. This, I believe, settles any debt I might have with Valentina." And with that he turned to leave the room.

At the door, he stopped and turned to Remy. "Nice work with those two guards, young man. When I heard they'd been murdered in their own homes and you were in town, I knew it had to be you. I take it you and I have no issues to resolve? That would not be good for you …"

"We have no issues," said Remy. "Your loss was as great as mine and I might have done the same as you if our places were reversed. We've both lost enough, and that's that."

Master Balcoff left. Radent stood quietly, shuffling his feet.

"So, where did you see Beth?" Leara asked, sizing him up and noticing how nervous he was. She could tell that he was an opportunist, looking to play the situation to his advantage.

"I met her and the man in Cember – a town in Rishan. Do you know it?" He switched glances between Remy and Leara.

Leara knew his type and understood that he was trying to spot some weakness between her and Remy that he might be able to exploit. "Never been there," she replied. "Where is this Fernish?"

"The dark-skinned man she travelled with is from there." He stopped flitting his gaze and focused on Leara. "If they were in Cember, then that's where they were going. They have trades and agreements in Cember because it's the only place they can go into the mist to the northern region."

"You've been to Rishan, I take it, and this northern region?" asked Leara.

"Not exactly. Rishan, yes. The North of Fernish, no." He paused, and his tone became ominous. "You avoid the North if you want to stay alive. They don't welcome visitors. The other parts aren't that friendly, either." Then with a sly smile he added, "But it's possible to get in there sometimes to trade."

"Can you take us there?" Leara was certain that this was his bargaining chip. He was selling himself as an essential part of any plans they might have.

"You two? No. You won't last two minutes on the other side of any mist – never mind Rishan."

"What use are you to us then?" asked Leara, leading him to the offer he was sure to make.

"Balcoff promised to cut my nuts off and feed them to me if Mistress Valentina wasn't satisfied with my service. But he hasn't paid me a single coin for my efforts or the news I brought to him."

"So, you want money?" asked Remy.

"I was a mist walker for Master Brigges – do you know what that means?"

"No …" Remy replied uncertainly.

"It means I know what's on the other side of the mists. I know where to go. I speak some of the languages and I can guide a team – I can find this Beth woman. I was hoping the Mistress would pay for such a service."

This was the offer Leara had been expecting. "You've never met Valentina, then," she scoffed. "She makes Balcoff look like a baby in these matters, and she doesn't take kindly to extortion."

"It's not extortion. I will give good service for fair payment. But I will need equipment, and strong men and women to accompany me, as it's really not safe travelling the mists. If you want to go to North Fernish you will need a small army. They're a vicious lot."

Leara considered this for a few moments. "You will stay here. Two of Valentina's guards occupy the suite next door. You can stay with them for now. If you try to flee or disappear, you'll find out what it's like to be a mist guide with only one leg."

Radent let out a small chuckle. "Can I have food, drink? A bath even? And a change of clothes?"

"That can all be arranged. I will send a message to Mistress Valentina today and she can decide what we do next."

***

Valentina's told them to bring Radent to the jungle in Deline. They were to take the airboat to Fallon where they would join a team of wagons and carriages bound for the campsite near Anding Town. Leara was to ask Lissa Tormain and Piero Bloor to maintain a lookout for Beth in

Arities and communicate any news should she return; for this, they would be handsomely rewarded.

There were thirty drawn carriages in the team waiting outside the gates of Fallon. Their occupants had made camp, waiting for Leara's arrival. The wagon master had received these updated orders at the message station when they first entered the city. Having been on the road for a considerable time, he was impatient to reach their final destination.

"I've known Valentina since she was a little girl," said the grumpy old man, "and I'm not sure her late father would approve of all this". Despite his age, he was still tall and slim with long grey hair indistinguishable from his grey beard, and he managed the convoy of wagons with an air of authority as great as that of the Mistress herself.

"I'm sure she has good reasons," replied Leara.

She took her seat beside a man called Senay on the lead wagon. Twelve mounted soldiers rode ahead of them; behind them, an array of wagons, carriages and personnel, including children and soldiers, followed, as well as a selection of livestock. They were wary of attacks from predators and were well prepared. So far they'd travelled a great distance from Castle Worthmere and those who had started out as novice travellers were now well and truly seasoned. They had only lost ten people along the way, all of them soldiers.

"Cities won't like it, either," Senay grumbled, "the Mistress building a settlement outside her own lands. Bound to cause trouble it is."

He moaned all the time, Leara accepted, but over the last couple of days she found reasons not to ride at the head with him. But today he had insisted.

"So why's she doing it, Leara?" He sounded genuinely concerned.

"I don't know. I've been in the city a while so I'm out of touch," she replied honestly, with a soft sigh.

"I know Valentina's bite is a bad one," Senay said, "but I like to think she trusts me. I was friends with her father and her husband before he passed away."

"Husband?" Leara asked with shock and surprise.

"You didn't know?" He looked directly at her now, then turned to face forwards, changing the subject. "We've heard rumours that we're going to live beyond the mist. That's not true, is it?"

"How long was she married?" Leara had one line of enquiry now.

"Two years. Her father arranged it but they seemed happy together. Then one day he had a mystery illness and died within days." He switched subjects again. "There's a story, too, about some green stones … Are you sure you don't know anything about this?"

"If the Mistress wants you to know anything, she'll tell you herself," was all Leara could say. Then she paused, realising that this was also true regarding her former husband. Valentina only told anyone what she wanted them to know, even her.

"Everyone here is nervous. Most of them have lived in the shadow of Castle Worthmere for generations. They're loyal, but no one likes change."

When they reached the turn-off from the hidden trade road to the campsite, they entered a broad road with trees and vegetation cut well back. The once small campsite was now a large settlement, with newly constructed buildings and boundary lines that were still expanding.

An officer was waiting for them. "Leara, you are to take the man you brought directly to Mistress Valentina," he instructed.

Leara and Remy escorted Radent down a new side road to the area where the mist usually appeared. There they found yet more new buildings. Another officer approached them. "Sorry, Leara. The mist has become somewhat erratic of late. We've not seen it for three days. Best you take one of the huts and wait it out. The longest interval so far has been seven days."

The newly constructed buildings at the site where the mist appeared would accommodate them while they waited. Twenty male and female soldiers waited in the barracks station, waiting for their turn to cross through the mist. Beside the barracks were six smaller outbuildings, only two of which were vacant. But one of the more senior soldiers offered his hut to them, he would share with a colleague, meaning each weary traveller would have a bed of their own. Leara told Radent that he wasn't to leave his hut and arranged a rotation of guards to be placed at his door.

She let Remy go exploring. He noticed how well the new streets of the settlement were organised, making it feel more like a village than a campsite. First he found the mess hall; he was hungry and craved a properly cooked meal instead of campfire food. Taking a large plate of vegetables and meat smothered in gravy, he sat at one of the long wooden tables. Six soldiers were talking openly behind him on another table.

"That's about thirty-eight we've lost now."

"Might be more than that," someone else chipped in gruffly. "And once the next mist appears there's bound to be more."

"It's not good here," continued the first voice. "Back at the castle there were risks, but I've never known these kinds of losses."

"Did you know that all the Mistresses and Masters have been sending teams through mists all over Parablion for years now?" said one of the women.

"Yeah, contractors and specially selected guards of Valentina's household, or so I've heard."

"How come we didn't know this before?" asked the first speaker.

Because it didn't concern you, thought Remy. Not until now, anyway.

"We don't remember," warned the gruff voice. "The sergeant says if we're caught talking about it outside the camp, we'll get our tongues cut out."

"Do you think he means it?" asked the female.

"Well, it's been a well-kept secret so far, so I would say so, yes," answered the gruff voice. "The Mistress is good to us and all her people, but we know she's capable of harsh punishments. I've heard stories that when she's off on her travels, someone always ends up dead."

"We must be staying here for a long time, seeing how she's brought people's families here all the way from the castle," said the first voice.

Gruff replied. "Rumour is she's done a deal with Anders Town that lets us stay here indefinitely."

Then the woman. "What kind of deal?"

"No idea but probably better trading prices."

"I wonder if they've caught any of the local villagers yet?" she asked.

The first man said, "I doubt it. No one's seen a single one since we invaded."

"Where've they gone, do you think?" This was another woman.

"Well, when they were in the village they could simply disappear into the jungle and you couldn't see them, even if they were mere feet away," said the gruff one. "I bet they're watching us – waiting to get their village back."

"There's no village to get back. The compound on the other side isn't much smaller than this one now," said the first speaker.

"Why do you think the mist isn't coming so frequently now?" said the second woman.

"No idea," answered gruff.

"Perhaps they're planning something. If they cut us off, for example then they only have to deal with them on the other side." suggested the first speaker.

"I don't like the sound of that," said the second woman.

"Me neither," added the first one. "Morale's always been good, but everyone's getting fed up now."

"Yeah," said the gruff voice. "Being a soldier used to be a good life – now every duty brings more risk."

Remy finished his meal, and left to discover what else had changed. The quartermaster's store had increased greatly in size, as had the stables and corral, which were still near the centre of the settlement. On the outskirts, protected by high spiked barriers, were new huts for newly arrived families, some of them finished, others still under construction. One area was now dedicated to trades – blacksmiths, saddlers, weapon smiths, leather-workers among others – and there was a well-guarded section for storing the supplies required to sustain a compound of this size. Remy recalled all the farming equipment on wagons that had come with them from Fallon. He had no doubt that this place was going to be permanent – for as long as the mist stayed, at least.

The last building he visited was the infirmary, where dozens of patients were bedded. No one challenged him as he walked through the first room. Many of them had insect-bite fevers and other strange jungle-related maladies. In another room, he found bandaged soldiers, some with limbs missing. It underlined the high cost of occupying the jungle. Remy wondered how long the Mistress's people would stay loyal under such circumstances.

Before settling down for the night, he visited Leara and told her everything that he'd heard and seen. She would know what to do and whether to tell the Mistress about it. Then he slept soundly on the first soft bed he'd laid on for a while.

Two days later, around mid-morning, the mist formed. Scores of people were alerted and gathered to wait their turn to cross over, but Leara, Remy and Radent went ahead of them all and passed through. Things had changed on the other side, too. In the clearing stood a new barracks and huts similar to the ones they'd just left behind, and a wide roadway led into the jungle towards the village. Soldiers were waiting around for their counterparts to arrive to relieve them of their duties. Once their replacements got through, they'd cross back to Parablion along with their wounded and sick.

Huge tree stumps decorated their route, some sixteen feet in circumference, felled for their timber. The cacophony of bird song, buzzing insects and bellows of unseen creatures was a sharp reminder of the dangers that surrounded them. Although the dense foliage skirting the wide road had been cut well back, there were no fences or barriers to prevent predators from emerging. As Remy wiped streams of sweat from his face, he remembered Valentina's warning that the smaller creatures here were the deadliest. He had slathered himself with the pungent ointment that kept the majority of insects at bay, yet he already had some bites.

The original village had gone altogether, replaced by a compound resembling the one on the other side of the mist. Leara asked for directions to reach Valentina and they were directed to the only two-storey building in the settlement. Two guards held sentry at the doorway. They prevented the three of them from entering the building without first being announced.

The inside of the spacious lobby was furnished with Parablion furniture. A wide staircase led to the upper level with several doorways off the landing. A servant greeted them and escorted them to a door on their right. They entered the room to find Mistress Valentina and, behind her, another woman and a couple of men. They weren't wearing any type of uniform and Valentina didn't introduce them.

"You must be Radent," she said.

"Yes, Mistress. It's nice to meet you." He gave a quick nod.

"I already have your news regarding where you last saw Beth Reach and the Fernish man, so what else can you offer me?"

"I know the lands beyond the mists and I can guide you through them and to the north of Fernish, where you'll find the woman you are looking for." He smiled weakly.

"Anything else?" Valentina's tone was flat and level, giving no indication of her mood.

"No, Mistress. It's just that I'm a seasoned mist walker. I hope that's of use to you."

Valentina drew her pistol and fired a dart at him before he or anyone else in the room could react. Radent reached for his own pistol, but the two men in the room set upon him, obviously expecting his response, and restrained him until the powerful sedative took effect.

"Leara," Valentina continued. "You will be going with Amena and Nesbur." She flicked her hand towards the hardy-looking woman with a scar running from her forehead across her left eye and down to her chin, and the younger more athletic man.

"Geles," she pointed to the older man "will travel some of the way with you, but he has a different route into Fernish. I've never asked you, Leara, are you afraid of heights?"

"I don't think so," Leara replied, feeling a little anxious.

"Good. Then you will leave immediately – while the mist is here."

"But we've only just arrived, Mistress," said Remy.

"I am aware of that. You, Remy, will be staying here. I have assigned you to Rust. He's a good soldier and he will start your training and education."

"I'm not going with Leara?"

"No. It's far too dangerous." Valentina held up her hand before Remy could raise any objections. "You need to train and improve in all areas. When you are good enough you will work for me as a mist walker, like these here."

The door opened and six soldiers filed into the room. They removed all Radent's weapons and shackled him in irons and chains before leading him away.

"Now, you need to be going, Leara. Don't miss the mist."

Within the hour Leara was on the road again. She rode her newly acquired gausent beside Amena, who explained where they were going and why. They had a two-day ride north to a known mist bank. There, they would cross to Ummit, a poisonous moss land and the only way to get from Parablion to Rishan, then they'd travel onward to Fernish. She explained that Valentina had assembled her and the other two mist walkers specifically because they'd all made it to Fernish before, and she (and she alone) had been as far as the northern region. Their mission now was to retrieve Beth, alive – at any cost. All of this was based on the assumption that Beth was still in Fernish.

"It will take us three days to cross the mosslands and you won't be able to eat when we're there. The poison in the air sticks to any surface and quickly impregnates food. It rapidly increases in toxicity when it does that. But you will be able to drink, conservatively, and when we get there you'll need to wash everything in saltwater. It's the only thing that neutralises the poison."

"Why are there so many of us?" Leara asked. As well as the three mist walkers and herself, and Radent in chains, there was a contingency of thirty-six armed soldiers.

"You, me and Nesbur are going directly into the northern region of Fernish along with three specially selected soldiers. The rest will enter the Fernish lowlands. They'll join us later. Our objective is to find Beth Reach and take her. If we can't take her, then we wait for Geles and the other soldiers to do so – by any means. Geles and the others are the back-up option. We have to make every effort to get hold of her before they catch up with us. These northern Fernish are really tough bastards, though, and their mist walkers are some of the best fighters I've ever seen. No matter what's ahead of us, it won't be easy. This Beth must be worth quite something ..." she mused.

They made camp where the mist was known to form. Four soldiers took their mounts to the nearby village of Irus, where they would stay until the mist walkers returned. The mist here appeared at dawn at fairly regular intervals. It formed afresh after their second night at the camp. A variety of prey animals gathered just before the mist arrived. Leara was astounded – surely their instincts would alert them to the danger?

"Giant frogs," Amena told her. "They guard this mist. Look at them! Twice the size of an average gausent and they will eat you if they catch you. Their tongues shoot out nearly twenty feet and once they've got you it's hard to escape. They pull you at great speed into those huge wide mouths and crush you. Their skin is dangerous too, coated in the toxin in far more concentration than what's in the air or on the plants."

The enormous frogs leaped about with their muscular tongues darting, feasting on small deer, wild pigs, rabbits, even birds. The smaller prey was gulped down immediately then their tongues shot out for more. Some of the frogs captured larger, heavier animals and crushed them in their gaping mouths before jumping back into the mist.

A large Parablion vember crashed through the undergrowth and mounted one of the frogs, flashing past them in a whir of grey and black. It raked its claws across the back of a frog and sank its sharp teeth in repeatedly, looking for a vulnerable spot. The frog ignored the animal tearing at its back, and within seconds it fell to the ground motionless, incapacitated by the frog's poisonous coating. Then the frog took the predator turned prey with a quick snap of the tongue and disappeared into the mist.

"Now!" ordered Amena. According to prearranged instructions they all charged forwards through the frogs towards the mist. Two remaining frogs managed to take a soldier each before accompanying the racing horde into the mist.

On the other side, Leara sank almost shin-deep in a soft, damp, thick moss that carpeted the ground. The air was wet, making it uncomfortable to breathe. It was not humid like in the jungle, but as though water hung in the air, and it had an aroma of wet dirt. Large huge-leafed plants rose twenty foot above them. The sun was already setting and they had orders to follow it.

A briefing was delivered by the mist walkers to everyone gathered on the mossy terrain. The tension was high. They were not to travel at night – when it was at its most dangerous. They were to wrap themselves completely in a broad leaf before sleeping, and wait until the light came the following morning before surfacing. When they wrapped themselves, they were to leave no gaps – if they did so they could be discovered by predators – or worse. Amena would instigate the morning move by waking those next to her, they, in turn, would wake others, and so on. There would be no roll call, no large mustering. They were to rely on their training to keep others in sight at all times. There would be deaths, unfortunately – not everyone would reach the next mist. They would encounter steep climbs and descents and sink-pools that looked just like the moss that lay everywhere, but which hid a thick ooze just beneath the surface that would suck them down until they drowned. They weren't to stop and help anyone who fell behind, whether they were stuck in a sink-pool, attacked by wild creatures, or overcome by the poison of the terrain. Although the air-borne toxin was weak, it would eventually overcome them if they were exposed to it for long. Speed was the only way to survive here and they had to reach the next exit point as quickly as possible.

Amena had agreed to oversee Leara because she was essential if they were to take Beth peacefully. Leara appreciated her guidance and assistance during the three hungry days it took to arrive on the sandy shores of Rishan, ten soldiers down.

Radent survived. Nesbur and Geles had seen to that. His leg irons had been removed but his wrist shackles remained in place; a leather strap around his neck attached to a lead had kept him in line. During the nights, Valentina's special mist walkers lay either side of him, sandwiching his leafy envelope between them. On the beach they let him go into the sea to wash, after secured his leg irons again, the leash still in place.

"Cember is three to four hours' walk from here," Amena told Leara. "There we will equip ourselves for Fernish and part with Geles."

After a far more pleasant walk over fertile green land, Leara saw on the distant horizon large stone stacks rising from the ground. As they got closer, she saw that they were towers, spread out as far as her eyes could see. This was Cember. She'd been warned to avoid any trouble here and not to grab or hold any of the towns people.

Amena and Nesbur said their farewells to Geles, leaving the older mist walker to continue further overland with the bulk of the soldiers and Radent, then they led Leara and three soldiers towards one of the stacks, mounting the steps and descending on the other side into the lush interior of Cember. They walked along a broad bright colourful street, illuminated by reflections of the sun's rays. Countless busy people in colourful robes rushed all around them. Their skin was quite pale, paler than Leara had expected and she was astonished at the lack of visible weapons – they were so necessary in Parablion.

"Right," said Amena. "Tonight we can rest, once we have picked up supplies. This might be our last decent sleep for a while now. Leara and I will get the food and sundries. You three go with Nesbur for the specialist gear. Listen to everything he tells you as though it were an order from Valentina herself."

Once the four of them departed Amena relaxed visibly; the change in posture and demeanour surprised Leara.

"I like it here," Amena said, her voice now free of its usual hardness and aggressive undertones. "There's rarely any trouble or hassle, but you still have to be careful."

Her features and eyes had softened, too. She was almost smiling. "First things first, though – a bath! These are the best bathing houses anywhere."

***

An attendant pulled a chain and steaming hot water flowed out into a large circular tub until it was filled. Amena stripped naked and climbed into it. Leara followed. When they were submerged and soaking up the delicious feeling, the attendant returned and took away their clothes. They would be laundered and brought back while they washed and relaxed.

"Where has Geles gone?" asked Leara.

"Oh. He's here too, in Cember. Just in a different area. They have a longer journey to the next mist they need to cross. They will hire mounts and ride to Ynew, about a day from here. Then they'll cross into the Fernish lowlands."

Leara ducked her head below the water. She resurfaced with a question. "What of Radent? How far behind us will they be?"

"It will take them maybe six more days than us to get to the northern region," said Amena creating a foamy lather with the soap in her hair. "That's assuming they can traverse the desert. Without the locals and the use of their tomeruscks, they won't be able to cross."

"Tomeruscks?" asked Leara.

"Giant silver-haired creatures that cross the desert without water. They drink gallons of water and bloat to hold it while they cross the hot sands for days. And they can carry a tent on their back that seats six, and all the equipment. Without them and a guide, Geles won't be able to follow us."

"How will he secure a guide? I thought the Fernish hated outsiders."

Amena, ducked below the water to rinse out her hair before rising to reply. "Geles has been visiting here for a while, establishing good relationships for Valentina. They hate mist walkers – even their own from the north. The lowlanders don't cross the mists. They wish there were no mists. Geles has learned their tongue. He picks up languages like and I would pick up ale in a tavern! That's were Radent comes in."

"How?" asked Leara.

"Of all the Masters and Mistresses, they hate Brigges the most. His mist walkers have been stealing their people for a long time now. Geles will tell them that Brigges is dead, and that Radent was the one stealing their people. The chief of one village in the lowlands might well recognise Radent, as he lost a daughter to Brigges – if he does, that serves us better. But Geles will convince them of Radent's guilt, regardless. He'll give them Radent as a gift and ask for a guide and tomeruscks to take them north. He can be very convincing. I'd be surprised if he doesn't succeed."

"What will happen to Radent?"

"They will bury him to his neck in the sand next to an anthill. No ordinary anthill, mind. The pain when these things bite is like a hot burn. It will take him days to die, very painfully, while the ants pick at him and slowly take every soft part of him back to their nest as food."

Leara wasn't entirely sure that allowing the Fernish to

torture Radent was necessary, but there was nothing she could do about that now. She wondered if Valentina knew what was to happen to Radent and decided, without doubt, that she did. There was so much that she still didn't know about her new lover, she realised.

"So how do we get into Fernish? You haven't told me much about how or why we are going ahead."

"Remember Valentina asking you about heights?"

"Yes."

"Well, our mist opens out onto the face of a mountain. A steep hard climb on rocky terrain. We may get lucky and step through onto a ledge, but most likely we'll be on an almost sheer face with a long drop below."

"The northern Rishan are good climbers, then?"

"They probably are, but they rely on maleks. They can ride up and down such terrain. We won't have maleks, so we will need to climb. The soldiers with us are experienced climbers, as is Nesbur. You're the only novice. What's more, we'll need to cross at night, and climb even higher to avoid their patrols around the mist. If they see us while we're climbing, we're as good as dead. Getting out we might have to risk the same. But if Geles arrives, we might be able to travel back over the desert."

"We're going to climb a mountain in the dark?"

"That's why we need Nesbur. He's not only a decent climber – his incant allows him to see in the dark for short periods of time. That should be enough for him to pick the safest route up the rock and secure some anchor points along the way to help us. You'll be the next to last to go through. I'll be behind you so I can collect any anchors that Nesbur uses."

"Sounds very risky."

"Oh, it is. Just don't look down! And make sure you have a good grip each time before moving up. I might be able to help you at times, and Nesbur and the soldiers will be able to pull you some of the way. We will all be roped together."

Washed and dressed in clean clothes they went shopping for supplies. Due to the vibrant fresh environment, Leara actually enjoyed the experience.

Later Nesbur dropped off her new gear. They were going to a hot climate, but because of the height he brought her warm clothing. The nights would be cold. He instructed her to wrap everything in the cloth he provided, as none of her equipment, packed or worn, could be allowed to rattle. The slightest noise would alert the Fernish patrols. Tomorrow they would cross overland, on foot, and that would allow them to check how well she had muffled her outfit and equipment.

They stayed away from the beach that night as they camped, just in case any Fernish mist walkers were making a crossing. Then, in the early morning, they gathered on the sand as the mist appeared. Crossing here not long after dawn would take them into the darkness of night on the other side.

***

Leara lost her footing almost immediately. She had done as instructed and crawled through the mist, taking a good hold of anything ahead of her. As her right hand passed out on the other side she thought she had a solid grip on the rock surface. However, as she moved on, the sudden change from horizontal to vertical completely disorientated her and she let go. The rope around her waist snapped taut – they had expected her to fall and drag Amena with her too. Amena reached out silently in the darkness and pulled herself back onto a solid surface – albeit vertical –and then she helped Leara get a good grip on the rock wall. Recovering quickly, and appreciating the precariousness of their situation, Leara found a firm handhold and began to climb, taking the tension off the rope. She gave it her best effort, but on more than half a dozen occasions she fell and found herself dangling in the darkness. The experienced climbers somehow managed to retain their hold and saved her. Amena climbed alongside her sometimes, helping her to find, reach and use the right footholds and handholds. There were some easier sections, but Leara's hands went numb in the cold so nothing was simple for her.

The rope tightened as Leara was pulled up the next section; she had no need to climb. As she broached a wide ledge, Nesbur whispered in her ear to put her back against the wall and stay still. There would be no more climbing tonight.

The dawn was magnificent. From their high vantage point they could see a great distance across the rock formations and out into the vast desert beyond. It seemed bleak and alien to Leara, with no safe way in any direction to flat horizontal ground. Looking along the ledge she saw the three soldiers and Nesbur, but no sign of Amena.

"Where's Amena?"

"Gone to find a safe place and get her bearings," replied the nearest soldier, a fresh-faced man who'd not long left his boyhood behind.

They ate cold rations and drank from their flasks while waiting for the mist walker to return. It was mid-morning when she did and the temperature had already started to become uncomfortable in their warm clothing.

"The climb's easier from here," Amena announced. "There are small tracks and a few areas to slide comfortably and then a wider outcrop that will be almost a walk, to a plateau. Their cave-village is to the south."

And at that, they set off again.

"How do you know about this place?" Leara asked Amena when they were finally on level ground.

"That's what we do, mist walkers, whether from Parablion or other lands. We explore, look for opportunities, answers. I've been doing this for two years now, but other lands have known about the mists for decades, maybe more. Valentina wants to know what's out there. One thing we have always got to ask about is whether Orestas Connroy ever visited any place we find. She is obsessed with that old spellbinder."

"Oh, yes. I'm aware of that."

"Trading out here is nearly impossible. If you can't carry it, then there's no way to get it through the mist, either because of terrains like the mosslands or predators. Then there's the language barrier. Here, if they catch us, they *will* kill us. I came here to scout with three others last year … and I was the only one that got back home. I've stayed away ever since."

"What's the plan now?"

"Well, we see if that woman is here. We keep out of sight. If we see her, we try and take her, or we wait for Geles and try to take her. If she's not here, we go home and tell Valentina."

They finally reached a flat plateau. Ahead of them were numerous other tabletops of rock; some below and some above. The maze of canyons and ravines that divided them formed a dark lattice of shadows that stretched for miles. It wouldn't be easy to navigate through them. They also needed to watch for predators that stalked the rocks, perfectly camouflaged amid their surroundings. In such a barren landscape, any potential prey was worth investigating. And on top of all that, there was the permanent risk of being spotted by one of the patrols.

They made camp early in the day, in a shaded hollow in one of the rock faces, not quite a cave but deep enough to hide them. Amena told them to leave their warmer clothing here, and the wrappings used to muffle their equipment. She doubted they'd need them again because if they found Beth she assumed a pursuit would follow and if they didn't find her, they would probably return with Geles.

"A couple of miles along in a straight line is the village." Amena pointed into the distance. "Getting there means climbing and walking through canyons and over flat plateaus, which adds a lot more distance and time."

Leara nodded.

"I know I said they live in caves, but that's not quite true," Amena explained. "What they have done is carved homes – with doors, windows, stairways and so on – into the rock wall. I don't propose we explore inside them as we have no way of knowing what's inside or how to hide our pale skin among these people."

"So what do you propose?" asked Leara.

"We find a spot to watch the space outside and look for another pale skin. Leara, we've never seen this Beth Reach, so you'll need to confirm that it's her. Once they see us they'll come after us relentlessly until they capture us or kill us; either way, we'll die."

She turned to Nesbur. "Hand out the eyeglasses now. You have to keep the lenses out of the sun. One flashy reflection will bring them straight to us. Stay back in shadow as best you can and do not angle the eyeglass to the sun."

A day and a half later, after climbing up and down rock walls, winding through dark shadowy ravines and crossing scorching plateaus, they were almost at the village. The six of them had climbed to a high point overlooking the flat-topped mountains around them. Amena scouted ahead with her eyeglass from a sheltered position. The others stayed low, not breaking the horizon. It was soon obvious that something had gained the Amena's attention.

"This is too easy," she said as she handed her eyeglass to Leara. "Look. In that direction. On top of that plateau, two away from where we are now, there are two stone buildings. A pale-skinned woman is sitting outside the smaller one. Is it her?"

Leara took the viewing position. She located the buildings but there was no one to be seen. Scanning the area, she was startled, astounded even, to see green stone pillars. Returning her gaze to the buildings, she observed an old dark-skinned man and a younger woman approaching the smaller building. Then Beth came out to meet them.

"That's her," declared Leara, returning to the group.

"Geles is perhaps four to six days away from us," said Amena.

"Or not coming at all," Nesbur reminded them all.

"We'll need to deal with that when it happens. Is this Beth dangerous?" Amena asked Leara.

"I've not seen her for a while, but she's most definitely not a spellbinder or a seeder and she's never had any real fight training."

"Then we should be able to handle her if we take her. Alive, remember! They are isolated from the rest of the village, but for how long we cannot know, so we take her now. Well, tomorrow, by the time we manoeuvre over there. Then we run and hide and head for the desert and wait for Geles. They won't expect us to go towards the sand, they'll expect us to go for the mist, and that might buy us time."

"And if Geles doesn't show up?"

"Then it will have to be the mist."

They moved on ever more cautiously, walking, hiding, climbing. Finally, they reached a ledge twenty feet below the flat plateau of the two stone buildings. Once they breached the surface there would be little to no cover. The only thing that would conceal them were the two buildings themselves. It would be dark in an hour and then they would move. Nesbur, using his incant, would establish where Beth was and then they would snatch her. No talking and instructions to kill anyone in their way. They could attempt to reason with Beth later, but being in and out as quickly as possible was the plan.

***

Beth said goodnight to Orldrey and entered her hut. The old man returned to his. That's when Amena gave her signal and the six moved silently across the plateau until they were behind the long building, concealed from sight. They waited for a short while, Amena allowing their objective to settle. Then she moved them forward.

Amena's plan was simple: ambush the woman, disable her, silence her, bind her and then go back the way they had come, lowering the captive on ropes. They'd left some lines anchored on the rock face so that they might escape quickly. Then they simply had to avoid capture until they met Geles.

Amena and Nesbur broke away and charged stealthily, followed by two of the soldiers. Amena had seen the soft glow of a hearth fire from inside. That would be all the light they needed. The hut only seemed to have one entrance and the room was too small for Beth to hide away, therefore her plan was for the four of them to crash through the door and pounce in the confusion.

Once inside, they immediately saw a bundle wrapped in the bed sheets and dived on top of it.

Three of them held the body down, while Amena pulled back the covers to expose the woman's face to strike her unconscious. But when she did so, a large black fist smashed into her face and she tumbled backwards onto the floor. The nearest soldier was grabbed by the neck and thrown towards the hearth. The next took a knee to his nose which exploded in a bloody mess. Nesbur took a foot to the head. Now free of his attackers, Jallon was free to stand. Stark naked and totally unarmed, he continued his onslaught. He wrestled the man with the smashed nose until he crumpled to the floor; took the other soldier's knife from the sheath on his belt and cut his throat.

As Amena tried to rise she saw her comrade felled by the muscular man. She could tell he was already dead; his arms went limp and he made no effort to clutch his severed throat to stem the flow of blood. Almost on her feet Amena saw that Beth was standing upright, as naked as Jallon, and watched her pounce on Nesbur as he drew his pistol. She knocked the pistol aside with ease and a dart fired into the floor. Amena was astonished by how quickly their target moved. She watched Beth grab Nesbur's wrist, preventing him from taking aim, as her free hand balled into a tight fist and struck him in the throat. The blow was precise.

Their victim was not as defenceless as they had been led to believe.

Nesbur was struggling to breathe and was choking as Beth knocked the pistol from his hand, but then Nesbur drew out his dagger with his other hand. Despite battling to breathe, Nesbur was still fighting. Beth simply ignored the man's feint and counter with the knife. Amena realised, as she closed the gap between them, that the naked woman was already ahead of Nesbur's attack. She struck his left temple hard with a knuckle extended from her fist. Nesbur's gaze lost focus. A second blow and he fell unconscious to the floor.

Amena reached out to grasp Beth but missed her entirely. She was on the move again, racing outside to following the naked man who was locked in combat with a female soldier. Amena went out behind her.

The two of them had rolled out on to the open ground beyond the hut and the naked man was on his feet, seemingly having the advantage.

Thud! Thud! Thud! Three arrows struck Jallon's chest, where his heart lay. Amena looked to the source and saw Leara with another arrow nocked and aimed at the naked woman.

Then a man rushed out through the door of the longer building, brandishing a sword in his right hand. The other soldier, lying in wait, lunged with his dagger at the old man's neck, but the man saw the blow coming and twisted to avoid it. The blade merely cut a fine line across his neck. He spun on his assailant and plunged his sword deep into his stomach, and sliced it upwards into his chest. The weight of the falling body took the sword with it, disarming the old man.

Amena felt the air go still, just for the briefest part of a second, and time seemed to slow. The woman soldier who had tumbled from the cottage, with the black man had her pistol half drawn from its holster and was staring at Beth. Leara, too, had a steady aim but had not yet loosed her arrow, watching the naked man who stood stock still, both hands clutching at the arrows in his chest. Then he fell limply to the ground. The old man was running towards them.

The stillness in the air shattered. A ball of flame, so hot that Amena could feel the heat from where she stood, engulfed Leara. With her pistol still aimed at Beth, the other woman was wrapped in crackling light and started convulsing grotesquely.

Beth was the source of both magical strikes. Not only had she released both attacks, but she was also holding them, prolonging their effect. The ball of fire surged more strongly and Leara turned black where she stood, her skin charred. The other woman soldier was still convulsing, her face turned blue and her swollen tongue protruded from her mouth. Her eyes bulged and popped, thick fluid bursting over her face before evaporating into the night air.

Amena wanted to move but she couldn't. One hand went up and felt a dagger protruding from side of her neck. She had seen the old man hurl a blade at her, but was so stunned by the outburst of powerful magic that her instinct was dulled; she hadn't thought to dodge out of its way.

Then the magic stopped, the flames died down and the charred remains of Leara and that of the convulsing grotesquely faced woman soldier crumpled to the ground. It was the last thing Amena ever saw.

"You'll be fine," whispered Beth, rocking her lover in her arms. "You will just heal like you always do."

Orldrey put a hand on her shoulder, and with the other he checked the fallen mist walker for a pulse, and did not find one. Leaving Beth with her sorrow, he walked away, towards her hut, knowing that there may still be danger close by.

"Help! We are under attack!" he hollered loudly and repeatedly as he cautiously approached the building. Inside he found one dead body and another, unconscious but still alive. Outside he heard other people arriving at the scene – friends, not foes.

Taking the unconscious man by the ankle, Orldrey dragged him outside. The warriors immediately took the intruder from him and hauled him away, taking him off the plateau to a secure holding.

The old man gave instructions to have the other bodies

removed and for everyone to move back, away from Beth.

Aving arrived and started issuing orders for those gathered to search every location nearby and to alert the patrols that they had intruders. Beth was oblivious to it all. She was silent now, her face buried against the man she loved.

She was still there when dawn broke. The plateau was clear of people. Only Orldrey watched over her from a seat outside his cottage. Beth finally got to her feet, lifting Jallon in her arms, cradling him to her bosom, then she walked slowly and steadily towards the Stones. She crossed the threshold without hesitation, and Jallon evaporated into a cloud of dust. Beth continued walking towards the centre of the Stones.

Orldrey watched with a heavy heart. He had lost his own love many years earlier but he still carried the scars. A solitary tear rolled down his cheek. He hoped Beth would recover, perhaps not completely, but enough to carry on life herself. Then Beth disappeared from view. Orldrey stood, thinking she had collapsed to the ground and he had missed it. But no, she had vanished from the plateau completely.

SEVENTEEN

Beth found herself back in the middle of the tall green stone columns. Pain assaulted her immediately, momentarily ripping her from her grief, but her instincts for survival kicked in and she raced away from the centre and the Stones, unsure of what was happening or where she was.

Once she was standing outside the perimeter, the pain faded. She looked around, realising where she was but not quite able to believe it.

"I thought this might be how you would return to us. I have waited every day," said a familiar voice.

At first she couldn't make out the silhouette of the small black man in the darkness, but when he stepped closer she recognised him as Copo.

"I hid. Silent. In secret place – tunnel that goes from chamber of Stones to jungle. Tiid help me so I can rest. But many days, many weeks I am there."

He clasped her hand in his, and pulled at it gently. "Now. Quick. We must not stand out here. Valentina visit often, sometimes just her. Sometimes with person to sacrifice."

He paid no regard to the fact that Beth was naked. "Quick. Follow me."

The tunnel was narrow, and at times they had to crawl. It was in absolutely darkness and Beth felt the swell of anxiety as her childhood phobia of confined spaces overcame her senses. She pushed back the irrational fear, only for it to be replaced by another. The cramped passageway had no supporting structure; it had simply been carved through rock and earth. What if it collapsed and buried them alive?

She didn't know how long they had been in there, but she was extremely glad to be breathing the hot, humid jungle air once again, and hearing the loud chatters and calls of the jungle animals. She lay flat on her back staring upwards into the green canopy above.

Copo stood nearby, waiting. She needed a moment, and with Copo paying attention to their surroundings rather than the naked woman sprawled before him, she felt that she had time for that. There were no signs or sounds of any hunting groups from Valentina's compound and she knew Copo would dismiss any lurking predators. After all, he had waited this long already – a few more minutes would not bother him.

Beth finally got to her feet. In those few moments she had contemplated her life, or rather, whether she wanted to continue living. She knew Jallon would not be proud of her if she simply gave up; nor would he expect her, a Guardian, to do so. She had a purpose, one she didn't yet know, but it was one that Jallon had dedicated his life to. She took some consolation from that. Her grief was all too real, but so was her desire to meet the expectations of her one true love. She also wanted – needed – to know why Valentina had sent people after her, a thwarted plan that had taken Jallon away from her.

"Are you well?" asked Copo.

"Well enough. Why have you waited for me?"

"To show you."

They strolled through the tangled undergrowth, easily finding their way along what sometimes seemed an impossible path. Beth had forgotten how much she had enjoyed the jungle and the carefree attitude of the villagers. She wondered how they were faring, and what impact Valentina's occupation was having on them.

Copo stopped suddenly. A large sabre-toothed, sharp-clawed beast of the jungle crossed their path. It sniffed at the air, taking in their scent, and then moved on, its tail flipping insects aside as it disappeared. Only then did it occur to Beth that she was naked, without the pungent ointment that keeps the insects at bay, yet she had not been bitten or stung once.

They came to a large pond that stank of stagnation. The foliage of the nearby plants had turned yellow and brown and the spot didn't look healthy – a blemish on the otherwise green lush thriving environment of the jungle. They skirted around the body of water and as they did so they came across several rotting animal carcasses.

"Is this what you want to show me?" Beth asked.

"Yes."

"Why is this happening?

"The jungle lose balance. Magic that keeps balance – now bad," Copo said.

"But why? How?"

"I show you."

They walked for a couple more hours until nightfall approached. Beth heard the noise first. The jungle was always, night and day, alive with the calls of animals and the sounds of insects, but the din she heard now was not natural here. They crouched down and Copo picked a careful path forward.

Torches and lanterns shone ahead, as far as she could see. They were within touching distance of a tall spiked barricade wall. Beyond the defences, she saw scores of buildings and vast numbers of Parablionions milling around within a large compound. Valentina had been busy, it seemed. Then it dawned on her – this was the site of the original village, now decimated – destroyed in fact – to make way for Valentina's occupation. She reached out and touched Copo with sympathy and he met and held her gaze. Then they turned and disappeared back into the darkness.

***

The hut was small. Not even Copo could stand up inside it, but they could both sit or lie down comfortably. From the outside it was total invisible, well camouflaged so that it blended in seamlessly with the surrounding vegetation. A dim light came from a transparent container with glowing insects inside; the container itself was woven from a kind of leaf Beth hadn't seen before. Tiid had joined them not long after they'd arrived, and now the three of them sat in a small circle facing each other.

"I'm sorry. I didn't know." Beth said. She was still naked; there was no clothing for her here and it didn't seem necessary anyway, to cover herself. So she didn't.

"No. Not your fault. We knew when no more predators come from mist, someone come through next," said Copo.

"Not what expected – but did expect some sort of problem," added Tiid.

"What can I do to help?"

"Tell us where you went? What you learned?" suggested Copo.

Beth opened up about everything. Her grief was raw but so far she had contained it, but now it overflowed as she told her tale. She recounted her escape with Nyser, how she walked into the Stones of Fernish and ended up in the jungle of Deline, about her love for Jallon and her recent loss of him.

"I had never cast those spellbinder spells before," she said. "I had no idea I could do that.".

"Strong ...", he struggled to find the right words, "emotion and want to strike back release something inside you? " said Tiid.

"Perhaps," was her reply.

"You see the centre of our Stones now?" asked Copo.

"Yes, I suppose I have."

"Was something Valentina want to possess?" questioned Tiid.

Beth thought back to her recent arrival. She recalled the intense pain, but also the fact that there was nothing other than hard rocky ground and surrounding green pillars at the centre of their group of Stones.

"There was nothing there!" she exclaimed with sudden realisation.

"Yes, we know. But could not tell you or Valentina. She not believe us," said Copo. "Orestas come back one day. Left knowledge and secrets – not something you can hold. When he come back last time, he give himself to Stones and was cloud of dust, like we all are one day."

"History says he died at home. I've learned that much," stated Beth.

"History can be written in many ways – depend on who writes it," suggest Tiid with a shrug.

"So Valentina will never leave here. There's nothing here for her to find, but she will never believe that." Beth could now see the dilemma they faced.

"This is problem we must solve. Her presence here harms the balance," said Tiid.

"Can't you just drive her out?" Asked Beth

"Perhaps. We are not warriors, but will fight if we need to – or have to. But she will just bring more soldiers," Copo said despondently.

"Then kill her," said Beth – without any emotion whatsoever. She knew it was a viable solution.

"You would murder?" asked Tiid.

Beth thought about it. She had taken more than one life now. In a fight, she would kill as necessary, but cold-blooded murder was not something she could bring herself to do – even if she created the pretence of a fight or battle to cover up such a deed. Perhaps she could hire someone to do it for her. But that, too, was indirectly the same; she couldn't do it. Maybe she could explain to Valentina that there was nothing left behind by Orestas; but again, the Mistress wouldn't believe her.

"No. I will not murder." Beth sighed, accepting totally

that she would not. "But, then, she cannot live forever. Her people will leave when she dies."

"Perhaps yes. Perhaps no." Copo said sadly – something Beth hadn't heard before from one of the locals. "When your people think they own something, they not want to let it go," he continued. "The more they here, the more imbalance."

"I don't have the answers," she admitted.

"Stay with us for while, Beth," said Tiid. "Learn something of us you not know before you become Guardian. Give you insight. Perhaps way forward."

"Where else would I go anyway?" she asked.

"Back to Fernish," Tiid responded without hesitation.

"Ah, but the journey would take far too long. And I have no coin or supplies." Beth heard the sound of her own defeat in her words.

"Why you need these things? You come by the Stones and you can go by the Stones," Copo said.

The following morning, Tiid re-introduced Beth to the villagers. They were all settled nearby, but their homes were hidden in plain sight, indistinguishable from the natural flora and landscape.

When they were on their own again, Beth questioned Tiid. "Copo said last night I should learn from your people something I don't already know. What did he mean by that?"

"Magic different everywhere, but you know that. Your magic – from Parablion – is destructive, aggressive, must be caught, held, then forced out. Magic not like work this way. Our magic – most magic – is in balance with environment and people. We exist as part of environment, part of all

318

things. Only take what we need so the jungle treat us well. You – from Parablion – do not have balance. Perhaps this is what he mean?"

Beth stayed with the villagers for a couple of days. She wore wrappings as clothing, provided by the women of the concealed village. She ate with them, cleaned, cooked and hunted with them, observing them in detail, trying to better understand the balance Tiid and Copo had referred to. She observed that they only took from the jungle what they needed, never storing or oversupplying themselves in any way. They were delicate with the plants and fauna, careful not to snap, break or damage anything they encountered. The animals, even the predators, paid them little attention. The villagers ate meat and so they killed, but they selected their prey with care, taking just old, injured or weak animals that would struggle to survive the hardships of the jungle. If they found no suitable prey, they ate fruit or root vegetables. At first, Beth saw this as submission or fear. They didn't want to threaten the food chain in any way, or threaten the larger animals and thus make themselves prey, or damage the jungle so that the smaller creatures, which ignored them usually, began to give them poisonous bites and stings.

One morning in the village, Beth awoke to find her own low hut occupied by a myriad of jungle creatures: small furry animals, snakes, spiders, large insects – spikes, fangs, claws and paws of every description. They were crammed inside her small lodging. She was scared initially, but once she realised they weren't harming her she relaxed a little. There had to be a reason for their presence. Carefully, avoiding stepping on or injuring any animal in her path, she left the hut. Copo was waiting patiently outside. She had no idea how long he'd been there. Maybe he'd put all the animals in her hut.

"They sense your grief and power, Beth," he said. "Do you know you still cry when you sleep? It will pass, but pain will always be with you." He smiled reassuringly at her. "Remember good things and cherish them, then you will move on."

"Did you put them there?" Beth point back inside her hut.

"No. They seek you out. Imbalance is growing – they wish to be your companion."

"Companion? But why?" Her face creased in puzzlement.

"Your spellbinders name them 'familiars'."

"I don't know anything about familiars. Only that spellbinders hold them in great favour."

"You have much to learn, Beth, but little time. Balance must be restored to jungle soon. Valentina began destruction, by sacrifice many of your people to Stones, by ravaging jungle. This the animals know. They sense that you are the only one who can restore balance."

"Why do I need a familiar now, then? What good will it do?" she asked.

"Perhaps you do not need one. You know Stones create magic. And create mist. They make sure mists are guarded by predators and other obstacles."

"Are the Stones alive, then? Is that what you're telling me?"

"No. Not alive. Only keep balance. Mists exist so Guardian move quickly across lands to Stone outcrops, to keep balance."

"How do you know all this, Copo?"

"It is why I exist. My predecessors, my descendants, and I – we pass on all knowledge we acquire through generations. We know Guardian is important and risks everywhere if no Guardian – or if Guardian does not keep balance. I am much like your Orldrey who you mention in Fernish."

Beth took all of this on board, but she was still curious. "So what is a familiar, then?" she asked.

"Your spellbinders take magic – turn it into destructive force. It upsets balance. Magic found solution – created bonds with familiars. Familiars connect to balance in perfect harmony. They help spellbinders focus, give them greater ability. So spellbinders care for them. Familiars balance out negative effects of destructive magic – so help balance good."

"Do spellbinders know this?"

"I think no. They simply desire extra ability that familiars offer."

"So why are all these animals inside my hut?"

"You have used destructive magic. Jungle is sick. They seek to give you balance so you might save us all."

"But I have no idea how to do that."

At that moment a huge male avemont entered the small clearing where they were seated. The apex predator of the jungle, as tall as Beth at the shoulders and twice as long, lean and muscular, with aggressive horns, savage fangs and razor-sharp clawed paws. It resembled a vember, although much larger and more powerful. Its black and green striped fur blended perfectly with the environment.

Copo and Beth froze when they saw it. If they ran or made a sudden movement it might alarm the beast. They needed to trust the balance – the magic that these people possessed to keep them safe. But that balance was under threat; so would it hold now?

The avemont sniffed at Copo, just inches from his face, then it turned towards Beth. It sniffed again; then again. Seemingly satisfied with the presence of the two people, it sat down in front of them. On its way through the jungle, it had caught the scent of the creatures inside the hut. Its ears rotated as it identified the other villagers and animals in the vicinity then, reassured that it was in no immediate danger, it lay down, its head lying against Beth's lap.

"Something new to tell," said Copo, smiling.

"What?" asked Beth, her gaze darting between him and the creature lying against her.

"Even the great avemont would be your familiar. The threat here must be grave indeed. We have very little time left, I think."

"I can't possibly take him as my familiar." She pointed at the beast, then quickly stopped in case it intimidated him in some way. "He wouldn't fit in any pocket."

"You must find solution soon. Time is dwindling ..."

"You're the one that knows everything, Copo. You tell me what I'm supposed to do," she implored.

"I only know what I know," replied the little man. His tone was calm and measured. "What has been passed on by my predecessors and the few other Guardians we meet. This Orldrey, he has much written knowledge you say. Maybe he has an answer in those books that not yet discovered."

"So things are so bad that urgent action is needed – and you want me to go and *read*?" There was despair in her tone.

"What else can you do?" he smiled reassuringly, as though they had all the time they needed.

So that was that. Beth would return to Fernish, even though she had no idea how to.

Beth stood in the cave with Copo and Tiid, staring at the green pillars. She knew they would cause her pain and how severe that pain would be. Yet she had been able to flee them without collapsing when she had arrived that way; that was some sort of progress.

"So how does this work?"

"On that, we cannot help you. You are the Guardian, not us."

Beth recalled how she had arrived. She had just lost Jallon. Her grief was such that she wanted to die herself. She no longer wanted to be where she was – and then she hadn't been. I should just want to be back at Fernish with all my heart, Beth thought. Maybe that's all it takes?

"See you soon," she said, and ran into the Stones. She headed straight for the centre, assuming that was the point of departure and arrival. The pain was instantaneous as she crossed the perimeter; she faltered, stumbled a little, but persevered. Fernish, Fernish, Fernish, she thought. Then the pain was gone.

***

It was early evening on the plateau and the cooling air was pleasant after the heat and humidity of the jungle.

Rettia was sitting outside the long stone cottage. She saw Beth and called for Orldrey. The old man offered his condolences, as did Rettia. Beth thanked them but quickly broke the sombre mood by declaring that they had a plight far more demanding than her grief to tackle. She wasted no time informing the stone keeper and historian of her recent experience and what she had learned in the jungle, and that the hope that a solution might lie in his collection of dusty books and tomes was all she had to work with at the moment.

"But there are so many books," said Rettia.

"And so many languages," added Orldrey. "I have no idea what many of them, contain. The mist walkers bring back what they think may be of interest, but I rely on those written by my own predecessors."

"Are there any in Parablion?" asked Beth.

"I would think so," replied Orldrey, "but your land has only been discovered in recent years."

"Yet Orestas walked the mists hundreds of years ago." said Beth.

"Perhaps he never told anyone of his origins?" suggested Rettia.

"Another mystery for another day. Show me the Parablion books," Beth said with new determination.

"Do you not wish to sleep first?" asked Rettia.

"No. I need to be doing something."

Orldrey assigned Rettia to work alongside Beth while he trawled through the other books. They worked till dawn, separating books into different piles. They sifted through hundreds of them, discarding many that were unintelligible to them. By the time daylight came through the windows of the cottage, they had filtered out twenty or so of particular interest.

Aving stood in the open doorway. "I was told you had returned."

He stepped into the room and Beth greeted him, accepted his sympathies for Jallon, and quickly and politely moved on to matters at hand.

"Do you seek me for a reason?" she asked. "Is there something you wish to discuss?"

"Very astute of you, Guardian. The man who was not killed when they attacked you, we have made him talk."

"I didn't know there was a survivor."

"We treated his injuries and nursed him, but he remained poorly – having him to question seemed too good an opportunity to miss. He speaks of a Mistress Valentina and how she will not stop until she has you. This woman is supposedly very powerful, with a great army. I would seek your counsel on this matter."

Orldrey told Beth to leave them. He and Rettia would continue to sort through the vast library for anything else that might be of use.

In the village, the people smiled and some bowed as Beth walked down from the plateau with Aving. It seemed they were all glad to see her back and well.

They entered Aving's home where the remaining eleven mist walkers were waiting in the large entrance hall with six other men and woman. The six were introduced as Aving's council before they went through to another room and approached a circular stone table with twelve chairs that had all been carved directly from the hard rock. The base of each chair was rooted in the floor; thick, sturdy and immovable. No daylight reached this room. Flickering torches created a blaze of dancing shadows.

"We have not sat here for many years," explained Aving as he offered Beth a seat next to his. The other council members sat down, but the mist walkers remained standing. "We normally sort most matters with a more casual encounter. However, we feel today requires a little more formality. There will be a great risk to the village and perhaps our way of life."

"What can I do?" asked Beth.

"The man that was captured was named Nesbur. Did you know him?" asked Aving.

"No. But you said his name in the past tense?"

"He died early this morning. He was with two other men, Leada and Astor, and three women, Amena, Leara and Tiana. Do you know them?"

"I knew Leara. She was once a friend." Beth noted to herself her own lack of emotion on the matter. She was not sure if she was bottling her feelings up, or just moving on. Either way, she wasn't concerned.

"And you know this Mistress Valentina?"

"Yes I do. Am I in trouble? You're asking so many questions." Beth looked at each mist walker for any signs of aggression towards her. There was nothing in their eyes, but that didn't mean they weren't poised for action.

"No, Guardian. I must apologise," assured Aving. "If this all seems grave and ill-boding it is because the man, Nesbur, told us that Mistress Valentina will not hesitate to bring her army here and kill everyone in the village. This we must take seriously."

"She is no doubt capable of doing that. I will leave immediately. If I am gone, she will not bother you."

"You cannot leave. You are the focal point of these villagers. Those from other villages mock us or think we are strange because we preserve the story of the Guardian and protect the Stones. You cannot leave," he insisted.

"But she will come for me."

"Then we will stand with you." Aving waved his hand across those present. "All of my people will stand with you. But we do not know how. We can fight, use the mountains to our advantage, but we do not know the enemy well enough to prepare properly. This is what we need to know from you. The mist walkers know of the Masters and Mistresses of Parablion, that they are people of power and influence, but we know little else."

"Mistress Valentina can be cruel and ruthless," admitted Beth. "She has unlimited resources, soldiers, spellbinders and more. She has occupied the jungle of Deline and she is destroying the balance there. She will not hesitate to come here. But it's me she wants, not you or the jungle."

"I have spoken with Orldrey while you were away. He tells me you cannot give this Mistress what she wants." Aving looked at the other council members who nodded in agreement.

"That's true," said Beth. "When I spoke with Orldrey, I believed it to be true, but now, having returned to the Stones in Deline, I know it is absolutely true."

"So giving yourself to her would serve no purpose, it seems?" concluded Aving.

"I guess so."

"Then we must prepare for war." The other council members voiced agreement with Aving.

"No!" Beth almost screamed. She could not be the cause of so many deaths.

"Then what would you have us do?" asked Aving.

Beth's head bowed; her shoulders sagged. She had just lost Jallon. She should be grieving alone, curled up in a ball somewhere. She was not in the right state of mind to save both the jungle and its people, and Jallon's people. She was a simple girl from the Malad District with no prospects. Why couldn't they all just leave her alone?

The minutes passed. No one spoke. No one moved.

"Stop being so selfish," said the voice inside her head – her own voice that originated from the Stones. "You are the only one who can end this. There is no one else. If you kill yourself, and I know you've considered it, who will help them then? What if Valentina finds the next Guardian after you have gone? Would you pass your burden to someone else? You know more than you realise. You had no idea how to cast the spells you used on the plateau, let alone cast both simultaneously and then sustain them. No other spellbinder can do that. There is knowledge in the Stones. If you do not exist, then the balance everywhere will be lost. It's not only the fate of these people, but of everyone. You finally need to accept that. Or are you still the fat useless girl your father said you are? Or are you the mother your unborn child will love and admire?"

She was pregnant. She carried Jallon's child. These were now her people in more ways than her simply being the Guardian.

Beth's heart swelled. She drew her shoulders back and straightened up as everyone looked upon her for answers. When her head rose, her eyes were burning bright with passion, framed by her flame-red hair. The sad, reluctant girl dressed in dirty wraps from the jungle was replaced by a woman, lean and strong – a capable fighter, seeder, spellbinder and Guardian, and soon to be a mother. The people of two villages needed her now, and one of them was her family.

"I have an alternative," she declared. "There may still be fighting and there may still be losses, but it will be on our terms and not Valentina's."

"Ough!" The mist walkers grunted in unison. This was their call of unity. They were with her and proud to be so.

"Tell me everything else this Nesbur told you."

EIGHTEEN

The tomeruscks were massive. There was only one waterhole that the desert people could easily access in the North and they knew it was monitored continuously by the northern people. Yet, it was not where they were heading. Geles and his remaining fifteen soldiers – he had lost two more to the desert – wanted to arrive unseen. Meeting up with Amena was a precarious gamble. She and her party might already be dead, and if they weren't, then they would be in hiding. There was a real risk that they would miss each other. However, Geles' orders were simple: find Beth, take the woman, and return to Valentina; if Amena had already found the woman, then assist her in every way. And if she had not, proceed alone.

However Geles needed to also work on the possibility that Amena had failed and been discovered and that his arrival may be expected. The northerners may well be monitoring his progress. Therefore he and his army had been, for quite a while now, attempting to move the six huge silver-haired beasts to a remote location at the foot of the rocky mountains.

Geles and the soldiers dismounted, taking their equipment with them. Their aim was to leave their desert guides and mounts behind, hopefully to reunite with them later. He knew the mission involved more risk than reward, but he had served Valentina for a long time now and he was loyal to her. He was sitting with his men for a well-earned rest.

"I would go home if I were you, Geles," came a loud voice from a shaded outcrop of rock above the Parablionions.

Everyone looked up, shading their eyes against the sun's glare, weapons at the ready.

"You are surrounded. We have the advantage of the high ground and we know the terrain. Lower your weapons. If we wanted you dead, you already would be."

Geles gave the order and all weapons were lowered, but remained ready.

"Who are you?" he shouted.

A woman stepped out from behind a rock, fifty feet above the soldiers on the ground.

"I am the reason you are here. I am Beth Reach."

"Who?" he parried. "We are simply exploring. Looking for new resources and trade agreements."

"Amena, Nesbur and Leara would say different," replied Beth.

Geles paused to consider his options. "Are they still alive?" he asked.

"No. They are all dead."

Another long silence.

"You know I cannot go back to Mistress Valentina with my tail between my legs," Geles called back. Beth heard both the sadness and resolve in his voice, he was not willing to fail Valentina with trying first, possibly at the cost of his own life.

"And you do not have to, Geles. Tell Valentina that I will come to her soon. You can use the waterhole to replenish and then return."

"She won't like that."

"Tell her that I am mourning the loss of someone close to me – someone Leara took from me. Once I have done that I will return and help her on her mission."

Six arrows thudded into the sand close to one group of soldiers who were attempting to move back into the shadows, out of sight.

"You are not in a position to bargain," Beth said.

"When?" Geles enquired. "When will you return?"

"I will be two or three weeks behind you. No more."

"Seems we have little choice."

***

Geles gave the order to load their equipment back onto the backs of the tomeruscks, then for their drivers and guides to set out back into the desert and the watering hole.

"Will they go, do you think?" Beth asked Aving, who was hiding in the shade behind her.

"They will do something stupid first. He won't want to return with only your message."

***

They travelled for a couple of miles, skirting the base of the mountains to the watering hole to the east. The tomeruscks' massive circular feet weren't suitable for climbing the rocky terrain, but they had no problems navigating close to the rocky outcrops that flowed into the desert and gradually disappeared below the sand. The journey gave Geles time to formulate a plan.

In the shadows of the outcrops, four soldiers dropped stealthily to the ground and hid until they were left far behind, before emerging and moving further into the high ground. This happened on another occasions, and Geles went with the second group.

The six tomeruscks arrived at the secluded watering hole, which was sheltered from the sun by high walls on all sides. The path into the watery haven was through a crack in the rock that kept the arid desert out. The huge beasts could barely squeeze through it. Spiny vegetation and grass grew around the large expanse of water for several feet around its edge. It was large enough to accommodate all six beasts with ease.

No one dismounted other than the guides to fill water containers for the return journey. The long trunks of the tomeruscks sucked up copious amounts of the life-giving water and poured it into their mouths. They started to swell as they readied themselves for the return journey across the desert. The remaining few soldiers stayed silent and hidden as they sat under the cover of the tents on the backs of the tomeruscks.

The sickening thud of hurled bodies surprised those who stood around the watering hole. They landed not far from the drinking beasts, having been thrown from a great height. There were seven of them, all soldiers. If they hadn't been dead before hitting the ground, they were now. The shocked onlookers remained hidden.

Beth knew that the mangled bodies of their comrades would grab the soldiers' attention below. She imaged them staring angrily, perhaps with fear, at their lifeless forms, knowing that Geles would most likely have told them not to reveal their numbers. She nodded and the body of Geles hit the ground too.

"Whoever is in charge now, you have my message," Beth shouted from her vantage point. "Take it to Valentina. Geles' orders died with him. You will best serve your Mistress now by returning and telling her what happened here. The price for your safe passage is to leave one of the tomeruscks behind, here at the watering hole."

Their thirst sated and water stocks replenished, five tomeruscks left the oasis. They took to the vast expanse of desert and disappeared over the horizon. The driver of the remaining animal had mounted alongside one of the others and gone with the group.

***

Nayas and Kynew approached Beth as she scanned through books at the table outside Orldrey's cottage. The two mist walkers assured her that all the remaining Parablion soldiers and the lower-region guides had now left the northern lands. They had followed them as far as they were able to and had left sentries to alert them should any try to return.

Beth thanked them for the update and then handed Kynew one of the books. The tome had illustrations of animals and vegetation from the jungle of Deline. Orldrey believed it had been written and illustrated by a former Guardian who had been gone for a long time. She asked them to arrange a mist walker to take it to Rishan and try to have it translated, not in its entirety – that would take too long – but to focus on anything useful contained withing its pages. The mist walker should only be gone for four days, as there would be more pressing matters to arrange.

Two days later Beth was feeling exasperated. They had looked through every book they could decipher and found little of use. Three very old Parablion spellbooks offered her new spells, but she wasn't sure she had the ability to cast them. She hadn't tried another spellbinder action since scorching Leara. Such power frightened her, and she remained reluctant to unleash it again without being trained to control it.

"You say you have hidden knowledge," said Orldrey, joining Beth at the table outside his cottage.

"There is knowledge in the Stones," she told him. "My inner voice says so and I know there is, but I don't know how to access it." The frustration was evident in her voice.

"The two spells that you cast – spellbinder magic. Had you seen them before or known about them before?" Orldrey casually picked up one of the books from the table.

"I've seen similar ones executed by others, but I've never known the symbols or patterns of focus they require."

"So, in a moment of desperation, when you needed something but didn't know what, the knowledge came to you."

"If you put it that way …" replied Beth, wondering where the conversation was going.

"You see, I came across a passage in one of my predecessors' journals. Just a short one, a couple of sentences, and at first I glanced past it. But it has played on my mind. It seems that Maddin, the Fernish Guardian, used to sit among the Stones for long periods of time. My predecessor thought that was how she gained her power ..." He paused momentarily to drive his point home. "But perhaps that was how she gained knowledge."

Beth stared out across the plateau at the stumpy green pillars. She hadn't entered them since finding out that she was pregnant. Her unborn child had already been within the Stones, both here and in the jungle, and she had no idea how that might affect the growing baby.

"You have access to two clusters of Stones, Beth." His voice brought her back from her reflections. "Perhaps if you spend time within them you may find answers?"

"The Stones of Deline still cause me great pain – far more acute than the ones here. Maybe because they are so much larger. To conquer the pain here I was unconscious for days. To conquer the pain in Deline, I may be unconscious for weeks, and I might not awake. More importantly, I may lose Jallon's child." Beth's despair was growing by the second. "And we don't have that much time, do we? The jungle and the balance are at more risk every day we do nothing."

"Then, without a greater advantage, there will be greater losses when we chase Valentina from the jungle," Orldrey said, and walked away, leaving Beth on her own.

He had once again sown a seed of thought in her mind for her to contemplate on. Her child's birth was months away, too long away to wait before entering the Stones again. It was a difficult choice – one she wasn't ready to make at that moment. She picked up another book and desperately searched its pages for something she might have missed.

The next day Kynew returned. She had taken the book to Rishan, as asked, and had found a translator. The work was written in the Temberian language. Nether the translator nor Kynew could transcribe the content into Parablion, but the mist walker had taken notes in her own language and committed yet more facts to memory. Orldrey read the notes aloud for Beth in front of Kynew and Rettia. Numerous questions followed, all of which Kynew answered as best she was able.

"I need to check this with Copo and Tiid," stated Beth finally. "If any of this is true, we may have our advantage."

An hour later, dressed and armed, Beth stood on the perimeter of the Stones. She hesitated as she stroked her swollen belly. She needed to visit Deline urgently. Travelling by the mist routes would take too long and was potentially as dangerous for her child as the Stones. Apologising to Jallon and her baby, she entered the Stones and travelled to the jungle.

Tiid was there, waiting, and thankfully there was no one else in the chamber.

A short while later she sat with Chief Mimambae, his five other councillors, and Tiid and Copo. She described her experience with Geles and warned them that some of the remaining soldiers would return soon, assuming they could safely navigate the mists. Then she disclosed the findings from the very old Temberian book. Her hosts were able to validate much of its content, but not all, which left some uncertainty in what Beth was proposing.

But the chief saw no alternative. New parts of the

jungle were sick and for the first time in long recollection a poisonous snake had bitten a villager. The woman survived, but she still needed constant treatment from the healers.

Beth promised to return every day for the following few days and told them they had to be prepared to act when the soldiers returned from Fernish. They must allow Beth's message to reach Valentina, but not allow her to prepare for what was to follow.

Arrangements to remove the Mistress from the jungle had begun.

NINETEEN

At night time, Beth slept among the Stones on the plateau, using a mattress and blankets from her cottage. If the green pillars did provide knowledge or power, she had decided to absorb as much of it as possible. On waking she would be back in Deline; fortunately the cavern was empty of visitors each time. There she caught up with Tiid on ongoing events in the jungle and discussed everyone's progress with the preparations.

During the days she trained alone. She had said farewell to the eleven mist walkers individually. What they were going to do was dangerous but they all accepted the risks. They served her now – well, they served the Guardian, Beth understood – but she knew they served her, too. When she stopped training, alone in the bowl of the canyon, she remembered each of them in turn, and hoped they would all be alive at the end of their ordeal. She also accepted the risk that not only might they lose their lives, but herself too.

Kynew was forefront in her thoughts, slim and slender,

short but strong, and very attractive. Then there was the tall and gangly Nayas, who shaved his head for reasons he wouldn't disclose. Unday was a burly man with little muscle definition, yet he seemed to be the strongest of them all. Enver was the youngest, a lean athletic woman with an almost constant smile. Stern Bourngh was the oldest and the most travelled. Uwayt was broad-shouldered, long-legged and their fastest runner. Iev was a quiet man and was extremely skilled with small blades. Jamena, a voluptuous woman with a heavy bosom, was their top archer. The muscular lean man Averus reminded her of Jallon, and he was unmatched with the mist walkers' Fernish swords. Oplee, with his craggy face, looked older than he was, seemingly older than Bourngh, despite being five years his junior; he had a natural aptitude for languages. Then there was Thonial, Jallon's younger cousin and the fastest in a fight; he moved so swiftly that he always seemed to be attacking from multiple directions simultaneously.

Beth realised that she loved and cared for them all. They were Jallon's people – her people now, she thought as she stroked her stomach.

The mist walkers had taken the recently acquired tomeruscks into the desert along with twenty other warriors from the village. It would be an arduous journey, but they had set out well prepared for the harsh environment. They would have to walk for two days and nights to a known mist that formed out in the middle of nowhere. This route would take them directly to the jungle of Deline. Predators were known to prowl the jungle side, and the Fernish side was defended by the vast open desert and scorching heat.

After she had trained with her bladed weapons, she

practised with her pistol. She would need to be at her best for any fighting that might happen; she hoped it wouldn't, but it seemed inevitable. Finally, she attempted spellbinder magic. This was her routine over the following days as they waited for the soldiers to return to Valentina.

She had been unable to reproduce to the same extreme level the searing heat and energy grip that had killed Leara and Amena's soldier, but she had at least been able to cast both spells to a lesser degree. She had successfully performed the knockback spell, and was now trying to master a new spell that she'd discovered in one of the spellbooks Orldrey had given her. She was pleased when she managed it, without ever receiving any formal training as a spellbinder.

Orldrey and Rettia continued to search through the books for anything that they might have missed. Any and every advantage would be of value. The old man also researched for a couple of things in particular; he went painstakingly through each book to determine the sex of each recorded Guardian, and for any mention of a Guardian who was pregnant. He concluded with surprise that Beth was the first female Guardian, but he didn't share this with her, concerned that it might alarm her in some way.

The people of Deline were also making preparations. They gathered every pot and container they could find and made extra ones from the natural resources around them. Inside these they secured snakes, spiders and other venomous creatures. It was a task that until recently would have involved little risk, but now that the balance in the jungle had shifted, and knowing one of their own had recently been bitten by a snake, they worked with utmost caution.

A group of them kept a constant watch on the compound and barracks at the mist line, waiting for the soldiers to return. At that point, their plans would be implemented. Their objectives had been explained to them by Beth. The most silent and evasive among them entered the compound under the cover of darkness to spy and get the lay of the land, so that they could be as prepared as possible for whatever outcome.

Everyone who was able readied their weapons, something many of them had never had to do before. Their hunters used small bows with short arrows tipped with a paralysing toxin taken from several slimy tree-dwelling creatures. They also used blow tubes and darts tipped with the same poisons. The only blades they possessed were for carving meat and skinning animal carcasses, but these were now sharpened for use against the Parablionions.

A number of them ventured deep into the jungle where they waited, hoping that their magic and relationship with the jungle would not leave them when they needed it most. This was put to the test one day as the Fernish mist walkers and warriors entered the jungle. The Delines greeted them and formed a circle around them, handing out the salve that kept insects away. This living shield would prevent the jungle predators attacking what might be perceived as intruders. Their magic held until they guided the Fernish to where they would be needed.

The mist between Parablion and Deline was forming less frequently. Copo had expressed his concerns about it to Beth, warning that one day it might never materialise again.

Beth was grateful that ten days or more were passing between appearances – it gave them more time to prepare. However, should the mists disappeared completely, Valentina might wreak even more havoc and generate more imbalance as she sought to use other mist routes to keep her presence established in the jungle.

Then two soldiers arrived at Valentina's encampment with the relief exchange. Fresh soldiers replaced the injured and those who were duty worn, but these two were escorted directly to Valentina. The concealed Deline observers had no doubt these were the men they had been waiting for.

TWENTY

Remy was practising his swordsmanship with Rust when the two soldiers were escorted through the compound towards the Mistress's building.

"Where's Leara?" he called out to them, but they paid him no heed.

Rust chastised him and demanded him to keep his attention on what he was doing. Remy ignored the directive. He wanted to know where Leara was.

"I'll be back soon," he said, sheathing his sword and abandoning his training.

Rust raised his arms in despaired as the boy ran off.

"Where's Leara?" he called out again.

The two soldiers still ignored Remy and their escort told him to leave them alone.

Valentina waited at her door. She didn't look very impressed with what was approaching. The sentries allowed the two soldiers entry but barred Remy who tried to follow them in.

"Mistress. Please?" he pleaded.

Valentina looked back at him, considered his request for a moment and then allowed him in. The four of them adjourned to a side room. Valentina instantly demanded their news. The soldiers started to describe their journey but the Mistress pulled them up straight away.

"Where is Beth? Answer that first," she ordered angrily.

"She remains in Fernish."

"Why?"

"She killed Amena, Mistress, and the team that went in at the north. She killed eight of our own, including Geles. She has an army of her own now. The northerners stand with her and they are formidable warriors."

"Leara's dead?" Remy stuttered.

"Be quiet!" barked Valentina.

Remy bit back a retort, sense prevailing over his emotions.

"Yet you two live? Were my orders not clear? I said to bring back the girl at any cost."

"She let us live so that we could deliver her message … Mistress" Both men were fidgeting nervously.

"What message?" demanded Valentina.

"She said that she is mourning the loss of someone who Leara killed. Once she has done that she will return to help you with your mission."

"Return when?" Valentina's hand rested on one of her holstered pistols.

"She said two or three weeks after we got back here."

"Huh." Valentina stared hard at both men. "Why should I believe this?"

"She could have killed us all, Mistress. But she let us live and sent us back with the message."

Remy heard the plea for mercy in the man's voice, and saw the other man with his gaze fixed on the floor. He was feeling increasingly anxious.

"But why should I believe your tale?" Valentina asked with increasing irritation.

"Because it's the truth, Mistress," the soldier insisted.

"And only you two remain alive?"

"Yes, Mistress. She let more of us live, but the journey back was perilous and only we made it back."

Valentina started to pace the floor.

"Who killed Leara?" asked Remy, who couldn't quite absorb the idea that his friend was dead.

"This woman – Beth – or maybe one of her warriors," replied one of the soldiers.

Remy was furious. "That bitch! I'll kill her myself when I see her again."

"Remy! You will do no such thing," Valentina shouted at him. "If I even suspect that you will try to, you will be gone from here. Do you understand?"

"Yes, Mistress," Remy said meekly, though he wasn't sure he meant it.

There was a loud knock on the door.

"What is it?" Valentina shouted out to the sentries.

"This, Mistress," one of them replied. He held a Fernish arrow in his hand. "It struck the door only a moment ago."

A note was wrapped around its shaft. Valentina opened it and read it aloud:

> *Mistress Valentina,*
> *I am here in the jungle of Deline. I wish to*

aid you in your quest, but first I need to know what you are looking for specifically. I am willing to assist you, provided that all your soldiers and people leave the jungle. If you do not leave, then we will be forced to make you. The Delines are not warring people, but they are willing to fight for what is theirs. The Fernish, however, are very able warriors and they will not hesitate to remove your troops.

This jungle is not your home. The Delines are able to bring all its resources down upon you, taking lives from the darkness. Your people will not see an enemy to fight, but when they do it will be a mighty Fernish warrior, not one of the smaller Delines.

We have already destroyed your supplies and stores. What arrived today is all that you have remaining. The next mist is likely to be many days away so you will need to ration your remaining supplies – but we will let you leave unharmed.

If you wish to talk, let me know. We are watching always.

Beth Reach

Valentina kicked the leg of her desk, hard. "Bitch. I will not be dictated to." And with that, she stormed from the room. Not knowing what else to do, the two soldiers and Remy followed.

"Get me the quartermaster!" she demanded as she marched briskly towards the store buildings.

The news from the quartermaster was grave. He visibly shook as he delivered it. All the perishable stock was spoiled. The food had a strange fungus growing all over it. The water in the barrels, had somehow turned foul and were no longer fit for consumption. Every reserved seedpod was damp and no longer functional, and no more had arrived with the last shipment. This meant the soldiers had only what they carried with them to recharge their pistols. The quartermaster finished his report and awaited his fate. The Mistress's eyes burned through him, yet she remained silent, although her fury was evident to everyone in the vicinity.

"Put extra guards on any supplies we have. Make them stand next to every item. No one is to get near to what remains."

"Yes, Mistress."

Valentina slammed the door behind her as she went out into the compound.

"I am here!" she shouted into the space around her. "So what's next?"

An arrow landed in the dirt several paces away from her. Another note. She read it out and Remy listened intently.

> *Recall all your patrols. Everyone must remain in the compound until the next mist. When you are ready to talk, walk to the east and I will meet you. Come alone. Come unarmed. If you fear for your safety, remember this arrow could have been aimed for you rather than next to you.*

Valentina gave the order to recall all personnel to the base and issued further orders than no one was to leave the compound. Everyone stationed at the barracks by the mist was also to return. Then she summoned her officers and stomped back to her lodge. Word of her fury spread like wildfire and her officers scrambled to the meeting that had been announced; no one wanted to get on the wrong side of her.

Remy and the two returning soldiers were now forgotten about, but they were barred from the officers' meeting so they retired to the mess hall. Remy asked them about their journey, and about Leara. They told him all that they knew, and a crowd gathered while they related their tale. Everyone knew something was wrong and they wanted to know what. They guessed that Beth was back in the jungle and all the signs told the more experienced among them that they were under siege.

An hour later, officers started barking their orders throughout the compound. The perimeter fences were checked over and reinforced. They consisted of large, high, portable frames with a central log to which long iron and wooden spikes were attached. Principally intended to be anti-predator obstacles, they could also be moved quickly to block a breach in another barrier. Every building was searched for hidden intruders. Sentries along the fence line were doubled. All alcohol was prohibited in the mess hall. If anyone had no specific orders, they were to bunk down.

The compound was on high alert. An attack was imminent at any time and everyone was to be ready to defend their position. They were digging in until reinforcements arrived.

Leaving all the commotion behind, Valentina walked east alone. The locals showed themselves fleetingly. Their message clear – she was surrounded.

Valentina entered a clearing where, on the far side, no more than ten feet away from her, stood Beth. At her side were two Fernish mist walkers, their swords drawn. On either side of the clearing, two other Fernish mist walkers held nocked arrows aimed at Valentina.

"I am here and I am unarmed. What can you offer me that might save your life?"

Beth ignored the threat.

Valentina studied the woman in front of her. The change from the soft weak unaccomplished girl she had collected at the Arities holding cells was astonishing. This woman looked confident and accomplished. Her eyes were bright and alert, her flame-red hair tied back in a ponytail. She was dressed in soft black leather but showed no signs of discomfort in the humid heat. A pistol and utility belt hung at her waist. The hilt of a sword was visible over her right shoulder, a dagger was sheathed at her boot and a large knife on her hip glinted in the sunshine. On her chest was pinned a circular brooch with central green stripes that reminded Valentina of the Stones. This woman was to be taken seriously.

"There is nothing at the centre of the Stones. I have been there. Orestas hid nothing there," Beth said.

"Why should I believe you?" Valentina replied as she surveyed those before her and looked beyond into the jungle. She suspected there were others there, hidden from sight.

"I am telling you the truth, Valentina. There is no way

for you to verify it, but you have my word."

"Your word," sneered Valentina. "I spent years searching for this spot – where Orestas left all his knowledge. There is no way I am leaving without what I came for."

"Orestas returned here to the Stones to perish," explained Beth. "He willingly walked into them and became dust. His knowledge returned to the Stones. It was never about books or spellbooks – it was he himself that he was referring to."

"I don't believe you!"

"I have learned a great deal while I've been away. The Stones hold knowledge and I can sometimes interpret that knowledge."

"You? How?" demanded Valentina, stepping a pace forward, ignoring the weapons raised at her.

"These people refer to me as the Guardian," replied Beth. "The Keeper of the Balance. I alone can access them and learn from them. If you tell me what you are searching for, I may have the answer or be able to find it for you."

"What makes you so special?" There was no derision, just curiosity and mounting anger.

"I don't know the answer to that. But all that I have said is true. I am your best chance to find what you have been seeking."

"And I am simply to believe anything you tell me?"

"I want to help you. I want to claim the jungle back for the Delines. Your presence here is making it sick. I don't want any more people to die unnecessarily. Tell me what you want and I will do my best to help you."

"Alright!" Valentina's rage came to the surface, as she

screamed the words. "I am barren. I can't have a child. There is no heir to take over when I am gone. That means everything my family has ever achieved over countless generations will simply be given to a stranger when I die."

"So adopt a child. Appoint someone to be your heir."

"That is not how it works with Masters and Mistresses, Beth. There is no way to change it." Valentina stood proudly now, her anger subsided. She was still a Mistress.

"What has Orestas to do with all this?" Beth asked.

"He lived for hundreds of years. If I can do the same, then I have more time to fix my situation."

"You seek immortality?"

"If that's possible, yes. But hundreds of years will serve me, too. So can you give me that secret?"

"No."

"Then you are useless to me, and if I believe what you say, so are the Stones." There was no anger in Valentina now, just a renewed determination. "I will simply have to rip them all down to find out whether you are telling me the truth. And if there is nothing at the centre of them, I will destroy this jungle to see if you have taken anything from them and hidden it elsewhere. If it's not here, I will do the same with Fernish. I will not stop until I have what I want."

"You will find nothing, Valentina. There is nothing to find. Leave the jungle and I will search for you, and if I can help you, I will. There's no need to wage a war on the Delines or the Fernish."

"That is where you are wrong. I cannot believe you. I cannot simply take you at your word. I need … I want to see for myself. I have been searching far too long to let a backstreet girl from Arities tell me I can't. If you want me out of the jungle, you will have to do it by force. Are you willing to sacrifice so many lives?"

Valentina didn't wait for an answer. She turned and walked back towards the compound, confident that no arrow would take her in the back and no one would stop her.

***

Beth translated the conversation for the Fernish mist walkers, Chief Mimambae and his council. Everyone remained committed to her plan and now it was time to implement it.

The mist walker Jamena reported that the Parablion compound was preparing for a siege. They had reinforced their perimeter and were constructing defensive positions within and showing no sign of retreat. She estimated that they had close to two hundred soldiers, which included around twenty spellbinders. Beth only had eleven mist walkers and twenty warriors, along with eighty able Deline villagers who ranged from young to old and had no experience of fighting. Valentina also had another two hundred soldiers on the other side of the mist, at the ready when it returned.

Copo had news from the other villages deeper in the jungle. They would not come to their aid. They would remain concealed in the Deline jungle, far away from this fight. They didn't see Valentina as a threat and they didn't share the same beliefs about the Stones as Chief Mimambae's people.

It seems they were outnumbered two to one, soon to

be four to one, and Valentina had highly trained and experienced soldiers. All Beth and her allies had was the jungle and the Stones.

The plan was still to drive Valentina from the jungle while keeping casualties to a minimum, but both the Fernish and Delines had already accepted this outcome was looking more and more unlikely. But they were steadfast and took to their appointed tasks and roles without hesitation. Ten of the Delines went to secure the Stones, in case Valentina should make a run for them. They would remain inside the cavern's entrance, guarding the passage. Their strategy was simple: they would block and obstruct the entrance, giving them the time, they hoped, for help to reach them should they be attacked.

The remaining locals surrounded the compound, hidden and dispersed. They began their attack.

Sentries all along the perimeter fence line started to fall. Silent darts struck them and they dropped to the ground. The alarm sounded and every soldier took arms. There was no visible enemy to fight but every man and woman on the perimeter lay prone, unable to move as paralysing toxins coursed through their veins. Word quickly spread that the fallen were still alive, but anyone who attempted to recover a fallen comrade was met by more darts.

Valentina commanded from her lodge. Reports came in and orders went out. Thirty soldiers had been incapacitated. One of the three officers that shared the command post pointed out the obvious – that if those darts were poisonous, then they would already have lost a significant number of soldiers.

The Mistress responded that Beth was too soft; she didn't have what it took to lead soldiers into battle and this weakness would be her downfall. Her counter was to move defensive positions closer to the perimeter, from where they would fire blind volleys of pistol slugs into the undergrowth. However, they were to preserve as much ammunition as possible. This would scare the invaders, she hoped, and should any be injured it would remind them that the situation was real and serious.

Her counter-move had the desired effect. It took the lives of three Delines and injured several others. An hour later, the paralysed men and women were back on their feet and the attackers had pulled back.

Kynew pointed out to Beth that it was time to increase the threat and the Guardian was forced to agree. The Fernish found their positions and launched arrows into the compound. They were far enough away to be out of range from the pistol fire and their targets were easy shots.

The Delines had extracted large quantities of a dark sap from certain trees. This sap was highly flammable and they used it to light fires in the damp humid jungle. Pods of the thick liquid were now attached to the arrows' tips and a wick set alight. The burning arrows spread the dark fluid on impact and instantly ignited in a ball of flames. The resulting fires were small but many, but all the structures inside the perimeter were made of timber. The soldiers attempted to smother some but finally had to resort to using their precious water to tackle others. Then the order came to leave the remaining buildings to burn – the water was too valuable a commodity. The fires burned through the night and in the morning many of the buildings had crumbled.

"They are showing no sign of retreat," Kynew advised Beth. "Any day now they will have reinforcements."

"The mist will be maybe six or more days yet," replied Beth.

"But it might also be today or tomorrow. It's time to threaten lives."

Beth was reluctant, but she'd always expected this time would come. Valentina was not a woman to be told to do anything. She would never take orders from someone she considered an inferior – a backstreet girl from Arities.

Over a hundred pots and containers were hurled into the interior of the compound. As they impacted they broke open and vast numbers of venomous snakes, spiders and other poisonous creatures swarmed forth. The aftermath of the attack was erratic but effective. Some pots landed far from their targets and soldiers were able to hack and slash at the deadly intruders; others were allowed to slither and crawl away. But many of them landed beside them, so they became victim to many fatal bites and stings. Twenty-six soldiers were lost in that attack.

Valentina received the report with little emotion. They were soldiers, this was their duty. Her command centre still stood. Parts of the building had burned but it was still solid and defensible. Specially selected soldiers, including her own Guard, defended her position. It was now time to push back. The mist could return anytime now and outside she had another two hundred soldiers ready and waiting. They needed to be alerted the moment the mist appeared and advance to reinforce her hold in the jungle.

Eighty soldiers with makeshift shields gathered in small groups in the compound. They raised their shields to form a perimeter and ceiling over them and then they broke from the compound at a pace, taking to the road towards the mist barracks. Valentina's move hadn't been expected and the arrows fired into the armoured convoy were few. Only six of the soldiers fell before they managed to reach the barrack buildings and set up their defences.

The next two days were a stalemate. The Delines had little sap left to burn the buildings of the mist barrack and it would take too long to gather enough of it to be effective now. What had remained of the sap had already been used in an effort to force the soldiers back to the compound, but they had easily combated the flames. Now they held a second fortified position.

Every moment, day and night, since the siege had started, Beth had searched her subconscious for anything the Stones might offer her. Yet nothing had presented itself. The old Temberian book had implied that the jungle would help them when threatened, that the mists would defend themselves in times of need, but so far there had been nothing, other than myriads of small animals offering themselves as her familiar. Those around her had grown accustomed to the snakes, rodents, birds, monkeys and boars that wandered out of the jungle to Beth and lay at her feet. She did not have time to solve the mysteries of a familiar now. She had no idea how to accept one, or choose one. If it was important, she could do so after Valentina was driven out.

"We need to take the barrack building by the mist," Kynew insisted. "If word gets to the other side quickly, they will have time to come through in force. Then we will be overrun. If we do take it, those on the other side will hesitate, with no orders to act on. I don't think Valentina is planning to leave – no matter what we do. So we hold back those reinforcements. Then once Valentina is isolated again, we take the compound too."

Beth was reluctant to follow this advice, but Chief Mimambae and his council and all eleven mist walkers agreed on it. However none of them would act without Beth's instruction. She studied all the faces around her. How many would she see again if she approved their proposal? How many would be lost on both sides of the fight? After a moment of sad contemplation and with sincere regret, she issued the order.

Beth, as their Guardian, was not permitted to partake in the fighting. She would stay back at a safe distance with Oplee as her protector and Tiid as her translator. Kynew would lead the assault on the mist barracks. She and the other Fernish would take the fight to the soldiers, along with fifteen Delines who were strong enough and willing to fight at close quarters. The other Delines would line the road and defend it should soldiers from the compound try to aid their comrades at the mist boundary. However, the darts and arrows they would fire were now laced with a deadly poison – not the one that caused non-fatal paralysis.

The fifteen Delines and ten Fernish warriors took aim and fired a salvo of arrows at any open doorways and windows in the mist barracks. The defending soldiers hunkered down under cover. Every time someone showed themselves, more arrows peppered the area around them. As the first flight struck, Kynew charged with her remaining troops. The mist walkers engaged first, bursting through doorways, closely followed by the Fernish warriors. When the fight came to close quarters the archers charged, creating a second-wave assault.

Beth watched from a concealed spot back in the cover of the jungle. She heard the clap of pistols, the bursts of magic, the screams and cries. The fighting was inside the buildings and she couldn't see the devastation or the tide of battle. Then the fighting spread out into the open and she saw her mist walkers move with amazing skill and agility. Their swords killed and dismembered with every powerful blow. The Fernish warriors also fought impressively alongside the brave Delines. But death preyed on both sides and men and women fell – Parablionions, Fernish and Delines.

The sounds of battle and the shrill alarm reached the compound. As anticipated, reinforcements were dispatched. Looking up towards the wide clear roadway, Beth watched as her people fell long before they reached the clearing.

When the avemont appeared it startled them. Oplee raised his swords immediately, while Tiid fell to the floor as the huge beast leaned over his shoulder. The apex predator did not appear to be aggressive.

"Wait!" said Beth, stopping Oplee before he could strike. The animal nuzzled Beth. It meant them no harm, but she didn't have time to deal with the animal now. Her people and many more were dying in front of her and more would continue to do so.

"The mist," called Tiid, pointing towards the clearing. The wispy grey fog was starting to form.

The Fernish and Delines had the advantage. No reinforcements had reached the barracks from the compound but new soldiers would soon break from the mist. They might be surprised by what they encountered, but they were trained and disciplined, and it wouldn't take them long to recover their wits and join the fighting. The alert would get back to the Parablionions and yet more would come through. The jungle defenders would be quickly overrun. They had lost.

Beth buried her head in the black and green fur of the avemont that would not leave her side, and she cried. She clasped a horn with one hand and grabbed a handful of its fur with the other.

"You simply accept him," said the calm voice of her inner self. "It's that simple. Once you do, your magic will have better balance and, as your familiar, he will help you focus."

Three score of Parablion soldiers marched into the clearing. The scene before them was a bloody affair. A large number of their comrades lay slaughtered on the ground. They reacted almost immediately and charged into the fray. Commands went back into the mist calling for hundreds more soldiers to converge on the jungle clearing.

The jungle burst into life. Predators of all sizes raced, galloped and assailed the boundary of the mist. Beth led the charge, mounted bareback on her avemont, who clawed and tore his way into the melee, swatting Parablion soldiers aside with ease, inflicting deep fatal wounds. The fresh onslaught created panic and disruption among all the Parablion soldiers. They turned and fled, the savagery of the new wave, the superstitious fear of mist monsters driving them back, only to be followed through the mist by the predators. The mist remained for nearly fifteen minutes.

The fighting on the jungle side was over in five. The number of predators diminished as they snatched bodies and returned to the jungle.

No more soldiers crossed from Parablion.

When the mist was gone, Beth slid from her mount and surveyed the scene of slaughter. Many bodies had been taken, but a large number lay scattered about. Only the Fernish and Delines remained standing, but their numbers were fewer. Beth's fury rose insider her and burned. It was time to end this. She turned and marched up the roadway towards the compound.

The route to the camp was littered with more bodies, far too many to count. The brave soldiers had tried valiantly to aid their comrades but failed nonetheless. Such a waste. Valentina did not deserve such loyalty.

Beth stormed up the cleared pathway, the huge avemont padding behind her. The concealed fighters in the jungle came forward and joined the advance. Kynew and Oplee came to her sides now, both blooded from battle. Iev and Jamena flanked her, alongside Tiid and Copo. The others fell in behind the avemont.

The entrance to the compound was open and everywhere other than Valentina's building was deserted. A bunker had been built before its door, the only way in and out. Shielded behind the sacks and barrels were ten soldiers with pistols ready.

Beth halted, out of range of the weapons as her army welled around her. This time the odds were in her favour, but she had seen enough friends die today already.

The presence of her familiar, a majestic beast in its own environment, in a jungle thick with the magic generated from the large outcrop of Stones, bolstered her. She felt powerful, formidable, and in complete control.

"Lay down your weapons and you will be allowed to leave peacefully," she called out at the bunker guards.

A single pistol shot was their answer, totally ineffective over the distance between them.

"Everyone stay here," Beth said to her army. "I will deal with this."

She stepped forward, calmly and confidently, and advanced on the bunker. Before she entered within pistol range she broke into a run and charged them. She had no weapon drawn as she did so. The claps of pistols resounded as they fired freely at her.

Every slug stopped short, striking an invisible shield that had formed around her from head to toe. This was the spellbinder spell from the books Orldrey had given to her, which she had attempted to master on the plateau. It seemed such a simple task now; an easy use of magic.

Beth stopped at the wall of the bunker.

"Lower your weapons," she commanded.

One of the officers, just a young man, stood and fired point-blank at Beth's head. The slug disintegrated against the invisible barrier. Beth raised a hand and the man convulsed and fell to the floor. Crackling lights danced all over him, but they ceased quickly. He would live.

"Drop your weapons."

The soldiers complied.

Behind her, the Fernish and Delines advanced together. Kynew gave orders to take the prisoners and to search the compound for any other survivors – to be taken alive wherever possible. Then Beth, Kynew, Oplee, Iev and

Jamena entered Valentina's lodge.

Beth already knew which room Valentina was in, somehow sensing her presence there. Instructing the others to stand back, she opened the door. Valentina fired at her instantly. The slug bounced off Beth's shield. Valentina tried to fire again but was unable to. She attempted to raise a hand to dispense magic but failed in that too. Beth had locked her immobile using a spell of her own. Then the Guardian entered the room and her mist walkers followed.

Remy screamed, leaping from his place of concealment behind the door. His small dagger was raised high and aimed at Beth's heart. Iev reacted instantly, catching the boy's arm and slamming him to the floor, striking him unconscious.

Beth took hold of Valentina and indicated that she should drop her pistol, which she did without hesitation.

"I didn't want this," Beth said to her.

"You should have known it was inevitable," replied Valentina, fire burning in her eyes. "I cannot give up my quest ... no matter what the cost."

"Orestas was a healer," said Beth. "He used magic to heal. I didn't know that until this very moment, but you did, didn't you?" The realisation had come unbidden. Beth understood that the knowledge was from the Stones, but it was only revealed when she needed it.

"I have read such. I thought it might be why he lived so long, but I could never find any spells that could confer even the slightest healing effect."

There was more Beth wanted to say.

"I'm pregnant. Leara killed the father. I didn't intend to kill Leara, it just happened. The Stones give me power.

I'm still getting used to it and don't understand it all yet, but there is also knowledge that surfaces at opportune times. This is what happened when I killed Leara and Amena. I am not a murderer. And I do not want to take any more lives, today or ever. I think I can help you now."

Beth took hold of Valentina by her hips and squeezed firmly. The Mistress started to pull away but stopped suddenly. Beth felt something changing inside Valentina, inside her womb. Her hands became warm and began to hurt slightly. The two stayed locked in their strange engagement for over a minute. Then Beth released Valentina and stepped away.

"You are no longer barren," said Beth.

The room was eerily silent. Valentina held her stomach, gently caressing it.

"Nonsense! How can …? What did …? Why would …?" The words tumbled from her mouth.

Then silence returned while the Mistress slowly recovered her composure.

"I do feel different," she held both hands to her stomach. "But how do I know you are not deceiving me?"

"Simply go forth and multiply and never return to the jungle," said Beth. "The truth will become evident to you soon enough."

"If you are tricking me, I will be back."

"You have your life. So many today do not. Take what you have now and leave peacefully. If what I have done is as I say, then your quest is over."

Beth gestured and the mist walkers apprehended Valentina. The war was over.

EPILOGUE

J oellen ran among the green Stones on the plateau. Her grandmother, Jallon's mother, despaired. She was barely walking properly and she constantly fell over as she tried to run, bumping and banging herself against the Stones. She was covered in grazes and bruises, but the toddler paid them no mind. They were already healing as she picked herself up and raced a few more steps before falling again.

Beth appeared among the Stones.

"Mamma," Joellen cried and raced towards the Guardian, falling face down at her mother's feet.

Beth picked up her daughter, wiping the dirt from her face, and kissed her. Joellen hugged her neck tightly.

Copo and Tiid had bid farewell to the Guardian as she entered the tall green pillars in the cavern. Beth no longer suffered pain when she entered. Both of the men were concerned when she collapsed inside them and didn't move for fourteen days. But now everything was fine.

Beth visited them from time to time. The mist to

Parablion was infrequent now, and when it did appear, predators gathered to defend it. The jungle had recovered and the sickness had receded. The balance had been restored.

Valentina had recalled all her people to her homelands. They no longer needed to occupy the jungle of Deline. Her son was six months old now. She had carefully selected a male to breed with and paid him well for the service. But he was long gone now.

She had also set Remy free with a healthy source of coin stored at the temple banks for him to make his own way in life. He and Beth had made their peace while he was held in the mist barracks in Deline, until he returned home with the surviving Parablionions.

Valentina sent him to be tested for magic. He had shown enough skill to perhaps become an accomplished spellbinder, but she left that choice to him.

ABOUT THE AUTHOR

Andy Sharp resides in Merseyside, UK, where he writes, paints art and takes the occasional photo. More can be discovered on his webpage www.penphotopaint.com.

This is his first book in the series, look out for more to follow the adventures of Beth, Remy, and Valentina.

If you enjoyed this book, please leave a review on Amazon.co.uk.

Lightning Source UK Ltd.
Milton Keynes UK
UKHW020657270222
399279UK00005B/564